Dedication

To Richard Patzer
A good-hearted, generous man
Our Husband, Father, and Grandfather

Vengeance

Vengeance is in my heart, death in my hand.
Blood and revenge are hammering in my head.

Shakespeare

Sanctuary of the Madonna of Monte Berico

Prologue

A.D. 1645

I know what it is like to be dead, because I was once dead to the world. Dead to everyone who I believed loved me. Dead to everyone who knew me well enough to call me by name. Dead and buried.

My friends and family in Vicenza believed the plague that ravaged the city had struck me down; and that my body lay buried and decaying in my ancestral crypt. They were wrong, of course, for I was very much alive. The only certain way to know someone is dead is through cremation or decapitation. Thankfully, that did not happen in my case.

The warm blood of a woman of thirty-two years courses through my veins. My eyes are ardent and clear, my body still curvaceous and firm, my face and hands are soft and pink, and my spine upright and dignified. My hair is the only thing that has changed. Before I died, it was the color of roasted chestnuts. Afterwards, it turned as white as the snow blanketing the Alps, though my curls remain as thick as ever.

Once, several years ago, I confessed my story to a compassionate priest. He listened to me without interruption, but I sensed his unmistakable scepticism.

When I finished speaking, he hinted that I might be mad, and with a pitiful gaze, he gave me a menial penance. I never told my story to another soul again.

Several years have passed, but the need to tell my tale has not left me, so I have decided to take pen to parchment. Now that enough time has passed and I can no longer be prosecuted for my crime, I can write the truth without fear. Here in the Sanctuary of the Madonna of Monte Berico, a person's past is irrelevant, a matter between them and God. Here I can dip the plume in my own blood if I choose, and no one will oppose me.

These days, the silence of a cloister surrounds me; an imposing, dignified tranquility within a haven of perfect calm. The sole thing to disturb the silence is the gliding of leather soles upon stone floors and the tolling of bells that announce the Canonical hours.

The sanctuary sits high upon a hill overlooking Vicenza. The Blessed Virgin appeared on this hill twice with a promise to rid the people of the plague if they vowed to build a church on the spot. The people honored their promise, but I am a living testament that the plague returned centuries later.

Now, amid the rose bushes and stone pathways of the convent's cloister, I can raise my burdened heart like an overflowing goblet, and spill it on the ground, emptying it to the last drop of vexation contained therein.

What a terrible thing it is to bury the remains of a loved one in a cold stone crypt or a hole in the sodden earth. Repulsive creatures hide deep in that dark. Things vile and abhorrent; slithering worms, sinister insects with unseeing eyes and worthless wings.

What would happen if, after they lowered someone's coffin into its vault or hole in the ground, they learned they had made a mistake? What would happen if the crypt or coffin were not as secure as everyone believed? What would happen if desperate, panicked fingers opened the coffin in the dark? What would happen if their loved one did not die, but instead returned to the love and fidelity of friends and family? Would their loved ones be happy to see their dead relative? Or would they regret their sudden reappearance, especially if they had inherited their wealth?

I believe most people are fake. Few truly mourn the dead. Fewer still, remember them with any real affection. Of all this, I am certain, for I have experienced it firsthand.

Now, long after my ordeal is over, I want to narrate the events of one short year; the most agonizing year in my life; a year in which a sharp thrust from the stiletto of time stabbed me in the heart and opened a wound that still drips tainted blood to this day.

With deliberate care, I dip my plume into the inkwell and whisper a prayer for God to forgive me. Then word by word, I begin to inscribe the story of my sin; a transgression that can never be cleansed. This is my dreadful tale...

Chapter One

A.D. 1628

I Carlotta Mancini, was born rich and noble. My mother died while giving birth to me. Many years later, my father, Count Federico Mancini, died and left me sole heir to our family villa and surrounding lands. I was sixteen years old, then, alone, and a wealthy contessa.

At the time, people predicted a dire future for me. Because I was rich and titled, I suspected some, with spiteful anticipation, wanted to see my downfall. For a while, I became the object of their malicious predictions. The most popular tidbits of gossip foretold that I was destined for bride theft or that I might become victim to a greedy nobleman's unscrupulous whims to usurp my wealth.

None of this happened, of course. Before he died, my father had the foresight to hire a governess and companion named Annunziata Cardano, a widow with a daughter my own age. He also hired a physician, a graduate of the University of Bologna, well versed in legal matters, to oversee my finances, my future, and to act as my guardian. My father's forward thinking not only guarded my wealth, it allowed me to have a say in my own destiny.

Together with my governess and her daughter, I dwelled in the villa, a miniature palazzo of white marble situated on a hill overlooking the city of Vicenza. Frescos and elegant statues decorated the numerous rooms and halls within the rambling two-storey structure. Fragrant groves of cherry and lemon trees, where nightingales warbled love-melodies, fringed my lands. Sparkling fountains with stone basins and cascading water refreshed hot summer days. Here, I lived peacefully for two happy years, surrounded by books and pictures, undisturbed by the world.

Of young, eligible men, I saw little or nothing. In fact, I avoided them altogether. My wealth attracted the attention of parents with marriageable sons who sought invitations to visit. I refused them all. My governess warned me to tread carefully around male society and I had taken her warnings to heart. Ignorance was not always the safest course, as I would someday come to learn.

My one dear friend, Beatrice Cardano, Annunziata's daughter, disagreed with her mother's thoughts about men and often chided me good-naturedly for avoiding them. "Oh, Carlotta," she would say. "A woman cannot know joy until she has sipped nectar from masculine lips, experienced the clasp of eager arms round her waist, or heard the beat of a passionate heart against her own."

I always smiled at her words, but never responded. They failed to change my mind. Yet, I loved to hear my friend speak. Beatrice's melodious voice was a joy and her eyes could convince with more fluency than speech. I loved Beatrice, selflessly, honestly, with that rare tenderness shared by young girls for one another.

I was as happy in Beatrice's company, as Beatrice seemed to be in mine. We passed most of our time together, Beatrice also having lost her father. She was as poor as I was rich, so I always gave Beatrice my gently worn garments without wounding her pride. We had much the same tastes and shared the same sympathies. I treasured nothing as much as I did our friendship. We were inseparable.

Annunziata also warned me that destiny permits no one to continue in blissful happiness. Fate could not tolerate it. Something trivial, a glance, a word, a touch, could shatter a friendship. A love deemed deep and lasting was so fragile it could disappear like straw in the wind. Yet, I refused to believe it; a folly I would soon come to regret.

One muggy afternoon toward the end of May, Annunziata accompanied me to Mass in Vicenza. Beatrice was not with us, having remained at home with a headache. Afterwards, trapped among the crowd exiting the church, I lost sight of Annunziata.

Alone, I strolled through the streets, savoring my moment of freedom and delaying my return home. At the far end of a crowded, narrow street, I heard chanting and caught a glimpse of black robes approaching. Priests and nuns walked towards me in a long procession. Clerics swung gold censers heavy with incense while nuns followed, row upon row, in black and white habits, each with a prayer book in hand. A statue of the Virgin Mary, carried on the shoulders of four burly youths, led their way. I paused at the side of the street to watch them pass. One face beamed like a star from among the four young men; one face of rugged, near perfect handsomeness lit by two luminous eyes, large, round, and of the darkest brown. His curved mouth smiled to provoke. His golden hair glimmered beneath the sun's rays.

I gazed at him, dazzled, excited. Here was a man, the gender Annunziata had warned me to mistrust and avoid, a man of my own age, eighteen, or twenty at the most. I drank in his soul-tempting glance and captivating smile. He was the most beautiful person I had ever seen. My eyes remained on him until the procession passed and he faded from my sight. In that moment of time, although I did not realize it, one era of my life had closed forever, and a new one had begun.

Of course, upon my return home, I made inquiries through the good physician, my guardian in all things. It took a few days for him to discover the identity of the young man I had seen carry the Madonna. His name was Dario Gismondi and he was the only son of a ruined nobleman of dissolute character, who had lost his fortune gambling. Fortunately, he had had his son educated in a Benedictine monastery renowned not only for its strict discipline, but for a vast library of rare books. The physician assured me that Dario was as trustworthy as the sun rising each morning, and I had no reason not to believe him. Once my guardian gained whatever assurances he needed to ensure it was a good match, he began negotiations to arrange our marriage. Much to my delight, Dario's father agreed. What better match could there be for an impoverished son than a wealthy contessa alone in the world?

Our courtship was brief and as sweet as a cup of honeyed wine. There were no impediments to block our union. We were married at the end of June.

Beatrice Cardano graced our nuptials with her presence. "Brava, Carlotta," she exclaimed, her eyes all aglow after we were declared married. "You have finally heeded me, and in the process, you have secured the handsomest man in the region, in the world."

I pressed my friend's hand, and a touch of remorse stole over me. Beatrice was no longer first in my affections, but I could not regret this. I glanced at Dario, my husband, bedazzled and overcome with love for him. The dreaminess of his large lucid eyes crept into my soul, and I forgot everyone but him. With him, I experienced a delirium of passion and touched the highest peaks of joy.

Our first days together passed with near bliss and the nights spun a web of rapture around us. I never tired of Dario. For me, he grew finer with each passing day. Within a few months, he knew my soul, my deepest thoughts. He discovered how certain looks could draw me to his side like a devoted slave. Did he love me? Oh, yes, I believed he loved me as all husbands love their wives, as something that belonged solely to them. In return, I begrudged him nothing, idolizing him, raising him to the stature of a god. He was an extraordinary man, sharing my passion for collecting exquisite jewels.

We kept an open house. Our home became a meeting place for all the nobility in and around Vicenza. Everyone respected and admired Dario's beguiling face and polite humility. Beatrice was loudest in her praise of my husband, and the respect and kindness she displayed toward Dario endeared her even more to me. I trusted and loved her as if she were my sister, and I treated her as one. I deemed my life perfect. It was filled with love, wealth, family, and friendship. What more could a woman desire? Nevertheless, there was more joy to come. Within a year, I gave birth to a daughter, fair as the jasmine that grew thick in the woods surrounding my palazzo. We named her Chiara. Minutes after her birth, wrapped in soft, embroidered cashmere, the fragile mite lay in my arms. The baby opened her eyes. They were large and dark brown as Dario's were. Heaven itself lingered in their pure depths. I kissed the innocent face. Dario and Beatrice did the same, and those clear, quiet eyes of my infant daughter regarded us all with a strange half-inquiring solemnity. A bird, perched on the bow of a tree outside the bedroom, broke into a low, sweet song. Too exhausted to stay awake any longer, I handed my daughter back to the wet nurse, who waited to receive her.

After Dario and the servant left the room, Beatrice laid

her hand on my shoulder. "You are a good woman, Carlotta."

"Indeed. Why do you think so?" I asked with a half-laugh. "I am no better than any other woman."

"You are less suspicious than most people." Beatrice turned away and played with the tassel of her belt.

I glanced at my friend in surprise. "What do you mean *amica*? Have I reason to suspect anyone?"

Beatrice laughed and resumed her seat at the edge of the bed. "Why, no," she answered, with a frank look. "But the world is always filled with suspicion. Jealousy's stiletto is ever ready to strike, justly or unjustly. Children are well versed in the ways of vice. Penitents confess to priests who are worse sinners than they are, and fidelity is often a farce." She paused a moment, a touch of sadness in her eyes. "Is it not wonderful to be you, Carlotta; a woman happy in her home, with all the confidence in the world?"

"I have no cause to be suspicious of anyone," I responded. "Dario is trustworthy and righteous."

"True." Beatrice looked at me and smiled. "He is as pure as a flawless diamond and as unapproachable as the farthest star."

I concurred, but something in her manner bewildered me. What a strange conversation. Our talk soon turned to different matters and I thought no more of it. I did not know it then, but her words would soon return to haunt me.

Chapter Two

A.D. 1631

A plague struck Vicenza, razing the population like a destructive demon. Its vile touch was indiscriminate, striking down scores of people, both young and old, who dropped in the streets to die. Fear, superstition, and utter selfishness reigned among the people. The illness struck its victims without warning. There were no physical signs. Brutal and virulent, it began with a cough and headache, followed by chills, fever, and shortness of breath, which left one exhausted and prostrate. Nausea, vomiting, back pain, and soreness in the arms and legs followed. Bright light became unbearable. Very few survived. Death came quickly, within two or three days. No one understood how it spread or how one contracted it. Many believed breathing the same air as those afflicted would bring it on. Whoever contracted the plague suffered great pain before taking their last breath.

When the pestilence struck a house or family, they were likely all to die if they remained together. Frightened, people abandoned their homes and relatives to flee to another town or village. Mothers barricaded doors against their own children, otherwise the authorities would board up their home and lock them all inside. Physicians could rarely be found, for they were not immune to the illness.

Those who could be found, demanded vast sums before they would enter a home to tend the sick. Most of those afflicted died alone, without confessor or sacraments, their bodies reeking until the *beccamorti* arrived to cart them away like rubbish.

Churches dug trenches, wide and deep, to receive the dead. The *beccamorti,* who passed with wagons to collect the dead, would toss them in, layer upon layer atop each other. Priests could not toll bells. Ordinances banned them from doing so because it disheartened the healthy as well as the sick. All fruits were forbidden entrance into the city. None of the guilds were operating. All the shops were shut, taverns closed; only apothecaries and churches remained open. Very few dared walk the streets. The plague enriched apothecaries, doctors, *beccamorti,* and vendors who tended to the sick or sold poultices of mallow, nettles, mercury and other herbs necessary to draw off the infirmity. No birds trilled until late in the evening, when the nightingales in my gardens broke out in an animated surge of song, part cheery and part glum.

But, in the wooded hills outside my palazzo, the breeze wafted moderate and fresh. I had taken all precautions necessary to prevent the contagion from attacking our household. In fact, I would have insisted we all leave Vicenza, but I feared our flight might drive us straight into the arms of the disease.

Dario did not seem nervous. Brave men seldom are. Their stoic courage makes them think they are invincibile, able to fight off any threats. As for our daughter, Chiara, now two years old, she was healthy and active as any child of that age, a blossom ever open to the sun.

Beatrice, Annunziata, and a small retinue of servants lived with us. I permitted no one to leave the palazzo for any reason. We existed on bread made from flour stored in our pantry, milk from our goats, whatever we could grow in our garden, and meat from the chickens or sheep we raised ourselves. I made sure everyone bathed regularly, rose and retired early, and remained in perfect health.

We entertained ourselves. Among his many other gifts, Dario had a beautiful voice. He sang with tender expression, and on many evenings, when I sat with Beatrice in the garden after putting little Chiara to bed, Dario would serenade us with luscious tones and beautiful songs. Beatrice would often join him, her delicate and clear voice chiming in as exquisite as a cascade of water from a fountain.

For many years thereafter, I would recall the sight of them singing together; their voices and united melody mocking me. The pungent fragrance of orange-blossom still floats towards me on the air and a yellow moon burns round and full in the dense sky. I remember how they leaned their two heads together, one fair, the other dark – my husband and my best friend, two people whose lives were a million times dearer to me than my own. Those were the happiest of days. Days of self-delusion always are.

As spring ebbed into summer, the plague spread with appalling persistence. The people of Vicenza became mad with terror. And still, my family remained unaffected. It was as if Chiara was our good luck charm against the plague. Her innocent mischievousness and chatter distracted us from our fears.

On one of the coolest mornings of the scorching summer, I woke earlier than usual. Dario slept soundly at my side. The fresh breeze outside tempted me to rise and stroll through the garden. I dressed softly, careful not to disturb him. As I was about to leave the room, some instinct forced me to turn and look at him once more. How enticing he was, smiling in his sleep.

My heart fluttered with love as I gazed down at him, chest bared, one naked, muscular leg above the covers. We had been married for three years and my passion and love for him had increased. I raised one of his golden locks that shone like a sunbeam on his pillow, and kissed his forehead. Then I left him.

A gentle breeze met me as I stepped outside. As I walked past the outside hearth, I noticed Dario had forgotten his silver tinderbox there. I ran my fingers over the engraved scrollwork around our intertwined initials, C and D, recalling his smile when I had given it to him as a gift. How happy I had been to give it to him. How happy he had been to receive it. My heart warmed at the memory as I slipped it into my belt purse to return to him later.

I strolled along the garden paths. A draught scarce strong enough to flutter the leaves invigorated me after the heat of the past few days. Absorbed in thoughts of family and household, I wandered further than I intended and found myself on a path long abandoned. Curious, I followed the winding footway. Overgrown with trees and foliage, it was shady and cool. I continued down the narrow path until I glimpsed rooftops through the leafage of the trees. The path had brought me to the perimeters of Vicenza. Fearful of the plague, I knew I should not continue and I turned round to return home.

A sudden sound startled me; a moan of intense pain, a smothered cry emitted by some poor creature in torture. I turned in that direction, and saw, lying face down on the grass, a boy, a little vegetable-seller of eleven or twelve years of age. His basket of wares stood beside him, a tempting pile of vegetables, lovely but dangerous to eat in this time of plague.

"What ails you?" I asked, leaning close to him, placing my hand on his forehead. The heat of his body burned my palm. His fetid breath scorched me when he coughed.

He shuddered as he looked at me with pitiful eyes set in a beautiful face, scarlet with suffering. "The plague, *signora*," he moaned. "The plague. Keep away from me, for the love of God. I am going to die."

I hesitated. I had touched the boy and inhaled his breath. For myself, I had no fear, but for my husband and child, I did. For their sakes, I must be vigilant. Yet, I could not abandon this poor boy and resolved to help him. "Courage, do not lose heart. Not all illnesses are the plague. Rest here till I return. I am going to fetch a healer for you."

The little fellow looked at me with incredulous, wretched eyes, and tried to smile. He pointed to his stomach, and tried to speak, but to no avail. Then he writhed about in the grass like a wounded animal.

I left him and hurried away. Soon, I reached a small piazza bathed by the sun's intense heat. I noticed a few worried-looking men standing uselessly about. To them, I explained the boy's predicament and beseeched them for assistance. They all hung back. No one offered to accompany me, not even for all the silver coins I offered them. Annoyed at their cowardice, I hurried on in search of a healer.

Through the streets I went, making inquiries. Several hours passed before I found a healer and knocked on her door.

The sallow-faced, wrinkled, old woman listened to my account of the condition in which I had left the little vegetable-seller. Then she shook her head and refused to follow me. "He is as good as dead," the hag said with callous curtness. "Better hail one of the *beccamorti*. They will fetch his body."

Frustration rose inside me. "You refuse to help him?"

The healer bowed her head with sarcastic politeness. "*Signora* must pardon me. If I touch a plagued corpse, I would endanger my own health and I would be unable to help others who may need me. I bid you a good-day."

The Contessa's Vendetta

Then she disappeared, slamming the door in my face.

Exasperated, and though the heat and the putrid odour of the sun-baked streets made me feel faint and sick, I forgot all danger to myself. I stood in the middle of this plague-stricken city at a loss as to what to do next.

A sombre, but gentle voice greeted me from behind. "You seek aid, *signora?*"

I spun about.

A tall, lanky monk, whose cowl partly concealed his pallid features, stood before me. I greeted him respectfully and explained my need.

"I will go at once." He spoke with compassion. "But I fear the worst. I have remedies with me, but it may be too late to help the boy."

Relief coursed through me. I had come upon a cleric who faced the pestilence without fear when others I had met had scuttled away like frightened rabbits. "I will bring you to him," I offered. "I would not let a dog die unaided, much less this poor lad, who seems friendless and without kin."

The monk studied me as we walked. "You do not reside here?"

I gave him my name and described the location of my home.

By his nod, he indicated he knew of me.

"At that height we are free from the pestilence," I said. "I understand the panic that prevails in the city, but the situation is made worse by the cowardice displayed for those poor souls who have been afflicted."

"But what else can the people do? Their hearts are set on life. When death, common to all, enters their midst, they are like babes scared by a dark shadow."

"But you, dear brother," I began, and stopped to cough, conscious of a sharp throbbing pain in my temples.

"I am a servant of Christ. The plague holds no fear for

me. Unworthy as I am, I am ready and willing to face all manner of death." He spoke with firmness, yet without arrogance.

I looked at him with admiration, and was about to speak, when a curious dizziness overcame me. I clutched his arm to prevent myself from falling. The street rocked like a ship at sea, and the skies whirled round me in a blur of blue. The feeling gradually passed, and I heard the monk's voice as though it came from a long way off, asking me what was the matter.

I forced a smile. "I believe it is the heat," I said. "I feel faint, feeble. I had best stay here. Please see to the boy. *Dio.*" My weakened legs collapsed beneath me and I experienced a shooting pain, bitter and harsh as though a sword had been plunged into my flesh.

I sank to the ground shuddering. Without hesitation, the lanky monk helped me to my feet. He half carried, half led me to a nearby inn. Inside, he helped me sit on a wooden bench and called for the proprietor, a man he seemed to know very well. Although I felt very ill, I was conscious and could understand everything that was happening around me.

"Attend to her well, Giovanni," the monk said. "She is the Contessa Carlotta Mancini. You will not regret caring for her. I will return within an hour."

"Contessa Mancini. *Santissima Madonna.* She has caught the plague."

I knew it was possible, for it took only a few hours before one contracted the plague after exposure.

"Hush, fool," the monk exclaimed. "You cannot know that. A stroke of the sun is not the plague. See to her well or, by Saint Peter, there will be no place for you in Heaven."

The landlord appeared terrified at the uttered curse. He retreated and returned with pillows to place beneath my head. The monk held a glass to my lips. It contained some herbal mixture, which I swallowed without thought.

"Rest here, my lady," he said with a calming tone. "These people will treat you kindly. I will hasten to the boy and in less than an hour will return to you again."

I restrained him with my hand on his arm. "Wait," I murmured. "Let me know the worst. Do you think I have the plague?"

"I hope not," he replied with compassion. "But it is possible. You may have contracted it from the boy. It does not take long for the plague to spread from one person to another. If this is the case, you are young and strong. You can fight it. Do not be afraid."

"I am not afraid, but please promise me one thing. Send no word of my illness to my husband. You must swear it. Even if I am unconscious or dead, swear you will ensure no one takes my body back to my villa. I cannot risk making my family ill. Swear it. I cannot rest till I have your word."

"I swear it, my lady," he answered, solemnly. "By all I hold sacred, I will respect your wishes."

His words reassured me. The safety of my loved ones was certain. I thanked him with a mute gesture, too weak to say anything more. He disappeared from my sight.

I lost all semblance of time. My thoughts meandered into a confusion of bizarre delusions. I could see the interior of the room where I lay. The landlord polished his glasses and bottles, casting anxious glances in my direction. Groups of men peered at me through the doorway, but the moment they saw me, they fled.

A cloud floated above my face and in its center, a face emerged. "Dario. My love, my husband," I cried, stretching out my arms to clasp him. Instead, I realized the landlord held me in his embrace. I struggled to push him away.

"*Cretino!*" I shrieked. "Let me go, my husband's lips

are the only ones to kiss me, not yours, let me go."

Another man advanced and seized me. He and the landlord overcame me and forced me back on the pillows. Exhaustion robbed me of strength. I ceased to struggle. The landlord and his assistant stared down at me.

"She's dead," one of them whispered.

I heard them. Dead? Not me. The pain my chest was unbearable, my breathing shallow because of it. Scorching sunlight streamed through the open door of the inn. Thirsty flies buzzed with persistent loudness. Voices sang, though I could not distinguish the words.

I yearned for Dario. What had Beatrice said about him? *As pure as a flawless diamond and as unapproachable as the farthest star.*

That idiotic landlord still buffed his wine-bottles, his fearful round face oily with heat and grime. I did not understand why he was there, for I saw myself resting on the banks of a cool river where huge trees grew wild and a drowsy lion slept in the sun, its jaws open wide and eyes aglitter with hunger. A boat slipped silently through the water. In it, I beheld a woman, her features similar to those of Beatrice. The woman drew out a long thin stiletto as she approached. Brave Beatrice. She meant to attack the lion on the shore. She stepped onto the bank and passed the lion, unaware of its presence. Instead, she headed straight toward me with a rapid, unwavering step. I was the one Beatrice sought. Beatrice thrust the cold metal stiletto into my heart and drew it out dripping with blood. Once, twice, three times she stabbed me, and yet, I did not die. I thrashed about and moaned in torment. Then a dark shadow came to stand over me.

Two dark eyes looked into mine. "Be calm, my lady. I commend you to Christ." He made the sign of the cross on my forehead.

It was the monk, and I was happy to see he had

returned from his errand of mercy. Though I struggled to speak, I managed to rasp out an inquiry about the boy.

The holy man crossed himself. "May his soul rest in peace. I found him dead."

Dead? So soon? I could not understand it and drifted off again into an addled state.

Time passed. Intense, intolerable pain, tortured me. Through my delirium I heard muffled, sad sounds like chants or prayers. I also heard the tinkle of a bell, but my mind lurched with thoughts and visions that seemed both real and false at the same time. "Not to the villa," I shrieked. "No, not there. You shall not take me. A curse upon anyone who disobeys."

It seemed as if someone had dragged me into a deep hollow. The monk stood above me. I could not plead with him, could not move a limb, but through the narrow slits of my closed eyes, I caught a glimpse of a silver crucifix sparkling above me. With one last cry for help, I fell down, down, into a void of dark oblivion where time had no beginning and no end.

Chapter Three

Silence and total blackness engulfed me. The gloom held me trapped. Dreamy visions fluttered through my mind, at first vague, but later more clear. In what horrifying darkness was I? Slowly my senses returned, and I remembered my illness. The monk, the innkeeper, where were they? Where had they put me? I was lying on my back upon a very hard, uncomfortable surface, without so much as a pillow, or sheet.

A prickling sensation shot through my veins. My hands were warm and my heart beat strongly. I struggled to breathe. Air. I must have air. I raised my hands, but they struck wood above and around me. A horrible realization flashed into my mind: someone had buried me alive in a coffin. They must have believed me dead from the plague.

Terror and fury blazed through me. I wrenched and scratched at the wood surrounding me with the entire force of my body. I strained to push open the closed lid, but my efforts were in vain.

Icy drops of sweat trickled down my forehead as I gasped for breath. Summoning my energy for one last attempt, driven by desperation, I hurled my body hard against one side of my narrow prison. It cracked and split, but no light showed through the crack, and a horrid new fear beset me. If they had buried me in the ground, what good was it to break open the coffin and let in the damp, maggot-ridden mold? It would choke and silence me forever. I recoiled at the thought and wavered on the verge of madness. A scream flew from my lips; a sound that rasped like the rattle in the throat of a person about to die. Yet, I breathed easily. Even in my bewilderment, I was conscious of air. Blessed air was rushing in from somewhere.

Encouraged, I felt around with both hands until I found the crack in the wood I had made. With frenzied swiftness, I yanked and heaved at the wood, but made little progress. After regaining my breath and wiping the sweat from my forehead, I tried again. Splinters cut into my fingers; my desperation kept me focused on the task. Soon, the opening widened and with one more push and kick, the entire side of the coffin gave way.

I managed to force up the lid and stretched out my arms. No weight of earth impeded my movements. Nothing but empty air encircled me. Instinctively I leaped out of the unbearable coffin and fell to the ground, bruising my hands and knees on a stone pavement.

From somewhere beside me, something heavy fell with a loud, splintering crash.

In the darkness, I breathed deeply of cool, musty air. With difficulty and pain, I raised myself to a sitting position. My limbs felt cramped and I shivered in the cold dampness.

When my muddled thoughts cleared and some of my hysteria dissolved, I pondered my situation. My illness had likely rendered me unconscious. The innkeeper must have believed me dead of the plague, and panic-stricken, had thrust me into a flimsy coffin and nailed it shut with inept haste.

Had they laid me in a sturdier casket, or buried me in the earth like other victims of the plague, who knows if I could have freed myself? I cringed at the thought. One question remained. Where was I? I searched for an answer, but could not arrive at one.

I remembered telling the monk my name. He knew that I was the sole descendant of the noble Mancini family. The holy man must have done his duty. He had seen me laid in my ancestral vault, sealed since my father's burial. The more I thought of this, the more probable it seemed.

The Mancini vault; its forbidding gloom had terrified me when I followed my father's coffin to his assigned stone niche. Somewhere in the dark was my mother's heavy oaken casket, hung with tattered velvet and ornamented with tarnished silver. I felt sick and faint. Trembling with cold, I would not feel better until I breathed fresh air beneath an azure sky. Trapped in my family burial chamber, I was a prisoner with little hope of escape.

I recalled that a heavy door of closely twisted iron barred the entrance to the vault. From there, a flight of steep steps led downward to where I now sat. Could I feel my way through the dark to those steps and climb up to that door? But it was locked and the vault was in a remote section of the cemetary. Even the keeper might not come near it for days, perhaps weeks. I would starve or die of thirst.

Tortured by such thoughts, I stood erect. The cold stone floor chilled my bare feet to the marrow. Fearful of contagion, they had left me fully clothed in the same ivory and wine-colored gown with its tabbed bodice, long stomacher, and virago sleeves I had worn the day I fell sick. Since donning it, my world had changed horrifically.

I raised my hand to my neck. When I touched the gold chain and medallion engraved with the initials of my husband and daughter, a flood of sweet memories rushed over me. I raised the round pendant to my lips and pressed my kisses and tears, scalding and bitter, upon it. Life was worth living while my Chiara and Dario's smiles lit the world. I resolved to fight; to climb out of this crypt, no matter what dire horrors awaited me.

Dario, my love. In the black gloom, I pictured his handsome face that shone like a beacon in my mind. His mournful eyes beckoned, as though I could hear him sob alone in the empty silence of our bedchamber, his hair dishevelled, his face haggard with grief. My little Chiara, too, would wonder why I did not come to kiss her good night. How I missed my baby. And Beatrice, my dearest friend. I fretted over how profound her sadness would be.

I must escape these grim confines. How ecstatic they would be to see me again, to know that I was alive. Oh, how they would welcome me. Dario would sweep me into his arms, my beloved daughter would cling to me, Beatrice would shed tears of joy at my appearance. I smiled, picturing our reunion. My happy home blessed by faultless friendship and staunch fidelity.

In the distance, a church bell tolled the hour. One, two, three... I counted twelve strokes. My pleasant thoughts faded and the grim reality of my situation troubled me anew. Did the bells announce midday or midnight? I could not tell.

It had been early morning when I took that ill-begotten path into Vicenza. It must have been before midday when I met the monk and sought his assistance for the young lad who had suffered and died alone. If my illness had lasted a day or two, as was the case with most victims who died of the plague. I might have died the following day or the next. In that case, they likely buried me before sunset. These might be the bells of midnight struck on the very day of my burial. I felt certain it could be no more than three days after contracting the illness, otherwise I would be in severe thirst.

I trembled; a tense fear crept over me. Something dreadful resounded in the tolling of those midnight bells that echoed cruelly on my ears, the ears of a woman pent up alive in a crypt with the putrefying bodies of her ancestors. I tried to suppress my terror and summon my courage. I must escape this hell. With my hands before me, I slowly and carefully felt my way to the steps of the vault.

A long piercing cry, intense and miserable, echoed through the hollow arches of my tomb. Blood curdled in my veins. I broke out in a cold sweat. My heart beat so stridently that I could hear it thump against my ribs. The shriek seemed to come from inside the vault, and this time a flurry and flutter of wings followed it. *It is only an owl*, I whispered aloud in an effort to still my rising panic, only a harmless companion to the dead. But how did it get in here? If it could enter, it could also depart.

Hopeful, I moved cautiously onward. Suddenly, from out of the darkness, the owl sprung at me with wretched malice. I fought with the creature as it circled my head, pounced at my face, and beat me with massive wings I could feel, but could not see. I struck at it relentlessly. The repulsive confrontation seemed to last forever. Although ill and lightheaded, I battled the beast. Finally, the huge owl halted its assault. It emitted one last vicious screech then vanished into some black corner. Every nerve in my body shook as I tried to regain my breath.

Blindly groping with outstretched hands, I continued on my way to where I believed the stone staircase might be, but instead, I bumped into a hard and cold horizontal barrier. I ran my hands over it. Was this the first step of the stairs? It seemed too high. I stroked it cautiously and touched something soft and sodden like wet velvet. Beneath the cloth, my fingers traced the oblong form of a coffin. A realization shot through me and I withdrew my hand swiftly. Whose coffin was this? My father's? Or was it my mother's oak casket?

A deep sense of despair swept through me. All my

efforts to find my way through the vault were fruitless. Lost in the overwhelming blackness, I did not know in which direction I should turn. With shocking realization, the direness of my circumstances became clear. Thirst tormented me. I fell to my knees and wept.

My sobs rang through the vault's arches; the sound strange and horrific to my own ears. If I could not escape this agony soon, I would go mad, confined in this place of death and darkness, with decomposing cadavers as my sole companions. I buried my face in my hands, forcing myself to remain calm and keep my mind from surrendering to the madness that threatened to possess me.

Then, from somewhere in the distance, I heard a cheerful sound. I raised my head and listened to the trill of a nightingale. How it reassured me in this hour of despair. I praised God for its existence and sprang up laughing and weeping for joy at its shower of lustrous warbles. A rush of courage surged through me, invigorating me with hope and vitality.

A new idea came to me. I could follow the nightingale's voice. It sang harmoniously, optimistically, and I resumed my journey through the blackness. In my mind, I pictured the bird perched on one of the trees outside the vault, and believed that if I could move towards its voice, it would guide me to the staircase I so desperately sought.

Stumbling along, I felt weak and my legs quavered beneath me. This time nothing impeded my progress. The nightingale's song drifted closer. Hope that had nearly faded, bounded once more into my heart. Barely aware of my own movements, the golden melody of the song drew me as if I were in a dream.

My foot tripped over a stone and I fell forward. I felt no pain; my limbs were too numb with cold. I raised my aching eyes in the darkness and cried out. One meager ray of moonlight, no thicker than a blade of straw, flickered down on me and revealed the lowest step of the stairway. I could not see the door of the vault, but I knew that it must be there at the top.

Too exhausted to move, I lay still as a stone, gazing at the solitary moon-ray, and listening to the nightingale, whose melody rang out with clarity. The low-pitched bell of earlier now rang out the first hour of the day. Soon, it would be morning. I decided to rest until then. Completely exhausted, I rested my head against the cold stones as if they were silk pillows. Within a few moments, I put all my miseries out of my mind and drifted into sleep.

Chapter Four

A biting sting on my neck woke me. Nauseated and dizzy, I raised my hand to my throat and closed my trembling fingers around a winged and slimy, flesh and blood horror fastened to my skin. Its abhorrent grip drove me to hysteria. Wild with revulsion, I screamed as I clasped its plump bulk and ripped it away, flinging it hard and far into the vault. I could hear it flapping about in the darkness until it settled somewhere.

I continued to scream, terrified. Had I reached the edge of insanity? Fatigue finally silenced me. Gasping for air and in my weakened state, my entire body trembled. After a length of haunting silence, I tried to regain control over my fears.

The moonbeam no longer shone into the vault. Instead, a stream of dull grey light took its place. I could now see the entire staircase and the closed iron grate at the top. With desperate haste, I crawled up the steps. Grasping the iron grate with both hands, I shook it hard. My efforts were in vain; the locked grate would not open.

"Help me," I screeched. My voice echoed over the desolate tombstones. Absolute stillness replied.

I stared through the tightly weaved black rods. Beyond lay verdant grass and lush trees beneath a glorious sky already flushed with the peach and rose-tinted hues of a rising sun. I drank in the pure, revitalizing air.

A long, wild grapevine dangled within reach, its leaves sodden with dew. I squeezed one hand through the grate and picked a few fresh, leafy fragments, ravenously stuffing them into my mouth. They tasted more delectable than anything I had ever eaten and they relieved my parched throat.

The sight of the sky and earth calmed me. The nightingale had ceased its melodic song. In its place, I heard the gentle twitter of awakening birds. My breathlessness soon eased.

As my terror abated, I leaned against the stone archway and glanced back down the steep stairway. Something white lay on the seventh step from the top. Curious, I descended and saw that it was a partially spent thick wax candle, the type used by the Church for funeral masses, likely from my own. Now, if only I had a means to light it. Then I remembered Dario's tinderbox. I reached into the purse attached to my belt. It was there. I pulled it out along with a few silver coins, a thimble, a fan, my visiting card case, and the ring of keys belonging to various doors in my villa. They must have buried me in haste for they had taken none of my possessions. The silver tinderbox was especially valuable. Only fear of contagion would have kept someone from taking it.

The knowledge that I could strike a flame and light the candle made me almost giddy with relief. The sun had not yet fully risen and it might be hours before anyone came to the graveyard and discovered me.

An unusual idea came to mind, and the more I thought about it, the more I wanted to do it. I needed to see my coffin. Possessing the tinderbox had chased away my fears and gave me the courage to do it. I picked up the candle and after two strikes of the steel, I managed to light the char-cloth, which I then used to light the candle. At first, it flickered, but after a moment, the flame became steady and

The Contessa's Vendetta

strong. The candle would not last long, perhaps an hour, two at the most. I shaded it from any draughts with my hand, cast a parting glance at the daylight that shone temptingly through the iron grate, and descended back into the murkiness.

Lizards slithered away as I descended the steps. The moment the candle flame permeated the darkness, I heard the flurry of wings and a feral cry. Hideous creatures lived in this house of the dead, but armed with my light, I had the confidence to defeat them all. My descent seemed so short compared to my climb in the impenetrable dark, and I soon found myself back in the vault's depths.

Now I could see. High walls enclosed the small room. Horizontal niches in the wall, one above the other, held narrow caskets containing my ancestors' bones. I held the candle high above my head and looked around with morbid curiosity until I found what I sought – my own coffin.

It lay in a niche five feet from the ground, its fractured wood proof of my struggle to free myself. I advanced for a closer look. It was a flimsy box, unlined, of plain wood, and shoddily crafted. Thank goodness it had been so poorly made, otherwise I might never have escaped from it.

I peered inside. Something shone from within – an ebony and silver crucifix. The good monk must have laid it on my breast before they closed me into the coffin. My heart warmed at his thoughtfulness. In my struggle to free myself, the cross must have dropped off my chest. I raised it to my lips, kissed it, and made up my mind that if I ever met the monk again, I would tell him my tale, and show him the cross as proof of my ordeal. I had no doubt he would recognize it.

Had they put my name on the coffin lid? I leaned closer to look. There it was, painted on the wood in coarse, black letters. CARLOTTA MANCINI. The date of my birth followed it and then a short Latin inscription stating that I had died of the plague on August 15, 1631. Only Saturday, yet an eternity seemed to have passed since then.

I turned to my father's resting place. The velvet pall over his coffin had begun to disintegrate. Next to him, was another coffin covered with a worm-eaten, frayed cloth upon which I lay my palm. This was my mother's coffin; she who had given me life, who had first embraced me and from whose loving arms I first beheld the world. I recalled my mother's portrait that hung in the dining hall of my villa. The artist had captured her in full youth; a light-haired beauty, whose delicate complexion was as lovely as a ripening peach against the summer sun. Now, all that loveliness lay in this damp hole, decaying into bone and dust. I shuddered at the thought.

I knelt in front of my parent's desolate stone niches and prayed for their blessing. While I prayed, the candlelight caught a small object glittering on the ground. I leaned over to retrieve it. A thick, golden chain upon which hung a pendant of a ship, dangled from my fingers. Its fine artistry and intricate details astonished me. Only the most talented of goldsmiths could have created such an ornament, likely for some nobleman, for there was nothing feminine about this piece. Upon its masts, flew sails painted with white enamel and studded with pearls. Sapphires, rubies, and diamonds decorated it from bow to stern. I clutched it in my hand and glanced about to discover where the treasure could have come from.

An unusually large coffin lay sideways, toppled on the ground. I lowered the candle to the ground and observed a vacant but damaged niche below the one where my own coffin had been. I recalled that when I had broken free, I had heard a crash. It must have been this coffin, big enough to contain a huge man, that had fallen. What ancestor had I dislodged? Had the rare jewel in my hand come from a skeleton's throat?

Curious, I bent to examine the lid of the enormous casket. It bore no name and no mark except for a stiletto roughly painted in black. I had never seen this casket in the vault before. How had it come to be here? Eager to learn more about the mysterious coffin, I rested my candle in an empty niche and carefully laid the chain and ship pendant beside it.

I stepped closer to the coffin and applied both hands to a fractured corner, pushing and yanking to tear it open. After a loud crack and splinter, a leather pouch fell out. I picked it up and weighed it in my hand. When I unlaced it, I discovered it was full of gold coins. Excited, I seized a large pointed stone and began to thrust it repeatedly against the casket. I toiled hard and long, but finally managed to smash it open.

Stunned, I stared at the contents. No decomposing body met my gaze. No discolored or putrefying bones or skull mocked me with empty eye-sockets. Instead, I looked upon a treasure worthy of a king's ransom. Items of immeasurable wealth filled the casket. I counted fifty large leather pouches crammed with gold and silver coins. Others brimmed with priceless jewels - necklaces, crowns, bracelets, brooches, and other articles of masculine and feminine adornment. Some contained loose precious stones including diamonds, rubies, emeralds, and opals, all of unusual size and lustre, uncut and ready for a goldsmith to set.

Beneath the bags lay bolts of silk, velvet, and cloth of gold, each one carefully wrapped in oilskin and perfumed with camphor and other spices, all of unsurpassed quality and in a faultless state.

Among the cloths lay two gold serving trays with four matching goblets, all magnificently engraved and ornamented. I also discovered other riches such as small ivory statues, a belt of gold coins linked together, a delicately painted fan with a handle set in rubies and sapphires, an impressive steel stiletto in a jewelled leather sheath, and a silver mirror framed with amethysts. At the very bottom of the chest lay more leather purses filled with *soldi* and *denari* likely amounting to millions and millions of *scudos* - an amount far surpassing the revenues I had inherited from my father. I plunged my hands deep into the leather bags, fingering the riches, letting them fall through my fingers in a golden cascade. Amazement and wonder conflicted with my confusion. Where could such a treasure have come from? Many of the items appeared ancient, perhaps even Roman antiquities. I knew it well, for I had collected such treasures for several years.

My heart leapt with excitement. I let out a giddy, nervous laugh. Then it struck me. The treasure was mine. I had found it in my family crypt and had the right to claim it. But who had placed it there without my knowledge? The answer came easily. I now understood the meaning of the painted black stiletto on the lid of the coffin. It was the mark of a violent and notorious brigand named Cesare Negri who with his misguided band of thieves, ruthlessly haunted Vicenza and its surrounding areas. He was wanted by the authorities for theft and murder. People feared him. The cut-throat's cunning impressed me. He had calculated well, thinking no one would disturb the dead, much less break open a coffin. But all his shrewd planning had failed. I had found it. A dead woman returning to life deserved something for her trouble. Despite the fact this was an ill-gotten hoard, I would be foolish not to claim to it. After all, I was the sole owner of the vault. Besides, I deserved the treasure more than a villain like Cesare Negri, for I would find some honorable use for it.

I pondered the situation for a few moments. If this

treasure were indeed the spoils of the formidable Negri, how had it come to be here? Likely four sturdy scoundrels had carried the coffin here in a bogus funeral procession for a non-existent companion. Yet the question remained, how had they gained access to my ancestral vault? Did they possess a duplicate key?

All at once, a gust of air blew out my candle. I found myself in darkness once more. I had my tinderbox, and could light it again, but the gust of wind must have come from an opening somewhere. I looked round and noticed a ray of light emanating from a corner of the niche where I had left the candle and pendant. I approached and reached out for the items. A solid current of air blew through a hole large enough to fit three fingers. I relit my candle and examined the hole at the back of the niche.

Someone had removed four granite blocks in the wall. In their place were thick, loosely placed, wooden tiles. I pulled them off, one at a time. A pile of brushwood lay behind them. As I cleared it away, I discovered a tunnel large enough for a person to pass through. My heart beat with excitement as I clambered up. At the other end, I could see a glimpse of blue sky. I crouched down and crawled through it.

Within moments, I stood outside the vault, my bare feet upon soft, green grass and my body beneath an emerging blue sky. I fell to my knees and wept with joy. I was free. Free to resume my life, my love, my marriage to my beloved Dario; free to forget, if I could, the horror of my live burial.

Thankful, I prayed, heaping numerous blessings upon Cesare Negri. I owed the famous lout my gratitude, not only for the fortune he had left, but also for my freedom. He or his followers must have dug the secret passage into the Mancini vault for their own nefarious purposes. The authorities had been seeking him for quite some time and there was a price on his head. The villain was in hiding somewhere. Even if I were to discover his whereabouts, those who sought him would receive no aid from me. There was no reason for me to betray him. He had been my savior. Besides, no one could ever accuse me of stealing stolen property.

Bathed by the morning light, I rejoiced in my deliverance. Happiness the likes of which I had never known radiated through my body. When Dario saw me once more, he would love me more fondly than before, for although our separation had been brief, but terrible, the knowledge that I was alive would endear us to each other even more.

And my little Chiara. I could not wait to swing her again beneath the orange boughs and listen to her delightful squeals. I would clasp Beatrice's hand and the joy of our friendship would flood both our hearts. Tonight I would lay my head upon Dario's chest and listen to his heartbeat after our lovemaking. My head spun with dazzling, euphoric visions.

The sun had fully risen now. Long golden sunbeams stroked the treetops. I felt as if I would die from all my euphoria. I would share it all with Dario tonight when the moon rose and the nightingales returned to sing their love-songs. Full of such joyful fantasies, I inhaled the pure morning air for several more moments, and then went back down into the vault.

Chapter Five

Aided by the light of my candle and the meager sunlight that filtered into the crypt, I repacked the treasure. I kept two leather bags for myself - one full of jewels and the other of coins. To my relief, the casket had suffered little damage when I had forced it open. I secured the lid, and despite my weakness, I managed to push it to the darkest corner of the vault. Fighting for breath, I disguised it beneath three heavy stones then wiped the sweat from my brow and paused to catch my breath.

Next, I removed the rope belt at my waist and secured my treasure to it. Then I raised the hem of my filthy gown to below my breasts and held it in place with my elbow. I knotted the belt around my waist before lowering my gown over it to disguise the booty.

Straightening my gown, I ran my hand over my hair. I could tell it was in disarray too. I must look a fright. I did not want anyone to see me in so dirty and disheveled a condition. With all the money I carried, I had more than enough to purchase a gown, but where could I find one? Unfortunately, I did not know. All my life, I had ordered gowns from exclusive dressmakers who came to my villa with bolts of material to choose from and later for fittings.

Must I wait until nightfall before I could escape this tomb? No. I could not bear to linger in these gruesome surroundings a moment longer. Throngs of beggars swarm the streets of Vicenza in every manner of rags, dirt, and misery. If taken for one of them, it would matter little to me. Whatever problems I might encounter on my way home would be short-lived.

Satisfied that I had placed the brigand's treasure-filled coffin in a safe position, I hung the ship pendant round my neck. It would make a fine gift for Dario, whose fondness for gold jewelry surpassed my own. After one last glance about, I climbed out through the tunnel.

I used the same logs and brush to disguise the opening, and then stood back to examine my handiwork. I could detect no signs that a passage lay behind it and whispered a prayer of thanks to Cesare Negri for having created such a clever cover-up. All that remained was for me to declare my identity, drink and eat something, purchase a new garment, and then return home.

I stood on a grassy knoll and looked about. In the distance, I could see the outskirts of Vicenza. A sloping road wound toward the city and I walked in that direction. The sun beamed down with searing vibrancy on my uncovered head. With each step, my bare feet sunk into the scalding hot dust of the road.

Yet, I cared little about all the unpleasantness. I was ecstatic to be alive and it showed with every buoyant and jaunty step I took. Soon I would be home with Dario and Chiara. My eyes and head throbbed under the shimmering brilliance of daylight. A shiver or two ran through me as I walked - remnants of my near fatal illness, but I was confident that it would pass in a day or two. Enfolded in the loving arms of my family, I knew I would make a full recovery.

I strode valiantly onward, at first encountering no one. Then I came upon a small fruit cart laden with baskets brimming with lemons, apricots, peaches, and melons. The driver was sleeping across the front seat, his hat over his face. His donkey munched the roadside's green grass. Every now and then, the creature raised its head to look about and set off a delicate jingle from the small bells on its harness.

At the rear of the cart, the fruit piled in various baskets lured me. My hunger and thirst near unbearable, I nudged the sleeping man's foot. He awoke with a start. At the sight of me, his eyes widened with fear. He leaped down and dropped to his knees in the dust trembling. "*Madonna Mia.* Saint Peter. I implore you, *per favore,* spare my life."

I could not help myself. I burst out laughing at his ludicrous reaction. What could be so fear provoking about a small woman like me other than the filthy state of my clothing?

"Please, do not be afraid," I said, holding out several coins. "All I want is to buy some fruit from you."

Quivering, he rose and studied me with misgiving. He grabbed two peaches and three apricots and handed them to me without saying a word. The man snatched the coins from my palm, bounded back into his cart, and flogging the poor donkey until the creature kicked back with anger, clattered down the road emitting a cloud of dust in his wake. Amused at the absurdity of his terror, I watched until he disappeared from my sight. Did he think me a ghost who would raid his cart?

I ate the ripe, sweet, refreshing fruit as I walked along. I encountered more people the closer I came to Vicenza; farmers and venders who paid me no notice. I avoided making eye contact with them and hurried past as fast as possible.

On reaching the city's perimeter, I turned into the first street. Dense with houses and foul-smelling, I continued forth until I happened upon a ramshackle cottage with a broken shutter through which I noticed a shabby array of used garments hanging on strings of coarse twine.

Among the desolate samplings of used garments, I could see many intriguing and charming objects - shells and coral, beads and bracelets, dishes carved out of wood, animal horns, painted fans, and old coins to name a few. A monstrous wooden statue stared down from a shelf between a chipped vase and a worn pair of boots, as though it scrutinized the peculiar assortment of goods with dim-witted bewilderment.

An old woman sat mending a tattered gown at the open door. Deep furrows scored her wrinkled, sun-weathered face, the color of brown parchment. Only her blue, bead-like eyes shone with life. They roved left and right with restlessness and suspicion. She saw me approach, but feigned absorption in her work. I stopped before her and she raised her gaze to mine, her eyes glaring with inquisitiveness.

"I have travelled a long way." She was not the type of person I could entrust with my secrets. "I lost some of my clothes in an accident. Can you sell me a gown? Anything will do. I am not particular."

The old woman laid her mending on her lap and looked at me through narrowed eyes of startling blue. "Are you afraid of the plague?"

"No. In fact, I have recovered from it," I replied with composure.

She stared at me from head to foot, and then broke out in a shrill cackling laugh. "Ha. Excellent. Just like me, another woman who is unafraid. The plague is a beautiful thing. I love it. I buy clothes that have been stripped from the corpses. They are usually in perfect condition. I never wash them and I sell them immediately. And why not? Those afflicted with the illness die. Better for them they die sooner than later." The old hag crossed herself.

The Contessa's Vendetta

I glared down at her with an air of disgust. She repulsed me as much as the beast that had fastened itself on my neck when I slept in the vault. "Will you sell me a gown or not?"

"*Si, si,* of course." She rose stiffly from the bench. Short of stature and misshapen by age and infirmity, she looked more like the warped limb of an ancient olive tree than a woman. I followed her as she hobbled into her dark shop. "*Vieni dentro,* come inside. Choose whatever you like. I have a great variety to suit all tastes and sizes. Here's a good one, the dress of a noblewoman. What strong wool. Made in Paris. The woman who wore this was French; a comely, jovial woman who drank wine like water, and she was rich too. The plague took her swiftly. She died drunk and cursing God. A marvellous way to die. One of her servants sold me her gowns for five *scudi,* but you must give me ten. That is a fair profit, is it not, especially for someone as old and poor as I am who must work hard to earn enough to feed herself?"

I cast aside the wool gown she held up for my examination. "I'm not worried about the plague, but find me something better than the cast-off clothing of a wine-soaked French woman. I would rather wear the dismal garb of a house servant."

A raspy laugh escaped the old woman's withered throat. "Good," she croaked. "I like that. You are old, but cheery. Everyone should laugh. And why not? Death always laughs and taunts us."

She plunged her knobby fingers into a chest stuffed with a variety of garments, mumbling to herself all the while. I stood beside her, bewildered by her words. *You are old, but cheery.* Why did she think me old? She must be blind, I thought, or in her dotage.

Suddenly she glanced up. "Speaking about the plague, did you know that it took one of the richest, most beautiful women in all of Vicenza? She was young too, strong and full of life; someone who looked as if she would live forever. The plague touched her one morning and before sunrise the next day, they nailed her into a coffin. They carried her into her big family vault; a cold lodging compared to her grand marble villa on the heights yonder. When I heard the news, I scolded God for taking Contessa Carlotta Mancini."

My heart pounded in my chest, but I composed myself enough to appear indifferent. "And why is she so special that she should not deserve to die?"

The old woman straightened from her stooped stance and stared at me with her keen blue eyes. "Who was she? I can see you know nothing of Vicenza. Have you not heard of the wealthy Mancini family? I wished the contessa to live a long life. She was clever and bold, but always good to the poor. She gave away hundreds of *scudi* in charity. I have seen her often, even on the day she got married." Her crinkled, parchment-like face screwed itself into a malevolent expression. "Bah. I hate her husband, a handsome man, but weak and as vile as a snake. I used to watch them both from the streets as they drove along in their fine carriage and I wondered how it would end between them. I knew their marriage could not last. I wanted her to be the victor over him. I would even have helped her kill him to free her from that cursed marriage. Instead, God made a mistake. She is the one who is dead and that snake lives on and now has all her wealth."

I listened to the old wench with loathing, but interest too. Why should she hate my husband? Perhaps she hated all young, handsome men. If she had seen me as often as she claimed, why did she not recognize me? "What did Contessa Mancini look like? You say she was beautiful. Did she have dark or golden hair? Was she slim or tall?"

Pushing aside an errant wisp of gray hair from her

forehead, she stretched out a tawny, garbled hand as though pointing to a vision. "She was a beautiful woman, as straight and tall and as slim as you are. Your eyes are hollow and weak while hers were bursting with life and luminous. Your face is haggard and pallid, but hers was lucent and of a clear olive tint that glowed with vigor. Her hair was glossy black, not snow-white like yours."

I flinched with fright. Had I changed that much in so short a time? Had the horror of spending a night in the crypt made such a severe impact upon my appearance? White hair instead of my ebony locks? I could hardly believe it.

Perhaps Dario would not recognize me and would doubt my identity. If need be, I could verify I was Carlotta Mancini. All I had to do was show him the vault and my own splintered coffin inside it.

While I contemplated all this, the old woman carried on with her ramblings. "Ah, *si*, she was a fine woman. I used to rejoice that she was so wise. She could have poisoned that snake of a husband so he could tell no more lies. I wanted her to do it. I would have gladly provided her with the poison. Had she lived, I am certain she would have done it one day. That is why I am sorry the contessa died."

It took intense effort master my emotions so I could speak calmly to this spiteful old crone. "Why do you hate the contessa's husband so much? Has he done you any harm?"

She straightened as much as she was able and stared at me with unrelenting force. "I'll tell you why I hate him. You are an intelligent woman," she answered with a sneer at the corners of her vile mouth. "I like intelligent women, but sometimes they're easily fooled by men. That's when a woman should take revenge. I was intelligent and strong myself once. You are old, so will understand. Dario

Gismondi has done me harm. When his horse knocked me down in the street, he laughed at me. I was hurt, but I saw his lips widen and his white teeth glitter. He has an enchanting smile, the people will tell you. So innocent. Someone picked me up, but it wasn't him. His carriage drove on. His wife was not with him otherwise I know she would have stopped to help me. But it doesn't matter, because he laughed and it was then that I saw the likeness."

"The likeness?" Her story annoyed me. "What likeness?"

"Between him and my husband," she replied, fixing her cruel eyes upon me with increasing intensity. "Oh, *si*. I know what love is. I married a man as handsome as a morning in spring with eyes as gentle as a tiny child who looks up and asks you for kisses. I was away from home once. When I returned, I found him sleeping with a black-browed beauty from Venice as brash and as brazen as a lioness. While they slept, I made my way to her side of the bed and put my stiletto to the whore's throat, signalling for her to keep her mouth shut. I forced her to the ground and knelt upon her chest. I looked down into her eyes and smiled. 'I won't not hurt you. All I ask is that you keep your mouth shut.' She stared at me, mute with fear. I gagged her then bound her hands and feet so that she could not move. I took my stiletto and went to him. His face looked so peaceful as I plunged the keen bright blade through the hairy white flesh of his chest. His brown eyes glared wide and imploring, while his heart's blood welled up in a crimson tide, staining the bed linens with a brilliant burgundy hue. Behind me, his whore moaned out in agony. He flung up his arms and sank back on his pillows dead. I drew the blade from his body, and with it cut the bonds of the Venetian slut. I then gave her the stiletto. 'Take it as a remembrance of him. In a month he would have betrayed you as he betrayed me.' She raved like a mad woman and

The Contessa's Vendetta

rushed from the room straight to the constable. I was tried for murder, but it was not murder - it was justice. The judge found extenuating circumstances. Naturally. He had a wife too. He understood my case. Now you know why I hate that rogue at the Villa Mancini. He is just like the husband I slew. He has the same slow smile and the same child-like eyes. I tell you again, I'm sorry that his wife is dead. It vexes me to think of it. In time, he would have driven her to kill him, of that I am certain."

Chapter Six

The old woman's story turned my blood cold. For our entire married life, I believed that everyone who met or knew Dario, respected and admired him. I could not deny that when my husband's horses knocked down this old woman, an event he had never mentioned to me, it was careless of him not to stop and at least inquire as to the extent of her injuries. He was young and thoughtless, but I did not want to believe he could be so heartless. It horrified me to think that he had made an enemy of this aged and poverty-stricken wretch, but I said nothing. I had no wish to betray myself to her.

She waited for me to speak and grew impatient at my silence. "Was it not fair vengeance I took?" she asked with childlike zeal. "God himself could not have done better."

"I think your husband deserved his fate, but I cannot say I admire you for being his murderer," I responded brusquely.

She turned on me in an instant and flung both of her hands above her head with frenetic motion. "You call me a murderer? How dare you. *He* murdered *me*." Her voice escalated into shrillness. "I died when I saw him asleep with his whore. That vision killed me. It was the devil rose up inside of me to take swift revenge. That same devil is in me now, a brave devil, a strong devil. That is why I do not fear the plague. The devil inside me frightens away death, but someday the evil will leave me." Her voice sank into a frail, pathetic tone. "*Si*, it will leave me and I shall find a dark place where I can sleep; I do not sleep much anymore. You see, my memory is very good, and when one thinks too much, one cannot sleep. Even though many years have passed, I still see my husband every night. He appears before me wringing his hands, his brown eyes piercing. I hear his terrorized moans and see his wretchedness." She paused, and then like a woman waking from sleep, she stared at me as if she saw me for the first time, and broke into a low chuckling laugh.

"What a thing the mind is," she muttered. "Strange, very strange. See, I remembered all that and forgot about you. You want a new gown and I need to be paid for it. If you do not want the fine gown of the French noblewoman, I will find you something else, but you must have patience."

She rummaged through a mound of garments at the rear of the shop. She looked so scrawny and forbidding that she reminded me of an aged vulture stooping over carrion. Yet, there was something pathetic about her too. In a way I pitied her; a poor dim-witted wretch who had lived a life filled with bitterness and aggravation.

How different my life was in comparison to hers. I had suffered only a day or two of anguish over my illness; trivial in comparison to the constant torment in her mind. She hated Dario for a single act of thoughtlessness. Well, no doubt, he was not the only man whose existence annoyed her. She was probably hostile towards all men.

I felt sympathy for her as she searched among the shabby garments that provided her with a paltry livelihood. I wondered why death, so vigorous in slaying the strongest, should have overlooked this downhearted ruin of human misery for which the grave would have been a welcome release.

She turned round at last with a triumphant wave. "I have found it," she exclaimed as she raised a gown up and laid it against her body. "This one will suit you. She who wore it was about your height and it will fit you as well as it once fit her."

It was not the servant's garb I expected, but it would suffice. The emerald-colored gown consisted of a whaleboned bodice and three separate skirts. Large, elbow length sleeves were of several layers — two of black silk, and the final top layer of emerald silk, which was slashed so that the black layer beneath was visible. The lower part of the sleeve was gathered into a narrow band and fastened with black ribbon ties. The center front panel of the bodice was embroidered in a floral pattern with silk and metallic thread. The first of the three skirts was split-fronted and gathered onto a waistband and fastened at the center front by means of ribbon ties. The second skirt was in black, but unsplit and also gathered onto the waistband as was the third, which was of a heavy turquoise satin. She spread out the garment before me.

I studied it with disinterest. "Did the former wearer kill her husband?" I asked with a clear wince.

The old rag-picker shook her head. "Not her. She was a foolish woman who killed herself."

"How? By accident or intent?"

"She knew very well what she was doing. It happened two months ago. All for the sake of a blue-eyed naval officer who had promised to marry her as soon as he returned from a long voyage. On the day his ship sailed into port, she met him on the quay, but before she could greet him, another woman flung herself into his arms and they kissed. I am not talking about a brotherly kiss either, rather, one that was long and lingering, the kind that women dream about. When he noticed her, he laughed. Just that and nothing more. She was tall and pretty, but she staggered, her face grew pale, her lips quivered. She bent her head a little, turned, and before anyone could stop her, she dove from the edge of the quay into the waves that closed over her head. She did not try to swim; she just sank down, down, down like a stone. The next day her body floated ashore, and I bought her dress for five *scudi*. You may purchase it for ten."

"And what became of the naval officer?" I asked.

"Oh, he is enjoying his life. He has a new lover every week. He doesn't care."

I drew out my purse. "I will take this gown," I said. "You ask ten *scudi*, but here are twelve. For the extra two you must show me to a private room where I can dress."

"You are most generous." The old woman quivered with greed as I counted the money into her withered palm.

"You may change in my room. It is not much, but there is a mirror, his mirror, the only thing of his worth keeping. Come this way."

Stumbling along, almost tripping over the muddled collection of clothing that lay strewn about the entire floor and in every nook and cranny, she opened a small door and led me into a vile smelling room furnished with a dismal pallet bed and one broken chair. A small square pane of glass admitted adequate light. Next to the crude window hung the mirror she had alluded to, a beautiful item set in ornate silver, the costliness of which I at once recognized, though I dared not yet look into the glass at myself.

With pride, the old woman showed me that the door to this narrow den of hers locked from within. "Here is the gown. You can take your time putting it on. Lock the door if you wish. The room is at your service." She nodded several times and left me.

I followed her advice and locked myself in. Then I stepped to the mirror and looked at my reflection. A bitter pain struck me. The hag's sight was excellent, for she had described me well. I looked old. Even if I had endured twenty years of suffering, I could not have changed so dreadfully.

My illness had thinned my face and carved deep lines into it. My eyes had sunk deep into my head and they bore a wild look that reflected the terrors I had suffered in the vault. Most obvious of all, my hair had indeed turned completely white from shock; all my ebony tendrils gone.

Now I understood the alarm of the man who had sold me fruit on the road that morning. My appearance was horrendous enough to startle the bravest of men. Indeed, I scarcely recognized myself. Would Dario recognize me? I feared he would not. Pain stirred within me, forcing tears in my eyes. I brushed them away in haste.

I must be strong, I thought. What did it matter whether my hair was black or white? What did it matter that my face had aged, as long as my heart was true? For a moment, perhaps, Dario might grow pale at the sight of me, but when he learned of all that I had suffered, I would become dearer to him than ever before. One of his soft embraces would make up for all my anguish and would be enough to make me young again.

Thus, I uplifted my sinking spirits and dressed in the wrinkled emerald gown. The gown was a little loose, leaving plenty of room to disguise the leather bags of coins and jewels from the brigand's coffin still secreted around my waist.

When I completed my hasty toilet, I glanced one last time at the mirror, this time with a half smile. True, my appearance had changed, but I did not think I looked quite so bad. The dress enhanced me. My snow-white curls clustered around my face and the anticipation of reuniting with my husband and daughter brought some luster back into my sunken eyes and color into my hollow cheeks.

I knew I would not always look so worn and wasted.

Rest, perhaps a change of air, would soon restore brightness to my complexion. Perhaps even my white tresses might transform back to their dark richness. But what if they remained white? Well, I knew of many people who went to great lengths to dust their hair to make it as white as possible. It was the fashion these days. Many would admire the stark contrast between my young face and old, white hair.

Now that I had finished dressing, I unlocked the door of the stifling little chamber and called out for the old rag-picker.

She came shuffling along with her head bent. As she approached, she raised her eyes and threw up her hands in astonishment. "*Santissima Madonna.* You are a fine woman. What a pity you are so old. You must have been quite an elegant beauty when you were young."

Half in jest and half to humor her, I curtseyed before her. "There is plenty of elegance in me still, you see."

She stared, laid her yellow fingers on my bared arm with a kind of ghoul-like interest and wonder, and helped me rise up with soppy admiration. "Beautiful," she mumbled. "Like a butterfly. Your beauty could win anyone's heart. Ah, I used to be beautiful like that once. I was clever at flirting, clever with the men. One word from me and I could cut a man down as if he were butter. You could do that too if you liked. It's all in the wit. A brave mind unafraid to strike with a single word; a conviction unafraid to kill with one stroke."

She gazed at me through bleary, watery eyes as though anxious to know more of my character and temperament.

I turned from her and called her attention to my own discarded garments. "You may have these, though they are not of much value. For another three *scudi* please find me some stockings and shoes."

She clasped her hands and inundated me with

gratitude for the additional sum. Declaring by all the saints that she and the entire contents of her shop were at the service of so generous a lady, she at once produced the articles I asked for. I put them on, and then stood up ready to make my way home.

Because my appearance had changed so much, I decided not to go to Villa Mancini by daylight for fear that I would startle my husband and daughter. My unforeseen arrival might give everyone too great a shock. I would wait till the sun had set, and then go up to the house by a back way I knew of, and try to speak with one of the servants. I might even encounter my friend Beatrice and she would break the joyful news of my return from death to Dario and Chiara and prepare them for my altered looks.

While these thoughts flitted through my mind, the old rag-picker regarded me with her head tilted to one side. "Are you going far?"

"*Si*," I answered. "Very far."

She detained me by placing her hand on my sleeve. A glint of madness shone from her eyes. "Tell me, I will keep the secret. Are you going to a man?"

I looked down at her, half in disdain, half in amusement. "*Si*, I am going to a man."

She broke into repugnant laughter that contorted her face. I looked at her with disgust. Shaking her hand off my arm, I made my way to the door of the shop.

She shuffled after me, wiping away her merry tears. "Going to a man," she croaked "Ha. You are not the first, nor will you be the last that has done so. Going to a man. That is good. Go to him, go. You are strong. You are wise. And when you find him in the arms of another woman, kill him. *Si*, *Si*, you will be able to do it easily. Go and kill him." She stood in her doorway, impertinent and smirking, her stunted figure and evil face reminding me of a dwarf-devil.

I bade her good day in an apathetic tone, but she did not respond as I walked away. I made the mistake of looking back and saw her in the fullness of her madness, still standing on the threshold of her miserable dwelling, her depraved mouth working itself into all manner of grimaces. With her warped fingers, she gestured as if she had caught something and throttled it.

I went on down the street, her last words ringing in my ears, '*Go and kill him.*'

Chapter Seven

Although it was late morning, the day already seemed insufferably long. I strolled leisurely through the streets of Vicenza, but thankfully, did not encounter anyone I knew. Fearful of the plague, the affluent citizens of my social circle had either fled or locked themselves away inside their own homes just like I had.

The plague's ravages soon became apparent. On almost every street, a funeral procession passed me by. In one doorway, a group of *beccamorti* were shoving a deceased woman into a coffin far too small for her body. It revolted me to see how they folded up her arms and legs and crammed her into the crude casket. I swore that the sound I heard was her bones cracking at the roughness. Stunned, I watched the disorganized proceedings for a minute or so before I approached them. "Are you certain she is dead?"

At first, my question rendered the men speechless. Then the burliest one burst out into a laugh that shook his corpulent belly. "*Corpo di Cristo*, if I believed this one was still alive, I'd be the first to twist her neck and put her out of her misery, the nasty hag. The plague never fails. She is most certainly dead." To prove his point, he grasped a handful of her hair and bashed her head repeatedly against the coffin.

Appalled, I walked away upset at the loss of human compassion that I had witnessed.

When I reached a main street, I noticed a group of people who glanced around anxiously and spoke in low voices. One of their whispers reached me. "The Doge of Venice. The Doge." All heads were turned in the same direction. I paused to look too.

Down the street, a group of men walked towards us at a leisurely pace. Among them, I recognized the Doge of Venice, Francesco Erizzo, who had been elected in April after his predecessor died from the plague. His election had been nearly unanimous. The vote had been forty to one in his favor. There were those, however, who believed his election fraudulent. Regardless of what anyone said, I knew him to be a good, honest man.

"That white-haired beauty would make a fascinating subject for a painting," I heard him say in a rich, deep voice to one of his attendants, as he pointed directly at me.

His words almost caused me to spring forward and throw myself at his feet to tell him my tale. But I hesitated to betray myself. How cruel that he, a dear aquaintance, did not recognize me and was about to pass me by when we had conversed on many occasions. I visited Venice several times a year and had attended many a ball within the splendor of the Palazzo Ducale where we had encountered each other and entered into exquisite conversations. But that Carlotta Mancini existed no more. A white-haired woman with an unfamiliar face had usurped her place. Not even my friend, the doge, recognized me.

I refrained from approaching him. Instead, I followed him at a respectful distance, as did many others. He wandered through the most plague-ridden streets as unconcerned as if he strolled through a garden of roses after a pleasant dinner.

He walked without worry into the most dilapidated of homes to observe the dead and dying. He spoke heartening words to grieving mourners who gazed at him wide-eyed through their grateful tears. The doge dropped silver coins into the hands of the anguished.

A mother knelt at his feet, raised her infant to him, and implored his blessing, which he gave.

One golden-haired girl flung herself at his feet and kissed them. Then she leaped up in triumph. The doge smiled, rested his hand on her head as a tolerant father would, and said nothing as he walked on.

A small cluster of men and women huddled outside a hovel listening to the shouts and cries that came from within. As I approached, I could see two *beccamorti* arguing and swearing at three women who wept. At the center of all this agitation, a coffin stood on end awaiting its occupant. One of the doge's attendants announced his presence. The people outside the door stepped back to allow him room to approach. The strident hues and cries from within ceased as the *beccamorti* bared their heads and the women stifled their sobs.

"What is wrong here, my friends?" Erizzo asked in a placid and concerned tone.

Everyone fell silent. The *beccamorti* looked glum and mortified. Then, a woman with a round, but strained face, her eyes crimson with grief, elbowed her way through the gathering and stepped into the doorway to face the Doge.

"May God and the Holy Virgin bless you." Her voice quavered with emotion as she pointed to the *beccamorti*. "All would be well if those shameless pigs would leave us alone for an hour. One short hour. The girl is dead, and Giovanni, poor lad, refuses to let her go. She died from the plague and he has wrapped his two arms round her tight. We have begged and done all that we can, but he refuses to let them take her away. I fear if we force him, he will lose his mind, *poverino*. One hour, that is all we need; enough time for the priest to arrive who will help us persuade Giovanni."

The doge raised his hand and entered the miserable dwelling. His attendants followed and I, too, could not resist placing myself near the doorway to see what would happen.

The scene I glimpsed was so heartbreaking that I could hardly bear to look upon it. Erizzo uncovered his head and stood silent beside a pallet bed where the body of a young girl lay, her beauty not yet marred by death. Except for her stiffened limbs and ashen pallor, she looked asleep. A man lay stock-still across her body, his arms wrapped round her, his face upon her cold breast that would never again respond to his warm embrace. A solitary ray of golden sunlight shone into the dark room, shedding light on the spectacle - the prostrate couple on the bed, the upright stature of the benevolent doge, and the solemn and concerned faces of the people who surrounded them.

"See. He has been that way since she died last night," the woman whispered. "He has clinched his hands so tight around her, we cannot even shift a finger."

The doge advanced and touched the shoulder of the grieving admirer. "*Figlio mio*. My son." He spoke with exquisite tenderness.

There came no answer. The women, moved by the doge's endearing words sobbed and the men wiped away tears of their own.

"*Figlio mio*. I am your doge. Do you not wish to greet me?"

The young man raised his head from the breast of his beloved and gave the doge a blank stare. His shattered face, matted hair, and feral, hollow eyes gave him the appearance of someone trapped in a nightmare from which there was no escape.

"Your hand, my son," said the doge with military-like authority.

Gradually, half-heartedly, as if a powerful force compelled him, he loosened his right arm from the dead woman he had clasped for so long, and yielded his hand to the doge.

Erizzo grasped it within his own and held it tight. He looked the grieving lad full in the face. "When it comes to love, there is no death," he said.

The young man's eyes met his for a long moment, and then his rigid expression softened. He yanked his hand back and erupted into a dirge of tears.

Erizzo shielded him with his arm and raised him from the bed. The doge lead him away sobbing and handed him into the arms of his worried mother. The torrent of tears had likely saved the youth from madness.

Applause greeted the doge as he passed through the small crowd of people who had witnessed what had happened. He acknowledged them with a sincere bow, left the house, and signalled to the *beccamorti*. They could now complete their heart-rending duty. The people praised the doge with cheers and ardent blessings as he continued on his way.

I watched his retreating figure till I could see him no more. I felt that I had become more resilient in the presence of such a hero. In my life, I have encountered few men as true and virtuous like Francesco Erizzo of the Venetian Republic. Even now my heart warms when I think of him.

As soon as the doge vanished down the street, I decided to visit the small inn where I had fallen ill. After a few missed streets, I found it. The door stood open and I glanced inside. Giovanni, the fat landlord, polished his glasses as though he had never left off. In the corner was the wooden bench upon which I had lain and where I had died.

"*Buon giorno signora,*" the landlord said when I entered.

"Good day," I said returning his greeting. I ordered some wine and bread then sat myself at one of the little tables while he bustled about to serve me.

"You are new to Vicenza" he asked as he dusted and rubbed a cup for my wine.

For a moment, his question confused me and I stumbled to gather my wits. My appearance was so altered, he did not recognize me. "Relatively new," I answered. "And you? How goes the situation with the plague?"

The landlord shook his head and his expression turned woeful. "*Dio mio,* my God, do not speak of it. The people are dying like flies in honey. Only yesterday, goodness, who would have believed it?" Pressing his palms together as if in prayer, he waved them back and forth before him as he looked up to Heaven and sighed.

"What happened yesterday?" I asked, even though I knew what he would tell me. "I am a stranger in Vicenza and eager for news."

Perspiring, Giovanni laid the cup of wine and half-loaf of bread on the marble top of the table. "Have you heard of Contessa Mancini?"

I shook my head and bent my face over my wine cup.

"Ah, well, it does not matter," he groaned. "There is no Contessa Mancini anymore. She is gone. She was rich, they say, yet as vulnerable as the rest of us. Fra Cipriano of the Benedictines carried her in here yesterday morning because she fell ill with the plague. She died in a matter of hours." The landlord caught a mosquito and killed it. "As dead as that *zanzara. Si,* she lay dead on that very wooden bench opposite to you. The *beccamorti* took her away before sunset. Life in Vicenza has become like a bad dream."

I pretended to be engrossed with breaking off a piece of the bread and dipping it into the wine. "Whether a person is rich or not makes no difference. The rich must die just like the poor."

"Ah, that is true, very true," assented Giovanni. "All the money in the world could not save the blessed Cipriano."

I tensed, but regained my composure. "What do you mean?"

"*Si,* Fra Cipriano. He deserves to be canonized a saint one day, the poor man. I speak of the holy Benedictine brother who brought Contessa Mancini here so ill. Little did I know that God would soon call him too."

A sickening sensation settled in my heart. "Is he dead?"

"As dead as a martyr. He caught the plague, I suppose, from the contessa, for he was bending over her to the last. He sprinkled holy water over her corpse and laid his own crucifix upon it in the coffin. Then he went to Villa Mancini to deliver the news to her family."

My poor Dario. "How did her husband take the news?"

The landlord shrugged his bulky shoulders. "How should I know? The reverend brother said nothing, save that the man turned away from him. But that is not so unusual. A man never lets another man see him cry. As I said before, the good brother Cipriano presided over the contessa's burial, and he had scarce returned from it when the illness seized him. He died this morning at the monastery." Giovanni crossed himself. "May his soul rest in peace.

I pushed away my meal untasted. The bread choked me and the wine tasted sour. I fought back tears for the gracious, tolerant monk who had sacrificed his life for me and the young boy I had asked him to help. One hero less in this brutal, heartless world. I sat quiet, lost in my mournful thoughts.

The landlord looked at me curiously. "Does the wine not please you? Have you no appetite?

I forced a smile. "Your story about the death of the good brother stripped me of my appetite. Vicenza seems such a terrible place right now. There is nothing to hear but stories of the dead and dying."

Giovanni gave me an apologetic expression. "Well, truly, there is very little else. The plague is everywhere, touching everyone, and it is the will of God."

As he finished speaking, a woman who strolled past the open door of the inn caught my gaze. It was Beatrice Cardano. My dear friend. I yearned to run out and embrace her, but something in her look and manner restrained me.

She walked with a smile on her face and a posy of roses in her hands, similar to the roses that grew in such profusion on the upper terrace of my villa. Shocked, I stared at her as she passed. She looked happy and tranquil, happier indeed than I had ever seen her. Yet, I, her best friend, had died only yesterday. With such recent sorrow, how could she smile so happily and carry such beautiful roses? These were not the signs of mourning.

For one long moment, I felt the sting of hurt. Then I laughed at my own over-sensitivity. After all, what did it matter that she bore a smile and carried roses? A woman could not always be answerable for the expression in her face. As for the flowers, perhaps she might have gathered them in passing or Chiara might have given them to her. Beatrice did not appear to be mourning, but with my recent death, there would have been no time for her to procure black vestments.

Satisfied with my own self-reasoning, I made no attempt to follow Beatrice. I let her go on her way unconscious of my existence. I would wait, I thought, till the evening. Then all would be explained, all would return to normal.

I turned to the landlord. "How much do I owe you?"

"Pay what you can," he replied. "I am never hard on strangers. Times are bad, or you would be welcome to it for nothing. Many a day I have done the same for new visitors to Vicenza, and the blessed Cipriano would assure me that St. Peter would remember me for it."

I laughed and tossed him a gold coin. He pocketed it at once and his eyes twinkled. "Such an overpayment is most generous, but the saints will make it up to you, never fear."

"I am sure of that," I said as I rose. "*Arrivederci.*"

He responded with amiable heartiness, and then began polishing his glasses anew.

For the remainder of the day, I strolled the less travelled streets of Vicenza, pining for the dark pink splendor of sunset, which would return me safe into the arms of my family, of love and contentment.

Chapter Eight

The evening arrived at last. A delicate breeze carried the sweet fragrance of flowers and cooled the heat of the day. A grandeur of colors blazed in the sky, its magnificent tints sending luster against walls and rooftops. My longing for home urged me forward, yet I held myself back, forcing myself to wait until the sun sank below the horizon, till the glow of its fading light died, and the moon rose languidly into the night sky.

Finally, when night had fully fallen, I turned onto the road that led to Villa Mancini. My heart raced, my limbs quivered with anticipation, each footstep impatient. Never had the way seemed so long.

At last, I reached the gate, but it was locked. The sculptured lions on either side frowned down upon me. Beyond, I could hear the splash and tinkle of the fountains as I inhaled the scents of the roses and periwinkle.

My home. My family. I had no intention of entering through the main gate. I took one long, loving look, and turned left into a small private gate that led into an avenue of trees. This lane had been my favorite place to walk, for it provided cool shade on hot days and was rarely used by anyone other than myself. Beatrice sometimes joined me, but usually I walked alone. I enjoyed strolling the shadowed path reading a good book or giving myself up to the *dolce far niente,* the sweetness of doing nothing, and my own fancies.

The path led to the rear of the villa where I hoped to find Annunziata. I would carefully approach her first. The trees rustled in the darkness as I stepped further along the moss-grown path. Sometimes the nightingales broke into melody before falling silent again. Moonlight filtered through interlacing boughs, casting shadows on the ground. Faint aromas floated in the air, shaken from orange boughs and trailing branches of white jasmine.

I hurried forth, my spirits rising with every step, the closer I came to my destination. Sweet anticipation drove me. I longed to be embraced by my beloved Dario, to see his lustrous eyes looking fondly into mine. I was eager to see Beatrice's delight at my appearance. Chiara would be in bed, but I would tiptoe into her room and watch her sleep, for my happiness would not be complete till I had kissed her round face and caressed her curls, the color of spun gold.

I heard a sound and came to a sudden stop. What could it be? I strained to listen. It sounded like a ripple of pleasant laughter. A shiver shook me from head to toe. It was my husband's laugh. I recognized its rich baritone ring. Iciness squeezed my heart. I paused, unsure. How could he laugh so easily, so soon after my death?

I caught a glimpse of white through the trees. Acting on impulse, I stepped behind some dense foliage through which I could see without being seen. His clear laugh rang out once again; its intensity painful to my ears. He sounded happy, even merry. He wandered in the moonlight joyous-hearted, while I had expected to find him shut in his rooms grieving. We women are such fools when we love a man.

A terrible thought struck me. Had he gone mad? Had the shock and grief of my unexpected death affected his mind? I shuddered at the thought. Bending apart the

The Contessa's Vendetta

boughs behind which I hid, I looked out. Two figures were walking towards me; my husband and my best friend, Beatrice Cardano.

There was nothing unusual about seeing them together. Beatrice was like a sister to me. It was her duty to console Dario over my loss. But I saw much more than that. His arm was around her shoulder and she leaned against him for support.

An angry curse threatened to break from my lips. Death and the horrors of the vault were nothing compared to the anguish that coursed through me. To this day, the memory of that moment burns in my mind like an inextinguishable fire.

My hands clenched into fists in an effort to beat back my bitterness. I fought to restrain the ferocious rage that awoke within me and I forced myself to remain motionless and silent in my hiding-place.

I observed their betrayal. I witnessed my honor stabbed to death by those whom I most trusted, and still I remained silent. Beatrice and Dario came so close to my hiding-place that I could hear every word they uttered and watch their every gesture.

They paused within three steps of me, his arm still around her shoulder and hers around his waist. She rested her head on his shoulder just as I had done with Dario a thousand times. She wore a pure white gown except for the blood red rose at her breast fastened with a diamond pin that flashed in the moonlight. How I wished it were blood instead of a rose at her breast. How I wished it was a stiletto that jabbed into her body instead of a diamond pin that pierced her gown.

But I had no weapon. I could only stare at them, dry-eyed and mute. Dario looked handsome as ever, exceptionally so. No trace of grief marred his fine-looking features. His eyes were as clear and gentle as ever. His lips were parted in that fetching smile that was so endearing, so trustworthy. I heard him speak in the old enchanting tone of his low voice that made my heart leap and my brain reel.

"Foolish Beatrice," he said with amusement. "What would have happened, I wonder, if Carlotta had not fortunately died."

I held my breath as I awaited the answer.

Beatrice laughed carelessly. "She would never have discovered anything. You were too clever for her, Dario. Besides, her conceit saved her. She had such a high opinion of herself that she would not have deemed it possible for you to love any other woman."

My husband, that paragon of manhood, sighed restlessly. "I am glad she is dead. But we cannot be careless, Beatrice. We must not be seen together yet. The servants will talk. I must go into mourning for at least six months...and there are many other things to consider."

Beatrice's hand played with the jeweled necklace she wore, a favorite of mine.

He bent and kissed the location on her neck just above the pendant. Ah, my dear husband, do not let your conscience prevent your enjoyment, I thought as I crouched behind the trees, the wrath inside me making the blood beat in my head like a hundred drums.

"No, my love," she replied to him. "It is a pity Carlotta is dead. Alive, she made an excellent screen. She was an unaware guardian of propriety for both of us, as no one else could be."

The boughs that covered me creaked and rustled. My husband looked uneasily about.

"Hush," he said, nervously. "She was buried only yesterday."

"And her ghost could be about, especially on this path. I wish we had not come here. It was her favorite place to walk."

"She was the mother of my child. We must think of that, too," Dario added with a slight tone of regretfulness.

"You don't think I know that?" Beatrice exclaimed. "I curse her for every kiss she stole from your lips."

I listened astounded. Here was a new philosophy: wives were thieves. They *stole* kisses and only lovers or mistresses were honest in their intimacy. Oh, my dear friend, how near you came to death in that moment. Had you seen my face peering through the dusky leaves, you could have known the force of the fury pent up within me.

"Why did you marry her?" she asked, after a little pause

Dario toyed with one of her curls that rested against his chest. He looked at her with a frown and shrugged his shoulders. "Why? Because I was tired of the monastery and all the stupid, solemn ways of the monks. It was an unbearable location for an education. Also because she was rich and I was horribly poor. I cannot bear to be poor. Then there is the fact that she loved me." His eyes glimmered with malicious triumph. "*Si*, she was mad for me and—"

"You loved her?" Beatrice demanded almost fiercely.

"I suppose I did, for the first few weeks. As much as one can ever love a wife. Why does one marry at all? For convenience, money, position. She gave me these things, as you know."

"You will gain nothing by marrying me, then," she said, jealously.

"Of course not. Besides, have I said I will marry you? You are very agreeable as a lover, but otherwise, I am not so sure," he said teasingly. "And I am free now. I can do as I like. I want to enjoy my liberty, and—"

Beatrice laid her hand, aglitter with my rings, against his lips.

In response, Dario snatched her close to his breast and

held her tight, his face engulfed with passion.

"You cannot deceive me, Dario," Beatrice said with a giggle. "I have endured much because of you. From the moment I first saw you on your wedding day with poor Carlotta, I loved you desperately, completely, and without shame. I knew you would be unfaithful to Carlotta, so I bided my time. And only three months after your wedding, you came to me, willing and eager. With my touch, words, and glances, I gave you all you sought. Why try to deny it now? You became my lover as much as Carlotta's. No, you belonged more to me because you loved me. And though you lied to your wife, you dare not lie to me. Carlotta was easily tricked. A married woman must be vigilant when it comes to a husband, for if she relents, she has only herself to blame when her man wanders into another woman's arms. I repeat, Dario, you are mine, and you shall always be so." The impetuous words coursed rapidly from her lips as she thrust herself into his arms.

I smirked bitterly as I listened and stared.

He pushed her away.

The fierceness of her embrace had crushed the rose she wore, and its scarlet petals drifted on the breeze to scatter on the ground at their feet.

Dario's eyes flared and an irritated frown tapered his brows. He glanced away from her in silence, the silence of derision.

His manner seemed to upset her. She caught his hand and kissed it. "Forgive me, *caro*. I did not mean to mock you. It is not your fault you are so handsome, so beautiful, so appealing. You are my heart and soul. Let us not squander words in worthless irritation. We are free, Dario. Free to pursue our dreams. Carlotta's death is our good fortune. We can now be together for the rest of our lives."

He grinned and drew her into his embrace.

Her lips met his.

I observed them, agonized, as they held each other in a staunch embrace.

He weaved one of her ebony curls around his jeweled finger. "So impulsive, so jealous. I have told you many times that I love you." He laughed. "Do you not remember that night when Carlotta sat out on the balcony reading, and we were singing together in the library? Did I not tell you then that I loved you more than her? I truly meant it, you know."

Beatrice smiled, and placed her hand on his that still held her curl. "I believed it, and still do," she said. "But you must expect me to be jealous. Carlotta was never jealous; she had complete trust in you. She thought herself better than you. A woman who spent her days at church and in charity work, leaving her husband to his own devices; a woman who preferred to read instead of look after him. She was the mistress of her own fate and deserved to lose you. But I am jealous of the ground you tread, of the air that touches you, and I was jealous of Carlotta." Her eyes darkened with fury. "If any woman dared now to come between us, I would make her regret it."

Dario gave her a look of reproval. "Must you be so cross, and over nothing?" He kissed her. "I am happy that I am your only love. Come, it's chilly out here. Why don't we go back inside?

I watched as my husband led his lover away. Arms entwined, they strode toward my villa, and then I saw them pause.

"Do you hear the nightingales?" Beatrice asked.

I believed the entire world could hear their burst of melody. It erupted from every tree around us. The chaste, fervent tones penetrated the air like the peal of bells, singing their love-songs with perfect rhapsody. Creatures untainted by lies, unsullied by betrayal.

Beatrice shivered and drew her wrap tighter about her shoulders. "I hate them. Their noise is enough to damage one's hearing. And Carlotta used to be so fond of them. Poor, stupid Carlotta."

Without averting my eyes, I watched them walk away, their consciences untainted, as though no shadow of vengeance loomed over them, as though retribution did not follow their steps. Between the dark boughs, I gazed at their receding figures till the last glimmer of my husband's face and Beatrice's white gown vanished behind the thick foliage.

Slowly, I came out of my hideaway and stood where they had stood, reconciling myself with the hateful truth. My mind reeled. Prisms of light spun before my eyes. The solid earth swayed beneath my feet. Was I a ghost who had returned to witness the ruin of all that was precious in my life? The man I had loved was not the same person. He was lower than a vile snake, someone all men would despise and point a scornful finger at. *That* creature was my husband, the father of my child. He had cast mud on his soul by choice. He had selected evil and crowned himself with shame instead of honor.

What should I do? I tortured myself with this question. I stared blankly about as if the trees and earth might provide an answer. What should be done with him and with her, my treacherous friend and betrayer of a husband?

I noticed the fallen rose petals. They lay on the soft ground, round and soft and scarlet. I stooped and picked them up, holding them in my palm. They carried a sweet fragrance even though they had adorned the breast of a woman who reeked with lies. I wanted to kill her.

I remembered the miserable rag-picker who told me she had taken her revenge on the day she had discovered her husband and his lover. I had foolishly let my opportunity pass. But there were many ways to settle a score. I must seek my vengeance wisely to inflict the longest and cruelest agony upon my betrayers. How sweet to slay the sinners in the act of sinning, but I was a Mancini and I must not bloody my hands directly. There were other means to accomplish such a task. I must plan it out carefully. I hauled my tired body to a nearby tree and slid down to the ground, the dying rose-petals in my clenched palm.

A rush of blood surged through my veins. I looked down at the clothes I wore, the former garments of a suicide victim. *She was a fool,* the old rag-picker had said. *She killed herself.* There was no doubt about it; the woman had been a fool to forfeit her own life. I would not follow in her footsteps, or at least not yet. I had something to do first, as long as I could follow through without remorse. My thoughts swirled in my head in a jumble of confusion. The scent of the rose petals I held in my palm sickened me, yet I refused to cast them away. I wanted them as an eternal reminder of the betrayal I had witnessed.

I reached for my purse and dropped the wilting petals inside. Then I remembered the two leather pouches I had concealed beneath my gown; one filled with gold, the other with gems. The horror of being buried alive returned to me; my grim fight for life and freedom. Life and freedom. Of what use were they to me now, save for one thing – revenge?

I was not wanted. No one expected me to return. The large fortune I had possessed was now my husband's by decree of my own last will and testament. But I possessed new wealth; the hidden hoard was sufficient to keep me in luxury for the rest of my life. A rush of excitement throbbed in my veins. Wealth. Gold could purchase anything, even vengeance. But what sort of vengeance? The type I sought must be distinctive. It must be sophisticated, persistent, and absolute.

An evening wind swayed the leaves of the trees. The nightingales chirruped sweetly and the moon shone brightly against the impenetrable indigo sky. Heedless of the passing time, I sat still, trapped in bewildered thoughts. Once betrayed, nothing in life can restore happy days long past. So I have learned, and so many more after me must learn.

A white-haired beauty. The words of the doge tumbled about in my tortured thoughts. I was greatly changed and looked worn and old. I doubt anyone would recognize me. The innkeeper hadn't. And neither had the rag-picker.

All at once, an idea came to life; a plan of retribution so diabolical, so bold, and so unspeakable, that I recoiled as though I had been stung by a wasp. I rose and paced back and forth as outrageous ideas tossed about in my mind. Amid all my wonder, details began to form. I deliberated over every circumstance that might spoil my plot, and then resolved each one.

My despair disappeared. Let sailors' lovers and rag-pickers resort to murder and suicide as fit outlets for their wrath. As for me, I would not blight my family's good name with a vulgar crime. No, retribution by a member of the Mancini family must rise above such common methods and must be taken with confidence, calm, and careful forethought - no haste, no fury, no fuss, no scandal.

I paced slowly, calculating every scene of the bitter drama I would soon enact. My thoughts cleared and I breathed more easily. Bit by bit, I became very collected. Regrets for the past disappeared. Why should I mourn the loss of a love that was never mine in the first place? It was not as if they had waited till my death. No, their deceit began within three months of my marriage and endured for three years after that. And in all that time, I had suspected nothing.

Now I knew the extent of my injury. I was a woman enormously wronged, grossly duped. My sense of justice and self-respect demanded that I punish those who had played me false. The love I once felt for my husband died. I plucked it from my heart like a thorn from my flesh and flung it away with disgust. Infinite contempt replaced my deep fondness for Beatrice Cardano. I also scorned myself for hurrying home with so much joy and love in my heart, like a merry fool marching to her own execution. But the delusions of my life existed no more. I possessed the strength to avenge myself and the craftiness to accomplish it.

My plan now complete, I drew from my breast the crucifix the dead monk Cipriano had laid with me in my coffin, and kissing it, I raised it aloft, and swore never to relent, never to relax, never to rest, till I fulfilled my vendetta.

The nightingales paused their song. The wind scattered a shower of jasmine blossoms at my feet. Symbols that my past with its days of sweet illusion and dear remembrance had withered and perished forever. Henceforth my life would be like a blade of steel; firm, bitter, and indestructible. I knew what must be done and I resolved to do it.

I walked back down the lane, swung open the private gate and stepped back onto the main road. A loud clang made me glance up as I walked past the main entrance of the Villa Mancini. I glanced beyond the gates to my beloved ancestral villa.

Beatrice Cardano stepped out onto the upper balcony. She glanced lazily outwards in my direction, her beautiful face clearly visible in the bright moonlight. But all she saw was a white-haired old woman passing by the front gates.

Her look only rested upon me for a brief second before she withdrew it.

An insane desire possessed me to scream at her, to rush back and climb the trellis to spring at her throat, to throw her in the dust at my feet, to spit at her, and trample upon her. But I repressed my fierce emotions. I had a better game to play. I had an exquisite torture in store for her. Vengeance ought to ripen slowly in the heat of intense wrath. So I let my dear friend, my husband's consoler, dream her dreams without interference.

I re-entered Vicenza, and found lodging at a small convent. There, in a tiny cell meant for guests, my recent illness, fatigue, and roiling emotions threw me into a deep slumber. But the most soothing opiate was the knowledge that I had armed myself with a practical plan of retribution, more terrible than any human had ever before devised.

Chapter Nine

The following morning, I rose early, eager to set my plan in motion. After acquiring a small lantern, a hammer, and some nails, I set out for the cemetery. Not a soul was in sight when I arrived. A blessing, for now I could work freely without worrying about being accidentally discovered by someone.

At the Mancini vault, I removed the shrubs and debris, and uncovered the secret passage. Despite my fear and aversion, I entered. Once more, the cold and dark surrounded me. The dreadful memory of my ordeal resurfaced. My anguish flooded back, but I refused to allow it to distract me.

I lit the lantern and glanced about. The coffin with the treasure lay undisturbed where I had hidden it. Raising the lid, I removed all the gold coins I could find, hundreds and hundreds of them, and tucked it into the pouches secreted beneath my gown. I also took several pieces of masculine jewelry to add to the ship pendant I had first found and that still hung from my neck. With the tools, I repaired the damage I had made to the casket when I had forced it open, and nailed it up tight so that it looked untouched. This work did not take me long, for I was in a hurry. I planned to leave Vicenza this very day and would not return for several weeks.

I glanced one last time at my own coffin, undecided

whether to repair it too so that it would appear my body still lay inside. I decided to leave it as it was, broken and forced open. One day soon, it would serve its purpose. I crawled through the secret tunnel and carefully covered it back up behind me. Then I returned to the convent to spend one last night.

My first task was to hire a lady's maid and a steward to oversee business matters, for no woman should travel alone. The nuns at the convent suggested I hire Santina, a young woman of eighteen years, and her elderly father, Paolo. The nuns assured me of their good nature and diligence at any tasks assigned to them. I agreed. They both suited me perfectly. It pleased me to see how eager they were to come with me. We liked each other instantly and I showed my gratitude by leaving the abbess a sizeable donation.

The next morning, I hired a coach, which took us to Venice. There I made inquiries and learned a ship would soon leave port headed for Pescara. Since Pescara would suit me as well as any other place, I sought out the captain of the vessel.

He was a cheerful man with a sun-battered, olive-colored complexion. When I expressed my desire to take passage with him, his smile revealed a wide gap between his two yellowing and overly large front teeth. He charged me a fair and moderate sum, but which I learned later was actually three times the usual fare. But the charismatic scoundrel swindled me with such charm and politeness, I did not let it bother me. I would rather be duped by a friendly, polite man than receive fair value for my money from a brusque boor who lacked the good manners to wish me a good day. Besides, I could afford to be generous.

We left port about mid-morning. While Santina and

Paolo settled us all in our quarters below deck, I sat idly on the vessel's edge. The sun shone bright, and a cool breeze blew. The water rippled against the sides of our vessel with a gentle cadence. I looked down into the clear waters of the Adriatic, blue as an ocean of sapphires, and retreated into my thoughts, reflecting on the past as well as the future. Lost in contemplation, a touch on my shoulder startled me. I looked up.

The captain of the brig stood beside me, smiling. "You are enjoying the beauty of the water, *dama*?" he said courteously.

"Why do you call me *dama*?" I inquired brusquely. Surely the used clothing of the drowned woman I still wore could not be mistaken for those of a noblewoman.

The man shrugged and bowed courteously. "Ah, I understand. As the *dama* pleases."

I looked at him sternly. "What do you mean?"

The captain pointed a brown finger at my hands. "These are not the hands of a woman who launders or scrubs a house clean."

I glanced down at them. True enough, their delicate softness betrayed me. The sharp-witted captain had noticed the contrast between my supple hands and the inferior quality of my gown, though no one else I had come in contact with, had noticed. At first I was embarrassed, but after a moment's pause I met his gaze. "And what of it?"

He gave me an apologetic look. "I did not mean to offend, *dama*. Not at all. Please understand. Your secret is perfectly safe with me. I am prudent and do not gossip. You, *cara dama,* must have good reason for concealing your identity, I am sure. You have suffered; it is evident in your face. There are far too many things that bring sorrow into one's life." He tallied them on his fingers. "There is love, there is vengeance, there are disputes, there is a loss of wealth, any of these will drive a person away. You, *dama*, are entrusted to me while on this ship and I assure you of my discretion and best service."

He tipped his hat with such polite charm that in my disheartened state, his act touched me deeply. Wordlessly, I extended my hand to him and he kissed it with respect.

"Do you mind if I enjoy a cigar?" he asked.

"Please, do not hesitate on my account."

"Excellent," he answered, showing his sallow, lackluster teeth in his amused smile. He pulled one out of his short jacket and lit it from the flame of a nearby lantern someone had forgotten to distinguish or which had been left burning for this very purpose. He inhaled deeply and let out a puff. "A cigar of the finest quality, a gift from a man who will smoke nothing but the best. Ah, Cesare Negri, what a generous man he is."

The familiar name startled me and words remained trapped in my throat for a few moments. What twist of fate kept putting this notorious bandit in my path? "You know the man?"

"I know him very well, indeed. While I was docked in Venice, he found me alone on the brig; my men had gone ashore. He told me the authorities were after him and offered me more gold than I had ever seen in my life if I would take him to Pescara. From there, he could get to one of his hiding-places. If I refused, he threatened to slit my throat. He brought a woman named Teresa with him. Even though I knew he was a scandalous rogue, I agreed to take him and assured him I would not betray him. My agreement seemed to surprise him, for he smiled that dark smile of his, which might mean gratitude or murder. Teresa placed her hands on mine, tears in her pretty, blue eyes. She told me I was a good man and that I deserved the love of a good woman."

I looked at him with a gnawing at my heart. Here was

another self-deluded wretch like me who believed in dreams and love. "You are a happy man." I forced a smile. "You have a guiding star for your life as well as for your boat; and a woman that loves you and is faithful to you? Is it so?"

He raised his hat politely and smiled. "Si, *dama*, my mother."

I was deeply touched by his unexpected reply; more deeply than I cared to show. A bitter regret stirred in my soul. Why had my own mother died so young? Why had I never known the same joy that shone through the sparkling eyes of this common sailor? Why must I be forever alone, with a curse of a man's lie on my life to weigh me down so miserably? Something in my face must have revealed my turmoil.

"The *dama* has no mother?" he asked softly.

"She died when I was a child."

The captain puffed lightly at his cigar as we stood together in the silence of compassion.

"You spoke of Teresa? Who is Teresa?" I asked to divert the topic of our conversation away from me.

"No one knows who she is. She loves Cesare Negri, and that is all I know. Such a tiny thing, and as delicate as foam on the waves. And Cesare, you have seen Cesare, *dama*?"

I shook my head.

"He is huge and coarse and mean as a wolf. Teresa is like a small cloud in the sky. She is tiny and light with hair that ripples with curls, soft eyes and hands, not strong enough to snap a twig in two. Yet Cesare would do anything for her. She is the one soft spot in his life."

"I wonder if she is true to him," I muttered, half to myself and half aloud.

The captain's brows rose. "True to him? One of Cesare's own band of thugs, as ruthless and handsome a cut-throat as ever lived, fell madly in love with Teresa. He pursued her like a beaten mongrel. One day he found her alone and tried to kiss her. She reached for the knife she kept at her waist and stabbed him with it. She did not kill him. Cesare did that later. To think of a little woman like that with such viciousness in her. She boasts that no man, save Cesare, has ever touched so much as a ringlet of her hair. *Si,* she is true to him; more's the pity."

"You do not believe her false?" I asked.

"No. A false man or woman deserves death. Still, it is a pity Teresa has fixed her love on Cesare. Such a vile man. One day the authorities will capture him. Then he will face the galleys for life, and she will die. You may be sure of that. If grief does not kill her quickly enough, then she will kill herself, I am certain. She is as slight and frail as a delicate flower, but her soul is as strong as iron. She will have her own way in death as well as in love. They say it is usually the weakest-looking women who have the most courage. In her case, this is very true."

A sailor who came to ask the captain a question interrupted our conversation. With an apologetic smile and bow, the talkative captain left me to my own reflections.

I was not sorry to be alone. I needed a reprieve in which to think, though my thoughts revolved solely around vengeance. *A false man or woman deserves death.* Even this simple Venetian mariner agreed.

Go and kill him. Go and kill him. The rag-picker's words repeated in my mind until I found myself nearly pronouncing them aloud. My soul sickened when I thought about Teresa; mistress of a loathsome villain whose name was spoken with fear. Even she remained faithful, keeping herself free from the wicked touch of other men. She was proud of being faithful to a man whose temper was treacherous and unpredictable. A woman who took pride in her fidelity to her blood-stained lover, while Dario, the wedded husband of a noblewoman descended from an ancient and unsullied noble family, could trample upon the dignity of our marriage and cast it away like rubble in the dust. Dario, a man so low and vile that even this common woman, Teresa, would pollute herself to touch him. What had Cesare Negri done to deserve the priceless gift of a true heart? What had I done to merit such foul deceit as that which I now must avenge?

I thought of Chiara, my darling child. Her memory fell upon me like a ray of light. In all the tumult I had suffered, I had nearly forgotten her. Poor little flower. Hot tears stung my eyes as I conjured the vision of her soft round face, her trusting eyes, her pink lips puckering to give me an innocent kiss. What about her? Once I fulfilled my vendetta, I must take her with me far, far away into some quiet corner of the world, and devote my life to her. One day she, too, would become a beautiful woman, and I would teach her to be much wiser than I had been when it came to matters of the heart.

Poor Chiara. She was a flower born of a poisoned tree. Oh, we women have serpents coiled around our lives in the form of handsome, but false men. If God has given us children by them, the curse descends upon us threefold. There is nothing more torturous than to see innocent babes look trustingly into the devious eyes of an adulterous husband, and call him *Papa*.

For the rest of the day I remained very much alone except to share my meals in the cabin with Santina and Paolo. The captain spoke pleasantly to me whenever our paths crossed, but nimble opposing winds made it necessary for him to attend to the management of his vessel instead of yielding to the love of chatter inherent in him.

The weather was wonderful, and despite the shifting

and tacking about to seize the unpredictable breeze, the brig sailed rapidly over the shimmering Adriatic, at a rate that promised our arrival at Pescara by sunset of the following day.

As evening arrived, the wind blew a bit stronger, and by the time the moon soared high into the sky, we were scudding along at a tilt, the edge of our vessel leaning over to kiss the waves that gleamed like silver and gold, flecked here and there with flames from a brilliant sunset.

We skimmed near the bows of a magnificent ship. An English flag fluttered from her mast. Her sails glittered white in the moonbeams. A man, with a tall athletic figure stood on deck, his arm around the waist of a young woman beside him. It took only a minute or two to pass the vessel, yet I saw this loving duo with clarity. I pitied her. Men's unfaithfulness tears apart the hearts of women.

Later that night, I returned on deck and stared up at the countless stars that sparkled in the restful indigo sky; my gaze lingering till it seemed that our ship had also become a star, and was sailing through space with its iridescent companions.

The world was filled with men and women who lived and loved and lied to one another. Vague ideas and strange opinions fluttered in my thoughts. I relived the anguish of my burial in the crypt. I forced myself to recall the scene I had witnessed between Dario and Beatrice. I meditated on every small detail. And my desire for vengeance grew ever more powerful. There was no remedy for a woman betrayed and whose pride was sullied by a cheating man. No law existed to punish him. So therefore I must seek justice on my own. I must be counsel, jury, and judge, all in one and render justice so there could be no appeal. But I took it a little further. I would also be the executioner for the unique penalty I had devised.

So, I mused with my face upturned to the sky,

watching the light of the moon shining down on the sea like a shower of silver, while the waves slapped gently against the sides of the ship. Lost in such thoughts, a long time passed before I turned away and retired to my quarters where Santina waited to attend me.

Chapter Ten

The brig sailed into Pescara's harbor an hour before sunset. It had scarcely reached dock when a band of guards, heavily laden with matchlock muskets and swords, boarded the vessel. Their sergeant produced a document authorizing them to search the brig for Cesare Negri.

In his usual gregarious manner, the ship's captain smiled and welcomed the military emissaries as though they were his dearest friends. While his aides distributed cups to the unexpected visitors, he uncorked a flask of wine. "In my opinion, Cesare Negri is somewhere in Vicenza."

The sergeant cocked his head and stared at him doubtfully.

"I speak the truth." The captain filled the man's cup. "There is a reward for Negri's capture, is there not? And I am not a wealthy man. Therefore I will do everything I can to assist you."

The sergeant's gaze narrowed. "We received information that Negri escaped from Vicenza. His escape was assisted by a man named Ernesto Paccanini, owner of the coasting brig *Laura Bella* who ships goods between Venice and Pescara. You are Ernesto Paccanini and this is the brig *Laura Bella.*"

"Ah, I see you are a very astute man." With

exuberance, the captain slapped the sergeant on the back causing the wine to spill from the cup he held uncomfortably in his hand. "You are correct about my name and that of my brig, but you are wrong about Negri." He wagged his finger back and forth in denial then broke out into a laugh. "But I do not wish to quarrel with you. Have some more wine. Hunting for thiefs is thirsty work. Let me refill your cups, my dear friends. I have plenty more below deck."

The officers drank the proffered wine. The youngest-looking of the group, a brisk, handsome fellow raised his cup. "Bravo Ernesto. Let us all be friends together. Besides, what harm is there in accepting a thief and murderer as a passenger? No doubt he paid you better than most."

It was evident to me that the man's deliberate levity was a means to trap the captain into an accidental confession.

But the captain was smarter than he looked and would not be caught. Instead, he raised his hands and eyes with feigned alarm. "May the saints forgive you for thinking that I, a simple seaman, would accept one *scudo* from such a bandit. I would be cursed for the rest of my life. You are mistaken, sergeant. I know nothing of Cesare Negri, and I have never encountered the lout."

He spoke with such sincerity that the officers appeared perplexed, yet it did not deter them from thoroughly searching the brig. They questioned everyone on board, including myself, but did not learn any further information. Though they glanced curiously at my white hair, they seemed to think there was nothing suspicious about me, a woman and her servants travelling alone for a brief vacation.

After more of the captain's pleasant cordialities, the guards departed with puzzled expressions over the incorrect information they had received that Negri may have been on board.

As soon as they were out of sight, Ernesto cavorted about the deck like a child in a garden, and snapped his fingers defiantly. "Those idiots. How dare they think to force me, Ernesto Paccanini, to betray a man who has given me good cigars. Let them hunt in every town and city. Cesare may rest comfortably without the authorities to disturb him."

I advanced to bid the captain farewell.

"Ah, *dama*, I am truly sorry to part company with you. I hope you will forgive me for not betraying poor Signor Negri who trusts me."

"I wish there were more men in the world like you. *Arrivederci.*" I handed him the fare for our passage. "Please accept my sincere thanks. I shall not forget your kindness. If you ever need a friend, send to me."

He gave me a curious look. "But how can I do that if the *dama* does not tell me her name?"

I had pondered this during the night. I knew I must assume a new name, and I had decided to adopt that of an old school-friend, a girl to whom I had been profoundly attached in my earliest youth, and who had drowned before my eyes while bathing in the Venetian Lido. So I answered Ernesto's question at once and without effort. "Ask for Contessa Giulia Corona. I shall return to Vicenza shortly. Seek me there and you will find me."

The captain doffed his cap and bowed. He straightened with a grin. "I was correct that the *dama's* hands were those of a woman of noble rank. I know a lady when I see one. *Arrivederci, dama.* Command me when you will. I shall be happy to serve you again."

I gave him my warmest smile and Santina, Paolo, and I stepped from the brig onto the dock.

"*Mille grazie,*" I called out to him.

And thus I left him, standing bareheaded on the deck

The Contessa's Vendetta

of his small vessel, waving good-heartedly as I walked away. His ideas of right and wrong were odd, and he lied better than many people who told the truth. I could not dislike him.

We went immediately in search of a place to stay. I engaged three rooms for several weeks at the finest inn I could find.

My second need was to purchase clothes. I found a quaint dressmaker's shop where I ordered numerous gowns to be made in the finest materials - brocatella, gold cloth, silks, damasks, brocades, and velvets. Santina was also to receive several gowns, not as fine as mine, of course, but appropriate enough for a lady's personal maid. By the look of delight on her face, I knew her new gowns of linen and lace pleased her. I did not forget Paolo either, who received new shirts, doublets, and jerkins.

I gave the dressmaker my new name and the address of the inn. She served me with flattering humbleness and allowed me the use of her private back-room, where I discarded the drowned woman's gown for a ready-made gown constructed in an elaborate brocade, its bodice embellished with embroidered roses and foliage with colorful beading. The main skirt was in a deep cream silk, opening at the front to show a brocade panel, enhanced with pearls.

Thus arrayed, we returned to the inn where I would spend the coming weeks preparing for the act of retribution that lay before me.

I needed to find a safe place for the coins and gems I kept hidden on my person. I sought out the leading banker in Pescara. After introducing myself with my fake name, I explained how I had recently returned to Pescara after several years' absence. He received me with utmost cordiality. Despite his astonishment at the vast wealth I presented to him, including the bag of jewels, most of which, because of their remarkable size and lustre, seemed to daze and impress him, he accepted it all and arranged for its safe keeping,

As payment, I gave him a fine sapphire and two rose-cut diamonds, all unset. "Please have a ring made for yourself," I said as I placed the gems into his sweaty palm.

His eye widened with surprise. "But I cannot possibly accept such a gift."

"But I insist," I said in my most commanding voice. "It is the least I can do to compensate you for protecting my riches."

He did not argue any further. His covetous desire to possess the exceptional stones prevailed. He swiftly tucked them into his waist pouch then inundated me with his gratitude.

I could not help but smile. My bribe had worked. Not only had I secured his services, but he either forgot or saw no need to ask me for personal references, which would have been impossible for me to provide.

With this matter attended to, I turned my attention to my next dilemma – how to disguise myself so that no one would ever recognize me, either by appearance or gesture, as the late Carlotta Mancini. Already, my face had filled out and I looked young again. The spark of life and freedom glimmered in my eyes once more and I knew it would give me away to anyone who once knew me. What should I do about my tell-tale eyes?

An idea immediately came to mind. I decided to feign weak eye-sight made worse by the sun's brilliance. A pair of spectacles would cover my eyes and much of my face. From a small shop specializing in Venetian glass, I purchased a hand-held mirror and a pair of dark-tinted spectacles. Ribbons attached to the silver frames kept them looped over my ears so I would not need to hold them in place with my hands. When I returned to my room at the inn, I examined myself in the mirror. The eye glasses disguised my most distinguishable features perfectly. Together with my white hair, I looked like a woman in her mid fifties with an eye impediment.

The next thing to do was to change the brisk, but clear diction of my voice and eliminate the expressive hand gestures those from the Veneto area are prone to. I trained myself to speak in a different voice, hardening my accent and speaking with forethought and detachment. I injected sarcasm and curtness while taking care to keep my hands and head still.

This all took much time and effort. As luck had it, a middle-aged English woman had taken a room at the same inn as myself. Her reserved indifference never wavered. Like a human block of ice, she carried herself with a permanent air of gloom. With practice, I learned to imitate her almost to perfection. I kept my mouth shut in the exact manner of her pig-headedness, walked with the same erect stiffness, and looked at the world around me with similar haughty condescension. When I overheard a waiter refer to me as 'the white viper' I knew I had succeeded.

Another idea came to mind to help me prepare for my journey home. I wrote a courteous letter to the owner of Vicenza's newspaper, which we had always received at Villa Mancini. Enclosing fifty *scudi*, a very generous amount, I requested that he insert the following words in his next issue:

> *Contessa Giulia Corona, who has been absent from Vicenza for many years, will soon return. Possessed of fabulous wealth, she intends to make her home here once more. There is little doubt that society's leaders will welcome the distinguished dama into their brilliant social circles with much enthusiasm.*

The owner printed it word for word and sent me a copy of the newspaper with a note of thanks.

My plan was now complete. All that remained was to return to Vicenza and set it in motion.

On the second last day of my stay in Pescara, Santina and I sat in two padded chairs beside an open window in the inn's dining hall. I had sent Paolo to purchase several trunks for our return journey. She embroidered a handkerchief while I read a book. I had grown used to Santina's reserved, but agreeable manner. A comfortable bond existed between us. Eager to please, she seemed happy with her new life as my maidservant, just as I was with her silent efficiency. More importantly, she watched the changes I underwent, quietly accepting them with nary a challenge.

Church bells tolled the call to Vespers. Although the gorgeous colors of the sunset lingered in the sky, a cool breeze blew in from the Adriatic sea.

My new persona of a somewhat callous and churlish woman who had experienced life and hated it, had already become second nature to me. Hourly practice had made it so. In fact, I doubted I could easily return to the carefree mannerisms that had once belonged to Carlotta Mancini.

As I read quietly, a loud clamor caused by the shouts of a crowd floated in through the window and startled me. I leaned out and looked up and down the street, but could see nothing. As I pondered what the noise could mean, an excited waiter entered the room. "Cesare Negri. They caught him, *poverino*. They have him at last."

Though powerfully drawn by this news, I refused to allow my interest or excitement to show. I held taut to the new personality traits I had worked so hard to ingrain.

"Then they have caught a great scoundrel indeed. I congratulate the authorities. Where is Negri now?"

"You need only walk around the corner, and you will see him bound and fettered in the piazza, may the saints have mercy on him. The crowds have flocked there like vultures. I am going there myself. I would not miss it for a thousand lire." He ran off excited.

I tossed my book onto the chair. "Come, Santina. Let us see this infamous rogue for ourselves."

Her eyes widened, the name now familiar to her from our time on the brig, but she gathered our belongings and followed me out the door.

We strolled to the piazza. At the center of a muttering crowd were a troop of mounted guards with drawn swords flashing in the pale evening light. Men and horses stood as motionless as bronze statues. They were stationed opposite an office of the guards, where the chief officer had dismounted to make his formal report regarding Negri's capture and sentence before proceeding further.

Encircled by the vigilant guards, with his legs strapped to a robust mule and his hands manacled behind his back, I caught a glimpse of the notorious Cesare Negri; a man as dark and fierce and thunderous as a storm.

A mane of long, thick, dishevelled curls hung in a tangled mess upon his shoulders. His bushy black mustache and beard covered his sinister features. I caught a glimpse of yellowed teeth as he gnawed his lip in helpless rage and misery. From beneath bushy brows, his eyes blazed with wrath. He was a huge, brawny man, barrel-chested and muscular. His manacled hands were huge, formidable enough to kill a man with one blow.

He was dressed unremarkably in a shirt of plain linen tucked into black breeches, and tall narrow boots with turned-over tops. His throat and chest heaved with the pent-up anger that raged within him. His menacing form was set off by a peculiar effect of color in the sky. A lengthy band of pink and maroon clouds burned on the olive-tinted faces of the multitude who stared with misguided admiration on the brutal face of the notorious murderer and thief who had so terrorized the country. Everything about him was hideous and dreadful. I could find no redeeming feature about him.

I pressed my way through the crowd to get closer.

I saw Negri move his bound upper body abruptly.

The guards pointed their swords at him in warning.

The scoundrel laughed and tossed his head back. "*Porca miseria*. Do you think a man tied hand and foot like me can escape? I am trapped, you fools." He tilted his head in the direction of a man in the throng. "Tell that man to come forward. I have a message for him."

The guards looked first at one another, and then at the crowd with bewilderment, unsure which man to call out to.

Impatient, Cesare elevated himself as much as he could in his awkward trussed up posture, and shouted, "Filippo Barocco. Capitano. You think I cannot see you? I would know you even in hell. Come and show me your face. I have a parting word for you." His gravelly voiced echoed over the crowd who fell into a shocked silence.

There was a sudden commotion as people made way for a young man to pass. He was a lanky, feeble-looking fellow with a pasty complexion and eyes that glimmered with aloofness as well as scorn. Dressed meticulously in his guard's uniform, he elbowed his way to the front with the ease of a spoiled dandy. He came to stand beside Negri and stared at him scornfully. "So they caught you at last, Cesare. You called me and here I am. Say what you have to say."

"Hey, *faccia di merda*. Shit face." Negri looked like a feral lion ready to spring upon its prey. "You betrayed me. You followed me. You hunted me down. Teresa told me

The Contessa's Vendetta

everything. She is yours now. You won. Go and take her. She waits for you. Make her tell you how much she loves you, if you can."

Something threatening in the ruffian's glare startled the young man. "What do you mean, you bastard? *Dio.* You haven't killed her, have you?"

Negri broke out into a savage laugh. "Me? I had nothing to do with it. She killed herself. She snatched my knife out of my hand and stabbed herself with it, preferring to die rather than see your lying white face again or endure your foul touch. Try to find her if you can. Her body lies dead up in the mountains, but her soul smiles down upon us from Heaven. Her last kiss was for me. Me — only me. Now get out of my sight." He coughed and spat in his face. "May the devil curse you."

The guards rattled their swords and Negri received a blow to the chest from the butt of a musket. He curled forward momentarily. Slowly he straightened and resumed his furious scowl and fake indifference.

The man whom he had cursed staggered and seemed about to fall. His pale face became ashen. He disappeared into the crowd catatonically, as if he was unsure whether he was alive or dead. The news he had received had brought about his shock, wounding him deeply.

I approached the nearest guard and slipped a silver coin into his hand.

"May I speak with Negri?" I asked, cautiously.

The man hesitated. He glanced about and eyed the office. Then he nodded. "For an instant, but keep it brief."

I approached Negri. "Have you any message for Ernesto Paccanini? I am a friend of his."

He stared at me and then a smirk arose on his face. "The captain is a good man. Tell him that Teresa is dead and I am worse than dead. He will know for certain that I did not kill Teresa. I could never do such a thing. She shoved the blade into her breast before I could stop her." He shook his head. "It is better this way."

"She killed herself rather than become the property of another man?" I asked.

Cesare Negri nodded. I had to look twice at him, for I could swear I saw tears glistening in the depth of his sinful eyes.

The guard gestured for me to come away, so I withdrew. Almost at the same moment the troop's commanding officer exited the office, his spurs clinking against the cobblestone road. He mounted then shouted a command. The crowd moved back as horses were put to a quick trot. In a few moments the entire band, with the hulking form of Cesare Negri swallowed in their midst, disappeared down the street.

The people broke up into little groups talking excitedly of what they had witnessed. They returned to their homes or work. In a very short time, the piazza was empty.

I sat with Santina upon a bench near the center of the piazza. In my mind I pictured the beautiful Teresa lying dead and alone in the mountains with a self-inflicted wound that had freed her from the love and persecution of men. There *were* some women who preferred death to infidelity. How strange. Common women must be capable of killing themselves for such a reason. Daintily fed, silk-robed women like me would never stab themselves with a vulgar stiletto. Rather, we might retaliate by choosing a lover, or a score of lovers. Or, as in my case, launch a diabolical vendetta.

As I sat, I found myself glancing at the guards' office. On an impulse, I rose and entered the building determined to ask for the details of Negri's capture. I was met by an intelligent-looking man who greeted me cordially.

"Oh, *sì,*" he said, in answer to my inquiries, "Over the

years, Negri has given us a great deal of trouble. But we suspected he fled Vicenza for Pescara, where he went into hiding in the nearby mountains. A few stray bits of information gleaned here and there led us right to him."

"Was he caught easily or did he put up a fight?"

"He surrendered like a gentle lamb, *signora*. One of our men followed the woman named Teresa who lived with Negri. He traced her up to the corner of a narrow mountain pass where she disappeared from his sight. He returned to report this and we sent out an armed party in the middle of the night to find him. Two by two, they surrounded the location where we thought he was hiding. With the first beam of morning light, they rushed in upon him and took him prisoner. They tell me he showed no surprise. He merely said, 'I expected you.' They found him sitting next to the dead body of his mistress; she was stabbed and still bleeding. There is little doubt he killed her, even though he swears he is innocent. The man lies as easily as he breathes."

"But I thought he was the leader of a large band of men? Where were they?"

"We captured three of his men two weeks ago, but we can find no trace of the others. My guess is that Cesare dismissed them and sent them far and wide throughout the entire country. At any rate, they are disbanded. When criminals are separated, there is no danger."

"What will happen to Negri now?" I asked.

"A big strong man like him? It will be leg irons, the whip, and the galleys for him, for whatever remains of his sorry life."

I thanked him and returned to the piazza where Santina awaited me. Based on what I had just learned, I was reassured that the treasure I had discovered in my family vault was safely mine. A grim smile curled my lips. If Negri knew how I had been wronged, I had little doubt he would be happy that his hidden riches were destined to help me carry out an elaborate vendetta.

Any difficulties towards my goal had been smoothed out. The path before me was clear, without obstacles. God himself seemed to be on my side, and why not? Is He not on always on the side of the just?

Oh, Dario. I will be home soon. Those who are unfaithful should never let down their guard. Just because one goes to church and prays, God is not deceived. My husband attended church regularly, kneeling before sacred altars, his eyes upturned to Christ, but each word he uttered was blasphemy.

One day soon, all his lies would turn on him like a curse. Prayer is dangerous for liars. And he was the biggest liar of them all.

Chapter Eleven

By the middle of September, I found myself once more in Vicenza. The heat of summer had dulled into the gentle warmth of early autumn. News that a decrease in plague victims had eased the panicked, frightened population. Businesses were opening and society once more resumed its entertainments.

Santina, Paolo, and I disembarked in Venice shortly after midday. I immediately hired a carriage to take us into Vicenza. There, I secured the most amazing suite of rooms in an imposing, elegant villa where the ravages of the plague had killed the entire family except for the matriarch, a kind, middle-aged woman who was more than relieved to receive my generous payment.

My affluence and rank enthralled her. I mentioned that I needed to purchase a carriage and horses, the services of a launderess, and a few other trifles of the sort, and added that I trusted her recommendations on how or where I should best acquire all that I sought. She became my eager servant in all things, and through the good will of people she knew, I acquired all that I desired and was thoroughly satisfied. Through word of mouth, knowledge of my vast wealth, munificence, and abundant disbursements travelled. People hurried to attend my every wish.

Hence, on the evening of my first day in Vicenza, I,

the fabricated Contessa Giulia Corona, the coveted and advantaged noblewoman, took the first few steps towards fulfilling my vendetta.

It was one of the most exquisite evenings I had ever experienced. A light breeze blew and the falling sun shone with an opalescent glow amid radiant clouds of rose and lavender. After the evening meal, I called for Paolo to prepare my carriage and drive me to my favorite coffee house. Beatrice and I frequented it regularly on evenings like this and I suspected she might be there. The coffee house hosted literary and musical readings and we had both learned to love the newly discovered dark fragrant beverage that arrived in Venice from Arabic countries.

The gleaming white and gold salon was crowded, and due to the cool evening, many tables had been pushed out into the street. People played chess, gossiped, and drank coffee and wine. A celebratory air existed due to the good news that the pestilence that had ravaged the city for so long would soon disappear.

I glanced around. There, unmistakably, sat my former friend, my disloyal adversary, Beatrice Cardano, alone at a table near the window, reading a copy of Vicenza's newspaper. Dressed in black, the solemn color suited her light skin and ideal features well. As she raised a cup to her lips, a diamond on the ring of her left hand glittered against the evening light. It was of extraordinary size and brilliance. Even at a distance I recognized it as mine.

Was it a love gift or a memorial for the cherished companion she had lost? I studied her through contemptuous eyes for a moment, and then collecting myself, I strolled toward her and sat at the empty table next to hers.

She glanced apathetically at me over the top of her publication, but there was nothing interesting at the sight of a white-haired woman wearing ugly, dark-colored

The Contessa's Vendetta

spectacles, so she returned to her reading. I rapped my fan against the table to summon a waiter and ordered coffee.

Something in my attitude seemed to catch Beatrice's interest, for she laid down her paper and looked at me with a little more interest and unease.

And so it begins, my friend. I turned my head and pretended to be absorbed by the view outside. My coffee arrived and I paid for it with an extraordinarily generous gratuity. The impressed waiter buffed my table with enthusiasm. He gathered several publications and books that lay about and set them down in a pile at my right hand.

"Do you know Vicenza well?" I asked this likeable young man in my well-practiced, disguised voice.

"Oh, *si, gentildonna.*"

"Can you tell me the way to the house of Contessa Carlotta Mancini? She is a wealthy noblewoman of this city."

Ha! I had struck a cord. From the corner of my eye, I saw Beatrice twitch as if stung, and then quickly collect herself.

The waiter shrugged and shook his head sadly. "Ah, *Dio. La poverina,* the poor woman is dead."

"Dead," I exclaimed, with feigned shock and surprise. "At such a young age? But that is not possible."

"Eh. It is the truth, signora. *La pestilenza,* for which there is no remedy, struck her down. The plague does not spare the old or young, the rich or poor."

I leaned my head on my hand as if overcome with shock. Then I looked back up at him. "Oh dear, I am too late. I was a friend of her mother's. I have been away for many years, and I wanted to meet the young woman whom I last saw as a child. Does she have any relatives living? Was she married?"

The waiter, whose features had turned mournful in

respect of my feelings, perked up immediately. "Oh, *si*. Signore Gismondi, her husband, lives up at the villa, though I believe he receives no one since his wife died. He is young and handsome. There is a little child too."

A swift movement by Beatrice forced me to turn my gaze in her direction and I regarded her through my spectacles.

She leaned forward with all the elegance I remember so well. "*Scusa*, signora. I knew Contessa Mancini better than anyone in Vicenza. I would be happy to answer your questions."

The unforgettable melody of her voice struck me. For an instant, I could not speak. Rage and anguish nearly suffocated me. Fortunately it passed swiftly. Slowly, I nodded. "Could you introduce me to the relatives of Contessa Mancini? Her mother was dearer to me than a sister. Permit me to introduce myself." I handed her my visiting card.

She accepted it, and as she read the name printed upon it, cast me a look of respect mingled with pleased surprise. "Contessa Giulia Corona. How fortunate to meet you." She raised the newspaper. "Your arrival has already been heralded in this journal, so I am well aware that you are to receive a hearty welcome. I am only sorry that the distressing news of Contessa Mancini has darkened your return here after so long an absence. Permit me to express my hope that it may be the only news that clouds your visit."

She extended her hand to me. A cold shudder ran through my veins. Could I touch her? I must if I was to act my part, for if I refused she might think it strange or rude. One false move on my part and I would lose the entire game I had so craftily prepared.

With a forced smile I held out my gloved hand. She clasped it in her own and the affectionate weight smouldered through my glove. I could have cried out in misery, so acute was the torment I endured. But it passed. From that moment on, I knew I could touch her often and with indifference. Only this once did I allow it to gall me to the quick.

Beatrice did not notice my reaction. She was in an exceptional mood and turned to the waiter who had watched us make each other's acquaintance. "More coffee," she ordered, and then looked at me. "You do not object to another coffee, Contessa? No? That is good." She removed a silver card case from her purse. "And this is my card."

The case was finely engraved with flowers, leaves, and scrolls that surrounded the Mancini coat of arms and coronet with my own initials engraved thereon. It was mine, of course, I thought with grim amusement. I had not seen it since the day I died.

"I am Beatrice Cardano. Come, let us share a coffee together."

I smiled. The waiter vanished to execute his orders and Beatrice joined me at my table.

"A fine antique," I remarked, putting out my hand. She happily relinquished the silver card case to me. I turned it over and over in my hand. "Lovely and expensive. Was it a gift or an heirloom?"

"It used to belong to my late friend, Contessa Carlotta Mancini. The monk who saw her die found it in her purse. That and other trifles she wore on her person were delivered to her husband, and—"

"He gave it to you as a memento of your friend," I said, interrupting her.

"Why *si*, that is exactly the truth. *Grazie.*" She took the case as I returned it to her with a frank smile.

"Is Signore Gismondi young?" I inquired.

"Young and extremely handsome," Beatrice replied enthusiastically. "I doubt if sunlight ever fell on a more enchanting man. If you were a young woman, Contessa, I would not tell you of his charms for fear of losing him to you, but your white hair assures me you can be no rival to me. Although Carlotta was my friend, and an excellent woman in her own way, she was never worthy of the man who married her."

"Is that so?" I asked coldly, as I suffered yet another stiletto-thrust to my heart. "I only knew her when she was a young girl. She seemed to be warm and loving, generous to a fault, and most kind-hearted. Her mother thought so, and I confess I thought so, too. I often received reports about how well she managed the vast fortune she inherited. She donated large sums to charity, did she not? And was she not a lover of books?"

"Oh, *si*, that is all true," Beatrice said impatiently. "She was a most virtuous and moral woman, if you like that sort of thing. Reflective, philosophic, a perfect *gentildonna*, swollen with pride, gullible, and a great fool."

My fury rose but I forced myself to stifle it, recalling the importance of playing the role I had crafted for myself. Instead, I broke out in forceful laughter. "*Brava*. I can see what a shrewd woman you are. You have no liking for moral women. Excellent. I agree with you. I've lived long enough to know that an upright woman and a fool are one in the same. Ah, here is our coffee. You and I, *cara*, must become friends."

My unexpected outburst seemed to startle her. Then she gave a hearty laugh herself just as the waiter set down our coffees.

"And this poor weak-minded friend of yours, was her death sudden?"

Beatrice leaned back in her chair and turned her flushed face up to the sky where the stars were starting to sparkle. "She rose early and set out for a walk on a hot August morning. At the perimeter of her estate, she came upon a young boy struck down by the plague. Carlotta stopped to help him and hurried into Vicenza to find a healer. Instead of a healer, all she could find was a monk. She was leading him to the boy, who had already died, when she herself was struck with the pestilence. The monk carried her to a common inn, where she died, all the time shrieking demands that no one must take her, alive or dead, to her villa. She showed good sense in that at least, for she did not want to bring the contagion to her husband and child."

"Is the child a boy or a girl?" I asked, carelessly.

"A girl, no more than a baby; a tedious little thing just like her mother."

My poor little Chiara. My blood throbbed with indignation at Beatrice's apathy, for she had often embraced Chiara and pretended to love my poor, motherless child. No doubt her father cared little for her too, and I saw that she was, or soon would be, a snubbed and companionless little thing in the household. But I said nothing. I sipped my coffee with a preoccupied air for a few moments. "How was the contessa buried?"

"Oh, the monk who was with her saw to her burial, and I believe, administered last rites. He ensured she was buried with the proper respect in her family vault. I attended the funeral."

"You were there?" My voice almost failed me.

Beatrice raised her eyebrows with astonishment. "Of course. Why are you surprised? I was the contessa's dearest friend. We were closer than sisters. It was natural, even necessary, that I should be with her until she reached her final resting place."

I managed to recover. "I see. Because of my age, I'm nervous of disease in any form. I would think the fear of contagion might have kept you away, too."

"Me?" she laughed. "I have never been ill a day in my

life, and I have no fear whatsoever of the pestilence. I suppose I took a risk, though it never entered my mind at the time. I should have perhaps, because I learned the monk died the next day."

"Shocking," I murmured over my coffee-cup. "And you had no fear for yourself?"

"None at all. To tell you the truth, I know I will never die of any kind of disease." Her features became solemn. "An odd prophecy was made about me when I was born, Whether it is true or not, it kept me from panicking while the plagued struck so many people in Vicenza."

This was news to me. "And may I ask what the prophecy foretold?"

"Oh, certainly. I was told that I would die a violent death by the hand of a friend known to me. Of course, I never believed the absurd prediction. It's nothing more than an old wive's tale. In fact, it is now more ridiculous than ever, considering that the only friend I have ever had, or am likely to have, is dead and buried, namely, Carlotta Mancini." And she sighed slightly.

I raised my head and looked at her. Beneath the shelter of my dark spectacles, she could not see the scrutiny of my gaze.

A faint tinge of melancholy shadowed her face. She seemed deep in thought, almost sad.

"You loved her well then, in spite of her foolishness?" I asked.

She came out of her reverie and smiled. "Loved her? No. Absolutely not. Nothing so strong as that. I liked her, but only until she married."

"Ah, then her husband must have come between you?"

She flushed slightly and drank down what remained of her coffee. "*Si*, he came between us. A woman changes after marriage. But we have been sitting a long time. Shall we walk a little?"

The Contessa's Vendetta

For some reason, she did not wish to talk about Carlotta anymore. I rose slowly as befit someone whose joints had stiffened with age. "It is getting dark. I will dismiss my carriage and driver so we can walk and enjoy the night air. It would please me if you would accompany me to my villa. I need to retire early, for I suffer from a chronic complaint of the eyes." I touched my spectacles. "We can talk on our way. Then I will have my driver take you home. I can pay you for your company if you wish."

"Thank you, but no payment is required. In six months time I shall be comfortably wealthy," she answered gayly.

"Indeed. Are you inheriting a small fortune?"

"Well, not exactly. I am going to marry a wealthy man. That is almost the same thing, is it not?"

"Congratulations." My heart pulsed with a torrent of pent up anger. I knew very well what she meant. In six months time, she planned to marry my husband. According to social etiquette, six months was the minimum waiting period before a man should remarry, and even that was considered so short as to be barely decent. Six brief months. Much could happen in that span of time. Unimaginable things. Undesirable things. Carefully measured tortures. Punishments, rapid and harsh.

I asked Paolo to follow us home. Wrapped in dark thoughts, I strolled beside her. The moon had risen and now shone brilliantly above us. The evening exuded splendor, harmony and serenity, but my hands trembled with a curtailed desire to strangle the cheat who promenaded so boldly beside me. Ah, if she only knew my inner thoughts. Her face would lose its slipshod smile. Her manner would not be so lighthearted, so fearless. I studied her as she hummed a tune, but when she realized I was looking at her, she looked at me. "You have traveled far and seen much, Contessa?"

"I have."

"And which country has the most handsome, wealthiest men?"

"The business of life has kept me away from male society," I answered coldly. "I devote myself solely to protecting my wealth. Gold is the key to all things; far more important than a man's love. I could have had love if I had desired it, but I didn't. Now, I cannot tell the difference between a handsome face from an ugly one. I was never interested, nor attracted to men. At my age, I am set in my ways, and I refuse to change my life to accommodate any man."

Beatrice laughed. "You remind me of Carlotta. She used to say exactly the same things before she married, though she was young and had none of the life experiences which have made you sceptical, but she certainly changed her point of view very quickly when she met her husband, and it did not surprise me."

"Why? Because he is so very handsome?"

"*Si*, he is a ruggedly good-looking man. But you will soon see him. As a friend of his late wife's mother, you will call upon him, will you not?"

"Why should I? I have no desire to meet him. Besides, a grieving widower will likely not receive visitors."

My show of utter indifference was genius. The less I appeared to care about meeting Signore Gismondi, the more Beatrice wanted to introduce me to him, my own husband. And thus she worked towards her own demise.

"Oh, but you must go to see him. I know he will be happy to receive you. Your age and your familiarity with his late wife's family will garner his most cordial courtesies. Besides, he is not really inconsolable—" She paused suddenly.

We had arrived at the entrance of my rented villa.

I looked at her steadily. "Not inconsolable? What do

you mean? Is he not grieving for his wife?"

Beatrice broke into a forced laugh. "Why no. He is young and light-hearted, and in the fullness of good health. One cannot expect a young, virile man like him to mourn very long, especially for a woman he never cared for."

We had arrived at the villa's front steps. "Please come inside. We can share a glass of wine before my driver takes you home." I paused and gestured for her to follow. "You say he did not care for her?"

Buoyant because of my sociable invitation and pleasant manner, Beatrice seemed to relax, and linking her arm through mine, we ascended the steps together. "My dear Contessa, how can a man love a woman whom he is forced to marry? His father thrust Carlotta upon him because of her wealth. That is the only reason. As I stated earlier, my late friend was utterly blind to the handsomeness of her husband. She was cold as marble and preferred her books. Naturally, no man could love a woman like that."

By this time we had reached the front entrance, and as I threw open the door, I saw that Beatrice took in the costly fittings and luxurious furniture with a discerning eye. I gave her a chilly smile. "As I said before, *carissima*, I do not understand men and care nothing about their interests, who they love and who they hate. Try this wine. I am told it comes from the finest vineyards in the Veneto region."

She accepted the glass and sipped the wine as if she were an expert. "Superb," she murmured, taking another sip. "You live like a princess, Contessa. I envy you."

"Please do not say that. You have youth and health and beauty, and, as you have hinted, love. All these things are far superior to being rich. At any rate, I do not believe in love. As for me, I prefer luxury, comfort, and ease. I have suffered much in my life. Now that I am older, I have earned my rest and the right to enjoy whatever is to come in my future."

"How very sensible of you." Beatrice leaned back against the satin cushions of the chair in which she sat. "Do you know, Contessa, now that I look at you, I believe you must have been a great beauty when you were young. You have a lovely figure for a woman of your age."

I smiled stiffly. "You flatter me. Of course, I was never considered hideous, but I believe that a woman's attractiveness always ranks second to her courage and strength, and of both, I have plenty."

"I do not doubt it." She regarded me with an expression of faint unease. "It is a strange coincidence, but I think there is an astonishing resemblance between you and my late friend, Carlotta. You are both tall and your figures are similar."

I poured myself some wine and took a long sip to steady my hand. "Really? I am glad that I remind you of her, if the reminder is a pleasant one."

Beatrice frowned and didn't respond to my remark. She studied me hard, and I returned her look steadily, without embarrassment. Finally she smiled, and finished drinking her glass of wine. Then she rose to go.

"You will permit me to mention your name to Signore Gismondi, I hope? I am certain he will receive you, should you wish to meet him."

I faked vexation. "The fact is, I dislike conversing with men. They are always too logical, and their seriousness wearies me. You have been so kind that I will give you a message for the signore, if you don't mind delivering it. However, if you do not plan to see him soon, please do not trouble yourself."

She blushed a little. "On the contrary, I will be seeing him this evening. It will be my pleasure to convey your greeting to him."

"Oh, it is no greeting." I noted her discomfort with a

careful eye. "It is a mere message, which will help you understand why I was so anxious to see the young woman who is dead. When I was young, the elder Contessa Mancini did me a tremendous service. I never forgot her kindness. You see, I never forget a good or a bad deed, and I have always wanted to repay her in some manner. I am getting old, and I own many fine, priceless jewels. I collected them all these years and reserved them to present as a gift to the daughter of my old friend, as an expression of gratitude. Her untimely death has prevented me from fulfilling my intention. Because the jewels are of little use to me, I would like to present them to Signore Gismondi to give to his daughter one day. They would have come to her anyway, had her mother survived; so they should be hers now. If you will discuss this with him and learn his wishes with respect to this matter, I shall be indebted to you."

"I am more than delighted to do so." Beatrice rose and prepared to leave. "What a pleasant errand. Beautiful young girls love jewels, too. *Arrivederci*, Contessa. I hope that we may meet again soon."

"I have no doubt we will," I answered, quietly, but with the coolness which I had so painstakingly practiced, and we parted. From the window I watched her approach the awaiting carriage.

How I cursed her as she stepped jauntily in. How I hated her composed, easy manner. I watched the poise of her delicate head and shoulders and noted her confident steps, her mindful arrogance. Her entire demeanour showed off her sense of superiority and utter confidence in the future that awaited her once the stipulated six month mourning period for my sudden death ended.

Just before she entered the carriage, I saw her turn and pause. She looked back and then raised her face to the sky, to the cool breeze. The light of the moon fell full on her features. She appeared like a finely-cut cameo against the dense dark-blue background of the evening sky.

I gazed at her with the enthrallment of a hunter watching a stag just before an arrow is shot to kill it. She was in my power and had deliberately entered my trap. Now, she lay at the mercy of someone who had no mercy. She had said and done nothing to deter me from my plans. Had she spoken with the least bit of tenderness for Carlotta Mancini, her friend and benefactor, had she uttered one generous word to revere my memory, had she expressed even a solitary regret for my loss, I might have changed my course of action so that my retribution against her would have been lighter than his. For I knew very well that Dario, my husband, was the worst sinner of the two. Had Beatrice shown the least sign of regret or affection for me, her supposed dead friend, the scales would have turned in her favor. Despite her treachery, and how he must have encouraged her, I would have spared her any torture. But she gave me no sign, had spoken no word, had shown neither hesitation nor pity, and I secretly rejoiced because of it.

These were my thoughts as I watched her standing beneath the moonlight, on her way to see my husband. That much, I knew for certain. She was going to console him, to soothe his aching heart.

She stepped into the carriage and I watched as it drove out of sight. I waited until I caught the last glimpse of it, and then I left the window satisfied. My vendetta had begun.

Chapter Twelve

Early the next morning, while I was enjoying a leisurely breakfast in the dining room, Beatrice called on me. Paolo escorted her to me, and then he silently left us. I let her stand awkwardly before me as I waited for her to break the silence.

"I apologize for disturbing your meal, Contessa, but Signore Gismondi bid me to come and see you with an urgent request I was compelled to obey," she said. "We women often find ourselves the servants of men, do we not?"

"No, I cannot say that I find that statement true in my case." Delighting in her initial discomfort, I motioned for her to take a seat. "Please make yourself comfortable. May I offer you some pomegranate juice?"

"*Grazie*, but I have already breakfasted. Please do not let me disturb you. Signore Gismondi wishes—"

"You saw him last night?" I interrupted.

A touch of pink tinted her cheeks. "*Sì*, for a moment or two; only to give him your message. He thanks you and would like you to honor him with a visit before he can accept your gift of jewelry for his daughter. Because of his bereavement, he has not received visitors, but for you, a close friend of his wife's family, he extends a warm welcome."

"It is seldom that I receive so gracious, so tempting an

invitation." I gave her a meager smile. "But I regret that I cannot accept it. Please give Signore Gismondi my regards in your kindest words"

She gave me a puzzled look. "Do you mean that you will not visit him? You are refusing his invitation?"

I smiled. "I mean, Signorina Cardano, that I am accustomed to having my way and I make no exception for any man, regardless of how fascinating he is or from what class he comes from. I have much business to conduct in Vicenza and that is my first priority. When it is concluded, I may attempt a few social visits, but for now, I am not ready to meet with him. I am fatigued from travel and as a result, a bit curt, and not up to social niceties. But I promise you, with a little rest, my nerves will settle, my patience for etiquette will return, and I shall be better prepared to call upon him. For now, I trust you will make a fitting apology on my behalf for declining his gracious invitation."

Beatrice's look of astonishment faded, transformed itself into a smile, and then into a full laugh. "Oh, Contessa. You truly are a fascinating woman. I am almost inclined to believe that you truly hate men."

"Oh, not at all," I said with composure as I peeled and sliced a fragrant peach. "Hatred is a potent emotion. One must experience true love before one can hate. I do not hate men, rather, I am apathetic to them. They are nothing more than encumbrances to women. I find men a burden, needy, and terribly demanding."

"Yet many a woman longs for such a burden."

I gave her an intense look. "Women can be so blind. Men seize upon any pleasure that comes their way. Led by hot animal impulses, which we women mistake for love, they snatch up beautiful women and once they have their way with us, we become worthless to them." I held up the stone from the peach I had just eaten. "The fruit is gulped down and only the bitter core remains."

Beatrice shrugged. "I do not agree with you, Contessa, but neither do I wish to argue with you. For a woman of more senior years such as yourself, you may be right, but for one who is young, whose life stretches before her with promise and love, the embrace of a man is as necessary as spring rain to a newly planted seed. Surely there must have been a time when you loved a man?"

I expelled a short laugh. "Oh, I did at one time indulge in such a love with all its dreams and fancies. He was a good man, nearly a saint. But a friend I highly respected told me I was not worthy of him. I became so persuaded of the man's great goodness and my own unworthiness of him, that I left him."

She looked flabbergasted. "That was a most peculiar reason for abandoning a man you truly loved, was it not?"

"I agree, it was very peculiar, but it was enough of a reason for me. But I do not wish to discuss this any more. Rather, let's speak of something more pleasant and interesting. Yesterday, we spoke of many things, but when you mentioned to me that you painted, I was most intrigued. Will you show me your work?"

"Whenever you wish, though I fear they are not worthy of your attention. They are all at my studio."

"Nonsense," I said with starched civility. "A woman should never underestimate her skills or talents. Allow me to call on you this afternoon. I have some time to spare if that will suit you."

"It will suit me indeed." She gave me a gratifying look. "But I fear my paintings may disappoint you. It is not easy for a woman to practice her skills as an artist, as you must be aware. So my gift for art is not well honed yet."

I smiled, for I knew very well that she lacked artistic talent, but I made no remark. "Regarding the jewels I wish to bestow to the young Mancini girl, I would also like to present a few tokens of my appreciation to Signore Gismondi. I did not mention it earlier, but I had planned to leave them with Contessa Mancini too. They belonged to my father and I have no male heir to inherit them. Would you like to see them?"

"Oh, I would like to very much. They are unique and rare, I suppose?"

"*Si*, indeed. All my jewels are. I have been somewhat of a collector of fine and rare jewelry," I answered as I crossed to the chest in the corner. After unlocking it, I removed a large, elegantly carved, oak jewel-chest, which I had especially made for me in Pescara. It contained the golden chain upon which hung the spectacular ship pendant decorated with sapphires, rubies, and diamonds that I had discovered in the vault, a ruby and diamond studded man's ring, a thick gold bracelet, and a cross heavily embedded with fine emeralds. I had all the pieces reset by a talented goldsmith in Pescara so that although they were similar, they looked nothing like the originals.

Beatrice let out a sigh of admiration as she lifted the dazzling baubles one at a time and studied their bulk and brilliancy.

I waved my hand casually over them. "They are nothing more than trinkets, but they may please Signore Gismondi and are quite valuable. I would be honored if you would take them to him as a precursor to our future visit. I am certain you can persuade him to accept them until I can personally deliver the remainder of the jewelry I had planned to give to his wife had she lived. They really should belong to him and his daughter and he must not refuse to receive them."

Beatrice paused and looked at me with sincerity. "You will visit, will you not? He may rely on it?"

"You seem very anxious for me to do so," I said. "May I ask why?"

"I believe the count would be embarassed if you gave him no opportunity to thank you for such magnificent gifts. Otherwise, I fear he may not accept them."

"Please do not worry," I said with my warmest smile. "He shall soon thank me to his heart's content. I give you my word that within a few days I will call upon him. In fact, you have already offered to introduce me. I am pleased to tell you that I've changed my mind and now gladly accept his invitation."

She seemed delighted and squeezed my hand. "In that case, I will be happy to take these jewels to him. And may I say that had you searched the whole world over, you would not have found a man more suited to show them off. I assure you his handsomeness is beyond comparison."

"No doubt," I said with a nod. "I must take your word for it, however, for I am a poor judge of men's faces or bodies. And now, my dear, please do not be offended if I seek a few moments of solitude. I shall arrive at your studio later today to view your paintings."

Beatrice rose to leave. I placed the jewels in a leather-covered wooden case, strapped and locked it, and then handed it to her with its key. She gushed with appreciation, almost fawning over me, in fact.

And thus I discovered another defect in her character, a flaw which, as her friend in former days, I had never before noticed. With little encouragement, she would become a flatterer, a groveling servant to the affluent. As friends, I had believed her to be beyond reproach, never heartless, and a person who despised duplicity. But it was all a mere delusion. More treachery by my nearest and dearest. And now that I was no longer deceived? Was the destruction of my delusions worse than the delusions themselves? I believed so as my old friend took hold of my hand and bid me farewell that morning. How I longed to trust her like I once did, but I could not. That had all been swept away by a tidal wave of lies. I watched her leave carrying the box of jewels for my husband.

After Beatrice left, I paused to re-ponder every aspect of my plan. There was still much to do. Part of my plan was to establish myself as a person of great importance in Vicenza and I had written numerous letters and sent out visiting-cards to affluent families. I summoned Santina and Paolo to help me finalize these arrangements and attend to other minor business matters.

Santina was a perfect lady's maid, as Paolo was a faultless steward. They were both silent, discreet, admirably trained. Neither of them asked questions. They were too dignified to gossip, and both bestowed me with instant and unconditional obedience. They completed their duties, going beyond my expectations by attending to details that kept me comfortable and content. I rejoiced in my good fortune in having found and hired them both.

Occupied thusly, the hours passed swiftly, and in the afternoon, I made my way to Beatrice's studio. I had no need to consult the card she had given me, for I was already familiar with the studio's location. After all, it was I who had paid for and acquired it for her. It was a curious, charming place, located at the top of a steep hill. I had passed many a happy hour there with Beatrice before my marriage, reading a book or watching Beatrice paint her unsophisticated scenes and people, most of which I cheerfully bought as soon as she completed them. The quaint porch, now overrun by star-jasmine looked forlornly recognizable. My knees weakened at the pang of regret I experienced in remembering the past, but I recovered. I tugged the bell cord and heard its familiar melodic tinkle.

Beatrice opened the door, her face animated and glowing. "Come in, come in," she said cordially. "Please excuse the mess. Everything is in a state of disorder. I don't have many visitors. Mind the step, Contessa. It is a little loose and I do not wish to see you stumble."

She ushered me up the narrow flight of stairs to the sunlight-filled room where she worked. Glancing around, I immediately noticed the room's neglect and disarray. It was obvious she had not been there for quite some time, though she had made a half-hearted attempt to tidy it before my arrival. A large vase of elegantly arranged flowers rested on the table. I noticed that Beatrice had not begun anything new and I recognized all the old finished and unfinished paintings, now caked with dust.

I sat in a cushioned chair and looked at my betrayer with a fault-finding eye. She had donned a gray gown instead of the black one she had worn earlier that morning. Her face was pale and her eyes extraordinarily luminous. She looked her best and I could understand how my lazy, pleasure-seeking husband might be easily attracted by her beautiful form and features. I spoke a part of my thoughts aloud. "You give the appearance of a true artist."

She blushed a little and beamed. "You are very kind to say so." A delighted sense of self-importance glowed in her expression. "But you are flattering me. By the way, before I forget, I wish to let you know that I have fulfilled your request."

"To Signore Gismondi?"

"*Si*. He was not only astonished, but elated at the magnificence of the jewels you sent him."

I laughed. "Good. Now let us talk about the picture you have on the easel there. May I see it more closely?"

She pushed the easel closer to me. It was badly done, a gaudy landscape colored by the setting sun depicted in colors that appeared artificial. Nevertheless, I praised it enthusiastically and purchased it for five hundred *scudi*. Encouraged, she then produced four other similar paintings. Of course, I purchased these too at heavily inflated prices.

When we finished our transactions, Beatrice seemed jubilant. She opened a bottle of wine and poured us each a small goblet, chattering away ceaselessly. I listened to her politely, laughed at her anecdotes, all of which I had heard before, duping her vainglorious spirit into thinking I cared about what she spoke of. I let her natter on, let her bare her full personality to me, and saw it for what it truly was: a fusion of self-absorption, greed, sensuality, and callousness, with flitting glimpses of friendliness and understanding. This was the woman I had loved like a sister, a person of paltry intelligence and doubtful values. This worthless, frivolous, turd of humanity was the same being for whom I once bore such steadfast affection.

The clip clop of hooves stopping at our door interrupted our conversation. I set down the glass of wine I had just raised to my lips, and looked at Beatrice steadily. "You are expecting a visitor?" I inquired.

She seemed ill at ease, smiled, and dithered.

"I am not sure, but—" The bell tinkled and Beatrice rose with a word of apology to answer it.

I sprang from my chair. My instincts knew very well who it could be. With concentrated effort, I steadied my nerves. I forced my racing heart to slow down, adjusted my dark glasses more securely over my eyes, and straightened myself. I waited. I heard Beatrice ascend the stairs. A heavier step accompanied her lighter ones as she spoke to her companion in whispers. Another instant passed and she flung the door of the studio wide open with the haste and reverence due for the entrance of a king. There was a rustle of fine wool, a subtle scent of horse sweat and leather in the air, and then I stood face to face with my husband.

Chapter Thirteen

Dario's incredible handsomeness stole my breath away. My gaze swept over him with the same captivation that had befuddled me the first time I saw him. His solemn black mourning clothes only enhanced his stunning appearance. Without doubt, he was the most majestic looking man I had ever encountered, and I, his late wife, still trembled in the wake of his splendor.

He stood gallantly in the doorway with a disarming smile on his lips. Pausing, he studied me for an instant. I became so tense, I realized I was holding my breath, and had to force myself to appear calm.

"*Buon giorno*, do I have the pleasure of meeting the gracious Contessa Giulia Corona?" The sound of his deep voice flooded the room.

I could not utter a word. All speech seemed trapped within me. Shock scorched my mouth. My throat faltered with constrained fury and anguish. I could only respond with a slight nod.

He walked toward me and extended his hand with the confidence I had so often admired. "I am Signore Gismondi. When I learned from Signorina Cardano that you planned to visit her studio this afternoon, I could not resist coming to personally thank you for the exquisite gifts you sent. The gifts are truly wonderful. Permit me to offer you my sincere thanks."

I accepted his outstretched hand and squeezed it hard as he raised it to his lips for a kiss, but he was too well-mannered to show any reaction. By now, I had regained my composure and was eager to begin my charade. "Oh, but it is I who must thank you for accepting the trivial ornaments, especially in light of your recent loss. You have my deepest condolences. Had your wife lived, no doubt she would have gifted them to you, and they would have carried a more profound sentiment for you. I am grateful to you for accepting them from such an undeserving hand as mine."

His face turned pale and he shuffled his feet uneasily. He stared at me intently. Behind the shelter of my dark spectacles, I met his stare with confidence. Slowly he let go of my hand. I gestured for us to sit in a chair. He fell into it with the effortless ease I was so familiar with. Like a corrupted king, he studied me pensively.

Beatrice brought us wine, a dish of fruit, and some sweet cakes. "I can see we surprised you," she said to me with a bit of a giggle. "I trust that you have guessed that the signore and I planned this encounter to catch you unawares. We had no way of knowing when you could visit the signore, and he was so anxious to thank you personally that we arranged this meeting. How amusing. Come, Contessa, you cannot deny that you are delighted with our little surprise."

"Indeed I am," I responded, unable to disguise my derision. "Anyone would be delighted. I understand the special honor Signore Gismondi extends by permitting me to meet him after such tragic circumstances."

The moment I spoke these words, my husband's face turned wistful and sad. "Ah, my poor Carlotta. How tragic that she is not here to greet you. She would have been so excited to meet you, a friend of her mother. She cherished her mother more than anyone." He shook his head. "I still cannot believe she is dead. Such a terrible loss. I will always mourn her passing."

I could not believe the ease with which he assumed such profound grief.

I glanced at Beatrice. She coughed and her cheeks reddened. She was not as good an actress as he was an actor.

Studying them both, I could not decide whether my contempt or disgust was stronger. "In someone as young and handsome as you are, time will be quick to heal your wounds. Although your wife's death is most regretful, do not allow grief to consume you. It is futile. A lifetime of opportunity and many happy days await you and you deserve to experience it all to its fullest."

His angst-ridden expression evaporated like morning dew beneath a hot sun. "I appreciate your good wishes, Contessa, but a visit from you will go a long way toward easing my grief. You must promise to visit."

I hesitated.

Beatrice looked amused. "I warned him how uncomfortable you are with men, Contessa," she said with a touch of mockery in her tone.

I cast her a cold glance and turned to face my husband. "Signorina Cardano is perfectly right, I often avoid the company of men, but have no defense against the smile of an Adonis like you." I gave him a slight curtsey to emphasize my point.

His expression lightened. How he treasured his handsomeness and I knew it sparked his desire for conquest. With languid grace, he removed the glass of wine I was about to raise to my lips and fixed his dark brown, deep-set eyes upon me with a smile. "Your compliment pleases me and you must, of course, pay me a visit tomorrow, for Adonis' demand obedience. Bea—, I mean Signorina Cardano, I trust that you will accompany the contessa to my villa?"

Beatrice nodded stiffly, her look sullen. "I am glad to see, that you succeeded in persuading the contessa when all my attempts failed."

He laughed. "But I am a man and most men are used to having their way. Don't you agree, Contessa?" And he raised an eyebrow, amusement and spite merging in his expression. When he noticed Beatrice's annoyance, he delighted in teasing her still further.

"I do not know, Signor," I answered him. "I know almost nothing about the ways of men, but I am convinced that you must be right, whatever you say. Your eyes would convert a pagan."

Again he gave me one of his magnificently radiant, sensual, direct glances, and then he rose to leave.

"This has truly been a visit by Adonis – pleasant, but short," I said.

"We shall have a longer visit tomorrow," he replied, smiling. "You promised, so please do not disappoint me. Come in the afternoon, as early as you like. Then you can meet my daughter, Chiara. She is very much the image of her poor mother."

Dario extended his hand and I placed mine upon it. He raised it to his lips, smiled as he withdrew it, and then looked at me, or rather at the glasses I wore. "Do you have trouble seeing?"

"Ah, *si*, it is a most dreadful condition. My eyes are overly sensitive to light, but I should not complain, for the weakness is common in someone of my age."

"You do not seem old." His eye scrutinized my unwrinkled, soft skin, which could not be masked.

"Not old? With my white hair?" I exclaimed as I brushed away a loose curl.

"Many a young woman's hair has turned gray," he said. "At any rate, it is common when in one's prime. And in your case, it is quite attractive." With a deep bow given only to me, he departed.

Both Beatrice and I hastened to the window to watch him enter his carriage, which waited for him at the front door. The same carriage and pair of bay geldings I had given him for his birthday. The driver slapped the reins and the horses entered into a brisk trot. In a few moments, the elegant conveyance disappeared from sight. When I could see nothing more than the cloud of dust stirred up by its revolving wheels, I turned to my companion. She bore a grim expression and her brows were pinched in a frown. The green-eyed snake of jealousy had taken its first bite. The bow he had given me in farewell instead of Beatrice had stabbed her pride.

Woe the blindness of women. With all our abilities; with all the world before us to conquer, we crumble at an abusive word or rude gesture by a man, whose strongest affection is paid to the mirror that reflects him in the most becoming light. How simple my vengeance would be, I thought, as I studied Beatrice.

I touched her on the shoulder. She returned to the moment, away from her unsettling daydream, and forced a smile.

"What are your thoughts?" I asked with a gentle laugh.

Lost in thought, she gave me no answer.

"Do not be desolate, my friend," I said cheerfully as I linked my arm through hers and turned her away from the window. "It is said that one's wit should be sharpened by the glance of an intelligent eye. So why does your speech seem blunted? Perhaps your emotions are too profound for words? If so, I am not surprised, for the man is exceedingly fine-looking."

Her gaze flickered over me. "Did I not say as much?" she exclaimed. "Of all the men in this world, he is flawless. Even you, Contessa, with your distrust of men, even you were affected by him."

I pretended to ponder her words. "I was?" I responded with feigned astonishment. "Affected? I disagree, however, I do admit I have never seen a man so striking in appearance."

She unlinked her arm from mine, and stared at me. "I told you so. And now I feel I must warn you."

"Warn me?" I asked with insincere alarm. "Of what? Against whom? Surely not Signore Gismondi, to whom you have been so eager for me to meet? Does he have a disease? A contagious malady? The plague? Is he deceitful or dangerous or untrustworthy?"

Beatrice laughed at the concern I flaunted over my own safety - an angst which I delivered in an almost comic manner, but she looked a bit reassured too. "Oh, no. I meant nothing of the kind. It is only fair of me to forewarn you that he can be very seductive and his romantic behavior would flatter any woman who was not aware of his alluring ways. It might lead you to believe yourself the object of his desire, and—"

I broke out laughing. "Your admonition is unwarranted. Do I look like the type of woman who would attract the attention of such a handsome man? At my age, the idea is preposterous. Why, I am old enough to be his mother, and yours too. To be his lover? Impossible."

She gave me an attentive look. "He thought you did not seem old at all," she murmured, half to herself and half to me.

"Oh, most certainly he made a small, flattering remark to me." A thrill ran through me at the knowledge the attention he paid me tormented her. "I accepted the compliment in the nature that it was meant - kind-heartedness. Sadly, I am only too aware of how decrepit and unattractive I must appear in his eyes in comparison to you."

Her cheeks flushed. "You must forgive me if my warning seemed too severe. The signore is like a brother to me. In fact, my late friend Carlotta encouraged a brotherly and sisterly affection between us. Now that she is gone, I feel duty-bound to watch over him and protect him. He is youthful and carefree. Surely you understand what I am saying?"

I nodded. I understood her perfectly. She wanted no more thieves to threaten what she herself had stolen. I could not disagree with her point of view. But I was the rightful owner of all that she had claimed, and naturally, I had an opposing view. I said nothing and pretended to be bored by our conversation.

Seeing this, Beatrice dropped her dismal tone and became an engaging ally once more. After we agreed on the time for our visit to the Villa Mancini the following day, our conversation turned to matters concerning Vicenza, its society, and their way of life. I commented on the people's immorality and unfettered values to draw my companion out and measure her character more thoroughly, even though I believed I understood her views well enough already.

She laughed delicately. "Immorality is a matter of opinion. What is accomplished by marital fidelity? Why should a woman tie herself to one man when she has enough love for fifty? The good-looking youth she marries is likely to become a portly, vulgar, crimson-faced, good-for-nothing, troublemaker by the time she has reached the full bloom of womanhood. Yet, for as long as he lives, society and all its laws favor men."

"People should repent their sins, but they rarely do."

"Why should they? What good can come from regretting anything? Will it mend matters? Who is to be pacified or pleased by our remorse? God? My dear Contessa, there are very few of us nowadays who believe in

God. The best thing we can do is enjoy ourselves while we live. Life is short and when we die there is nothing."

"That is what you truly believe?" I asked.

"*Si*, to eat, drink and be merry, to live life to its fullest, because tomorrow we die."

I had no desire to disagree with her. I only wanted to understand what dwelled in her shallow heart to convince me of her utter worthlessness. I tested her further. "There truly is no need to be virtuous unless it suits us. The only important thing is to avoid public scandal so that our more pleasant activities do not suffer."

"That is exactly right," she said with a smile. "We women must guard our reputations and avoid scandal. A man's reputation, however, is not so easily tarnished. Before he marries, and after he marries, he is totally free. He can take a dozen lovers if he likes, and if he manages them well, his wife need never be the wiser. She has her lovers, too of course. Why not? When an injured wife learns the truth about her husband's infidelities, there is a devil of an argument, a moral one, the worst kind. But a clever man can always steer clear of scandal and gossip if he likes."

Contemptible bitch. I glanced at her pretty face and figure with unveiled disdain. With all the advantages I had given her, she was a bitch to the core. "I see you have a comprehensive understanding of the world and its ways. I admire your views. From what you told me, you have no sympathy with marital sins, do you?"

"Not in the least. They are far too widespread and absurd. To me, the wronged wife always cuts such a pathetic figure."

"Always?" I raised an eyebrow.

"Well, usually, she does. What can she do to resolve the problem if her husband refuses to relinquish his affair?

"Very true," I said with a forced laugh, exasperated by

her despicable flippancy. She met my gaze with merriment and fearless candor. Her opinions did not shame her, rather she seemed to glory in them. The warm sunlight played upon her youthful features, yet the sight of her sickened me. The sooner I could crush her the better, for I would rid the world of one less traitor. The thought of my dreadful but justified vendetta swept through me like an ill wind A shiver ran through me.

I must have displayed some outward sign of discomfort, for Beatrice frowned. "You look tired, Contessa. Are you ill?" She reached out her hand to grasp mine.

I waved it firmly away. "It is nothing. I only felt a little faint, likely due to a recent illness I am recovering from." I glanced out at the window. The afternoon was fading fast into evening. "You must excuse me. I should return home. I will send a servant to collect the pictures to save you the trouble of sending them to me."

"It is no trouble—" began Beatrice.

"Please do not worry," I interrupted. "I am perfectly capable of arranging things to my own preference. As you know, I am quite independent and wilful."

She nodded and smiled; the smile of a toady; a smile I hated.

"At least allow me to accompany you back home," she offered.

"*Grazie,* but no. It is not far and I look forward to a few moments of pleasant quiet."

The truth was that I could not stomach another moment with her. My strained nerves could take no more. I yearned to be alone. If I remained with her a moment longer, I feared I would be tempted to wrap my hands around her neck and strangle the life out of her. It took my entire will to wish her farewell with friendly, but forced courtesy.

She extended copious thanks for purchasing her pictures.

"Please, there is no need to thank me. I am proud to own such beautiful art." My false compliment seemed to flatter her. I turned and left the room.

She accompanied me down the stairs and watched me from the doorway as I walked away with the slow and careful step of an elderly woman. The moment I knew I was out of her sight, I quickened my pace, a tempest of conflicting emotions roiling inside me.

When I passed through the front doors of my home, the first thing that met my eyes was a large gilded bowl filled with fresh fruit placed prominently on the entrance hall's center-table.

"Santina," I called out. "Who sent this?"

She removed the attached letter and handed it to me.

It was written in my husband's own firm penmanship:

To remind the contessa of her promised visit tomorrow

Fury ran through my body like fire. I crumpled the parchment and flung it to the floor. The sweet aroma from the ripened peaches, lemons, grapes, and figs offended my senses. "Take these away at once," I said to Santina. "Take them to the *Convento della Carita*. The orphans there will appreciate them."

Santina took the basket and carried it out of the room. I breathed with relief the moment its fragrance and color left my sight. How cruel to receive a gift from my own orchards. Vexed and heartsick, I fell into an easy chair. Within moments, however, the irony of the gift made me laugh.

So. My husband takes another step on the path of infidelity, bestowing his attentions upon a woman he knows nothing about, except that she is staggeringly rich and alone in the world. Wealth. It forces those swollen with pride to their knees. It makes the determined become submissive. Man is ever at its command. The more wealth Dario possesses, the more caresses and kisses he can aquire.

I smiled with indignation as I recalled Dario's languid gaze when he said, *you do not seem to be so old.* I knew the meaning behind his words and recognized the greed in his eyes. We had been married for so long that I knew him well. My journey towards vengeance appeared smooth, almost too easy. I could see no complications, no hindrances. My betrayers had strolled willingly into my trap.

Bathed in my own cold blood, questions kept echoing in my mind. Was there any reason for me to be merciful towards them? Had they demonstrated one decent attribute? Was there any honor, any shred of honesty, anything virtuous in either of them to justify my pity? And the answer I came to was always the same. No. Shallow to the heart's core, they were cheaters and liars. Even the guilty passion they shared between them was hollow, without sincerity except to pursue their own pleasure and suit their own self-indulgence.

Dario, during that fateful conversation I had so painfully overheard at my villa, had hinted at the possibility of tiring of Beatrice, and she had just finished confessing that it was unreasonable to believe a man could be faithful to one woman all his life.

No, they were more than worthy of the calamity that fast approached them. Women like Beatrice and men like Dario are common, malicious creatures who deserved to be exterminated. And this I would do, but in my own good time.

Chapter Fourteen

"Welcome to Villa Mancini," Dario greeted me with a broad grin.

His words sounded strange, almost dreamlike. Yet, this was no dream. I stood with him and Beatrice on the lush green lawns of my garden. My beloved veranda with its climbing roses and fragrant jasmine beckoned. My grand villa, my childhood home where I had once been so happy, rose up before me nestled amid lush trees and terraced gardens in all its splendor. Its ethereal beauty swept my breath away. How I missed strolling in the gardens bursting with lemon trees and fragrant flowers. A sharp ache jammed my throat. I wanted to weep. My dear home; how dazzling, yet sad, it appeared. I had expected it to be in ruins; mistreated and uncared for without my loving touch, but thankfully, it was not.

I glanced at Beatrice and silently promised myself to never allow her to become mistress here.

My gaze returned to my villa. I noticed subtle changes. Someone had removed my favorite chair from its regular corner on the veranda. The cage that housed my beloved canaries, one orange and one yellow, no longer hung among the roses on the wall. And my dog, the smart little brown and white Lagotto Romagnolo, who excelled at searching out truffles, was nowhere in sight. What had become of poor Tito? He usually sniffed about the house and garden or slept on the lowest veranda step, basking in the sun. Incensed by his disappearance, I fought to contain my feelings in deference to the role I must play.

Dario waited for me to say something as I continued to look about. "Is something wrong, Contessa?"

It would be wise for me to be as pleasant as possible. "Oh, how could anyone be disappointed when they are beholding Paradise?"

Dario smiled.

Beatrice frowned impatiently, but said nothing.

My husband led the way into the house and the high-ceilinged *salotto* with its frescoed walls and wide windows that opened out to the gardens. In this room, the marble bust of me as a girl was missing. My virginal harpsichord handcrafted in Venice by Giovanni Celestini, distinguished by its exquisite casing ornamented with garlands of flowers and songbirds in magnificent inlay work, sat in its usual spot. My mandolin rested upon a side-table. Fresh flowers and ferns filled every Venetian glass vase in the room.

I seated myself and remarked on the beauty of the house and its surroundings. "I remember it very well," I added, quietly.

"You remember it?" Beatrice questioned as she sat beside me on my favorite damask wing settee.

"Of course. I used to visit quite regularly when I was a very young girl. Contessa Mancini and I played here together as children. The villa is very familiar to me."

Dario settled himself on an armchair across from us. "Did you ever meet my late wife?"

"Only once; she was little more than a babe in arms. I recall her father seemed greatly enchanted by her, as was her mother."

Dario steadied his eyes on me. "What was Carlotta's mother like?"

I paused a moment. Could I speak of that pure and

blessed woman to this foul, though handsome creature? I knew I must. "She was a beautiful woman unconscious of her beauty. All she cared about was to make others happy and to fill her home with a pleasant atmosphere of goodness and virtue. She died far too young."

A flash of malevolence flared in Beatrice's eyes as she looked at me. "How fortunate for her to have died before she could tire of her husband. Otherwise, she might not have been so happy."

My blood rose to a shocking heat, but I maintained my composure. "I do not understand you, Signorina Cardano," I said coldly. "The woman lived and died under the belief that being noble meant one must always behave honorably. She was a woman with great responsibilities and not one to spend her time in idle pursuits like many men and women of our generation. I am not as well versed in modern ideals of morality as you are."

Dario swiftly interjected to salvage the conversation from deteriorating. "Oh, my dear Contessa, pay no attention to Signorina Cardano. She can be rash and impulsive and often speaks recklessly, but she does not mean what she says. My poor wife used to become very vexed with her, even though she was fond of her."

Beatrice's eyes flamed, but he avoided looking at her.

"Because you know so much about the Mancini family, would you like to meet my daughter, Chiara?" Dario asked. "Shall I send for her, or are you not interested in children?"

My heart thudded with both joy and anguish at the thought of seeing my daughter. "I would love to meet my dear old friend's daughter."

My husband rang the bell and Giacomo entered. Giacomo, my old chief steward walked wearily and his aged features bore an injured expression. It saddened me to see him so.

"Please bring Chiara to me," Dario said.

While we waited, Beatrice engaged me in conversation. She tried to make up for her previous callous remark by agreeing to my opinions and nodding at everything I said.

After a few moments, the room's door handle turned slightly.

"Come in Chiara," Dario called out impatiently. "Do not be afraid."

The door creaked slowly open and my daughter stepped cautiously into the room. In the short span of time since I had seen her last, she had changed. Her face looked gaunt and she bore a miserable, frightened expression. The sparkle in her eyes no longer existed and it disheartened me to see her stand there with an aura of pained resignation. No smile graced her lips and her chestnut tresses were unbound and uncurled. She wore a yellow satin gown with a long pointed bodice and matching satin petticoat. The many tiny pleats that gathered in her skirt showed wrinkles and several stains. It was obvious she had been neglected. She walked toward us as hesitantly, pausing partway into the room to give Beatrice an apprehensive look.

Beatrice met my daughter's gaze with a scornful smirk. "Come, Chiara," she urged with a wave. "There is no reason to be frightened. I will not scold you unless you are naughty. What a silly girl. You look as if I am about to eat you up for dinner. Come and greet this woman. She knew your mama."

At this, Chiara's eyes brightened. Her steps became more confident as she came to a stop before me and placed her hand in mine.

The feel of her soft, tentative fingers almost shattered me. I lifted her onto my lap. Under pretence of kissing her, I buried my face in her hair and inhaled the aroma of childhood. Tears pooled in my eyes. Somehow, I managed to quell my emotions.

My poor, darling. I do not know how I maintained my composure under the power of her serious, but questioning gaze. She did not seem to be afraid of the black spectacles I wore and seemed content to sit on my lap as she studied me intently.

Dario and Beatrice observed her with indifference, but she ignored them and kept on staring at me. A sweet smile dawned on Chiara's face. Then she extended her arms, wrapped them around my neck, and kissed me.

At first, the affectionate peck on my cheek startled me, but intuitively, I pulled her tight to my heart and returned her embrace.

I stole a quick glance at Dario and Beatrice. Had they become suspicious? I discounted this thought. Beatrice herself had witnessed my burial. Reassured, I gave my child a warm smile. "You are a very charming young lady. I am told your name is Chiara, just like a pretty white star."

She became pensive. "Mama always said so too."

"Your mama spoiled you," Dario interrupted. "You were never as naughty to her as you are to me."

Chiara's bottom lip quivered, but she said nothing.

"Oh, goodness, naughty? You? I do not believe it," I exclaimed. "All little stars are good and brilliant and serene, aren't they?

She said not a word, but a deep sigh heaved from her tiny breast. Leaning her head against my arm, she raised her big round eyes to me. "Have you seen my mama? Will she come home soon?"

Stunned, I could not answer, but Beatrice did, and roughly. "Don't be foolish. You know your mama has gone away forever. You were too naughty, so she will never come back again. Now she no longer has to endure your aggravating disobedience."

What nasty words! At once, I comprehended the dire anguish my daughter must be suffering. They had convinced her that I had abandoned her because of her behavior. Poor Chiara must have taken this to heart; brooding upon it in childish innocence, blaming herself, confused. Yet, whatever Chiara was thinking or feeling, she did not give vent to it by tears or words. Instead, she looked at Beatrice and gave her a haughty, scornful look – the Mancini look; a look I had often seen in my father's eyes, and I knew were visible in my own from time to time.

Beatrice noticed it too and burst out laughing. "There. Now she looks exactly like her mother. It is positively astounding – completely Carlotta. She only needs one thing to make the resemblance perfect." Approaching Chiara, Beatrice snatched her disheveled curls and twisted them up on top of her head.

Chiara's face reddened and she tried to escape Beatrice's touch, hiding her face against me. The more she struggled, the more Beatrice tormented her. Her father did not interfere. All he did was laugh.

I sheltered her in my embrace, and stifled my indignation. "You must play gently and fairly, Signorina," I said to Beatrice. "An adult's strength turns into bullying against a child's innocence."

Beatrice emitted a nervous, uncomfortable laugh, ceased her mischief, and walked to the window. I smoothed Chiara's tumbled hair. "This *bimba* will have her revenge when she grows up one day. She will remember how she was teased, and in return, may tease back. Do you not agree with me, Signore Gismondi?"

Dario shrugged. "I do not agree, Contessa. *Sì*, she will remember the woman who teased her, but she will also remember the other who was kind to her – yourself."

Unused to being flattered by my own husband, I acknowledged the subtle compliment with an agreeable nod. Married couples are like candid friends, unafraid of speaking blatant truths to each other and avoiding the smallest morsel of flattery.

At that moment, Giacomo, my father's steward and mine, stepped into the room to announce dinner.

I set my daughter down from my lap. "I will come and see you again soon," I whispered into her ear.

She beamed and then obeyed her father's gesture to leave the room.

I watched her every step as she strode from the room. "What a charming child," I praised as soon as she disappeared from sight. "As beautiful and as lovely as her mother was at the same age."

My admiring comments received only a cold glare and no response from either my husband or his lover.

We all went in to dinner. As the guest, I had the privilege of being escorted by my spouse.

When we reached the dining room, Dario paused. "You are such an old friend of the family, Contessa, perhaps you will do me the honor of sitting at the head of the table."

"You pay me a great compliment, Signore," I responded as I sat in Dario's place at the head of my own table. Beatrice sat on my right and Dario on my left. Giacomo stood as always behind my chair, and I noticed that each time he poured my wine, he studied me with nervous curiosity, but I wanted to believe it was my odd appearance that accounted for it.

On the wall directly facing me, hung my father's portrait. My disguise permitted me to look at it intently and give vent to the deep sigh that broke from my heart. My father's eyes seemed to gaze into mine with heartbreaking compassion. I could envision his lips trembling in response to my sigh.

"Is that a good likeness?" Beatrice asked.

Her question startled me and I quickly collected myself. "The resemblance is so accurate that it arouses many memories in my mind, both bitter and sweet. Ah, the man was very proud."

"Carlotta was also very proud," Dario said. "Indifferent and haughty, too."

Liar! How dare he vilify my memory. Indifference was never in my nature, but now I wished that it had been. I should have been a block of ice incapable of thawing in the sunlight of his first smile. Had he forgotten all that I had done for him, all that I had given him? What a poor fool I was to have believed in his hypocritical caresses and feigned love. "It surprises me to hear you say that. The Mancini family may be noble, but every member was always kind and respectful of everyone. I know my friend always treated her family and dependants gently and kindly."

Giacomo coughed apologetically behind his hand. It was an old trick of his, which signified his desire to speak.

Beatrice laughed, as she held out her glass for more wine. "Giacomo remembers both the Mancinis. Ask him his opinion of Carlotta. He worshiped his mistress." She took a sip as if it could hide her sarcasm.

I turned to address Giacomo. "I do not recognize you, my friend. Perhaps you were not here when I used to visit the elder Contessa Mancini?" This was an attempt on my part to dispel any suspicions he may have about my true identity.

Giacomo rubbed his wrinkled hands nervously together. "I came into my lady's service only a year before the mother of the young contessa died."

"Ah, in that case, I missed making your acquaintance." I pitied the gentle soul when I noticed his lips tremble and how he looked so forlorn. "You knew the last contessa from childhood, then?"

"I most certainly did." His watery eyes roamed over me inquisitively.

"You loved her well?" I asked, watching him despite the hint of guilt I experienced at having to lie to this most caring, loyal servant.

"She was decency itself—an extraordinary, kind-hearted, generous woman. May the saints cherish her soul. Sometimes I cannot believe she is gone. My heart broke when I heard she died and I have never been the same since. My master will verify this; he is often dissatisfied with me." Uncomfortable, he turned his wistful gaze to Dario.

My husband frowned. I once believed that he frowned whenever he became irritated, but now I believed it was much more; it was a sign of his temper. "*Si*, indeed, Giacomo," he said harshly. "You are growing so forgetful that it is quite annoying. I have to repeat myself several times when one command ought to suffice."

Clearly troubled, Giacomo hung his head, sighed, and fell silent. Then, as if remembering his obligations, he refilled my glass, and retreated to his position behind my chair.

The conversation turned to mundane topics. Dario had always been an excellent talker, but this evening he surpassed himself. He was determined to charm me and spared nothing to succeed in his ambition. Witty remarks coupled with sharp satire and humorous stories briskly told, all flowed effortlessly from his lips. Although I knew him well, he surprised me with his glibness. I once thought him charming, even godly. Now, for the first time, I saw him for what he was – a devil disguised as an angel.

While he spoke, I noticed how Beatrice responded to his allure. The brighter and more amiable he became, the more she became silent and sullen. I pretended not to notice her mounting tension and I continued to draw her into the conversation, forcing her to give opinions on various subjects. She hesitated to speak at all; and when compelled to do so, responded with abrupt, snappish retorts.

Dario finally laughed at her gruff behavior. "You are quite ill-tempered this evening, Beatrice." When he noticed he had addressed her informally, he turned to me. "I always call her Beatrice. She has always been like a sister to me."

Beatrice glared at him and her eyes flashed dangerously, but she kept her jaw tightly clenched and did not utter a word.

Dario seemed delighted in jabbing at her pride and vexing her.

She stared at him in reproach and he burst out laughing.

Rising from the table, Dario made us a gallant bow. "I will leave you two ladies to finish your wine together. I know women love to share a little gossip and talk a little scandal. Afterward, please join me for a coffee on the veranda."

I watched as he strode from the room grinning after he poured more wine in our glasses. Beatrice sullenly eyed her reflection in the polished rim of a silver fruit-dish on the table in front of her. Giacomo had left the room and we found ourselves entirely alone.

I pondered my vendetta for a moment or two. The game held me in its fascination as if I played a shrewd game of chess. With the thoughtfulness of a cautious player, I made my next move. "What a fascinating man," I murmured before taking a sip of my wine. "Very intelligent too. I admire your taste in men, *Signorina*."

She seemed startled. "What do you mean?"

I gave her my most benevolent smile. "Ah, young blood," I sighed. "Do not be ashamed of your feelings. Anyone who fails to appreciate the affections of so ardent an admirer is truly a fool. Not every woman is lucky enough to have such a good chance at happiness."

"Do you think...you believe that...that I—"

"That you are in love with him?" I said. "Most certainly I do. And why should you not love him? I am sure that the late contessa would be pleased to see her handsome widower wed her best friend. Permit me to congratulate you and wish you all the success in your love." I took another sip of my wine. Pathetic fool! I had completely disarmed her and I could see any suspicions she harbored against me melted away like night's mist in morning light.

Her expression turned more cheerful. She took my hand and pressed it warmly. "Forgive me, Contessa. I fear I have been impolite and distant this evening. You have made me feel better. You may think of me as envious and silly, but I truly believed you were attracted to him. In fact, please forgive me, but I was daydreaming about how to...to kill you."

I burst laughing. "How very interesting, but you know the saying: the road to Hell is paved with good intentions."

"Ah, Contessa, how kind of you to accept my confession and not resent me, but truly, for the last hour I have been utterly inconsolable."

"Like all lovers, torturing themselves for no good reason. Well, I find it most amusing. When you reach my age, *carissima*, you will prefer the clink of gold and silver to the kiss and embrace of a man. How many times must I assure you that I care nothing for men." I raised my goblet. "Believe it or not, it is true." I took a long sip.

Beatrice drank her wine in one gulp. "In that case, I feel comfortable in confiding in you. I am in love with Signore Gismondi. In love. It is too weak a description for what I feel for him. The touch of his hand thrills me. His voice shakes me to my soul. His eyes ignite a fire inside me that I cannot extinguish. You cannot understand the joy, the pain—"

"You must keep calm," I said frostily as I listened to my victim reveal her true feelings. "You must keep your mind cool when your blood burns. Do you think he loves you?"

"Think. He has..." She paused and her face flushed. "I know he never cared for his wife."

"I know that too," I answered in a steady voice. "One cannot fail to notice it. It is evident in the dreariness of his voice when he speaks about her."

"It is no surprise. Carlotta was a restrained fool. She had no business marrying such a spirited, exceptional man like him."

My heart leaped with fury, but I controlled my voice, "It is best to let poor Carlotta rest in peace. She is dead. Whatever her faults were, her husband was true to her while she lived. He was faithful to her was he not?"

She glanced away then lowered her eyes. "Oh, certainly," she muttered.

"And you were a loyal and truthful friend to her, despite the appeal of her desirable husband?"

Again she answered huskily, "Why, of course."

I saw her hand tremble.

"Well, then, I believe the love you now bear for her widower is something she would approve of. Because you have both behaved appropriately and beyond reproach, I hope that you and Dario receive the reward you both so richly deserve."

While I spoke, she fidgeted and I saw her glance up at my father's portrait with agitation. I suppose she could see her dead friend's likeness there. Silence befell us for a few moments and then she turned to me with a forced smile. "And so you hold no interest in Signore Gismondi for yourself?"

"Oh, that is not true. I do have a very strong interest and admiration for him, but not in the way you think. If it will put you at ease, I can promise you that I shall never try to attract his attentions unless—"

"Unless what?" she asked, her face tense once more.

"Unless he happens to show an interest in me first, in which case it would be great fun to seduce him." And I laughed harshly.

She stared at me, her eyes wide. "Show an interest in you? Seduce him? Surely you jest. You would never consider such a thing."

"Of course not, *cara*," I answered, rising and patting her gently on the shoulder. "Women like me rarely pursue men like him, it is quite absurd. You are perfectly safe, my friend. Come, let us drink coffee with the handsome man awaiting us on the veranda."

Arm-in-arm we wandered out to the veranda. Beatrice's good spirits were restored and Dario seemed relieved. Apparently, he was wary of Beatrice — something I would be wise to remember. He smiled a welcome to us as we approached and Giacomo poured the fragrant coffee.

The moon had already risen and nightingales trilled their song in the nearby woods. I took my seat next to Dario and as I adjusted my gown around me, I heard a long mournful howl that soon turned into restless whines.

"What is that sound?" I asked even though I already knew the answer.

"Oh, it's that irritating dog, Tito, droning on again." Dario's face wrinkled with aversion. "The creature belonged to Carlotta. His whining can be very annoying at times."

"Where do you keep him?"

"After my wife died, he wandered about the house howling for days. I could not stand the relentless sound, so I had no choice but to chain him up outside."

The Contessa's Vendetta

My poor Tito, callously treated because he grieved for me. "I adore dogs, and I would love to see the poor animal. May I?"

"If you wish," he said without enthusiasm. "Beatrice, would you mind fetching the dog for the contessa?"

Beatrice did not move; she leaned back in her chair and sipped her coffee. "Me? I hope you will not mind if I refuse. The last time I went near the creature, it attempted to bite me. Perhaps you could ask Giacomo to unfasten the dog and bring it here."

Dario faced me with raised brows. "For some strange reason, Tito has taken a dislike to Signorina Cardano, even though he is loving and loyal to Chiara. Perhaps it is best if we leave the dog chained up for tonight. I would not wish to see either one of you harmed in any way."

I narrowed my gaze at Beatrice and wondered what she had done to merit such a reaction from Tito who had never behaved in such a way before. "I'm sorry to hear that, but I would still dearly love to see the poor creature, if only to give it a bit of comfort since it seems he misses his mistress."

Dario looked at Giacomo. "Please untie Tito and bring him to me."

Giacomo gave a slight bow and departed to attend to the task.

In a few moments, Tito's howling ceased and the nimble, whitish-brown creature came bounding across the moonlit lawn toward me at full speed. He yelped with joy, tail wagging and panting as he cavorted around me, licking my hands as I patted him.

Beatrice and Dario watched Tito's frenetic affection with unreserved amazement.

"See, I told you I have a special affinity with dogs. No matter the dog, I always receive the same reaction." With a touch of my hand on Tito's neck, he lay down quietly at my feet, tail still wagging, brown eyes never leaving my face. I had no doubt my loyal dog recognized me.

Meantime, Dario watched me with a look of confusion, his pallor lighter than moments before.

"You do not like this dog?" I asked, watching him closely.

He laughed, a little forcedly. "Oh, no, I like dogs, but I have never seen Tito react so strongly to anyone other than Carlotta. How very strange."

Beatrice, too, looked uneasy. "Very strange indeed," she said. "For once, Tito is completely ignoring me. Usually, he never fails to snarl or bare his teeth at me."

At the sound of her voice, Tito turned and gave her a discontented growl, which I immediately silenced by touching his head. My pet's animosity towards Beatrice surprised me. Prior to my burial, Tito had always been friendly towards her.

"I have owned many dogs over the years," I said. "And dogs can sense when someone likes them. No doubt Tito is responding to my love for canines." My air of indifference seemed to reassure my betrayers and after a few brief moments, the incident was forgotten.

It was getting late and I rose to leave. "I would be happy to chain up the dog before I go home so that he will not disturb your sleep by his howling."

Beatrice looked relieved and she walked with me to the kennel. I chained Tito and patted him affectionately. He wagged his tail and lay down on his straw bed with no resistance except for a brief, pleading look as I turned and walked away from him.

When we returned to the veranda, I thanked Dario for an entertaining evening and announced my departure.

"Please allow me to accompany you home in your carriage," Beatrice offered.

"That is very kind of you, but there is no need. I am

fond of late night rides and I do not have far to go."

Thus, I bade them goodnight and coldly kissed Dario on both cheeks. He beamed with pleasure. I wanted to shudder with aversion.

Beatrice walked me to the villa gates and watched me enter my carriage. With a quick flick of the reins, Paolo set the horses to a walk. I waved at Beatrice as I rode away, but the instant I saw her turn away and heard the villa gates clang shut behind her, I asked Paolo to halt the carriage. I descended and went back to the villa, moving along the outer wall to the rear of the residence to a thicket of laurel that extended almost up to the house. I swept the branches softly aside and pushed my way through until I came within hearing distance of the veranda.

Beatrice sat with Dario on the settee I had just vacated. She leaned her head against his chest. He tilted her chin up and gave her a long kiss.

"You can be very cruel, Dario," Beatrice said when they separated. "For a while, you had me fooled into thinking you truly liked that rich old contessa."

He laughed. "Ah, but I do, *carissima*. I believe that beneath those grotesque spectacles hides a striking woman. And did you see all the jewels she wore? They were of the finest quality and very rare. I'll bet there are plenty more and I hope she gives some to me so that I can add them to my collection."

"And if she were to give you more gifts, would you care for her, Dario?" A tinge of jealously echoed in Beatrice's voice.

"I sincerely doubt it."

"She is very conceited, you know. She told me she would never make love unless a man showed interest in her first, and then she would initiate it. How shocking. What do you think of that?"

He laughed. "How original and charming." He stood,

pulled her to her feet, and embraced her. "Come, let's go inside."

"You are shameless, Dario. You would flirt with your own grandmother." Beatrice laid her head against his chest tenderly. "Tell me the truth, Dario, do you not think she looks a little bit like Carlotta?"

"I confess I do think there is a resemblance. In fact, I think it is possible she might be a long-lost relative, perhaps even Carlotta's aunt, and wants to keep it a secret for some reason. Overall, I believe she is a good woman, and disgustingly, gloriously wealthy. I think it would be wise to treat her as a valuable friend, don't you? Come, *sposina mia*, it is time for us to go to bed."

They disappeared inside and shut the veranda windows after them.

Sposina mia. His little bride. I left my hiding-place and returned to my carriage. I felt confident they did not suspect my identity. It would be unusual if they did, for who would believe it possible for a dead woman to come back to life? Stupid fools. In this game of vendetta, it was I who held all the power and I resolved to play it out to the bitter end and with all due haste.

Chapter Fifteen

Two months passed and during that time, I spent my time wisely, establishing myself as a great noblewoman within Vicenza's society. My wealth garnered many invitations from the city's most affluent families who eagerly sought my acquaintance. No one cared whether I was intelligent, witty, or beautiful. My popularity rose when I appeared in my satin-lined, ornate carriage drawn by four Arabian mares as white as polished ivory, my luxurious box at the opera, my beaded silk gowns, and the never-ending display of jewels I wore.

I soon came to know everyone of importance in Vicenza. People spoke about me in the most opulent salons. Newspapers chronicled my lavish generosity. Rumors about my immense revenues spread from mouth to mouth on every cafe and street corner. Jewellers, dressmakers, shoemakers, and furniture makers stopped Santina and Paolo with small trinkets to solicit my attention or obtain my custom. They both discreetly tucked away these bribes, but told me about each one, providing the name and address of the person who made the request.

Even more startling were all the matchmaking mothers seeking to marry me to their sons. My garish spectacles did not seem to deter these politically inclined social climbers. On the contrary, they assured me how fetching I looked while wearing them, so eager were they to add me to their families as a daughter-in-law.

Stiff and insincere widowers thrust themselves forward as potential suitors eager to get their hands on my wealth and then dupe the old black-spectacled wife to their heart's content. I played along with their ogling glances and false compliments about my beautiful white hair and forged laughs at my horrendous attempts at humour, as they tried to trap me into marriage.

At the many social events I attended, I saw to it that my husband and Beatrice were included as a matter of course. At first, Dario retreated from all invitations, citing his recent bereavement, but I persuaded him otherwise. I convinced several male acquaintances to implore him to attend and tell him it was not good for so young a man to waste his time grieving. Thankfully, Dario listened to their advice and accepted the invitations he received, despite the fact that he did it only to please me.

On Beatrice I heaped all manner of rewards. To surprise her, I paid her debts at the local dressmaker. Apparently, all of my gowns that she had claimed for herself failed to satisfy her. Nevertheless, she appreciated it. I delighted her with many jewels and trinkets of small extravagance, toying with her like a cat to its prey. In this way, I won her confidence. Although I failed to trick her into confessing her affair with Dario, she kept me informed as to their progress. Clueless to whom she was confiding in, she told me many intimate details, and although the knowledge stirred my blood into wrath, I always managed to remain composed while it fueled my need for vengeance.

Sometimes, as I listened to her petty dreams that would never come true, an appalled bafflement would come over me. She seemed so sure of her future happiness, so certain that nothing could blight it. Traitor that she was, selfish to her heart's core, she failed to fathom the possibility of retribution. On occasion, a risky urge stirred me; a desire to caution her that she was a condemned woman with one foot on the brink of her grave; and to prepare for her death while she still had time. Often, I wanted to seize her by the throat, declare my identity, and accuse her of treachery. Thankfully, I always managed to bite my lips and keep a strict silence.

Beatrice loved a good wine; a secret flaw I knew about from our past together. Therefore, I encouraged her to drink at every opportunity. Whenever she visited me, I offered her the finest vintages. Often after a cordial evening spent in my apartments with a few other women of my class, she tottered away with slurred words and a deeply flushed face. I wondered how Dario would receive her, for although he saw no offense in his own drunkenness, he abhorred drunken vulgarity in a woman. *Go to your lover, my dear Beatrice,* I would think, as I watched her leave my residence staggering and laughing loudly as she went. *Dario will turn against you soon and will look upon you with disgust and repugnance.*

Dario and Beatrice welcomed me at Villa Mancini at any hour. I could sit in my own library and read my own books or stroll leisurely through my beautiful gardens accompanied by Chiara and an eager Tito. The villa was completely at my disposal, though I never passed a night beneath its roof.

I played my character of a prematurely aged woman well. Cautious in all interactions with my husband in Beatrice's presence, I guarded against any word or action that could rouse her jealousy or mistrust. I treated her with consideration and formality, but Dario was quick to perceive that my interest lay with him. As soon as Beatrice's back was turned, he would look at me with a knowing, mocking smile, or utter some disparaging remark about her while he complimented me. It was not for me to betray his secrets. I never disclosed to Beatrice that Dario regularly sent Giacomo to my apartments with fruit and flowers; or that Paolo carried gifts and similar messages from me to him. And this was all part of my plan, unfolding so perfectly.

By the start of November, my own husband was secretly courting me and I reciprocated his romantic behavior with equal secrecy. The fact that I was often in the company of other men piqued his vanity. He knew many sought my hand in marriage and resolved to win me for himself; and of course, I was determined to let him win me.

Beatrice never suspected anything between Dario and me. She had often mentioned how poor Carlotta had been too easily duped; yet never was there a woman more duped than she was. She was too self-assured of her own good fortune to see what was happening before her very eyes. I sometimes wished to stir up her distrust and hostility, but I could not do it. She trusted me as much as I had once trusted her. Therefore, the devastation that would befall her would be unexpected as well as lethal. It would be better that way.

In my numerous visits to the villa, I saw Chiara often. The poor little thing was naturally fond of me. Often, Annunziata would bring her to my rented villa to pass the time, just her and I. Chiara delighted in these visits, especially when I took her on my knee and recounted a tale about a girl whose mama suddenly went away, and how the child grieved for her until fairies helped her mother to return. It became her favorite. I spent as much time as possible with Chiara. I yearned to pull her to me in a fast embrace and relieve her grief and pain by confessing my true identity. Somehow, I found the strength not to do so, for it would ruin the plans I had spent so much time preparing. To compensate, I bestowed her with my full attention and unfettered love. The knowledge that soon, Chiara and I would be fully reunited was my solace. My patience would one day be rewarded.

At first, I was nervous around old Annunziata. After all, she had once been my guardian. Could it be true she did not recognize me? The first time I met her in my disguise, I held my breath in suspense, but because she was nearly blind, the good old woman could scarce make out my facial features. She truly believed Carlotta was dead.

Giacomo, however, did not. The old man had an obsessive belief that his young mistress could not have died so suddenly, and he grew so obstinate in this conviction of Carlotta being alive, that Dario declared him demented.

Annunziata talked of Carlotta's death to me. "It was to be expected, Contessa. She was too good, and the saints took her. God takes the best among us. Poor Giacomo will not listen to me, and refuses to believe she is dead. Poor man, he loved the mistress very much," she would say in a solemn voice. "I always knew my mistress would die young. She was as delicate as an infant and too kind-hearted to live long." Then Annunziata would shake her hoary head and reach for her rosary, muttering an Ave Maria for the repose of my soul. Much as I tried, I could never get her to talk in detail about her mistress' life, the one subject on which she remained ever silent. Once, when I spoke of the young contessa's beauty and good deeds, she scrutinized me, but said nothing.

It pleased me to see her strongly devoted to Chiara, who returned her affection. But as the days progressed, I noticed how my daughter became pale and gaunt and she became easily fatigued. Because of her increasing thinness, her eyes looked unnaturally large. I called Annunziata's attention to these signs of poor health.

"I have spoken to the signore about it," she answered,

"but he has taken no notice of the child's weakening condition."

I then mentioned the matter directly to Dario and offered to call a physician.

"Really, Contessa, you are too good." He gave me a grateful smile. "Chiara's health is excellent. Perhaps I overindulge her and permit her to eat too many sweet cakes, and she is growing rather fast. Nevertheless, you are very kind to think of her. But, I assure you, she is quite well and there is no need for a physician to visit her."

I was not so certain, but masked my worry lest it betray me.

Around mid November, something happened which forced me to accelerate my vendetta. The days became colder and I was in the process of organizing a few dinners and masque balls for the approaching winter season, when one afternoon Beatrice hurried into my apartment unannounced and slumped into the nearest chair with a vexed expression.

"What is the matter?" I asked. "Is it a matter of money? If so, permit me to help."

She smiled nervously. "*Grazie*, Contessa, but it is not that. It is...it is...*Dio*. How unlucky I am."

I put on an expression of profound concern. "Is it Dario? I hope he has not played you false. Is he refusing to marry you?"

She laughed with derisive triumph. "No, there is no danger of that. He would not dare to play me false."

"Would not dare? That is a rather strong statement." I gave her a hard look.

She blushed. "Well, I did not mean that exactly. Of course he is perfectly free to do as he likes, but I doubt he could refuse to marry me with all the attention he pays me."

"Not unless he is an outright scoundrel, but we both

know he is a most decent man, so have no fear. If it is not about love or money, then what is troubling you? Judging by your expression, it must be serious."

She twisted a loose thread on her sleeve; a green damask gown that had been a favorite of mine, turning it round and round her index finger. "I have to leave Vicenza for a while."

My heart pounded with excitement. She was leaving the field of battle, enabling me to reap victory. What good fortune, indeed. Fortune surely was on my side. "Going away? Where? Why?" I asked with false sincerity.

"My uncle is dying in Rome. He has no sons or daughters, so I am to inherit everything. For the sake of decency, I must be by his side and attend him in his final days. I do not know how much time he has left, but the solicitor insists I be present, otherwise the old man may disinherit me with his last breath. I do not think I will be gone for long, perhaps two weeks at the most." She gave me an anxious look and hesitated.

"Please say what you have to say, *cara*," I urged. "Do not hesitate to ask anything of me. I am only too happy to help."

Beatrice rose and walked to the window where I sat. She took the chair opposite to me, sat down, and laid a hand on my wrist. "There is something you can do for me and I know I can depend upon you. Watch over Dario. He will have no one else to watch over him and he is so handsome and can be impulsive at times. Watch over him as a mother would. After all, you are a family friend and this in itself merits your vigilance over him. You can prevent other women from meddling and pushing themselves upon him now that he is an eligible widower."

I rose from my seat with an air of false tragedy. "If any woman dared to come between you, I would make her regret it." I grinned as I said this. She had uttered those exact words when I had witnessed her with my husband that first time in the avenue.

Something about the words must have seemed familiar to her because she looked a little bewildered.

I hurried to change the topic of our conversation and became serious. "I apologize for my flippancy. I can see this subject is far too sensitive for you. Let me assure you that I will watch over Dario with the jealous scrutiny and the prudence of an elder sister even though I admit it is a task unsuited and repugnant to me. Still, I will do it so that you can leave Vicenza with an easy mind." I took hold of her hand. "I promise to be a true and worthy friend and demonstrate the same devotion and faithfulness you showed to your dead friend Carlotta. The past could not provide me with a better example of honesty and loyalty."

She tensed as if my words stung. All color drained from her face. Doubt shone in her eyes.

I feigned an expression of reassurance.

"*Grazie*. I know I can rely upon your loyalty and friendship," she said composing herself.

"You most certainly can, as confidently as you can rely on mine towards you."

Again, she winced.

I released her hand. "When are you leaving?"

"Early tomorrow morning. I'm taking the coach from The Black Horse Inn."

"Well, I am glad you told me." I glanced at the unsent invitations on my writing table. "I will delay all festivities until you return."

She gave me a grateful look. "Truly? That is very kind of you, but I did not mean to cause you any inconvenience."

"Think nothing of it, *cara amica*. The masque ball can wait for your return. Besides, it will be better for you if you know Dario will be relatively isolated during your absence."

"I would hate for him to be bored."

I showed no reaction to the insincere tone in her voice and smiled. "Oh, you need not worry about that." As if Dario would permit himself to be bored. "I will take care of everything and arrange small diversions like a quiet drive into the countryside or the opera to occupy him. Any dances, dinners, or musical evenings shall wait for your return."

Her eyes flashed with delight.

"You are very good to me, Contessa. How can I thank you?"

"Do not worry. The day will come when you will have an opportunity to thank me and show me your gratitude. Now, I am sure you have much to attend to and much packing. I will come and see you off in the morning," I dismissed.

My reassurance seemed to satisfy her and she left.

I did not see her again that day. I knew she was with my husband, no doubt extracting promises of fidelity from him. I envisioned him holding her in his arms, kissing her with passion as she beseeched him to be faithful, night and day, until her return.

I smiled coldly at this vision. *Si*, Beatrice, kiss him now to your heart's content, for you will never do so again. Dario will no longer bewitch you with his glance. He will no longer sweep your jealous body into his embrace. His kisses will no longer burn upon your curved sweet lips. Your day is done, my dear Beatrice. The final moments of pleasure born from your transgressions has arrived. Make the most of them. No one shall interfere. Drink the last drop of sweet wine. I shall not disturb your final night of love. Turncoat, swindler, and charlatan — may your wretched soul fall to ruin. Take one last look at Dario. May he murmur persuasive lies into your ears. *I will be true,* he will tell you, and I hope you believe him as I once did. May your parting be sweet, because this time, you will part forever. You will never see him again.

The next morning I met Beatrice in front of The Black Horse Inn. She appeared ashen-faced and weary, but she gave me a slight smile when I descended from my carriage, which had come to a stop behind the passenger coach headed to Rome.

I could see at once that she was in a foul mood. She scolded the old porter who struggled to load her heavy trunk on top of the conveyance. Tension surrounded her and it was a relief when she at last ascended into the coach. She carried a small leather volume in her hand.

"Is that an amusing book?" I asked.

"I do not know yet because I only recently purchased it. It is by Antonio Francesco Grazzini from Florence. In his writing, he delights in praising low and disgusting things and in jeering at what is noble and serious. His work is said to be both playful and bizarre." She held up the cover for me to see.

"*Sì*, I have heard of this book. *I Parentadi.*" The Marriages. How appropriate, I thought.

"The bookseller told me it is about a wife betrayed by her husband and the ensuing loss, romance, and unexpected discoveries."

"Ah, I see. Betrayal always brings excitement, but be forewarned; the ending may be tragic. You must lend it to me when you have finished reading it. I am always interested in such tales."

All was ready and the other passengers had boarded. I watched her alight. The driver was on the verge of driving away when she leaned out of the coach window and beckoned me to come closer.

"Remember," she whispered, "I entrust Dario into your care."

"Do not worry. I promise to do my best to replace you during your absence."

She gave me a troubled smile and squeezed my hand with gratitude.

These were our last words, for at that moment, the driver called out a warning, gave the reins a slap, and I watched the coach drive away.

A sense of unqualified freedom swept over me. Now I could do as I pleased with my husband. If I wanted to, I could even kill him. No one would interfere. I could visit him that evening, declare myself to him, and accuse him of infidelity before stabbing him in the heart. Then I could flee without suspect because the world believed I was dead.

But no, I would do none of that. My original plan was better, and I must keep to it and allow it to unfold with patience, even though my patience was difficult to keep in check.

Just as I was about to enter my carriage, I was startled by the unexpected appearance of Santina, who came upon me quite suddenly, out of breath from running. I slid over to make room for her in the carriage and she handed me a note marked *Urgent*. It was from Annunziata.

Please come at once. Chiara is very ill, and asks for you.

"Who gave you this?" I asked.

"Giacomo from Villa Mancini brought it," Santina said.

My heart sunk and a great fear rose within me. I bade Paolo to hurry to Villa Mancini first and then take Santina home afterward.

Despite the fact Paolo hurried, the ride to Villa

Mancini seemed to take forever. When we finally arrived, the gates were already open in expectation of my arrival. I ran from the carriage to the entrance. Before I could knock, Giacomo swung open the door, his face creased with worry.

"How is Chiara?" I asked him anxiously as I swept inside, mantle billowing behind me.

He shook his head solemnly and gestured to a sympathetic looking man descending the stairs. I instantly recognized him as a physician who practiced in the vicinity of the villa.

"How is the child?" I asked the physician.

He gestured for me to follow him into a side room and closed the door behind us. He shook his head. "It is a matter of flagrant negligence. The child has been in a weakened state for quite some time, and therefore an easy target for disease. She was once hale and hearty, that is most evident. If someone had summoned me when her symptoms first developed, I believe I might have been able to cure her. The nurse, Annunziata, tells me she asked the signore several times to summon me, but was always refused. She was afraid to enter the father's bedchamber to disturb him in the night, otherwise he might have checked on the child and summoned me. How unfortunate. Now, it is too late, there is nothing I can do."

I listened to his every word as if I were trapped in a nightmare. Not even old Annunziata dared enter her master's room in the night, despite the fact, the child was ill and suffering. And I knew why. Last night, while Beatrice lay in my husband's arms delighting in amorous embraces and lingering farewells, my little daughter suffered without a mother or father's comfort. Not that it would have made a difference, but I was fool enough to hope that one faint spark of fatherhood remained in Dario, the man upon whom I had squandered all my love.

The physician watched and waited as my mind raced with these thoughts.

"The child is asking to see you, Contessa. I persuaded Signore Gismondi to send for you, though he seemed reluctant because he feared you might catch the disease. Of course there is always a risk of contagion—"

"I am not afraid of contagion. I survived the plague when many others perished."

The physician bowed courteously. "Then there is little else to say, except that you should visit the child at once. I am obliged to leave for a brief while, but I will return shortly."

I gripped his arm to detain him. "Please stay. Is there any hope?"

A glint of sadness appeared in his eyes and he shook his head gravely. "I am afraid not, Contessa. You should prepare yourself for the worst."

"Nothing? Are you certain nothing can be done?"

"I am sorry. There is nothing more to be done except to keep her as quiet and comfortable as possible. I have given her a small amount of a tincture made with poppy, mandrake, and vinegar and left more with the nurse. It will help alleviate the pain, but you must not give her any more than necessary. I shall return to examine her again as soon as I return."

Stunned, I watched wordlessly as he left the room until Giacomo nudged my arm and offered to accompany me to the nursery.

"Where is Signore Gismondi?" I whispered as I followed him up the stairs.

"The signore?" he asked, eyes wide in astonishment. "In his bedchamber, of course. He would not think of leaving it for fear of infection." His tone carried a hint of sarcasm.

One more act that proved my husband's utter

heartlessness. One more nail in his coffin. I smothered the curse that rose to my lips. "Has he not seen his daughter?"

"Not since she became ill, Contessa."

Unimaginable pain, fear, and panic clamoured in my stomach as I gently pushed open the door to the nursery. The blinds were drawn shut to prevent the strong light from bothering my beloved child. Annunziata sat beside the small ivory bed, her face ashen and tense with anxiety.

At my appearance, she raised her eyes to mine. "Chiara has the fever in her throat. She took ill in the middle of the night. This morning she became worse. Why must it always be like this? God always take the good and virtuous. First the mother; now the child. Only the wicked remain."

"Mama," Chiara moaned weakly. She tried to raise herself upon tumbled pillows, her eyes wide, her cheeks scarlet with fever. She breathed with difficulty through parted lips.

Shocked at her appearance and the symptoms she bravely suffered, I placed my arms tenderly round her. She smiled softly and I pressed my lips upon her poor little parched mouth and kissed her. "Hush, *carina*, rest, and soon the pain will better." I adjusted her pillows and she sank back upon them obediently, her eyes never wavering from me. I knelt at her bedside, her small warm hand in mine, and watched her with desperation and yearning.

Annunziata moistened Chiara's lips with a damp cloth and tucked the bedcovers neatly around her.

I watched helplessly, unable to ease the pain endured so meekly by my little darling whose breathing grew quicker and fainter with every moment.

"You are my Mama, are you not?" she asked, a deeper flush crossing her forehead and cheeks.

A knot clogged my throat and I could not answer. Instead, I kissed the small hot hand I held in mine as I fought back my tears. I could not let Chiara see me cry.

Annunziata's eyes welled with tears and she shook her head. "Ah, *poverina*. Her time must be near because she sees her mother. And why not? She loved her with all her heart. I have no doubt her mother's spirit has come to take Chiara to Heaven." She fell on her knees, wrapped her rosary between her gnarled fingers and hands speckled with age, and prayed with deep devotion.

Chiara raised her arms to me.

I lay myself down on the bed beside her and rested her head against my breast. I knew I held my baby for the last time and struggled to stifle my profound grief.

"My throat aches so, Mama," she said, her breathing coming with great difficulty. "Can you make it better?"

"I wish I could, *piccolina*," I whispered. "I would take away all your pain."

She was silent a moment. "You have been gone for such a long time, Mama, and now I am too sick to play with you." A faint smile arose on her lips. "See poor Nina." Her eyes moved to the old battered doll that lay discarded near the foot of her bed. "Poor Nina. She will think I do not love her anymore because my throat hurts me. Give her to me, Mama."

As I obeyed her request, she hugged the doll with one arm, while she clung to me with the other.

"Nina remembers you, Mama; remember, you brought her from Rome, and she is fond of you, too—but not as fond of you as I am." Her dark eyes glowed with fever. She turned to Annunziata, who had buried her gray head in her hands as she knelt praying. "Annunziata," she said.

The old woman glanced up. "*Sì*, my *bambinetta*," she answered in an aged, trembling voice.

"Why are you crying?" Chiara asked with surprise. "Are you not happy to see my Mama?" A sharp spasm of pain seized her. Her body convulsed as she gasped for breath.

My child was suffocating and all my wealth, all my love could not help her.

Annunziata and I hurried to raise her up gently and supported her against her pillows; her agony passed slowly, but left her little face white and rigid. Sweat gathered on her brow.

"Hush, my sweetheart, try not to talk too much," I whispered in an attempt to soothe her. "Try to lie still so that your throat will not hurt."

She looked at me sadly. "Kiss me, then, and I will be good."

I kissed her and embraced her. She closed her eyes. A long silence ensued in which she did not move.

Time passed as I watched my daughter with terror and fear and helplessness.

Finally, the physician returned. He came to stand at Chiara's bedside, looking down on her. He shook his head and remained standing quietly at the foot of the bed.

At that moment, Chiara awoke and smiled angelically at the three of us.

"Are you in pain, my *bambola,* my doll?" I asked gently.

"No," she answered in a voice so faint, we almost had to hold our breath to hear her. "I feel much better now. Annunziata, you must dress me in my white frock now that Mama is here. I knew she would come home to me."

And she looked upon me with clear astuteness.

"Her brain wanders," the physician whispered *sotto voce*. "It will be over soon."

Chiara did not hear him; she nestled herself more comfortably in my arms. "You did not go away because I was naughty, did you, Mama?"

"No *carina*," I answered, hiding my face in her curls. "You were never naughty. You must never think that."

"Why do you wear those ugly black spectacles?" Her

voice was so feeble now that I could scarcely hear her. "Are your eyes hurt? Please let me see them."

I hesitated. Dare I humour her request? I glanced around. The physician had turned his head away and Annunziata was still on her knees, her face buried in the bedclothes, praying. I quickly slipped my spectacles down, and looked over them at my darling child.

"Mama," she uttered and stretched out her arms.

At that very moment, a fierce shudder shook her body.

The physician rushed forward.

I replaced my glasses and pushed myself away to make room for the physician to examine my suffering child.

Her face reddened and she tried to speak. Her beautiful eyes rolled upward. A sigh escaped from her lips, and then she sunk back on my breast. Her chest no longer rose and fell.

My sweet baby had left me. I stifled the fierce sob that threatened to explode and clasped her small, lifeless body to me, rocking back and forth in my grief. I released my tears and they fell hot and fast.

An enduring silence hung in the air; a profound, reverent silence. I knew the Angel of Death had entered and departed, taking my delicate little flower away forever.

Chapter Sixteen

"Please, come away now." The physician's voice, soft and kind, swarmed over me as if from a great distance to rouse me from grief. "The child is free from pain now," he said. "Her dream that you were her mother brought her comfort in her final moments. Come with me now. I can see this has been a shock to you."

I laid my darling's fragile body back down on the pillows and adjusted her brown locks around her angelic face. With a gentle sweep of my hand, I closed her upturned, blank eyes and folded her tiny hands together across her chest. Her cheeks still held the warmth of life when I bent down to kiss them for the last time. The remnants of a delicate smile lingered on her face, a smile so sweet, so magnificent in its simplicity.

Tears cascaded down Annunziata's weary, shrunken face. She rose awkwardly from her knees and laid her rosary on Chiara's folded hands. Her age-spotted hands trembled as she wiped her tears away with the edge of her apron. "Someone must tell her father."

The physician's expression turned sour. "Her father, as you call him, should have been here."

Annunziata shook her head. "For the duration of her illness, the child never once asked for him."

"How very tragic," the physician answered, his eyes unwavering from Chiara's face.

An awkward silence befell us. We stood round the small bed, gazing down at my baby; the flawless pearl of innocence whose spirit had left us far too soon. Why had God saved me and not her? She deserved to live, to laugh, to wed and have children of her own one day. Instead, she had died sad, neglected, forlorn. Numb with profound grief, I watched Annunziata shutting the blinds; a signal to the world that death had once more visited the villa.

The physician crooked his finger for me to follow him out of the room. We paused at the top of the stairwell and began our descent to the villa's second level.

"If you do not object, I will announce the child's death to Signore Gismondi," the physician said.

My grief was more than I could bear, and I struggled to fight it off. I must remain composed. "I appreciate it. I cannot speak with him right now."

"I completely understand. I hope he will show some pretence of grief."

By this time, we had reached the first landing and stood in the corridor.

"I doubt he will demonstrate emotion." My entire body trembled with a mixture of anger and anguish.

A grimace contracted the physician's face, and then he turned and disappeared down the corridor to Dario's bedchamber.

I sat in a chair that faced a small window, incoherent of everything except for the agony of my loss. Alone and in the quiet, I allowed my tears to fall freely. I hated myself for having been so blind and not having seen the repulsiveness of the man I had married. He had caused this. Because of his actions, I had left Chiara in his hands. Because of him, I planned my vendetta instead of confronting Dario and Beatrice immediately upon my resurrection. His guilt was clear. My pain was more than I could bear.

Absent-mindedly I studied the room's costly furnishings, vases, and ornaments, most of which Dario had wanted me to purchase during the first few months of our marriage. Once I had beheld them with pride. Now they disgusted me and all that they represented. Worthless trinkets, meaningless compared to the true values of humanity like love and family.

Soon, I heard the sound of footsteps and in a moment, the physician made his way back down the hall towards me bearing a sardonic expression. "He looked shocked, but he did not weep," he replied at my look of inquiry. He touched my arm in consolation. "The signore would like to speak with you before you go. He said he will not detain you long. It is obvious you have taken this very hard. You do not look well. I recommend you return to your home as soon as possible to rest. *Arrivederci.* If there is anything I can do for you, send someone to my home and I will come to you at once."

He took my hand in his and gave it a gentle pat. Then he left me and I heard the door close behind him. Again, I stared out the window, my arms folded across my chest, my body rocking back and forth, wrapped in torment.

I did not hear the stealthy tread on the carpet behind me, but I sensed someone's presence. I turned sharply around and found myself face to face with old Giacomo, who held out a note on a silver salver. He peered down at me with such sorrowful, inquisitive eyes that it made me uneasy.

"Our little angel is dead," he murmured in a thin, quavering voice. "Dead. What a tragedy. Misfortune has visited the villa too much. But my mistress is still alive. Contessa Mancini is still alive."

I paid no heed to his confused ramblings and read the message Dario had sent to me through him.

I am in mourning. Will you kindly send a letter of my dreadful loss to Signorina Cardano? I shall be much obliged to you. Dario

I looked up from the note and studied my old steward's wrinkled face. He was a short, stooped man whose attention was riveted on me. He clasped his hands together and muttered words I could not make out.

"Tell your master," I said, speaking slowly and harshly, "that I will do as he wishes; that I am entirely at his service. Do you understand?"

"*Si,* I understand," faltered Giacomo, nervously. "Contessa Mancini never thought me foolish. She always understood me well."

Anger, frustration, grief, and impatience melded together inside me and I could not prevent myself from lashing out at him. "I am tired of hearing about your mistress." My tone was cold and cutting and I cared not. "I weary of it. If she were alive, she would say you were in your dotage. Take my message to Signore Gismondi at once."

The old man's face paled and his lips quivered. He straightened his shrunken figure with dignity. "My mistress would never speak to me like that - never." Then his expression wilted and he shook his head. "Though it is just...I am a fool...mistaken...ah, quite mistaken. There is no resemblance." He paused. "I will take your message." With his shoulders sagging more than ever, he shuffled away.

My heart smote me as I watched him disappear. I had spoken far too harshly to the poor old fellow, but there had been no choice. His incessant scrutiny, his timidity when he approached me, the strange tremors he experienced whenever I addressed him, warned me to be on my guard in his presence. If by chance my devoted steward recognized me, it would spoil all my plans. For now, because of Chiara's death, my need for vengeance surged stronger and more desperately than ever before. One more sin against Beatrice's and Dario's black hearts.

I descended the stairs to the salon. From the writing desk, I penned a brief letter to Beatrice and after waiting for the ink to dry, sealed it. Gathering my mantle, I left the house. As I crossed the upper terrace, I noticed a small round object lying in the grass. It was Chiara's ball, the one she used to throw for Tito to catch and bring to her. I picked it up tenderly, held it in my hand as a flood of memories rushed over me. With a sigh, I placed it in my bag. I glanced up once more at the darkened nursery windows and waved a kiss of farewell to my little one lying there in her last sleep. Then fiercely controlling all the weaker and softer emotions that threatened to overwhelm me, on trembling legs, I hurried into my waiting carriage.

On my way home, I stopped at the inn where Beatrice had boarded her coach to Rome and asked the innkeeper to dispatch my letter on the next coach. She would be surprised, I thought, but certainly not grieved. Chiara had likely always been in her way. Would she rush back to Vicenza to console Dario, now a childless widower? Not she. She would know that he would need little consolation. She would accept Chiara's death as she had accepted mine - as a blessing and not a loss.

On reaching my apartments, I gave orders to Santina that I was not at home to anyone who might call. I passed the rest of the day in bed, locked in my dark room, the shutters closed tight, weeping, releasing my deep anguish in private.

When I had cried till I could cry no more, it was then that a vile coldness crept into my soul. My thoughts cleared. The last tenuous bond to my husband had crumbled like a lump of sun-baked mud. Our child, the one unsullied link in the long chain of falsehood and deception, no longer existed. The torment of her loss would haunt me forever. My only consolation was that Chiara no longer had to endure such horrendous misery. Now she was at peace, happy.

The tragedy of her parents' lives could now unfold without harming her. She was in God's care now. He had released her from every worldly menace, past and future, and that knowledge gave me solace.

Now, more than ever, I must see my vendetta to the end. It was a fire that burned within me, stronger, fiercer. Nothing was as important to me as the need to avenge Chiara and restore my self-respect and damaged honor.

Ten days passed since Chiara's death. I do not know how I survived those impossible black days, having to disguise every shred of my grief. My child's passing had only strengthened my resolve. The need for retribution kept me from falling into deep melancholy and drove me forward.

Dario had asked me to arrange our child's funeral and burial. It was a blessing, for I could not bear to think of her cherished body laid to rot away in the Mancini vault where I had endured so many horrors. Instead I chose a quaint spot in the cemetery, beneath the dappled shade of a glorious cherry tree with a stone bench nearby. Here we laid her to rest in the warm earth. I had sweet jasmine and pink roses planted thickly all about her grave. Her tombstone was of an angel carved in white marble. Upon it I had the words *A Vanished Star* engraved above her name followed by her birth and death dates.

Throughout this time, I visited Dario numerous times; always at his request, of course. Though for propriety's sake, he denied all other visitors. Each time, I marvelled at how he looked handsomer than ever; how the air of lethargy he assumed suited him perfectly. If he had experienced any grief over his daughter's death, it did not show. Rather, he looked rejuvenated, as if a burden had been lifted from his shoulders. Always wise to the power and allure he had over women, he now put his full energy into winning me.

However, now, my strategy had changed. I paid him scant attention and never went to him unless he pressed me to. All courtesies from me had ceased. He courted me, and I accepted his attentions with indifference. I played the part of a reserved woman, who preferred reading to his company. Sometimes, I sat with him in the salon, turning the leaves of a book and feigning to be absorbed in it, while he, from his velvet armchair, studied me with an insincere look of part respect and part admiration.

We had both heard from Beatrice. Although he never showed me her letter to him, he told me she had been distressed to hear of Chiara's death. The letter she had sent me, however, told a much different tale:

> *You can understand, my dear Contessa, that I am not much grieved to hear of the death of Carlotta's child. Had she lived, her presence would have been a perpetual reminder to me of things I prefer to forget. The child never liked me and would have been a great source of trouble and inconvenience; so, on the whole, I am glad she is out of the way. My uncle is close to death, yet, he clings to life. The physician promises me that it will not be much longer, otherwise I shall return to Vicenza and sacrifice my inheritance. I am restless and unhappy away from Dario, though I know he is under your safe and protective care.*

I read this particular paragraph to my husband,

watching him closely as I slowly enunciated the words contained in it. He listened, and his brows contracted in the vexed frown I knew so well.

His lips parted in a chilly smile. "I owe you my thanks, Contessa, for showing me the extent of Signorina Cardano's insolence. I am shocked that she wrote to you in such a callous manner. My late wife's attachment to her was so great that she now presumes to hold influence over me. I think she believes I am her brother and that she can interfere, as sisters sometimes do. I regret having been so patient with her and having allowed her far too much liberty."

How true, I thought as I gave him a bitter smile. My game was in full fervor now and I must make my moves with swift stealth. I could not afford the time to hesitate or to reflect.

I folded Beatrice's letter and replaced it in my purse. "I think Signorina Cardano is determined to be more than a sister to you."

"Then I fear Signorina Cardano is doomed to be disappointed," he said with a disdainful laugh. He rose and came to sit in a chair next to me. "Surely she is not so foolhardy as to hope I would marry her?"

"Indeed, that is exactly what she confided to me." Why did his duplicity continually catch me by surprise?

"I am flattered, but how can you believe I would even consider marrying her?"

And still, I struggled with his treachery. He seemed to have no conscience. Why had I been so blind to him all the years of our marriage? All the passionate embraces, the lingering kisses, the vows of fidelity, and words of caressing endearment meant nothing to him. He had blotted them all from his memory. For a brief moment, I pitied Beatrice. Her fate, in his hands, was evidently to be the same as mine had been.

"Did you truly believe I might return Signorina Cardano's interest in me?"

I knew I must respond. "Of course I did. She is young, undeniably attractive, and on her uncle's death will be quite wealthy. What more could you desire? Besides, she was your wife's friend."

"And that is exactly why I would never marry her. Even if I liked her, which I do not, I would not wish to stir up such a scandal."

"I do not understand. Why do you suppose there would be a scandal?"

"If I were to marry someone who was known to be my wife's most intimate friend, people might believe there was something between us before my wife's death. And I could not endure such slanderous scandal." He paused. "They might even think I murdered her. A perfectly innocent woman like Signorina Cardano could not possibly foresee society's condemnation."

And you Dario, are rancorous and cruel, yet you do everything in your power to gain everyone's good opinion. You think you have fooled everyone who knows you, and you wish to entrap me, but you will not. Despite my building anger, I had to answer him. "No one in my presence would dare slander you," I said with as much courtesy as I could summon. "But, if it is true that you have no interest in Signorina Cardano—"

"Of course it is true. She is low-class and unsophisticated. I believe she drinks far too much wine and I find her insufferable." His face had become somber as he looked down at his clasped hands.

"Then I feel sorry for Beatrice; she will be deeply hurt, but I confess that a small part of me is glad."

"Why?" he asked eagerly.

I glanced away modestly. "Because now other women have a chance to garner the attention of the handsome

Signore Gismondi."

He shook his head slightly. A fleeting expression of disappointment appeared, and then disappeared on his face.

"Other women would not aspire to such ambition or the belief it is her duty to watch over me." His eyes sparked with annoyance. "I suppose Signorina Cardano wishes to keep me for herself; a most brazen and stupid concept. There is only one thing to do; I will leave Vicenza before she returns."

"Why?" I asked.

"To avoid her and to put some distance between us to cool her ardor for me," he said, his face stone-like. "Lately, she frustrates me. I do not want her attentions and feel uneasy around her. But when I am with you, I am happy, peaceful, but I cannot allow myself to indulge in it."

The moment had arrived and I stepped closer to him. "Why not?" I said.

He half rose from his chair. "What do you mean, Contessa?" he faltered, his face hopeful. "I do not understand."

"You just said you are happy whenever you are with me, but that you cannot allow yourself to indulge in it. It seems to me that you could, if you were to take me as your wife."

"Contessa," he stammered.

I held up my hand to silence him. "I am perfectly aware of the disparity in years that exists between us. I am not young, healthy, or pleasant to look at. Trouble and bitter disappointment has made me what I am. But I have wealth, which is almost inexhaustible, along with position and influence." I looked at him steadily. "And beside these things, I desire to give you all you deserve. If you think you could be happy with me, do not be afraid to tell me so. I cannot offer you the passionate adoration of a young woman. My blood is cold and my pulse is slow, but whatever I can do for you, I will." I waited and gazed at him intently.

He opened and closed his mouth alternately, lost in thought. Then a triumphant smile curved his mouth. He raised his eyes to mine tenderly. He came close up to me; his fragrant breath fell warm on my cheek. His strange gaze fascinated me, and a sort of tremor shook my nerves.

"You mean that you are willing to marry me, but that you do not love me?" He laid his hand on my shoulder, his voice low and thrilling.

I remained silent, and for a moment, I battled the old foolish desire to let him draw me to his heart, to permit his lips to cover mine with kisses. But I forced the mad impulse down and stood mute.

He watched me as he lifted his hand and touched my hair. "*Si*, I believe you really do not love me, but I love you." He held his head proud as he uttered the lie.

I seized the hand whose caress stung me, and held it hard. "You love me? No, no, I cannot believe it. No man has ever loved me. It is impossible."

He laughed softly. "It is true though. The very first time I saw you, I knew I loved you. I never liked my wife, though in some ways you resemble her, and are quite different in others. But you are far superior to her in every way. Believe it or not, you are the only woman I have ever loved." He made the comment without flinching, with an air of conscious pride and virtue.

"Then I will marry you," I said, half stupefied at his manner.

"I will make you love me very much," he murmured, and with a quick, lithe movement, he pulled me softly against him and looked down at me with a radiant face. "Kiss me," he said, and stooped to kiss me with his false lips.

I would rather have placed my mouth on that of a poisonous snake, his kiss roused such fury within me.

He led me gently back to the couch he had left, and I sat down beside him.

"Do you truly love me?" I asked almost fiercely.

"With all my heart."

"And I am the first woman whom you have really cared for?

"You are."

"You never liked Signiorina Cardano?"

"Never."

"Did you ever kiss her with all the emotion as you have me?"

"Not once."

Dio. How the lies poured forth. A cascade of them and all spoken with an air of truth. I marvelled at the ease and rapidity with which they glided off his tongue. I took hold of his hand upon which he still wore the wedding ring I had once placed there and quietly slipped it off. Into his palm I placed a magnificent man's ring with a square cut emerald. I had long carried this trinket about with me in expectation of this moment.

"Oh, Giulia. How very lucky I am. How generous you are to me." Leaning forward, he kissed me then slipped the ring on his finger. "You will not tell Beatrice?" he said with anxiety in his tone. "Not yet?"

"No," I answered. "I will not tell her until she returns. Otherwise she would leave Rome at once, and we do not want her back just yet, do we?" And I adjusted his collar, while I pondered the rapid success of my scheme.

He grew pensive and distant, and for a few moments we were both silent. If he had known or imagined that he held his own wife in his arms, the woman he had duped and wronged, the poor fool he had mocked and despised, whose life had been an obstruction in his path, whose death he had been glad of, would he have smiled so sincerely? Would he have kissed me then?

He remained leaning against me peacefully for some moments. "Will you do me one favor?" he asked. "Such a little thing, a trifle, but it would give me such pleasure."

"What is it?" I asked.

"Take off those dark glasses. I want to see your eyes."

I rose from the sofa quickly. "Ask anything you like but that *caro*," I responded with some coldness. "The least bit of light on my eyes causes me acute pain; pain that irritates my nerves for hours afterward. Be satisfied with me as I am for the present, though I promise you, your wish will one day be granted."

"When?"

"On our wedding night," I answered.

"That is too long to wait," he said crossly.

"Not at all. We are now in November. May I ask you to allow me to set our wedding for the second month of the new year?"

"But my recent widowhood. Chiara's death," he objected.

"In February your wife will have been dead nearly six months. It is a sufficient period of mourning for one so young as yourself. And the loss of your child increases the loneliness of your situation. Society will not censure you for it."

A smile of conscious triumph parted his lips. "As you wish. If you, who are known in Vicenza as one who is perfectly indifferent to society's opinion, wish it, I shall not object." And he gave me a mischievous, amused look.

I saw it, but answered, stiffly, "You are aware, Dario, and I am also aware that I am not a typical 'lover', but I readily admit that I am impatient."

"Why?" he asked.

"Because, I want you to be my husband, to allow you

The Contessa's Vendetta

to completely possess me, and to know that no one can come between us, or interfere with us in any way."

He laughed. "Your dignity will not allow you to believe that you are in love with me, but in spite of yourself, you know you are."

I stood before him in almost somber silence. "If you say so, then it must be so. I have had no experience in affairs of the heart, and I find it difficult to name the feelings that possess me. I am only conscious of a very strong wish to become the absolute mistress of your destiny, and you of mine." Involuntarily, I clenched my hand as I spoke.

He did not observe the action, but he answered with a bend of the head and a smile. "I could not have a better future and I am sure my destiny will be bright with you in it."

"It will be all that you deserve," I half muttered, and then with an abrupt change of manner I said, "I must wish you goodnight. It grows late, and with my state of health being so tenuous, it is important that I retire to bed early."

He rose from his seat and gave me a compassionate look.

"You really suffer then?" he inquired tenderly. "I am sorry. Perhaps careful nursing will restore you. I shall be so proud if I can help you to attain better health."

"Rest and happiness will no doubt do much for me," I answered. "Still, I warn you that in accepting me as your wife, you take on a pitiful woman, one whose whims are notorious and whose chronic state as an invalid may in time prove to be a burden to you. Are you sure your decision is a wise one?"

"Quite sure," he replied firmly. "I love you and you will not always be ailing. You look so strong."

"I am strong to a certain extent," I said, unconsciously straightening myself as I stood. "But my nervous system is completely muddled. I—why, what is the matter?"

He had turned deathly pale and looked startled. I extended my arm to him, but he pushed it aside with an alarmed yet appealing gesture. "It is nothing. A sudden memory I recalled. Tell me, are you certain you are not related to the Mancini family, even distantly? When you stood up just now, you were so much like Carlotta that for a moment I thought you were her ghost."

"You are tired and still distressed over your daughter's death," I said calmly. "No, I am not related to the Mancinis, though I may have aquired some of their mannerisms. Many women are alike in these things." And pouring out two glasses of brandy, I handed one to him.

He sipped slowly, leaning back in his chair, and in silence we both looked out on the November night. There was a moon, veiled by driving clouds. A rising wind moaned dismally among the fading creepers and rustled the heavy branches of a giant cypress that stood on the lawn. Now and then, a few big drops of rain fell like sudden tears wrung by force from the black heart of the sky.

"Shut the window," my husband demanded harshly.

His abrupt, rude command caused me to frown.

At my look of reproach, Dario quickly changed his tone. "I do no know what came over me, but I felt bothered, very uncomfortable with you."

"That was hardly a complimentary way to speak to your future wife," I remarked, quietly, as I closed and fastened the window shutters in obedience to his request. "Should I not insist upon an apology?"

He laughed nervously.

"It is not yet too late," I resumed. "If you have second thoughts and would rather not marry me, you have only to say so. I shall accept my fate with composure, and will not blame you."

At this he seemed quite alarmed, and rising, laid his hand on my arm.

"Surely you are not offended?" he said. "I was not really bothered by you, you know. It was a stupid reaction, one I cannot explain. But you make me happy and I would not risk losing your love for all the world. You must believe me." He touched my hand with his lips.

I withdrew it gently. "If so, we are agreed, and all is well. Let us both try to take a long night's rest. Do you wish me to keep our betrothal a secret?"

He thought for a moment. "For the present, it would be best. Though," he laughed, "it would be delightful to see all the other men envious of my good fortune. Still, if the news were told to any of our friends it might accidentally reach Beatrice, and—"

"I understand. We must be discreet. *Buona Note.* May your dreams be of me."

He responded to this with a gratified smile, and as I left the room he waved. The emerald ring flashed upon his hand. The light from the wall sconces that hung from the painted ceiling highlighted his handsomeness, softening it into near godliness.

When I left the house and walked into the night air, heavy with the threatening gloom of a coming tempest, the vision of his face and body flitted before me like a mirage; hands that seemed to beckon me; lips that had left a scorching heat on mine. Distracted with such torturous thoughts, I boarded my carriage and returned home. There I stared out at the world from my room for what seemed like hours.

The storm broke at last. The rain poured in torrents, but heedless of wind and weather, I felt forsaken. I seemed to be the only human being left alive in a world filled with wrath and darkness. The rush and roar of the wind, the pounding rain that fell, were all unheeded by me.

There are times when one can grow numb under the pressure of mental agony; when the soul, smarting by some vile injustice, forgets. Such was my mood. An awful loneliness encompassed me; one of my own creation. There was nothing in all the world except me and the dark brooding horror of vengeance.

Suddenly, the mists in my mind cleared. I no longer moved in a deaf, blind stupor. A flash of lightning danced vividly before my eyes, followed by a crashing peal of thunder. In my thoughts, I saw to what end of a wild journey I had come. The memory of heavy gates, undefined stretch of land, and ghostly glimmers of motionless tombstones emerged. I knew it all too well - the cemetery. Another bolt of lightning flashed across the sky. I recalled the marble outline of the Mancini vault. There the drama had begun, but where would it end?

I conjured the vision of my lost child's face as it had looked in death, and then I experienced a curious feeling of pity. Pity that her little body should be lying stiffly out there, not in the vault, but under the wet sod, in such a relentless storm of rain. I wanted to pull her from the cold earth, carry her to a home filled with light and heat and laughter, warm her to life again within my arms.

As my mind tossed about these foolish fancies, slow hot tears forced themselves into my eyes and scalded my cheeks as they fell. These tears relieved me. Gradually my tense nerves relaxed, and I recovered my composure. Turning deliberately away from the window, I knew where I was going. Left alone at last in my sleeping chamber, I remained for some time before actually going to bed. I took off the black spectacles which served me so well, and looked at myself in the mirror with curiosity. Without my smoke-colored glasses, I appeared what I was, young and vigorous in spite of my white hair. My face, once worn and haggard, had filled out. My eyes blazed with life. I wondered, as I stared moodily at my own reflection, how it was that I did not look ill. All the mental suffering I had experienced, my intense grief over Chiara's death, my gloomy satisfaction over my vendetta, should have destroyed my features.

I wondered what Dario would say, could he behold me, unmasked as it were, in the solitude of my own room. This thought roused another vision in my mind, a vision which made me smile grimly. I was a betrothed woman. Engaged to marry my own husband; to be wedded for the second time to the same man. What a difference between this and my first courtship. Then, I was a fool, adoring, passionate, and devoted. Now, I was utterly ruthless and I must remain that way, for I had nearly reached the pinnacle of my vendetta.

I pondered the coming days and watched the end approaching neither slow nor fast, but steadily and silently. I was able to calculate each event in its due order, and I knew there was no fear of failure in the final result. I had formerly been very weak, fooled by my husband and friend. But now my strength worked like a demon within me. My hand had already closed with an iron grip on two false, unworthy lives, and I swore never to relax, never to relent until I accomplished my vendetta. Heaven and earth had borne witness to my vow, and now held me to its strict fulfillment.

Chapter Seventeen

Winter in Vincenza arrived with full force. The chilly air depressed my spirits. The people became carefree, their mood unaffected by the change of seasons. They drank more freely and kept their feet warm by dancing into the small hours of the morning. The plague was finally a thing of the past; a cleansing for the entire population. The sanitary precautions, so widely recommended to prevent another outbreak, were all neglected. The population tripped lightly over the graves of its dead as though they were covered with flowers and long forgotten. They thought only for today, not for what happened yesterday, or for what would happen tomorrow. All that, they left to God.

I could understand their foolishness, for many of the world's bitterest miseries come from looking too often to the past or future, and of never living in the present.

Carnivale was approaching. Carnivale with all its festivities, would soon reel through the streets of Vicenza with picturesque, brilliant madness. I was reminded of this coming festivity on the morning of December 21st when I noticed Santina trying to control her expression. Despite her efforts, she kept smiling as though something funny had flitted across her mind. She betrayed herself at last by asking me whether I planned to take part in any of the festivities. I smiled and shook my head.

Santina looked dubious, but finally summoned up her courage. "Will the contessa permit—"

"By all means, go, partake of the foolishness with everyone else. Take your time, enjoy the fun."

She was so grateful, she attended to me even more fastidiously than usual.

"When does the carnival begin?" I asked.

"On the 26th," she answered, with a slight air of surprise. "Surely the contessa knows."

"*Si, si,*" I said, impatiently. "I know, but I had forgotten. I am not young enough to keep dates of such celebrations in my memory. What letters have you there?"

She handed me a small tray full of different shaped notes, some from women who *desired the honor of my company* and others from tradesmen who *desired the honor of my custom*. Toadies, all of them, I thought contemptuously, as I flipped through the letters. One special envelope, square in form and heavily bordered in black grabbed my attention. The postmark *Roma* stood out distinctly.

"Finally," I breathed, excited. I turned to Santina who was giving the final polish to my breakfast cup and saucer. "You may leave the room," I said.

She curtseyed, the door opened and shut noiselessly, and she was gone.

Slowly I broke the seal of that fateful letter; a letter from Beatrice Cardano, a warrant self-signed, for her own execution.

My dear friend,

You will guess by the black trim on my envelope the good news I have to give you. My uncle is dead at last, thank God, and I am left his sole heir unconditionally. I am free, and shall return to

Vicenza immediately, that is, as soon as some trifling law business has been completed with the executors. I believe I can arrange my return for December 23rd or 24th. Will you oblige me by not announcing this to Signore Gismondi as I wish to surprise him. Poor man. He must have been lonely without me, I am sure, and I wish to see the astonishment in his eyes when he first sees me after so long an absence. You can understand this, can you not, or does it seem silly to you? I know you will humor me in my desire that the news should be withheld from Dario. How delighted he will be and what a joyous Carnivale we will have this winter. I do not think I ever felt more light of heart. Perhaps it is because I am so much heavier in purse. I am glad of the money, as it places me on a more equal footing with him, and though all his letters to me have been full of tenderness, I believe he will think even more highly of me now that I am somewhat nearer to his own rank. As for you, my good Contessa, on my return I shall make it my first duty to pay back with interest the rather large debt I owe to you. Thus my honor will be satisfied, and you, I am sure, will have a better opinion of me.

Your friend to command,
Beatrice Cordano

I read the letter over and over, burning the words into my memory as though they were a living flame.

All his letters to me have been full of tenderness. Oh, the miserable duped nitwit, fooled as I had been. And Dario, the traitor, doing his best to prevent her from entertaining the slightest suspicion or jealousy of his actions during her absence. So, he *had* written her; no doubt *letters* sweet as honey brimming over with endearing words and vows of fidelity, even though he had already accepted me as his wife. God. What a devil's dance of death they played.

On my return I shall make it my first duty to pay back with interest the rather large debt I owe you. Rather large indeed, Beatrice, so large that you have no idea of its extent.

...thus my honor will be satisfied. And so will mine in part.

...and you, I am sure, will have a better opinion of me. Yours to command. Perhaps I shall, Beatrice, for I have many commands for you. Maybe when all my commands are fulfilled to the bitter end, I may think more kindly of you. But not till then.

I paused to think for a few minutes, and then sitting down, I penned the following note.

Cara amica,

I am delighted to hear of your good fortune, and still more enchanted to know you will soon enliven us all with your presence. I admire your plan to surprise Signore Gismondi, and will respect your wishes in the matter. But you must do me a small favor. Things have been very boring since you left, and I propose beginning the gaieties afresh by hosting a Christmas Eve dinner in honor of your return, and your new wealth and status in society. It will be a feast for women only. Therefore, I ask you to oblige me by ensuring you return on that day, and when you arrive in Vicenza, come straight to my apartment so that I may be the first to welcome you home, as you deserve. Send me your answer and the arrival hour of your coach, and I shall have my carriage meet you. The dinner-hour can be fixed to suit your convenience, of course, but perhaps eight o'clock may suit? After dinner, you may leave to go to Villa Mancini. Signore Gismondi's surprise will be keener for having been slightly delayed. Trusting you will not refuse to gratify an old woman's whim, I am,

Yours for the time being,
Giulia Corona

Having finished this note in the disguised penmanship I had so patiently honed, I folded, sealed, and addressed it.

Summoning Paolo, I bade him to post it immediately. As soon as he left, I returned to my breakfast and tried to eat as usual. But my thoughts were too lively for appetite. I counted on my fingers the days. There were only four, between me and what? One thing was certain. I must see my husband, or rather, my betrothed. I must see him this very day. I then began to consider how my courtship had progressed since that evening when he had declared he loved me.

I had seen him frequently, though not daily. His behavior had been sometimes affectionate, adoring, timid, gracious, and once or twice, passionately loving, though the latter, I had always coldly curbed. For though I could bear a great deal, any sham of sentiment on his part sickened me. It filled me with such loathing that I feared my pent-up wrath might break loose and compel me to kill him swiftly and suddenly as one crushes the head of a poisonous adder; an all-too-merciful death for someone like him. I preferred to woo him with gifts. He was always eager to take whatever gift I presented him. From a rare jewel to a new horse, he never refused anything. After all, his strongest passions were vanity and greed. Sparkling riches from Negri's pilfered hoard; trinkets specially chosen for him — chains of gold, leather pouches filled with silver, silk for a new shirt — he accepted them all with a covetous glee he did not bother to disguise. In fact, he made it clear that he expected such things from me.

After all, what did it matter to me? Of what value was anything I possessed other than to assist me in carrying out the punishment I had destined for him? I assessed him with critical coldness. I saw the depravity he craftily concealed beneath his false virtue. Every day he sunk lower in my eyes, and I wondered how I could ever have loved so coarse and noxious a man. Handsome he certainly was, and as shrewd as gamblers, who, in spite of their addiction, I now considered less vile than the man I had wedded.

Mere beauty of face and form can be bought as easily as one buys a flower, but the loyal heart, the pure soul, the inner strength, the lofty intelligence which makes a man special, these are not purchasable and seldom found by good women like me. Yet, how was it that I who now loathed the creature I had once loved, could not look upon his good looks without a foolish thrill of passion awaking within me — passion that carried murder, admiration that was almost brutal, feelings which I could not control, though I despised myself for experiencing them. There is weakness in the strongest of us, and wicked men know well where we are most vulnerable. One dainty pin-prick well-aimed and all barriers of caution and reserve are broken down. We are ready to fling away our souls for a smile or a kiss.

I lost no time that day in going to Villa Mancini. I drove there in my carriage, taking with me the usual love-offering, this time, a thick golden bracelet. I recalled the words Beatrice spoke to me after Chiara was born. How mysterious they had seemed to me then; how clear their meaning now. *But the world is always filled with suspicion. Jealousy's stiletto is ever ready to strike, justly or unjustly. Children are well versed in the ways of vice. Penitents confess to priests who are worse sinners than they are, and fidelity is often a farce.*

When I arrived, I found my fiancé in his bedchamber, attired in a wine-colored velvet robe. He sat in an easy-chair in front of a sparkling wood fire, reading. His attitude was one of ease and grace, but he sprung up as soon as his valet announced me, and came forward with his usual charming words of welcome as if he were a monarch receiving a subject. I presented the gift with a few complimentary words uttered for the benefit of the servant who lingered in the room, and then added in a lower tone, "I have news of importance. Can I speak to you privately?"

He smiled and motioned for me to take a seat, and then dismissed his valet.

As soon as the door closed behind the man, I spoke at once and to the point, scarcely waiting till my husband resumed his easy-chair before the fire. "I received a letter from Signorina Cardano."

He tensed slightly, but said nothing. He merely bowed his head and raised his arched eyebrows with a look of inquiry as if to say, 'Why should that concern me?'

I watched him through narrowed eyes. "She is coming back in two or three days." Here I smiled. "She says that you will be delighted to see her."

This time he half rose from his seat, his lips moved as though he wanted to say something, but he held his silence and sunk back into the velvet cushions, his face anxious.

"She will likely be distressed when she learns of our engagement. It may be better for me to be the one to tell her. I advise you to visit some friends for a few days, till she has time to get used to our betrothal and accept the fact that you have chosen me instead of her. Then you can return. What do you say?"

He pondered my question for a few moments. "I think that may be a good idea. Signorina Cardano can be rash and hot-tempered at times. But surely you shouldn't have to face her alone. She may insult or offend you when she learns the truth."

"Oh, don't worry about me," I said, quietly. "Besides, I can easily pardon any outburst of temper on her part, in fact, I expect it from her. To lose all hope of ever winning your love will most definitely set off her fury. Poor woman." I sighed and shook my head with benevolence. "By the way, she tells me she has received letters from you."

I asked this question carelessly, but it took him by surprise. He caught his breath and stared at me with an alarmed look. When he noticed my blank expression, he regained his composure.

"Oh, *si*. I wrote to her once or twice on matters of business connected with my late wife's affairs. Unfortunately, Carlotta made her responsible for some trivial matters. She has no doubt exaggerated the number of times I have written to her. How ill-mannered of her to do so."

I let his lie pass without response. I reverted to my original theme. "What do you think, then? Will you stay here or will you go away for a few days?"

He rose and approached me. "I can visit the monks at my old school in Padua. There, I can devote some time to rest and contemplation and can plan for our future. What do you think?" He seized my hands and held them hard.

"I think it is a fine idea. None of us knows what the future holds. We cannot tell whether life or death awaits us. It is always wise to prepare for the future. Go visit your old friends, the monks, by all means. I am sure they will be happy to see you again. Please let them know that I will visit you there once Beatrice's reaction has been smoothed into resignation. *Sì*, go to Padua and while there, pray for yourself and pray for the peace of your dead wife's soul for me. Earnest, unselfish prayers uttered by someone as good as you, will fly swiftly to Heaven. And as for Beatrice, have no fear. I promise you that she will not bother us any more."

"Ah, you do not know her," he murmured, lightly kissing my hands. "She'll not let me go so easily and may give you trouble."

"I know how to silence her," I said, releasing him as I spoke, and watching him as he stepped closer to me. "Besides, you never gave her reason to hope you would be together, therefore she has no reason to complain or be upset."

"True," he replied with an untroubled smile. "But I hate hurting anyone. When do you think I should leave for Padua?"

I marvelled at how he could lie so effortlessly. I shrugged my shoulders with an air of indifference. "We are not married yet, so you are free to choose your own time and can suit yourself," I said coldly.

"Then, I will leave today. The sooner the better. My instinct tells me that Beatrice may return before expected. *Sì*, it is better to go today."

I rose to take my leave. "Then you will need some time to prepare." I straightened my gown. "Please leave me the address of where you will be staying and do not forget to let the monks know I may be visiting."

"Of course," he replied.

"Enjoy your time with the monks."

"I most definitely will."

"And will you, an untainted soul, pray for me?" I asked with a satirical smile, which he did not see.

He raised his eyes to mine. "I will indeed."

"Thank you." I choked back my contempt and disgust at his hypocrisy.

He stood before me, his hair glittering in the mingled glow of the firelight and the wintery sunbeams that shone through the window. "A kiss before you go?" he asked.

Chapter Eighteen

For a moment I lost my composure. I scarcely remember now what I did. I know I clasped my arms around his neck. I know that I permitted him to kiss my lips, throat and brow, and in the fervor of our embrace, the thought of how vile he was came swiftly upon me. I pushed him away with such suddenness that he caught the back of a chair to regain his balance. His face was flushed and he looked astonished, yet certainly not displeased. No, he was not angry, but I was thoroughly annoyed, bitterly vexed with myself for being so foolish. "Forgive me," I muttered.

A smile stole round the corners of his mouth.

"I should be the one to apologize," he said. "It was I who kissed you." His smile deepened. Suddenly he broke into a hearty rippling laugh that pierced me to my soul. Was it not the same laughter that had ripped my heart in half the night I witnessed his passionate conversation with Beatrice in the avenue? Had not the cruel mockery of it nearly driven me mad? I could not endure it. I sprung to his side. He ceased laughing and looked at me in wide-eyed wonderment.

"Don't laugh like that. It upsets me. Once, long ago, I loved a man. He was not like you; he was a liar. He lied to me with every word he uttered. He used to laugh at me, too. He trampled on my life and spoiled it. He broke my heart. It is all in the past now, and I never think of him anymore, except now, your laughter reminded me of him." I paused, taking in his lack of expression. "It's time for you to get ready for your journey, is it not? Please let me know if I can help you in any way. Travel safely and may the peace of a pure conscience be with you."

I laid my burning hand on his head. He thought this gesture was a motherly blessing. I thought, well, God only knows what I thought, yet if curses can be so easily cast, then this curse had just marked him. I dared not trust myself any longer in his presence, and without another word or look, I left him and hurried from the villa.

I knew he was startled and at the same time gratified to think he had moved me to such emotion, but I refused to look back at him to catch his parting glance. I could not because I was sick of myself and of him, and was weary of my broken spirit, for which there could never be a cure.

Soon, I grew calmer and the drive back to the hotel in my carriage through the dull December air calmed and restored me. The day was lovely, bright and fresh. A soft haze lingered above Vicenza like a veil of gray. In the streets, women strolled, eager to purchase their daily fare. Children, ragged and dirty, ran along, pushing the luxuriant tangle of their dark locks away from their eyes with smiles. Bells clashed and clanged from the churches in honor of Saint Thomas, whose feast day it was, and the city had an air of gaiety about it.

As I drove along I saw a small crowd at a street corner. A laughing crowd was listening to a wandering bard. He was a plump-looking fellow who had captured their interest.

I asked Paolo to stop so that I could listen to his tale. When he was finished, I tossed him three *scudi*. He threw them up in the air, one after the other, and as they fell, he caught them in his mouth, appearing to have swallowed them all. Then with a grimace, he pulled off his tattered cap and said, "*Ancora affamato*, Excellenza. I am still hungry," amid the renewed laughter of his amused audience.

A merry bard he was, and without conceit. His good humor merited the extra silver pieces I gave him, which caused him to wish me, "*Buon appetito* and the smile of the Madonna upon you."

Further on I came upon a group of fisherman assembled round a portable stove upon which roasting chestnuts cracked their glossy sides and emitted savory odors. The men were singing to the strumming of an old *viola da mano*, a guitar-like instrument. The song they sang was familiar to me.

Where had I heard it? It took a moment for me to recall it. It was when I had crawled out of the vault through the brigand's hole, when my heart had bounded with joy at the anticipation of being reunited with my family, when I had believed in the worth of love and friendship, when I had seen the morning sun glittering on the world and celebrated my release from death and my restored freedom. It was then that I had heard a voice somewhere in the distance singing that song and I had fondly imagined its impassioned words were meant for me. But that was then and it seemed like an eternity ago.

Now, the song sounded hateful, bittersweet. I wanted to cover my ears to shut out the sound of it. It reminded me of a time when I possessed a heart, a throbbing, passionate, sensitive thing alive to emotion, tenderness, and affection. Now my heart was dead and cold as a stone. My soul was heavily burdened. All I yearned for now was justice – stern, immutable justice, and I meant to have it.

Many would find it difficult to understand all the planning and the carrying out of such a prolonged vendetta as mine. Many will find it incomprehensible. Many are

The Contessa's Vendetta

incapable of carrying a lengthy deadly resentment against an unfaithful husband. They are too indifferent or may think it is not worth their while. But I can carry a vendetta for a lifetime. Many will think this is immoral and unchristian. Did Christ forgive Judas? The gospel does not say so.

When I reached my rented villa, I felt exhausted. I decided to rest and receive no visitors that day. Paolo accompanied me inside. Just as I was about to dismiss him, a thought occurred to me. I went to a cabinet in the room and unlocked a secret cupboard. Inside was a bottle of rare wine. I removed it and handed it to Paolo. "It is a hundred year old wine from Monemasia, the Venetian fortress on the coast of Laconia."

He did not show the least sign of surprise as he studied the burgundy liquid inside the dusty green glassed bottle with its round body and long neck. He ran his hand delicately over the label delicately ornamented with foliate scroll-work.

"Good wine?" I remarked, in a casual manner.

He nodded and examined the bottle critically. "It needs dusting, Contessa."

"Good," I said, briefly. "Then wipe it and put it back in the cupboard. I may need to serve this particular bottle of wine soon."

The imperturbable Paolo bowed and prepared to leave the room.

"Stay a moment."

He turned.

I looked at him steadily. "I believe you are a loyal and faithful man, Paolo," I said.

He met my glance frankly.

"The day may come when I shall perhaps put your fidelity to the test," I said quietly.

His dark eyes, keen and clear the moment before,

flashed brightly and then grew humid. "Contessa, you have only to command. I was a soldier once. I know what duty means. But there is a better service — gratitude. I may be only a poor servant, but you have won my heart. I would give my life for you should you desire it." He paused, half ashamed of the emotion that threatened to break through his mask of impassibility. He bowed again and would have left me, but I called him back and held out my hand.

"Shake hands, dear friend," I said, simply.

He caught it with an astonished yet pleased look. Stooping, he kissed it before I could prevent him, and this time literally scrambled out of my presence with his usual dignity.

Alone, I considered this behavior of his with surprise. This loyal man evidently loved me, but I knew not why. I had done no more for him than any other mistress might have done for a good servant. I had often spoken to him with impatience, even harshness; and yet I had somehow won his heart, at least so he said. Why should he care for me? Why should my poor old steward, Giacomo, still cherish me so devotedly in his memory? Why should my dog Tito still love and obey me, when my nearest and dearest, my husband and my only friend had both forsaken me and were eager to forget me? Perhaps fidelity was not the fashion any longer. Perhaps it was a worn-out virtue, left to the most humble, the poor, the animals. I sighed wearily, and threw myself down into an arm-chair near the window to watch the carriages roll past, their riders garmented in colorful winter cloaks.

The brassy jingles of bells attracted my attention. In the street below my balcony I saw a young man singing and dancing. His voice was hauntingly beautiful, his ballads heartwrenching. But what attracted me was not his superior tone, but his wistful expression of pride. I could not help but watch him. When his dance concluded, a young woman, his companion, held and jingled silver bells with a bright but appealing smile. Silver *scudi* were freely flung to her on his behalf. I contributed my quota to the amount. All that she received, she emptied into a leather bag, earnings for the both of them. She was totally blind.

I knew the couple well, and had often seen them. Their story was a sad one. The young man had been betrothed to the girl. She had been renowned for her skill in delicate embroidery, having received work orders from the Vatican itself to adorn papal gowns and decorations. With these meagre earnings she helped support her widowed mother and six younger siblings. Her eyesight, painfully strained over her delicate labors, suddenly failed her. Before long, she became totally blind. She lost her ability to work and her family soon found themselves destitute. She offered to release him from their betrothal, but he would not leave her. He insisted on marrying her at once and devoted himself to her completely, body and soul.

To earn a living to support her and her family, he sang in the streets. He had a skilled artisan teach her to weave baskets so that she might have some independence and a way to earn a living should something ever happen to him. She sold these baskets so successfully that she was making good trade.

They were both so young. She was not much more than a child with a bright face glorified by the self-denial and courage of her everyday life. He was only a year or two older, with a gentle spirit and a kind heart. No wonder he had won the sympathy of the warmhearted people of Vicenza. They looked upon him as a romantic hero. When he passed through the streets, leading his blind wife tenderly by the hand, there was not a person in the entire city who would dare insult or offend them. They treated the couple with great respect because they were good, innocent, and true.

How was it, I wondered dreamily, that I could not have won a man's heart like his? Were the poor alone deserving of respect and faith, love and loyalty? Was there something in a life of wealth and luxury that destroyed one's morals or virtues? Evidently, education had little impact, for had not my husband been educated among an order of monks renowned for their books and knowledge, their life of simplicity and sanctity? And yet, he was evil itself. Nothing had eradicated it. For him, even religion was a sham. He went through the motions only to disguise the true extent of his malevolence and hypocrisy.

My own thoughts began to weary me. To distract myself, I picked up a book of poems and began to read. The day wore on slowly enough. I was glad when evening arrived, when Paolo, remarking that the night was chilly, kindled a pleasant wood-fire in my room, and lighted the lamps. A little while before my dinner was served he handed me a letter stating that Signore Gismondi's coachman had just delivered it. It bore my own seal, and I opened it.

Beloved,

I arrived here safely; the monks are delighted to see me, and you will be made heartily welcome when you come. I think of you constantly. How happy I felt this morning. You seemed to love me so little. Why are you not always so fond of your faithful,

Dario?

I crumpled the note and flung it into the leaping flames of the newly lighted fire. There was a faint scent of cologne about it that sickened me because it reminded me of the brand he preferred and which I always associated with him. I would not permit myself to think of this so *faithful Dario* as he called himself.

I resumed my reading, and continued it even at dinner, during which Paolo waited upon me with his usual silent gravity and decorum, though I could feel that he watched me with concern. I suppose I looked tired. I certainly felt so, and retired to bed unusually early. The time seemed to me so long. Would the end never come?

The next day dawned, trailing its boring hours after it, as a prisoner might trail his chain of iron fetters, until sunset. Then, when the gray winter sky began to darken, Paolo brought me a note; a few scrawled words, a hastily written note that stilled my impatience, roused my soul, and braced every nerve and muscle in my body to instant action. The words were plain, clear, and concise:

From Beatrice Cardano, Rome
To la Contessa Giulia Corona, Vicenza.

I shall be with you on the 24th. Coach arrives at 6:30 P.M. Will come to you as you desire without fail.

Chapter Nineteen

Christmas Eve. An extra chilly day fraught with frequent showers of stinging rain. Towards late afternoon, the weather cleared. Dull, gray clouds began to break apart, revealing gaps of pale blue sky and golden sunshine. Vendors proudly set up their tables displaying their wares. The shops were brilliant with displays of food and glittering items to suit all ages and needs; a tempting array from bonbons to jewelry. Nativity scenes with baby Jesus lying in his manger decorated shop windows. Round eyed children stared fondly at the waxen images.

I intended to prepare an elegant feast for the party to honor Beatrice. I had requisitioned all the best resources. The villa's cook had transferred her daily work to her underlings, and focused her culinary intelligence solely on producing the magnificent dinner I had ordered. Paolo, in spite of himself, broke into exclamations of wonder and awe as he listened to and wrote down my orders for different wines of the rarest kinds and choicest vintages. The servants rushed about to obey my various requests with looks of immense importance. Santina, took the setting of the table under her scrutiny. The talk everywhere was all about the grandeur of my forthcoming feast.

About six o'clock I sent my driver with the carriage to meet Beatrice as I had arranged. Then, I checked the dining hall to ensure the scenery, side-lights, and general effects were all in working order. The room was octagonal in shape, not too large, and I had it exquisitely decorated for the occasion. The walls were hung with draperies of gold-colored silk and crimson velvet and interspersed with long mirrors ornamented with crystal candelabra, in which twinkled hundreds of lights under rose-tinted glass shades. At the back of the room there was a small conservatory full of rare ferns and subtly perfumed exotic plants, in the center of which a fountain flowed melodiously. Here, later on, a band of stringed instruments and a boys' choir would perform, so that sweet music might be heard without the performers being visible. One of the long French windows of the room was left uncurtained, simply draped with velvet as one drapes a painting, and through it my guests would be able to enjoy a perfect view of Vicenza in the wintery moonlight.

The dinner-table, laid for fifteen persons, glittered with silver cutlery, Venetian glass, and rare flowers grown in elite conservatories. The floor was carpeted with velvet pile, in which some grains of ambergris had been scattered. When walking over it, one's feet sunk into the softness, rich with the perfume of spring blossoms. The very chairs where my guests would sit were luxurious and softly stuffed, so that they could lean back or recline at ease. Everything was arranged with a lavish splendor befitting the banquet of the highest nobility, and yet with such accurate taste that no detail was omitted.

I was more than satisfied and returned to my room where Santina waited to help me dress for the party. Afterwards, I returned to the dining hall where I found Paolo wiping water stains from crystal wine glasses set on a tray on a sideboard.

"Paolo."

He tensed. "Contessa?"

"Tonight you will stand behind my chair and assist in serving the wine."

"*Sì*, Contessa."

"You will attend particularly to Sigorina Cardano, who will sit at my right hand. The rare wine in the cabinet I showed you earlier is meant only for her and no one else, not even me."

"Of course, Contessa."

"And take care to ensure that her glass is never empty."

"As you wish, Contessa."

"Whatever may be said or done," I went on, quietly, "you will show no sign of alarm or surprise. From the start of dinner, unless I tell you otherwise, your place is to remain by me, serving only Signorina Cardano."

He looked a little puzzled. "*Sì*, Contessa."

I smiled, and advancing, laid my hand on his arm. "Is the rare wine bottle wiped down and set out, Paolo?"

"It is ready, Contessa," he replied. "It sits ready in your cabinet."

"Good. You can leave me now and arrange the salon to receive my friends," I said with a satisfied gesture.

I looked into a gilded mirror that hung on one wall and studied my appearance, which I had taken particular care with. For this evening, I had commissioned a most extravagant gown in a silver-colored silk embroidered with a rich, floral pattern in gold and silver thread. Gems and pearls decorated the entire gown from bodice to hem. Tiers of delicate gold cloth formed my sleeves, which ran to my elbows. Around my neck I wore gold choker with a pear shaped pendant studded with diamonds. A set of matching earings decorated my ears. A jeweled and feathered hair ornament in my neatly coifed hair matched the color of my gown. The dress was a work of art in itself. The garment became me, almost too well, I thought.

It would have been better for my purposes if I could have appeared older and more serious.

While I waited, I sat and quietly read a book.

I had scarcely finished reading the first page when the rumbling of wheels in the courtyard outside made the hot blood rush to my face, and my heart beat with feverish excitement. I waited in the room, composed. The doors were flung open and a servant announced Signorina Cardano.

She entered smiling, her face alight with good humor and enthusiasm. She looked more beautiful than usual wearing a new mantle and matching travelling gown the color of the reddest wine. How appropriate and ironic for what was to come this evening, I thought.

"Here I am," she exclaimed, taking my hands enthusiastically in her own. "My dear Contessa, I am delighted to see you. What an excellent friend you are. A generous-hearted woman who always strives to make others happy. And how are you? You look remarkably well."

"I can return the compliment," I said, gaily. "You are more radiant than ever."

She laughed, well pleased, and sat down, drawing off her gloves and loosening her traveling cloak.

"Well, I suppose plenty of money puts a woman in good spirits and health," she replied. "But dear Contessa, you are beautifully dressed for dinner, and I am still in my travelling clothes. I am positively unfit to be in your company. You insisted that I should come to you directly on my arrival, but I really must change my clothes. Your man took my valise; in it are my dress-clothes for this evening. I shall not be long in putting them on."

"I know how you enjoy a glass a wine before dinner. Share one with me first," I said, pouring out some of her favorite wine. I glanced at the cabinet where the special wine waited. *Soon, my dear Beatrice, very soon you will enjoy the finest of wines; a bottle I have already opened and prepared solely for you.* "There is plenty of time. It is barely seven, and we do not dine till eight."

She took the wine from my hand and smiled.

I returned the smile. "It gives me great pleasure to receive you, Beatrice. I have been impatient for your return, almost as impatient as—"

She paused in the act of drinking, and her eyes flashed delightedly. "As Dario has been? How I long to see him again. I swear to you, I would have gone straight to the Villa Mancini had I heeded my own desire, but I promised you I would come here first. The evening you have planned will do just as well," she laughed with a covert meaning in her laughter. "Perhaps even better."

My hands clinched. "Why certainly. The evening will be much better," I said with forced gaiety. "You will find him the same as ever, perfectly well and perfectly charming. It must be his sincerity and clear conscience that makes him even more handsome. It may be a relief for you to know I am the only woman he has allowed to visit him during your absence."

"Thank goodness for that." Beatrice devoutly sipped her wine. "And now tell me, my dear Contessa, who is coming tonight? After all I am more in the mood for dinner than romance."

I burst out laughing harshly. "Of course. Every sensible woman prefers a delightful meal to a good man. Who are my guests you ask? I believe you know them all. First, there is Federica Marina."

"Federica? Goodness," interrupted Beatrice. "A haughty woman who challenges anything or anyone. Can she lower herself enough to share a meal with all of us?"

I ignored this interruption. "Anna Fraschetti and Emilia Giulano will also join us."

The Contessa's Vendetta

Beatrice laughed. "Emilia drinks too much, and if she mixes her wines, she may strike out at any of the servers before the dinner is half over."

"In drinking and mixing wines," I returned, coolly, "she will but imitate your own example, *cara mia*."

"Ah, but I can tolerate it," she said. "She cannot. Few women in Vicenza are like me."

I watched her narrowly, and went on with the list of my invited guests. "After these, comes Louisa Freccia."

"What! That raging bible devourer?" exclaimed Beatrice. "Every second word that comes out of her mouth is religious in some way."

"And the illustrious Cristina Dulci and Antonia Biscardi, aspiring artists like yourself," I continued.

She frowned slightly, and then smiled. "There was a time when I envied their talent. Now I can afford to be generous. They are welcome to the whole field of art as far as I am concerned. I have said farewell to the brush and palette. I shall never paint again."

True enough, I thought, eying the shapely white hand with which she stroked her cheek; the same hand on which my family diamond ring glittered like a star. She looked up suddenly.

"Go on, Contessa, I am all impatience. Who comes next?"

"More haughty mannered women, as I suppose you would call them," I answered. "Gilda D'Avencorta and Eugenia d'Angelo."

Beatrice looked astonished. "Goodness," she exclaimed. "They are the most bitter of enemies. Together in one room? Your choice surprises me."

"I thought they were your friends," I said, composedly. "If you remember, you introduced me to them. As for their enmity, my dinner table is no battlefield and will scarcely encourage any bitter discussions between them."

Beatrice laughed. "Well, no, but these young women would love to make it one. They will pick a quarrel for the mere lifting of an eyebrow. And the rest of your guests?"

"Are the inseparable sisters, Carla and Francesca Respetti, Elizabetta Mancona, Luciana Salustri, poet and musician, and the fascinating Ippolita Gualdro, whose conversation, as you know, is very charming. I have only to add," and I smiled half mockingly, "the name of Beatrice Cardano, a most true and loyal friend, and the party is complete."

"Fifteen in all including yourself," said Beatrice counting them on her fingers. "With such good company and a hostess who will entertain us like queens, we shall have a grand evening. And did you organize this banquet, merely to welcome back so unworthy a person as myself?"

"Solely and entirely for that reason," I replied. "And to introduce you into the higher ranks of society now that you are a wealthy woman."

She jumped up from her chair and clapped her two hands on my shoulders. "But why, in the name of the saints or the devil, have you taken such an interest in me?"

"Why have I taken such an interest in you?" I repeated, slowly. "My dear Beatrice, I am surely not alone in my admiration. Doesn't everyone like you? Are you not a favorite at dinner parties and social gatherings? Have you not told me that your late friend the Contessa Mancini held you as her dearest friend in all the world after her husband? Why do you underrate yourself?"

She let her hands fall slowly from my shoulders and a look of pain contracted her features. After a little silence she said, "Carlotta again. How her name and memory haunt me. I told you she was a fool. It was part of her foolishness that she loved me too well, perhaps. Do you know I have thought of her often lately?"

"Indeed?" and I feigned to be absorbed in

straightening a ribbon on my sleeve. "Why is that?"

A serious, meditative look softened the usually defiant brilliancy of her eyes. "I saw my uncle die," she continued, speaking in a low tone. "He was an old man and had very little strength left, yet his battle with death was horrible. I still see him, his yellow convulsed face, his twisted limbs, his claw-like hands tearing at the empty air, the ghastly grim and dropped jaw, the wide-open glazed eyes. It sickened me."

"Well, well," I said in a soothing way, still busy with arranging my ribbon. I secretly wondered what new emotion was at work in the volatile mind of my victim. "No doubt it was distressing to witness, but you could not have been very sorry. He was an old man, and, though it is an experience not worth repeating, we must all die."

"Sorry?" exclaimed Beatrice, talking more to herself than to me. "I was glad. He was an old scoundrel, deep into every sort of social villainy. No, I was not sorry, but as I watched him in his frantic struggle, fighting furiously for each fresh gasp of breath, I do not know why, but I thought of Carlotta."

Profoundly astonished, but concealing my shock beneath an air of indifference, I laughed. "Upon my word, Beatrice. Pardon me for saying so, but the air of Rome seems to have somewhat obscured your mind. I confess I cannot follow your meaning."

She sighed uneasily. "I dare say not. I scarce can follow it myself. But if it was so hard for an old man to writhe himself out of life, what must it have been like for Carlotta. We were friends; we used to walk arm-in-arm, and she was young and full of vitality; stronger, too, than I am. She must have fought death with every muscle and nerve in her body." She stopped and shuddered. "By Heaven, death should be made easier. It is a frightful thing."

Contempt arose in me. Was she a coward as well as traitor? I touched her lightly on the arm. "Excuse me if I say that this depressing conversation is tiring. I cannot accept it as suitable for our dinner party. And permit me to remind you that you have yet to get dressed."

My gentle sarcasm made her look up and smile. Her face cleared, and she passed her hand over her forehead, as though she swept it free of some unpleasant thought. "I believe I am nervous," she said with a half laugh. "For the last few hours I have experienced an ominous foreboding, and I can't seem to rid myself of it."

"No wonder," I returned carelessly. "You have been through a terrible time. Besides, the Eternal City smells of death. Shake the dust of the Caesars from your feet, and enjoy your life, while it lasts."

"Excellent advice," she said, smiling, "and not difficult to follow. Now I must get dressed for the party. Have I your permission?"

I tinkled the bell which summoned Santina, and bade her to assist Signorina Cardano. Beatrice disappeared with her escort with a laugh and a nod as she left the room.

I watched her leave with strange pity; the first emotion of the kind that had awakened in me for her since I learned of her treachery. Her allusion to that time when we had been young girls together, when we had walked arm-in-arm, had affected me more than I cared to admit. It was true, we had been happy then, two careless young girls with all the world before us. Dario had not yet darkened our world; he had not yet entered my life with his false face to turn me into a blind, doting madwoman, and to transform Beatrice into a liar and hypocrite. All this was his fault. All the misery and horror; he was the blight on our lives. He merited the heaviest punishment, and he would receive it. Oh, if only neither of us had ever met him. His good looks, like a sword, had severed the bonds of friendship between us; a bond stronger and more tender than the love of man.

Any regrets were useless now. The evil was done, and there was no undoing it. I had no time left to reflect. Each moment that passed brought me nearer to the end I had planned for them both.

Chapter Twenty

At about a quarter to eight my guests began to arrive. One by one they entered, all except the two Respetti sisters. While we waited for them, Beatrice made her grand entrance. She swept into the room with the confidence and charm of a beautiful woman who knows she is looking her best. The guests all greeted her enthusiastically, welcoming her back to Vicenza. Most of the guests were old friends of Contessa Mancini who were now eager to meet Contessa Corona. So they embraced and kissed Beatrice on both cheeks, all except for Federica Marina, who merely bowed her head with courtesy and asked about certain families of distinction who lived in Rome.

Beatrice was replying with her usual grace and ease, when Santina brought me a note marked *Immediate*. It contained an elegantly worded apology from Carla Respetti, who informed me that an unforeseen matter would prevent her and her sister from dining with us that evening. I therefore rang my bell as a sign that the dinner need no longer be delayed. Turning to my guests, I announced the absence of the two sisters.

"A pity Francesca cannot come," said Louisa Freccia, twirling one end of a long curl that cascaded from the right side of her coif. "She loves good wine, and, better still, good company."

The Contessa's Vendetta

"My dear Louisa," broke in the musical voice of Ippolita Gualdro, "you know that our Francesca goes nowhere without her beloved sister, Carla. Carla cannot come, so Francesca will not. Would that all women were so respectful and so close to each other."

"If they were," laughed Luciana Salustri, rising from the piano where she had been playing softly, "half the world would be at peace. You, for instance," turning to Gilda D'Avencorta, "would scarcely know how to occupy your time."

Gilda waved her hand in disapproval. "It is an impossible dream for all women to socialize as equals. Look at the differences in our births, breeding, and education. That is what makes us noble and different. We cannot be forced down to the lowest level of working class women. I do not think we could help them even if we wanted to."

"You are quite right," said Beatrice. "You cannot ask a race horse to pull a plow. I have always imagined that the first quarrel between Cain and Abel must have happened because of a difference in status as well as jealousy. Perhaps Abel was a negro and Cain a white man, or vice versa, which would account for the antipathy existing between the two races to this day."

Federica Marina coughed a stately cough, and shrugged her shoulders. "That first quarrel, as related in the Bible, was exceedingly vulgar. It must have been an unpleasant fight."

Ippolita Gualdro laughed delightedly. "So like you, Federica to say that. I sympathize with your sentiments. Imagine the butcher Abel piling up his reeking carcasses and setting them on fire, while on the other side stood Cain the green-grocer frizzling his cabbages, turnips, carrots, and other vegetable matter. What a spectacle. I myself prefer the smell of roasted vegetables to the rather disagreeable odor of scorching meat."

We laughed, and at that moment the door was thrown open. "Dinner is served," announced Paolo in a solemn tone befitting his dignity.

I led the way to the dining room. My guests followed talking and jesting among themselves. They were all in high good humor. None of them had yet noticed the bad omen caused by the absence of the Respetti sisters. But I had. My guests now numbered thirteen instead of fifteen. Thirteen at table! For anyone who was superstitious, it meant some misfortune would befall one of us. I wondered if any of my guests were superstitious? Beatrice was not, I knew, unless her nerves had been shaken after watching her uncle die. At any rate, I decided to say nothing to call attention to the circumstance. If any one should notice it, it would be easy to make light of it and of all similar superstitions.

I was the one most affected by it, for it had a curious and deadly significance. I was so pre-occupied thinking about it, that I scarcely listened to Federica Marina, who, walking beside me, seemed to be talking more than usual.

We reached the dining room doors, which were thrown wide in anticipation of our arrival. Delightful strains of music met our ears as we entered. Murmurs of astonishment and admiration broke from all the ladies as they viewed the lovely scene before them. I pretended not to hear their praise as I took my seat at the head of the table. Beatrice sat on my right and Federica Marina on my left. The music sounded louder and more triumphant, and while all the guests were seating themselves in the places assigned to them, a choir of young fresh voices broke forth in an aria.

An enthusiastic clapping of hands rewarded the unseen vocalists. When the music ceased, the conversation turned to general matters.

"By heaven," exclaimed Beatrice, "if that was meant as a welcome to me, *amica*, all I can say is that I do not deserve it. Why, it is more fitting for the welcome of one queen to another."

"Who better than for honest women like us to embrace and honor each other?" I asked. "Let us hope we are worthy of each other's esteem."

She flashed a bright look of gratitude and fell silent, listening to the compliments uttered by Federica Marina about my exquisitely arranged table.

"You must have traveled in the East, Contessa," said Federica. "Your banquet reminds me of an Oriental romance I once read, called *Vathek*."

"That's it exactly," exclaimed Beatrice "I think the contessa is much like Vathek."

"Hardly," I said, smiling coldly. "I lay no claim to supernatural experiences. The realities of life are sufficiently wonderful for me."

Antonia Biscardi, the painter, a refined, gentle-featured woman, looked at us and said modestly, "I think you are right, Contessa. The beauties of nature and of humanity are so varied and profound that were it not for our never-ending longing for immortality, I think we would be perfectly satisfied with this world as it is."

"You speak like an artist and a woman of even temperament," broke in Ippolita Gualdro, who had finished her soup quickly in order to be able to talk, talking being her chief delight. "For me, I am never content. I never have enough of anything. That is my nature. When I see lovely flowers, I wish I had more of them. When I behold a fine sunset, I yearn for many more such sunsets. When I look upon a handsome man—"

"You would have lovely men surrounding you ad infinitum," laughed Eugenia d'Angelo.

"And why not?" questioned Ippolita Gualdro. "Just

like a hot-house, where one is free to wander every day, sometimes gathering a gorgeous lily, sometimes a simple violet, and sometimes—"

"A thorn?" suggested Luciana Salustri.

"Well, perhaps," laughed Ippolita Gualdro. "I would gladly take the risk in order to find the perfect rose."

Elizabetta Mancona looked up. She was a thin woman with keen eyes and a shrewd face, which at a first glance appeared stern, but could with the least provocation, break into hearty laugher. "There is undoubtedly something fascinating about the idea," she observed in her typical precise way. "I have always believed that arranged marriages are a great mistake."

"So that is why you have never married. You are waiting for a love match," commented Beatrice with amusement.

"And what if I am?" Elizabetta Mancona's serious expression began to relax under her mocking wit. "I have decided that I will never be bound by the law to kiss only one man. Rather, I can kiss them all until I find the right one."

Merry laughter greeted this remark, which Beatrice did not seem inclined to take part in. "All?" she said with a dubious air. "You mean all except the married ones?"

Elizabetta surveyed her with comic severity. "When I said all, I meant all," she returned. "The married ones in particular. They need special attention, and often seek it out. And why not? Their wives have likely ceased to be amorous after the first months of marriage."

I burst out laughing. "You are very right, Elizabetta," I said. "And even if the wives are foolish enough to continue to deny them their bodies, the men deserve to be duped. And they usually are. Come, *amica*," I added, turning to Beatrice. "Those are your own sentiments, for you have often confided them to me."

The Contessa's Vendetta

She smiled uncomfortably, and her brows contracted. I could see that she was annoyed. To change the conversation I signalled for the music to recommence. Instantly, the melody of a *passacaglia* dance floated through the room. The dinner was now fairly on its way. The appetites of my guests were stimulated and tempted by the choicest, most savory meats and vegetables, prepared with all the skill of my first rate chef. Good wine also flowed freely.

Paolo obediently followed my instructions. He stood behind my chair, and seldom moved except to refill Beatrice's glass with the contents of the designated wine bottle. Beatrice was a self-disciplined and careful woman who was wise enough to know never to mix wines. She always liked to remain faithful to the first beverage she had selected. So she partook freely of the special wine Paolo kept pouring into her glass, without its causing the slightest flush to appear on her pale aristocratic features. The wine's warm, mellow flavor brightened her eyes and loosened her tongue enough that she spoke elegantly and often.

The merriment increased as the various courses were served. Bouts of laughter often interrupted the loud buzz of conversation, mingling with the clinking of glasses and clattering of porcelain. Every now and then Louisa Freccia sharing a favorite rumor, or Luciana Salustri recited a poem to give variance to the constant chatter about trite matters. I did my part to keep the banter light-hearted, though I mostly divided my conversation between Beatrice and Federica Marina, paying close attention to both, but especially to Beatrice.

We had reached that stage of the banquet when the game course was about to be served. The invisible choir of boys' voices had just completed an enchanting song, when a stillness, strange and unaccountable, fell upon us; a pause, an ominous hush, as though someone of supreme importance had suddenly entered the room and commanded everyone to be silent.

No one spoke or moved. The very footsteps of the waiters were muffled by the velvet carpet. No sound was heard except for the splash of the fountain as it flowed among the ferns and flowers. The moon, shining frostily white through the one uncurtained window, cast a long pale ray against one side of the velvet hangings; a spectral effect which was enhanced by the garish glitter of the wax candles.

The women glanced at each other with a sort of uncomfortable embarrassment, and somehow, though I wanted to speak and break the spell, I was at a loss, and could not find suitable words. Beatrice toyed with her wine-glass mechanically. Federica Marina appeared absorbed in arranging the crumbs beside her plate into little methodical patterns. The stillness seemed to last so long that it was like a suffocating heaviness in the air.

Suddenly Paolo, in his duties as steward, pulled out the cork of a champagne bottle with a loud pop.

It startled us all and Ippolita Gualdro burst out laughing. "Oh, dear," she cried. "At last we woke up. We must have all been struck dumb, staring at the tablecloth so persistently and with such gravity. May Saint Anthony and his pig preserve me, but for a brief moment in time, I dreamed I was attending a banquet with the dead."

"And you managed to hold your tongue, which is a miracle in itself," laughed Luciana Salustri. "Have you heard the legend about a sudden silence in the midst of a celebration? It is said that an angel enters, blessing everyone as he passes through."

"That story is more ancient than the church," said Elizabetta Mancona. "Nobody believes in angels anymore. These days, we call them men instead."

"*Brava*," cried Eugenia d'Angelo. "Your sentiments are the same as mine, with a very small difference. You believe men are angels, but I know them to be real devils, but I don't want to quarrel with you over such a small difference in interpretation." She raised her glass. "*Saluti*," and she sipped her wine nodding to Elizabetta Mancona, who followed her example.

"Perhaps," said the smooth voice of Louisa Freccia, "our silence was caused by the consciousness that something is amiss with our party. It is only a small inequity, which I dare say our hostess has not thought it worth mentioning."

Every head turned in my direction and then back to Louisa.

"What do you mean?"

"What inequality?"

"Explain yourself."

The questions were asked nearly all at once.

"Really it is nothing." Louisa lazily admired the dainty portion of pheasant just placed before her. "I assure you, only the uneducated would care about it. The Respetti sisters are to blame. Their absence tonight has caused the problem, but why should I upset us. I am not superstitious, but maybe some of you are."

"Oh, I see what you mean," gasped Luciana Salustri. "There are thirteen of us seated around this table. Oh, *Dio*, what a horrific omen!"

Chapter Twenty-One

At Louisa's exclamation, my guests looked warily at each other, and they were counting the number for themselves. They were intelligent, sophisticated women, but superstition ran deep in their blood. All, with the exception of Louisa Freccia and the ever-unruffled Gilda d'Avencorta, were definitely uneasy.

Beatrice also seemed bothered. She appeared tense and her face was flushed. Seizing her never-empty glass, she swallowed its contents thirstily, in two or three gulps as though attacked by fever, and pushed away her plate with a trembling hand.

I raised my voice and addressed my guests. "Our dear friend Luciana Salustri is perfectly correct, ladies. I noticed the discrepancy in our number the moment I learned the Respetti sisters could not attend, but I knew that you are all modern women who are not constrained by silly superstitions. Therefore I did not mention it earlier. The idea that misfortune might befall one of us because we are thirteen is ludicrous. As you are aware, the belief stems from the story of the Last Supper, where it was once believed that like Judas Iscariot, one out of the thirteen at the table must be a traitor and doomed to die. But we know better. None of us here tonight has any reason to worry. We are all good friends and kindred hearts, and I cannot believe this will affect anyone here. Remember also

The Contessa's Vendetta

that this is Christmas Eve, the most holy of evenings."

A murmur of applause and a hearty clapping of hands rewarded my speech.

Ippolita Gualdro sprung to her feet. "We are not terrified old women to shiver on the edge of a worn-out omen. Fill your glasses, ladies. To the health of our noble hostess, Contessa Giulia Corona." She waved her glass in the air three times. Everyone followed her example and drank the toast with enthusiasm.

I bowed my head in gratitude and the superstitious dread which had seized my guests passed. They resumed their conversations, merriment, and laughter, and soon it seemed as though the unpleasant incident was entirely forgotten.

Only Beatrice continued to be ill at ease, but even her disquiet slowly disappeared. Influenced by the quantity of wine she had drank, she began to talk boastfully of her new wealth, gowns, and jewels.

Soon Federica Marina became disgusted with her. She eyed Beatrice with an ill-disguised impatience that bordered on contempt.

I, on the contrary, listened to everything she said with civility, humoring her, and drawing her out as much as possible. I smiled smugly at her brash retorts. When she said something that was more than usually outrageous, I gave her a charitable shake of my head.

The dessert was now served, and the wine continued to flow. Paolo kept Beatrice's glass filled from the contents of the special green bottle, while the others shared the costly wines poured by the hired waiters. The result of all this wine was that the more reserved among us now became the most uproarious.

Antonia Biscardi, a quiet and modest painter, together with Cristina Dulci, usually the shyest of all, suddenly became animated, and uttered blatant nothings concerning their art. Louisa Freccia argued with Gilda d'Avencorta, both speakers emphasizing their points by thrusting their dessert-knives into the ripe peaches they had on their plates. Luciana Salustri sat back in her chair, her head reclining on the velvet cushions, and recited one of her poems in a low tone, caring little or nothing whether anyone was listening or not. The slick tongue of Ippolita Gualdro ran on incessantly, though she frequently forgot what she was talking about and became trapped in a maze of contradictory statements. The rather large nose of Elizabetta Mancona reddened as she laughed at nothing in particular. In short, the table had become a glittering whirlpool of exhilaration and intense silliness.

Federica Marina and myself were the only ones who remained composed. After the first glass of wine, she had declined any more, and as for me, I had not taken more than half a glass of a mild Chianti.

I glanced at my boisterous guests and noted their flushed faces, rapid gestures, and vibrant voices. I inhaled a long, deep breath, for I knew that in a mere two or three minutes, I would make my move.

I observed Beatrice closely. She had moved her chair a little further from mine, and was saying something confidential to Eugenia d'Angelo. Beatrice's voice was low and thick, yet distinct as she spoke about the charms of a particular man. What man, I did not stop to consider, but then it struck me that she was describing the physical perfections of my husband to Eugenia, the most inexhaustible of gossipers I had ever encountered in my life.

My blood rapidly boiled. To this day I recall how it throbbed in my temples, leaving my hands and feet icy cold. I rose from my seat, and tapped on the table to call for everyone's attention, but the clatter of tongues was so great that I could not make myself heard. Federica Marina tried to silence the crowd on my behalf, but in vain. At last, my attempts attracted Beatrice's notice. She turned round, and seizing a dessert knife, beat it against her plate so persistently that the loud laughter and conversation ceased.

The moment had come. I raised my head, fixed my spectacles more firmly over my eyes, gave Beatrice a covert glance, and prepared to speak. She had sunk back again lazily in her chair and was taking another sip of her special wine.

"My friends," I said, meeting their inquiring looks with a smile. "I wish to interrupt your mirth for a moment; not to restrain it, but to enhance it. I asked you all here tonight, as you know, to honor me by your presence and to welcome our friend, Signorina Beatrice Cardano."

Here I was interrupted by a loud clapping of hands and exclamations, while Beatrice murmured cordially between sips of wine. "You honor me too much, Contessa, too much."

I gave Beatrice a contrived smile and resumed. "This young and accomplished woman, who is, I believe, a favorite with you all, has been away for several weeks because of an urgent matter. I am certain she is aware of how much we have missed her pleasant company, but I am pleased to say that she has returned to Vicenza a richer woman than when she left. Fortune has done her justice, and now that she is abundantly wealthy, she is now free to enjoy all the rewards due to her."

The guests clapped again in agreement. Beatrice acknowledged them all with a casual, smug nod.

I glanced at her again. How tranquil she looked reclining among the crimson cushions of her chair, a brimming glass of wine beside her, and her lovely face upturned as she looked half drowsily at the uncurtained window through which the city glittered in the moonlight.

"I assembled you here tonight not only to welcome and congratulate Signorina Cardano on her good fortune, as you have done, but also for another reason which I shall now explain to you. It is something that concerns me and my future happiness, and I am certain you will offer me your good wishes."

Everyone remained silent, intent on my every word. "What I am about to say," I went on, calmly, "may very possibly surprise you. I have been known to you as a woman of few words, and, I fear, of abrupt and brusque manners."

I paused for cries of, "No, no," mingled with various compliments and assurances. I nodded with a gratified air, and waited for silence to be restored. "None of you would think me the sort of woman to catch a gentleman's fancy."

My guests exchanged looks of curiosity. Beatrice set down her wine glass and stared at me in blank astonishment.

"Old as I am, and a half-blind invalid besides," I continued, "it seems incredible that any man would look at me more than once in passing. But I have met a fine man who has found me not displeasing. In short, I am going to be married soon."

There was a pause. Beatrice rose slightly and seemed about to speak, but apparently changed her mind. She remained silent, but her face had turned pale. Hesitation among my guests passed quickly and everyone, except Beatrice, broke out with congratulatory words.

I remained standing, leaning my two hands on the table before me. "I am known for my aversion to men, but when one of the handsomest men goes out of his way to court me and show his fascination for me, when he honors me with special gifts and makes me aware that I am not too daring in my desire to wed him, what can I do but accept my good fortune with grace. I would be the most ungrateful of women were I to refuse so precious a gift from Heaven, and I confess I do not feel inclined to reject the opportunity that has presented itself to me. I therefore hope for your good wishes for happiness with my future husband."

Ippolita Gualdro sprung to her feet and raised her glass high in the air. Every woman followed her example. Beatrice rose to her feet unsteadily, her countenance pale, while the hand that held her full wine glass trembled uncontrollably.

"You will, of course, honor us by disclosing the name of the handsome man whom we will soon toast?" Federica Marina asked.

"I was about to ask the same question," said Beatrice, her voice hoarse, her lips dry. She appeared to have some difficulty in speaking. "Possibly we are not acquainted with him?"

"On the contrary," I returned, eying her steadily with a cool smile. "You all know his name well. To the health of my betrothed, Signore Dario Gismondi."

"Liar!" shouted Beatrice, and with a madwoman's fury, she dashed her brimming glass of wine at my chest. I stood tall and perfectly calm, wiping the rivulets of wine that dripped from my throat and down onto my gown with my napkin. The glass struck the table as it fell, splitting into shards.

"Are you mad or drunk, Beatrice?" cried Eugenia d'Angelo, seizing her by the arm. "Do you know what you have done?"

Beatrice glared about like a lioness at bay. Her face was flushed and swollen like that of someone suffering apoplexy. She was perspiring profusely. Her breath came and went hard as though she had been running. She turned her eyes upon me. "You whore," she muttered through clinched teeth, and then suddenly raising her voice to a positive shriek, she cried, "I will have your blood if I have to tear your heart for it!" Beatrice sprung at me.

Eugenia d'Angelo grabbed her by the arm arm and pulled her back. "Not so fast, not so fast, *cara*," she said, coolly. "What devil possesses you, that you insult our hostess?"

"Ask her," Beatrice slurred fiercely, struggling to release herself from Eugenia's grip. "She knows well enough. Ask her!"

All eyes were turned to me. I remained silent.

"The contessa is not obliged to give any explanation," remarked Louisa Freccia.

"I assure you, I am ignorant of the cause of such an acute reaction, except perhaps that Signorina Cardano aspires to wed my betrothed," I said.

For a moment I thought Beatrice might choke.

"Aspires!" she gasped. "Hear her. Hear the miserable bitch."

"*Basta*. That's enough," Elizabetta Mancona exclaimed scornfully. "You must be more sensible, Beatrice. Why quarrel with an excellent friend for the sake of a man who happens to prefer her to you. Men are plentiful, good friends are few."

"If," I resumed, still wiping the stains of wine from my gown, "Signorina Cardano's extraordinary display of temper is the outcome of disappointment, I am willing to excuse it. She is young and hotblooded. Let her apologize, and I shall freely pardon her."

"By my faith," said Federica Marina with indignation. "Such generosity is unheard of, Contessa. Permit me to say that it is altogether exceptional, after such an undignified and callous act."

Beatrice looked from one to the other in silent fury. Her face had grown pale as death. She wrenched herself from Eugenia d'Angelo's grasp. "Let me go," she said, savagely. "None of you are on my side. I see that." She stepped to the table, held out a glass to Paolo, who poured more wine from the green bottle into it and drank heartily from it. She then turned and faced me, her head thrown back, her eyes blazing with wrath and pain. "Liar. You two-faced filthy liar. You have stolen him. You have fooled me, but, you shall pay for it."

"Willingly," I said, with a mocking smile. I gestured with my hand to restrain the shocked exclamations of my other guests who obviously resented this fresh attack. "But excuse me if I fail to see how you consider yourself wronged. The man who is now my betrothed has not the slightest affection for you. He told me so himself. Had he experienced any such feelings I would never have never accepted his proposal, but as matters stand, what harm have I done you?"

A chorus of indignant voices interrupted me. "Shame on you, Beatrice Cardano," cried Ippolita Gualdro. "The contessa is right. Were I in her place, I would give you no explanation whatever. I would not have condescended to discuss it with you at all."

"Nor I," sniffed Federica Marina, stiffly.

"Nor I," said Elizabetta Mancona.

"Surely, Beatrice, you will make amends and apologize," said Luciana Salustri.

There was a pause. Each woman anxiously looked at Beatrice. The suddenness of the quarrel had sobered the whole party more effectively than a cold rain. Beatrice's face grew more and more livid. Her lips turned a ghastly blue. She laughed aloud in bitter scorn. Then, walking steadily up to me, with her eyes full of maliciousness, said, "You say that he never cared for me and I am to apologize to you? You are nothing more than a thief, a coward, a traitor of the worst sort. Take that for my apology!" And she struck me across the cheek with her bare hand so hard, that the diamond ring she wore, my diamond ring, cut my flesh and drew blood. A shout of anger broke from all present.

Beatrice stood still for a moment, as did I. Then I saw her raise her hand to her throat and try to swallow. Sweat glistened on her brow. With her free hand, she clutched her stomach. Her face turned a light gray color as she swayed. Leaning slowly forward, she heaved, vomiting the contents of her stomach at my feet. Then she fainted.

I bent down to touch her cold and clammy hand. Then I turned and touched Paolo, who, obedient to his orders, had remained an impassive but astonished spectator. "Paolo, see that Signorina Cardano is brought up to one of the bedrooms."

Paolo beckoned two waiters to lift Beatrice. They obeyed instantly. Speechless, the guests watched them leave. Servants immediately appeared carrying cloths, buckets, and mops to wash away the vomit.

I looked round at the rest of the assembled company with a smile at their troubled faces. "Ladies, our feast has broken up in a rather disagreeable manner, and I am sorry for it, especially beause it compels me to part from you. Receive my thanks for your company, and for your friendship. I hope to see you all again on my wedding day when nothing shall mar the merry occasion. In the meantime, I bid you all a good night."

They closed round me, pressing my hands warmly and assuring me of their sympathy and support over the quarrel that had occurred. I escaped from them all at last and reached the quiet room where Beatrice lay ill and moaning. At her bedside, I sat alone for a while. I heard the departing footsteps of my guests as they left by twos and threes. Now and then I caught a few words whispered in exchange by the waiters who were discussing the affair as they cleared away the remains of the dinner feast where death itself had been seated. Thirteen at table. One was a traitor and one must die. I knew which one. Beatrice. No presentiment lurked in my mind as to the doubtful result. Part of my vengeance would soon be fulfilled.

I looked down upon her. Her breathing was slow and shallow. Cold sweat dampened her face, tendrils of hair damp upon her skin. Oh, what bitter agony Beatrice Cardano must have carried in her heart when I made my stunning announcement. How she had looked when I said he never cared for her. Just like the things she had said about me. Poor wretch. I pitied her even while I rejoiced at her torture. She suffered now as I had suffered. She was duped as I had been duped. And each quiver of her convulsed and tormented face brought me satisfaction. Each moment that remained of her life was now a pang to her. Well. It would soon be over. At least in that, I would be merciful.

I went to the window, and drawing back the curtains, surveyed the exquisitely peaceful scene that lay before me. The moon was still high and bright. There was a heavy unnatural silence everywhere. It oppressed me, and I threw the window wide open for air. Then came the sound of bells chiming softly. People passed through the streets with quiet footsteps. Some paused to exchange friendly greetings. I remembered what day it was with a pang at my heart. The night was over, though as yet there was no sign of dawn. It was Christmas morning.

I looked back at Beatrice. Had I not suffered as she was now suffering? No, I had suffered more than she, for she would not be buried alive. I would take care of that. She would not have to endure the agony of breaking free from a cold grave to come back to life and find her name slandered and her place taken by a usurper. Do what I would, I could not torture her as much as I myself had been tortured. That was a pity. Death, sudden and almost painless, seemed too good for her. She must live long enough to recognize me before she died. That was the sting I reserved for her last moments. Beatrice had hurt me three times. Once in her theft of my husband's affections, once in her contempt for my little dead child, and once more in her slanders on my name. Then why were such foolish notions such as pity and forgiveness beginning to creep into my thoughts? It was too late now for forgiveness. The very idea of it only rose out of silly sentimentalism awakened when Beatrice alluded to our young days; days for which, after all, she really cared nothing about.

I turned to look at Beatrice again and would do so with uncovered eyes. I removed my spectacles and placed them on the bedside table. Vaguely, I wondered what the effect would be upon her. I was very much changed even without these disguising glasses. My white hair had altered my appearance, yet I knew there was something familiar in the expression of my eyes that could not fail to startle one who had known me so well.

As I studied her pained, suffering face, I experienced a passing shudder, but not because the air was chilly. It was because of the terrible certainty of killing the woman I had once loved, my dearest friend. I experienced a sick pain in my heart. And when I thought of Dario, the snake who had wrought all the evil, my wrath against him increased tenfold. I wondered scornfully what he was doing in the quiet monastery in Padua. No doubt he slept; it was yet too early for him to practice his sham of sanctity. He slept, in all probability most peacefully, while his wife waited for death to take his lover.

Beatrice moaned and opened her eyes, glazed with agony. She stared at me with a frantic faroff look. Suddenly she shuddered and gave out another smothered groan. A deep anguished sigh parted her lips. Sense and

The Contessa's Vendetta

speculation returned to those glaring eyes so awfully upturned. She looked upon my face without the dark glasses with doubt, and then she grew strangely shocked. Her lips moved and she tried to speak. She pointed at me. Her wild eyes met mine with a piteous beseeching terror.

"In God's name," she whispered. "Who are you?"

"You know me, Beatrice," I answered, steadily. "I am Carlotta Mancini, whom you once called friend. I am the woman whose husband you stole and whose name you slandered and whose honor you despised. Look at me well. Your own heart tells you who I am."

She uttered a low moan and raised her hand with a feeble gesture. "Carlotta? Carlotta?" she gasped. "She died. I saw her in her coffin."

I leaned more closely over her. "I was buried alive," I said distinctly. "Do you understand, Beatrice. Buried alive. I escaped, never mind how. I came home, only to learn about your treachery. Shall I tell you more?"

A terrible shudder shook her frame. Her head moved restlessly to and fro, the sweat stood in large drops upon her forehead. With my own handkerchief I wiped her lips and brow tenderly. My nerves were fraught to a brittle tension. I smiled as if on the verge of hysterical weeping.

"You know the dear old avenue where the nightingales sing? I saw you there with him on the night I returned from death. He held you in his arms and you kissed. You spoke of me and toyed with a flower."

She writhed under my gaze with a strong convulsive movement. "Tell me," she gasped. "Does he know you?"

"Not yet," I answered, slowly. "But soon he will, when I marry him."

A look of bitter anguish filled her straining eyes. "Oh, God, God," she exclaimed with a groan like that of a wild beast in pain. "This is horrible, too horrible. Spare me, spare—" A rush of vomit choked her utterance. Her breathing grew fainter and fainter; the livid hue of her approaching death spread itself gradually over her expression. Staring wildly at me, she groped with her hands as though she searched for some lost thing. I took one of those feebly wandering hands within my own, and held it closely clasped.

"You know the rest," I said gently. "You understand my vengeance. But it is all over, Beatrice, all over, now. He has played us both false. You drank poisoned wine all night, all part of my vendetta. It is over now. May God forgive you as I do."

"I must see Dario." She laboured to speak each word.

"He is gone. I sent him away to Padua."

Slowly I watched her expression of rage turn to one of understanding. She gave me a weak smile. "You won. You always win." A soft look brightened her fast-glazing eyes, the old girlish look that had won my love and friendship in former days. "All over," she repeated in a sort of plaintive babble. "All over now. God—Carlotta—forgive—"

A terrible convulsion wrenched and contorted her limbs and features, her throat rattled, and stretching herself out with a long shivering sigh, she died.

The first beams of the rising sun, piercing through the dark, moss-covered branches of the pine-trees, fell on her clustering hair, and lent a mocking brilliancy to her wide-open sightless eyes. There was a smile on her closed lips.

A burning, suffocating sensation rose in my throat. Rebellious tears tried to force a passage, but I refused to set them free. I still held the hand of my friend and enemy. It had grown cold in my clasp. Upon it sparkled my family diamond, the ring he had given her.

I drew the jewel off then I kissed that poor hand tenderly, reverently, as I laid it gently down.

Hearing footsteps approaching, I rose and stood with

The Contessa's Vendetta

folded arms, looking down on the stiffening form before me.

Paolo came up beside me. He did not speak for a moment, but surveyed the body in silence. "She is dead."

I nodded, unable to trust myself to speak.

"She apologized?" Paolo asked.

I nodded again. There was another pause of heavy silence.

The rigid smiling face of the corpse seemed to mock all speech. Paolo stooped and skillfully closed those glazed appealing eyes, and then it seemed to me as though Beatrice merely slept and that a touch would waken her.

"You must take some wine, Contessa. You look ill."

I glanced out the window. A golden radiance illuminated the sky, while a little bird rose from its nest among the grasses and soared into the heavens, singing rapturously as it flew into the warmth and glory of the living, breathing day.

Chapter Twenty-Two

Benedictine Abbey of Praglia

Later that night, Paolo helped me secretly deposit Beatrice's body at the rear of the church. Afterwards, as he drove me back through the streets of Vicenza, I bade him stop at the corner of the winding road that led to the Villa Mancini. There I alighted. I must leave Vicenza temporarily, until Beatrice's death became a thing of the past so that no suspicion would fall upon me.

I asked Paolo to continue on to my rented villa and have Santina pack my trunk in readiness to depart that evening for Venice.

He listened to my commands in silence. "Do Santina and I also travel with the contessa?"

"No, not this time," I answered with a forced smile. "I am heavy-hearted, and melancholy women are best left to themselves. Besides, remember the carnivale. I promised you and your daughter you were free to indulge in its merriment. If you come with me, you will feel obligated to take care of me, and I shall not deprive you of your pleasure. No, Paolo; stay here in Vicenza and enjoy yourself, and do not worry about me."

Paolo saluted me with his usual respectful bow, but his features wore an expression of obstinacy. "The contessa must pardon me," he said, "but I have looked upon death this night, and my taste is spoiled for carnivale. Again, the contessa suffers with sadness. It believe it is necessary that I should accompany her to Venice."

I saw that his mind was made up, and I was in no mood for argument.

"As you wish," I answered, wearily, "but believe me, you make a foolish decision. But do what you like. Arrange everything so that we leave immediately. Give no explanation to anyone of what has occurred, and lose no time in returning with the carriage. I will wait for you alone at Villa Mancini."

Paolo rumbled off in the vehicle. I watched it disappear, and then turned into the road that led me to my own sullied home. The place looked silent and deserted; not a soul was stirring. The silken blinds of the reception rooms were all closely drawn, showing that the master of the house was absent, or that someone lay dead within.

A vague wonder arose in my mind. Who was dead? Surely it must be I, the mistress of the household, who lay stiff and cold in one of those curtained rooms. This terrible white-haired woman who roamed feverishly up and down outside the walls was not me. It was some angry demoness risen from the grave to wreak punishment on the guilty. I *was* dead, otherwise I could never have killed the woman who had once been my friend. And she also was dead—the same murderer had slain us both—and he still lived. Ha! That was wrong and it was his turn to die next, but in such a torturous way that his very body would shrink and shrivel and descend into the furnaces of hell.

With my mind full of hot whirling thoughts like these I looked through the carved heraldic work of the villa gates. Here, behind these twisted wreaths of iron, Beatrice had once walked. There was nothing but compassion for her in my heart now that she was dead. She had been duped and wronged. Now I believed that her spirit would work with mine and help me to punish Dario.

I paced round the silent villa till I came to the private wicket that led into the avenue. I opened it and entered the familiar path. I had not been there since the fatal night on which I had learned of my own betrayal. How still were those solemn trees. How gaunt and dark and grim. Not a branch quivered, not a leaf stirred. A cold dew that was scarcely a frost glittered on the moss at my feet. No bird's voice broke the impressive hush of this Christmas morning. No bright-hued flower unfurled itself against the morning sun. Yet, there was a subtle perfume everywhere; the fragrance of unseen violets still closed in winter's slumber.

I gazed on the scene; a woman staring at a place where she once was happy. I walked a few paces, and then paused with a strange beating in my heart. A shadow fell across my path. It flitted before me, stopped, and remained still. Gradually, as if swirling in a mist, it turned into the figure of a woman standing in rigid silence, with the light beating full on her smiling, dead face, and also on a pool of vomit staining the grass at her feet. Sick horror seized me at this sight, and I sprung forward. The shadow vanished instantly.

It was a mere delusion; the result of my overwrought and excited condition. I shuddered involuntarily at the image my own heated imagination had conjured up. Would I always see Beatrice thus, I thought, even in my dreams?

Suddenly a ringing, swaying rush of sound burst into the silence. The slumbering trees awoke, their leaves moved, their dark branches quivered, and the grasses quivered. Christmas bells. And such bells. Their melody stormed the air with sweet eloquence, round, rainbow bubbles of music that burst upon the wind, and dispersed in delicate broken echoes.

Peace on earth, good will to men. Peace on earth, good will to men.

This was the melody the bells sang over and over again until my ears ached. Peace. What had I to do with peace or good-will? Christmas could teach me nothing. I was utterly alone in life, a murderer. For me, no bonds of family remained.

The song of the chimes jarred my nerves. Why, I thought, should the wild, erring world, with all its wicked men and women, presume to rejoice at the birth of the Savior? They, who were not worthy to be saved. I turned swiftly away. I strode fiercely past the elegant trees, now thoroughly awakened, which seemed to surround me with disdain.

I was glad when I stood again on the road, and was relieved to hear the rapid trot of horses, the rumbling of wheels, and saw my closed carriage drawn by its prancing white Arabians, approaching. I walked to meet it.

Seeing me, Paolo drew up instantly. He helped me into the carriage where I settled next to Santina, huddled beneath warm furs. Then I bade Paolo take me to Padua, to the Benedictine Abbey of Praglia.

The monastery was a two hour drive away. It was a good distance off the direct route and could only be reached by a side road, which from its rough and broken condition was evidently not used much. It lay at the foot of the Euganean Hills, between Padua and Abano Terme, along the ancient road to Este.

The building stood apart from all other habitations in a large open piece of ground, fenced in by a high stone wall. Paolo drew up before the heavily barred gates. I alighted, and bade him take the carriage to a nearby inn where he and Santina were to wait for me. As soon as he had driven off, I rang the monastery bell.

A little wicket fixed in the gate opened and the wrinkled face of a very old and ugly monk looked out. In a low tone, he demanded what I sought. I handed him my card, and stated my desire to see Signore Gismondi, if agreeable to the father superior. While I spoke he looked at me curiously. My spectacles, I suppose, made him wonder. After peering at me a minute or two with his bleared and aged eyes, he shut the wicket in my face with a smart click and disappeared. While I awaited his return I heard the sound of children's laughter and light footsteps running over the cobblestone passage inside.

"Robert," a young boy said. "Brother Maurizio is very angry with you."

"Keep quiet," another boy said in a more piercing tone. "I want to see who is there. I know it's a woman, because Brother Lorenzo's cheeks turned red."

Both voices broke into a chorus of renewed laughter.

Then came the shuffling noise of the old monk's footsteps returning. He evidently caught the two truants, whoever they were, for I heard him admonishing, scolding, and naming saints all in a breath, as he ordered them to go inside and ask the good Jesus to forgive their naughtiness. A silence ensued, then the bolts and bars of the huge gate were undone slowly. They swung open and I was admitted.

The monk guided me through a long, cold avenue lined by trees on either side. He looked at me no more and never spoke again till we entered the building. We entered a lofty hall glorious with sacred paintings and statues, and from there into a large, elegantly furnished room, whose windows commanded a fine view of the grounds. Here he motioned me to take a seat, and without lifting his eyelids, said, "Father Maurizio will be with you shortly, Signora."

I bowed, and he strode from the room so noiselessly that I did not even hear the door close behind him. Left alone in the reception-room, I looked about me with curiosity. I had never before seen the interior of an educational monastery. There were many paintings on the walls and mantelpiece; portraits of young men, some plain of face, others handsome. No doubt they had all been sent to the monks as mementos of former pupils.

Rising from my chair I examined a few of them carelessly. My attention was caught by a frame surmounted with a familiar crest and coronet. In it was my husband's portrait the way he looked when we married. I took it to the light and stared at the features dubiously. This was he—this slim, tall creature clad in dark sapphire blue. This was the man for which two women's lives had been sacrificed. With a sigh of disgust I returned the frame to its former position

The door opened quietly and a tall man clad in a black cossack stood before me. I curtseyed to him with respectful reverence. He responded with a slight nod. His outward manner was so composed that when he spoke, his colorless lips scarcely moved. His breathing never stirred the silver crucifix that lay glittering on his chest. His voice, though low, was singularly clear and penetrating.

"You are the Contessa Corona?" he inquired.

I nodded in the affirmative. He looked at me keenly. He had dark, brilliant eyes, in which the smoldering fires of many a conquered passion still gleamed.

"You wish to see Signore Gismondi, who is in retreat here?"

"If it is not inconvenient or against the rules—" I began.

The shadow of a smile flitted across the monk's pale, intellectual face; it was gone almost as soon as it appeared.

"Not at all," he replied, in the same even monotone. "Signore Gismondi is, by his own desire, following a strict regime, but today being Christmas, all rules are relaxed. The reverend father desires me to inform you that it is now the hour for mass—he has himself already entered the chapel. If you will share in our devotions, Signore Gismondi shall afterward be informed of your presence here."

I could do no less than accede to this proposition, though in truth it was the last thing I wanted. I was in no humor for church, prayers, or worship of any kind. How shocked this monk would be if he could have known what manner of woman he had just invited to kneel in the sanctuary. I offered no objection and he bade me follow him.

"Is Signore Gismondi well?" I asked as we left the room.

"He seems so," returned Brother Maurizio. "He follows his studies with exactitude, and makes no complaint of boredom."

We were now crossing the hall. I ventured on another inquiry. "He was a favorite pupil of yours, I believe?"

The monk turned his passionless face toward me with an air of mild surprise and reproof. "I have no favorites," he answered coldly. "All the young boys and men educated here share equally in my attention and regard."

I murmured an apology. "You must pardon my curiosity, but as the future wife of the man who was educated here under your care, I am naturally interested in all that concerns him."

Again the cleric surveyed me. He sighed slightly. "I am aware of the connection between you," he said, in rather a pained tone. "Signore Gismondi belongs to the world, and follows the ways of the world. Of course, marriage is the natural fulfillment of most young men's destinies. There are few who are called out of the ranks to serve Christ. Therefore, when Signore Gismondi married the esteemed Contessa Mancini, of whom everyone spoke of so favorably, we rejoiced, feeling that his future was safe in the hands of a gentle and wise woman. May her soul rest in peace. But a second marriage for him is what I did not expect, and what I cannot in my conscience approve. You see I speak frankly."

"I am honored that you do so, brother," I said earnestly, feeling a certain respect for this sternly composed, yet patient man. "Though you may have reasonable objections, a second marriage is, I think, in Signore Gismondi's case almost necessary. He is young and handsome and needs an heir."

The monk's eyes grew solemn and almost mournful. "His handsome face is his fatal, curse. As a young boy, it made him wayward. As a grown man, it keeps him wayward still. But enough of this, Contessa," and he bowed his head. "Excuse my forthrightness. Rest assured that I wish you both happiness."

We had reached the chapel door through which the sound of an organ poured forth surges of melody. Brother Maurizio dipped his fingers in the holy water, and made the sign of the cross, pointed out a bench at the back of the church as one that strangers were allowed to occupy. I seated myself and admired the picturesque scene before me.

There was the sparkle of twinkling lights; the bloom and fragrance of flowers. There were silent rows of monks, black-robed and bare-headed, kneeling and absorbed in prayer. Behind these men were a little cluster of youths also in black with drooped heads. Behind them, I could see one man's form arrayed in dark and elegant clothes; his black doublet of embroidered glazed linen stood out like a star against the somber vestments of the monks around him. The sheeny glitter of golden hair confirmed that he was my husband. How devout he looked bathed by the rainbow of colors from the stained glass windows. I smiled in dreary scorn as I watched him. I cursed him afresh in the name of the woman I had killed.

The stately service went on. The organ music swept through the church as though it were a strong wind striving to set itself free. Amid it all, I sat as one in a dark dream, scarcely seeing, scarcely hearing, inflexible, and cold as marble.

The rich deep voice of one of the monks in the choir singing the Agnus Dei, moved me to a chill. *Lamb of God who takes away the sins of the world.* No, there are some sins that cannot be taken away; the sins of faithless men.

Absorbed in thought, I knew not when the service ended. A hand touched me, and looking up I saw Brother Maurizio. "Follow me, if you please," he whispered.

I rose and obeyed him.

He paused outside the chapel door. "Pray excuse me for hurrying you, but strangers are not permitted to see our members leaving."

I nodded and walked on beside him. Feeling forced to say something, I asked, "Have you many boarders at this holiday season?"

"Only fourteen," he replied, "and they are children whose parents live far away. Poor little ones." The monk's stern face softened into tenderness as he spoke. "We do our best to make them happy, but naturally they feel lonely. We have generally fifty or sixty young boys here, besides the day scholars."

"A great responsibility," I remarked.

"Very great indeed," he sighed. "Almost terrible. So much of a man's after-life depends on the early training he receives. We do all we can, and yet in some cases our utmost efforts are in vain. Evil creeps in, we know not how. Some unsuspected fault spoils a character that we judged to be admirable, and we are often disappointed in our most promising pupils. Sadly, there is nothing entirely without fault in this world."

Thus talking, he showed me into a small, comfortable-looking room, lined with books.

"This is one of our libraries," he explained. "Signore Gismondi will receive you here, as other visitors might disturb you in the drawing-room. Pardon me," and his steady gaze had something of compassion in it, "but you do not look well. Can I offer you some wine?"

I declined this offer with many expressions of gratitude, and assured him I was perfectly well.

He hesitated. "I trust you were not offended at my remark concerning Signore Gismondi's marriage with you? I fear I might have been too hasty."

"Not so," I answered earnestly. "Nothing is more pleasant to me than an honest opinion. Unfortunately, I have grown accustomed to deception—" Here I broke off and added hastily, "Please do not think me capable of judging you wrongly."

He seemed relieved and gave me a shadowy, flitting smile. "No doubt you are impatient, Contessa; Signore Gismondi shall come to you directly," and with a small gesture, left me.

Surely he was a good man, I thought. I wondered about his past history—that past which he had buried forever under a mountain of prayers. What had he been like when young, before he had shut himself within the monastery, before he had set the crucifix like a seal on his heart? Had he ever trapped a woman's soul and strangled it with lies? I fancied not. His look was too honest and candid. Yet who could tell? Were not Dario's eyes trained to appear as though they held the very soul of truth?

A few minutes passed. Then came the shuffle of familiar footsteps. The door opened, and my husband entered.

Twenty-Three

He approached with his usual lion-like majesty and agile stride, his lips parted in a charming smile.

"So good of you to come, and on Christmas morning too." He held out his two hands as though he invited an embrace, and then paused. Seeing that I did not move or speak, he regarded me with apprehension. "What is the matter?" he asked. "Has anything happened?"

I looked at him and saw that he was worried. I made no attempt to soothe him. I merely gestured at a chair.

"Let us sit first," I said, gravely. "I am the bearer of bad news."

He waited for me to sit first, and then sank into the chair. He gazed at me nervously.

Watching him keenly, I observed his unease with deep satisfaction. I saw plainly what was passing through his mind. A great dread had seized him; the dread that I had discovered his treachery. Indeed I had, but the time had not yet come for him to know it. Meanwhile I could see he suffered a gnawing terror; suspense ate into his soul. I said nothing, but waited for him to speak.

After a pause, during which his face had lost all color, he forced a smile. "Bad news? What can it be? Some unpleasantness with Beatrice? Have you seen her?"

"I have seen her," I answered in the same formal and serious tone. "I have just left her. She sends you this," and

I held out my diamond ring that I had drawn off Beatrice's dead finger.

If he had been pale before, he grew paler now. All the brilliancy of his complexion faded into an awful haggardness. He took the ring with fingers that shook and were icy cold. There was no attempt at smiling now. He drew a sharp quick breath; he thought I knew everything that he and she had done.

I deliberately kept my silence.

He looked at the diamond signet with a bewildered air. "I do not understand," he murmured. "I gave her this as a remembrance of her friend, Carlotta. Why does she return it?"

Self-tortured criminal. I studied him with a dark amusement, but answered nothing.

Suddenly he looked up at me. "Why are you acting so cold and strange? Do not stand there like a gloomy sentinel; kiss me and tell me at once what has happened."

Kiss him. So soon after kissing the dead hand of his lover. No, I could not and would not. I remained where I was, unyielding, soundless.

He glanced at me again. "Do you not love me?" he murmured. "You could not be so stern and silent if you did. If there is bad news, break it to me. I thought you would never keep anything secret from me."

"I agree and that is what I mean to do," I said interrupting his complaint. "In your own words, you told me that your adopted sister, Beatrice Cardano, had become loathsome to you. Remember, I promised that I would silence her? Well, I have kept my word. She is silenced—forever."

He tensed. "Silenced? How? You mean—"

I rose and stood so that I faced him. "I mean that she is dead."

He exhaled a pent up breath, not of sorrow but of

The Contessa's Vendetta

disbelief. "Dead? That is not possible. Dead."

I bent my head gravely. "She became suddenly ill, perhaps from an illness she caught while in Rome. We spoke, and forgave each other in the moments before she died."

He listened intently. A little color came returned to his face, but he still looked anxious.

"Did she mention my name?" he asked.

I glanced at his troubled features with contempt. He feared the dying woman might have made some confession to me. "No."

He heaved a sigh of relief. He was safe now, he thought. His lips widened into a cruel smile. "What bad taste," he said, coldly. "Why she would not think of me, I cannot imagine. I have always been kind to her — too kind."

Too kind indeed. Kind enough to be glad when the object of all his kindness was dead. For he was glad. I could see that in the murderous glitter of his eyes.

"You are not sorry?" I inquired, with an air of pretended surprise.

"Sorry? Not at all. Why should I be? She was a very good friend while my wife was alive to keep her in order, but after my poor Carlotta's death, her treatment of me was quite unbearable."

Take care, handsome hypocrite, take care. Take care lest your poor Carlotta's fingers should suddenly nip your throat with a convulsive twitch that means death. Heaven only knows how I managed to keep my hands off him at that moment. Any beast of the field had more feeling than this wretch whom I had made my husband. Even for Beatrice's sake, I could have slain him in that very moment, but I restrained my fury. "Then I was mistaken? I thought you would be deeply grieved; that my news would shock you." I spoke in a calm and steady voice.

He sprung up from his chair like a pleased child and pulled me to him in an embrace. "No, not in the least. Rather, I did not want to burden you by making you feel more grief."

I looked at him in loathing and disgust. Every word he spewed from his lips was defamed. He did not notice my expression. He was absorbed, excellent actor that he was, in the role he had chosen to play.

"And so you acted sad because you did not wish to grieve me? Oh, you poor dear," he said, in a caressing tone, such as he could assume when he chose. "But now that you see I am not unhappy, you will be cheerful again? *Si?* Know that I love you." He held the ring out to me. "It is a small trifle, but because it once belonged to Carlotta, and to Carlotta's father, whom you knew, I think you ought to have it. Will you take it and wear it to please me?" He slipped the diamond signet, my own ring, onto my finger.

I could have laughed aloud, but I nodded seriously as I accepted it. "Only as a proof of your affection, *carissimo*, though it has a terrible association for me. I took it from Beatrice's hand as she lay dying."

"*Si*, I know. It must have been trying for you to have seen her dead. Try to forget the matter. Illnesses are very common occurrences, after all."

"Very common," I answered, mechanically, still regarding the handsome face, the powerful allure of his eyes, the golden hair. "But they do not often end so fatally. The result of this one compels me to leave Vicenza for some days. I go to Venice tonight."

"To Venice?" he asked with interest. "Carlotta and I went there often when we were first married."

"And were you happy there?" I inquired, coldly. I remembered the times he spoke of; journeys of such feral, foolish joy.

"Happy? *Si*. Everything was so new to me then. It was

delightful to be free and out of the monastery."

"I thought you liked the monks?" I said.

"Some of them, yes. The abbot is a kind man, but Brother Maurizio, the one that received you, I detest."

"Why?"

His lips curled mutinously. "Because he is so sly and silent. Some of the boys here adore him, but they have no choice, for there is no one else to love behind these strict walls.

"They have no choice? Must they?" I asked the question by rote, merely for the sake of saying something.

"Of course they must," he answered. "The boys are starved for love and attention, only they do not dare let the monks know. Since I have been here they follow me everywhere and ask me to tell them stories. And I do it because it vexes Brother Maurizio."

I was silent. What a curse love was. Its poison even finds its way into the hearts of children; young things shut within the walls of a secluded monastery, and guarded by the meticulous care of holy men.

"And the monks?" I said, uttering half my thoughts aloud. "How do they manage without love?"

A wicked smile, brilliant and disdainful, glittered in his eyes. "Do they manage without love?" he asked, half indolently. "I suppose they do in one way or another."

Roused by something in his tone, I caught his hand and held it firmly. "And you? Is it possible that you sympathize with those who participate in illicit lust?"

He recollected himself in time. "Not me," he answered, with a grave and virtuous air. "How can you think so? In my mind, there is nothing as horrible as deceit. No good ever comes of it."

I loosened his hand from mine. "You are right," I said, calmly; "I am glad your values are so correct. I have always hated lies."

"So have I," he declared with a frank look. "I have often wondered why people tell them. It is disastrous when they are found out."

I bit my lips hard to stop the accusations my tongue longed to utter. Why should I damn the actor or the play before the curtain was ready to fall on both? I changed the subject. "How long do you propose remaining here? Now there is nothing to prevent your return to Vicenza."

He pondered for some minutes before replying. "I told father superior I came here for a week. I had better stay till that time is expired. Not longer, because with Beatrice's death, my presence in Vicenza is necessary."

"Indeed. May I ask why?"

He laughed a little consciously. "Simply to put forth her last will and testament. Before she left for Rome, she gave it into my keeping."

A light flashed on my mind. "And its contents?" I inquired.

"Its contents make me the owner of everything she died possessed of," he said, with an air of quiet, yet malicious triumph.

Poor Beatrice. What trust she had placed in this vile, self-interested, heartless man. She had loved him, even as I had loved him – he who was unworthy of any love. I controlled my rising emotion, and merely said with gravity, "I congratulate you. May I be permitted to see this document?"

"Certainly. I can show it to you now. I have it here," and he drew a leather case from a pocket, and opening it, handed me a sealed envelope. "Break the seal," he added eagerly. "She sealed it up like that after I had read it."

With a reluctant hand, and a pained sympathy at my heart, I opened the packet. It was as he had said, a will drawn up in perfect legal form, signed and witnessed, leaving everything unconditionally to Dario Gismondi of

The Contessa's Vendetta

the Villa Mancini, Vicenza. I read it through and returned it to him. "She must have loved you very much."

He laughed. "Of course, but many people love me. That is nothing new. I am accustomed to be loved. But you see," he went on, reverting to the will again, "it specifies - *Everything she dies possessed of.* That means all the money left to her by her uncle in Rome, does it not?"

I nodded. I could not trust myself to speak.

"I thought so," he murmured, gleefully, more to himself than to me. "And I have a right to all her papers and letters." There he paused abruptly and checked himself.

Now I clearly understood. He wanted to get back his own letters to the dead woman, lest his intimacy with her should leak out in some way for which he was unprepared. Cunning devil. I was almost glad he showed me to what depths of vulgarity he would sink. In his case, there was no hope for me to show any pity or restraint. If all the tortures invented by savages or inquisitors could be heaped upon him at once, such punishment would be light in comparison with his crimes; crimes for which the law gives you no remedy but divorce. I grew tired of this wretched comedy.

"It is time to take my leave," I said stiffly. "Moments fly fast whenever I am with you, but I have many things to attend to before I leave for Venice this evening. On my return, will you welcome me?"

"You know it," he returned pulling me close until I rested my head against his shoulder.

For appearance's sake I was forced to remain in his partial embrace.

"I only wish you were not going at all. Do not stay away long."

"Absence strengthens love, they say," I observed, with a forced smile. "May it do so in our case. Pray for me while I am gone. I suppose you do pray a great deal here, don't you?"

"What else is there to do?" He held my hands. The betrothal ring on his finger and the diamond signet on my own, flashed in the light like the crossing of swords.

"Pray then for the repose of poor Beatrice's soul. Remember that she loved you, even though you never loved her. Who knows, but maybe her spirit may be near us now, hearing our voices, watching our looks?"

His hands grew cold.

"*Sì*," I continued, more calmly. "You must not forget to pray for her. She was young and not prepared to die."

My words affected him. For once, his speech failed. He seemed as though he searched for a reply and could not find one. He still held my hands.

"Promise me. And at the same time pray for your dead wife. She and poor Beatrice were such close friends. It will be kind of you to join their names in one prayer to God from whom no secrets are hid and who knows the sincerity of your intentions. Will you do it?"

He smiled, a forced, faint smile. "I certainly will. I promise you."

I pulled my hands away. I was satisfied. If he dared to utter such prayers, I knew he would draw the wrath of Heaven down upon him, for I looked beyond the grave. The mere death of his body would be but slight satisfaction to me – it was the utter destruction of his wicked soul that I sought. He should never repent, I swore. He should never have the chance to cast off his vileness as a serpent casts its skin, and then reclothe himself in innocence. He should never have the gall to seek admittance into that same Heaven where my little child had gone. Never. No church should save him. No priest should absolve him. Not while I lived.

He watched me as I fastened my mantle and began to

The Contessa's Vendetta

draw on my gloves.

"Are you going now?" he asked.

"*Si*, I am going now. Why? What has made you look so pale?"

For he had suddenly turned very white.

"Let me see your hand again; the hand on which I placed the ring."

Smilingly and with readiness I took off the glove I had just put on. "What is the matter?" I asked, with an air of playfulness.

He gave me no answer, but took my hand and examined it closely and curiously. Then he looked up, his lips twitched nervously, and he laughed a mirthless laugh. "Your hand, with that signet on it, is exactly like Carlotta's."

And before I had time to speak another word he broke out into a cold sweat and walked away to face the window. With both hands on the sill, he tried to steady himself and stop his heavy breathing.

I rang the bell to summon assistance. A lay-brother answered it. Seeing Dario's condition, he rushed for a glass of water and summoned Brother Maurizio who entered with his quiet, stoic demeanor.

Brother Maurizio took in the situation at a glance, dismissed the lay-brother, and took hold of the tumbler of water. He offered it to Dario who sipped some through clenched teeth. "What has happened?" he inquired in a stately manner.

"I really cannot tell you," I said, with an air of affected concern and vexation. "I told him of the unexpected death of a friend, but he bore the news with exemplary resignation."

"It is nothing," Dario said, somewhat recovered. "There was a resemblance between the contessa's hand and that of my deceased wife. At the sight, a jolt of grief passed through me."

"But that is absurd." I shrugged my shoulders as though I were annoyed and impatient.

A sarcastic smile flitted over the monk's face. "Ah, a tender heart," he said, in his passionless tone, which conveyed to me another meaning than that implied by the words he uttered. "We cannot perhaps understand the extreme delicacy of human emotion and we fail to do justice to them."

Here Dario looked at us plainly and heaved a long, deep sigh.

"You are better, I trust?" continued the monk, without any sympathy in his monotonous voice, and addressing him with some reserve. "You have greatly alarmed the Contessa Corona."

"I am sorry," Dario said.

I hastened to his side.

"It was nothing," I urged, forcing something like a lover's ardor into my voice. "It is my misfortune to have hands like those of your late wife, and I regret it. Can you forgive me?"

He was evidently conscious that he had behaved foolishly. He smiled, but looked worn and avoided glancing at Brother Maurizio, who stood at a slight distance, his body erect with a bland expression on his face and his silver crucifix glittering coldly on his still breast.

"I should leave," I announced.

"I am sorry you have to leave so soon. Good-bye. Write to me from Venice." He took my outstretched hand, and bowing over it, kissed it gently. He turned toward the door, when suddenly a mischievous idea seemed to enter his mind. He looked at Brother Maurizio and then back to me. "*Addio, amore mio.*" He threw his arms around me and kissed me passionately.

Then he glanced maliciously at the monk who had

lowered his eyes till they appeared fast shut, and breaking into a low peal of spiteful laughter, left the room.

I was somewhat confused. The suddenness of Dario's kiss had been a mere prank to vex Brother Maurizio's religious scruples. I did not know what to say to the poor cleric who stood with downcast eyes and lips that moved dumbly as if in prayer. As the door closed after my husband's retreating figure, the monk looked up.

"I apologize for the display—"

"Say nothing, Contessa," he interrupted me with a disapproving gesture. "It is quite unnecessary. To mock a religious man is a common amusement for young boys and men of the world. I am accustomed to it, though I feel its cruelty more than I ought to. Men like Signore Gismondi think that because monks have embraced God instead of women, we cannot understand love, tenderness or passion. They fail to realize that we, too, have our pasts. Pasts that would make angels weep for pity." He placed his hand on his heart. Then, composing himself, he returned to his neutral stance. "The rule of our convent, Contessa, permits no visitor to remain longer than one hour. That hour has expired. I will summon a monk to show you the way out."

"Wait one instant, please," I said, feeling that to enact my part convincingly, I must attempt to defend Dario's conduct. "My betrothed can be thoughtless at times. I really do not think that his parting kiss to me was meant to purposely annoy you."

The monk glanced at me. Disdain flashed in his eyes. "No doubt you think that was a show of his affection for you, Contessa. A very natural conclusion, and I am very sorry to enlighten you to the truth." He paused to gather the appropriate words. "You seem to be a sincere woman. Maybe you are the one destined to save Signore Gismondi. I could say much, yet it is wiser for me to be silent. If you love him do not flatter him. His arrogance and vanity are his ruin. With him you must always be firm and wise. Perhaps this may lead him to change. Who knows." He hesitated then sighed. "*Arrivederci*, Contessa. *Benedicite.*" He made the sign of the cross as I respectfully bent my head to receive his blessing before he left the room as noiselessly as he had entered it.

A moment later, a lame and aged lay-brother came to escort me to the gate. As I made my way down the stone corridor, a side door opened a little and two young faces peered out at me. For an instant I saw four laughing bright eyes. I heard a smothered voice say, "Oh, it's only an old woman."

My guide, though lame, was not blind. He noticed the opened door and shut it with an angry bang, which did not drown the ringing laughter that echoed from within.

On reaching the gates, I turned to my venerable companion and handed him twenty pieces of silver in his shriveled palm. "Take these to the father superior for me, and ask that Mass be said in the chapel tomorrow for the repose of the soul of the person whose name is written here." I handed him Beatrice Cardano's visiting-card. "She met with a sudden and unanticipated death, and please also pray for the woman who killed her."

The old lay-brother looked startled, and crossed himself devoutly, but promised that my wishes would be fulfilled.

I bade him farewell and departed, the monastery gates closing with a dull clang behind me.

Chapter Twenty-Four

Venice

I adored Venice; a dreamy, picturesque city where one can dream while enjoying the unusual, beautiful surroundings. To this splendid spot I came, glad for a rest away from my plot of vengeance, glad to lay down my burden of bitterness for a brief time, and feel human again.

I took residence in a humble lodging, living simply, and attended only by Paolo and Santina. I was tired of the luxury and ostentation I had been forced to practice in Vicenza and was relieved to live more simply for a while. The house in which I rented rooms was a large, picturesque home, and the woman who owned it was charismatic. Pride over her Roman background flashed in her dark eyes and was evident in her strong features, her statuesque dignity, and her free, firm tread which was swift without being hasty. She told me her history in a few words and with such eloquence that she seemed to live through it again as she spoke.

"My husband had been a worker in a marble quarry when a fellow worker had let a huge piece of the rock fall on him. My poor Antonio was crushed to death. I know the man killed my husband on purpose, because he was in love with me," she confided. "But I am a virtuous woman, and I refused to pay him any attention. When my dear Antonio's body was scarcely buried, that miserable murderer offered marriage to me. I accused him of his crime, but he denied it. He said the rock slipped from his hands. I cursed him, struck him hard on the mouth and cheek, and then screamed at him to leave my sight. He is dead now, and if the saints heard my curses, his soul is not in Heaven."

Her eyes flashed as she spoke. With her strong brown arms she threw open the wide casement of the sitting-room I had rented. She bade me view her orchard, a small strip of verdure and foliage.

She smiled, displaying her white teeth. "Venice has wonderful markets with spices and foods brought in by ships from all over the world. The rental of rooms from this house produces enough for my daughter and I to live on, but I am very careful to whom I rent my space. To common persons I would not open my door. When one has a girl, one cannot be too careful."

"You have a daughter, then?"

Her eyes softened. "One—my Lilla. I call her my blessing, and she is too good for me. She tends the garden well. When she brings the few vegetables we grow to market, it seems to me that her face and smile brings luck to the sale. She is past marriageable age, but she is reluctant to leave me, a poor widow, alone."

I smiled at her motherly pride and sighed. I had no

The Contessa's Vendetta

faith in humanity left. I could not even believe in Lilla's innocence. My landlady, Signora Monti as she was called, saw that I looked fatigued, and left me to myself.

During my stay, I saw very little of her. Paolo and Santina took care of everything for me, always meticulous over the smallest details to ensure my comfort. They attended to my wishes with such care. I was truly grateful and counted myself blessed to have found such loyal servants.

After we had been there for three days, Paolo tried to strike up a conversation with me. He had noticed that I always sought to be alone; that I took long, solitary rambles through narrow streets, over small bridges that crossed over the canals. As I listened, I kept my silence, making it difficult for him to continue the conversation. Not daring to break through my reserve, he let the matter drop and continued his work in silence.

One afternoon, after clearing away what remained of my midday meal, he lingered in the room. "The contessa has not yet seen Lilla Monti?" he asked with hesitation.

I looked at him in surprise. There was a blush on his olive-tinted cheeks and an unusual sparkle in his eyes. For the first time I realized that he was still quite young, and very handsome, a man not much more than forty years.

"Seen Lilla Monti?" I repeated, half absently. "Oh, you mean the landlady's daughter? No, I have not seen her. Why do you ask?"

Paolo smiled. "Pardon, Contessa, but she is beautiful. There is a saying where I come from: *Be the heart heavy as stone, the sight of a fair face will lighten it.*"

I gave an impatient gesture. "All folly, Paolo. Beauty is the curse of the world. Read a few history books you will will find the greatest conquerors ruined and disgraced by its snares."

He nodded gravely.

He probably recalled the betrothal announcement I had made at my banquet and strove to reconcile it with the inconsistency of what I had just said, but he was too discreet to utter his thoughts aloud.

"No doubt you are right, Contessa. Still, one is glad to see the roses bloom, and the stars shine, and the foam sparkle on the waves, so one is glad to see Lilla Monti."

I turned round in my chair to observe him more closely—the flush deepened on his face as I regarded him. I laughed with a bitter sadness. "In love, are you? So soon? We have been here only three days and you have fallen prey to Lilla's smile. I am sorry for you."

He interrupted me eagerly. "The contessa is wrong. I would not dare. She is too innocent. She is like a little bird in the nest, so soft and tender. A word of love would frighten her; I should be a coward to utter it."

Well, well, I thought. What was the use of sneering at the poor fellow just because my own love had turned to ashes in my grasp. I should not mock those who believed themselves in love. Paolo, once a soldier, now half courier, half valet, was something of a romantic at heart. Beneath his mask of formality, an amorous fire lay hidden.

I forced myself to appear interested. "I see, Paolo, that the sight of Lilla Monti has smitten you," I said kindly. "But why do you wish me to see this paragon of a woman, I do not know? Do you want me to regret my own lost youth?"

A perplexed expression flitted over his face "The contessa must pardon me for seeing what perhaps I ought not to have seen, but—"

"But what?" I asked.

"Contessa, you have not lost your youth."

I turned my head toward him again. He was looking at me with a bit of alarm, as if he feared an outburst of anger from me.

The Contessa's Vendetta

"Why do you think so?" I asked calmly.

"Contessa, I caught a glimpse of you without your spectacles the day Signorina Cardano died. Your eyes were beautiful; the eyes of a young woman, though your hair is white."

Quietly I took off my glasses and laid them on the table beside me. "As you have seen me once without them, you can see me again," I observed, gently. "I wear them for a special purpose. Here in Venice the purpose does not hold. Now that I have confided in you, beware you do not betray my confidence."

"Contessa, I would never do such a thing," Paolo said in a truly pained voice and a grieved look.

I rose and laid my hand on his arm.

"I was wrong, *perdonami*. You are an honest man and have served your country well enough to know the value of fidelity and duty. But when you say I have not lost my youth, you are wrong, Paolo. I have lost it. It has been killed within me by a great sorrowfulness. My strength, my suppleness of limb, my bright eyes, all these are outward things, but in my heart and soul lives the chill and bitterness of old age. In that way, I am very old; so old that I am tired of my life. But I do value and appreciate you, my friend." I forced a smile. "When I see Lilla, I will tell you honestly what I think of her."

Paolo stooped his head, caught my hand in his own, and kissed it, then left the room abruptly, to hide the tears that my words had brought to his eyes. He was sorry for me, I could see, and I judged him rightly when I thought that the mystery surrounding me had only enhanced his attachment to me. On the whole, I was glad he had seen me undisguised. I felt relieved to be without my smoked glasses for a time. For the remainder of my stay in Venice, I never wore them again.

Not long after our conversation, I saw Lilla. I had

strolled up to a quaint church with a fresco inside rumored to have been the work of artist Paolo Veronese. The sanctuary was quite deserted when I entered, and I paused on the threshold, touched by the simplicity of the place and soothed by the intense silence. I walked on tiptoe to the picture I had come to see. As I did so a girl passed me carrying a basket of fragrant winter narcissi and maidenhair fern. Something in her graceful, noiseless movements caused me to look at her, but she had turned her back to me and was kneeling at the shrine of the Virgin, having placed her flowers on the lowest step of the altar. She was dressed in a simple brown skirt with matching bodice and a white veil surrounding her rich chestnut hair that was coiled in thick shining braids.

I wanted to see her face, so I went back to the church door and waited till she should leave. Soon she came toward me with the same light step that I had already noticed and looked directly at me. What was there in those clear candid eyes that made me involuntarily nod in greeting as she passed? I do not know. It was not beauty. Though the woman was lovely, I had seen lovelier. There was something inexplicable and rare about her, a composure and sweet dignity that I had never beheld on anyone's face before. Her cheeks flushed softly as she returned my nod.

When she was outside the church door she paused, her small white fingers still clasping the carved brown beads of her rosary. She hesitated a moment. "If the contessa will walk a little further on, she will see a finer view of the lagoon."

Something familiar in her look, a reflection of her mother's likeness, made me sure of her identity. I smiled. "Ah. You must be Lilla Monti?"

She blushed again. "*Si*, Contessa. I am Lilla."

I studied her with sadness. Paolo was right. The young

woman was indeed beautiful; not with the forced beauty of society and its artificial constraints, but with a natural, fresh radiance. I had never seen anyone so spiritually beautiful as this woman, who stood fearlessly yet modestly regarding me. She was a little flustered by my scrutiny, and with a pretty courtesy turned to descend the hill.

"You are going home?"

"*Si* Contessa. My mother waits for me to help her with dinner."

I advanced and took the hand in which she held her rosary. "You work hard, don't you, Lilla?"

She laughed musically. "I love work. It is good for the soul. People are so cross when their hands are idle. And many are ill for the same reason." She nodded gravely. "It is often the case. Old Pietro, the cobbler, took to his bed when he had no shoes to mend. He sent for the priest who said he would die, not for want of money, because he had plenty and was quite rich, but because he had nothing to do. So my mother and I found some shoes with holes, and took them to him. He sat up in bed to mend them, and now he is as well as ever. And we are always careful to offer him more." She laughed once more and turned serious. "One cannot live without work. My mother says that good women are never tired, it is only wicked persons who are lazy. And that reminds me I must make haste to return and prepare your coffee."

"Do you make my coffee? Does Paolo not help you?"

The faintest blush tinged her cheeks. "Oh, he is very good, Paolo. He is a good friend and is glad when I make coffee for him too. He loves it so much and likes how I make it. But perhaps the contessa prefers Paolo to make your coffee?"

I laughed. For a grown woman, she was so naive, so absorbed in her duties. "No, Lilla. I shall enjoy my coffee more now that I know your kind hands have been at work.

But you must not spoil Paolo. You will turn his head if you make his coffee too often."

She looked surprised and did not seem to understand. Evidently, in her mind, Paolo was nothing more than a good-natured man whose palate could be pleased by her culinary skill. She treated him exactly as she would have treated one of her own sex. She seemed to think over my words as if they caused a conundrum, and then she apparently gave it up as hopeless, shaking her head and dismissing the subject. "Has the contessa seen the new bridge?" she said brightly, as she turned to go.

I asked her to what she alluded.

"It is not far from here," she explained, "The enclosed bridge is made of white limestone and has windows with stone bars. It passes over the Rio di Palazzo and connects the prison to the Doge's Palace. Some people believe that lovers will be granted eternal love if they kiss on a gondola at sunset under the bridge. It will please you to see it, Contessa. It is but a walk of ten minutes."

And with a smile, she left me, singing aloud for sheer happiness. Her pure lark-like notes floated toward me where I stood, wistfully watching her as she disappeared. The warm afternoon sunshine caught her chestnut hair, turning it to a golden bronze, touching up the whiteness of her throat and arms, and brightening the scarlet of her bodice. As she descended the grassy slope, I lost sight of her amid the stone façades of Venezia's homes.

Limestone Bridge
(Known as The Bridge of Sighs)

Chapter Twenty-Five

I heaved a sigh and resumed my walk. With every step, I came to realize all that I had lost in my life. This lovely young woman, near to my own age, with her simple fresh nature, had trapped the heart of a good, caring, and loyal man like Paolo. Why had I not attracted such a man and wedded him instead of the vile creature who had been my soul's undoing? The answer came swiftly. Even if a good man had been attracted to me when I was free, I could never have married him. Noblewomen must marry well educated gentlemen who are as wealthy and as well versed in the world's ways as they are, if not more so. And so we get the scoundrels while young women like Lilla too often become the household drudges of common workers, living and dying in the routine of hard work, and often knowing little more than the mountain-hut, the farm-kitchen, or the covered stall in the market-place. Women are often never so hopelessly, utterly fooled as in their marriages.

Occupied in various thoughts, I scarcely saw where I wandered, till a flashing glimmer of blue water recalled me to the reason for my walk. I stopped and looked around me. I had reached the corner where I could observe the structure. The view was indeed superb. Beyond the new bridge I could see the azure sea. The structure looked exactly as Lilla had described it, made of white limestone construction with barred windows stretching high above the canal that attached the Doge's palace to the prison. Two windows with stone bars appeared at the summit of the enclosed bridge. Despite the dismal reason for the bridge, it was beautiful from the outside. I had been inside the doge's palace several times, but had always entered by the front on the lagoon side – never from the rear of the residence. The bridge was lovely and I immediately understood why lovers in gondola stole kisses while gliding across the water beneath it.

I sat down on a bench to rest. Then I remembered the packet I had received that morning; a packet I had hesitated to open. It had been sent by Gilda D'Avencorta, accompanied by a courteous letter.

Contessa,

I am writing to inform you that Beatrice Cardano's body has been privately buried with last rites in the cemetery close to the funeral vault of the Mancini family. From all we can discern, this seemed to be her desire since she was a close friend of the lately deceased contessa. Within this packet, I have enclosed some letters found among Signorina Cardano's personal possesions. Upon opening the first one, in the expectation of finding some clue as to her last wishes, I quickly concluded that you, as the future wife of the man whose signature and handwriting you will recognize, should be made aware, not only for your own sake, but in fairness to the deceased. If all the letters are of the same tone as the one I unknowingly opened, I have no doubt Beatrice Cardano considered herself sufficiently injured by you the night you quarrelled. But of that you will judge for yourself, though I recommend you to give careful consideration to the enclosed correspondence before marrying Signore Gismondi. It is not wise to walk on the edge of a precipice with one's eyes shut. I have learned that Beatrice Cardano left a will in which everything she possessed was left unconditionally to him. You will of course draw your own conclusions. Please pardon me if I am guilty of too much zeal in informing you of all this. I have now only to tell you that all the unpleasantness of this affair is passing over very smoothly and without scandal. I have taken care of that. You need not prolong your absence further than you feel inclined, and I, for one, shall be charmed to welcome you back to Vicenza. With every sentiment of the highest consideration and regard, I am,

Your very true friend,
Gilda D'Avencorta

I folded this letter carefully and set it aside. The package she had sent me lay in my hand – a bundle of neatly folded letters tied together with a narrow ribbon, and strongly perfumed with the faint sickly cologne I knew and abhorred and Beatrice's favorite perfume. I turned them over and over; the edges of the note-paper had already become worn with use. Slowly I untied the ribbon. With methodical deliberation I read one letter after the other.

They were all from Dario, all very amorous, and all written to Beatrice while she was in Rome. Some bore the exact dates when he had declared his love to me, his newly betrothed. Letters burning and tender, full of the most passionate promises of fidelity, overflowing with the sweetest terms of endearment; with such a ring of truth and love throughout them that it was no wonder that Beatrice had not suspected anything, and that she had believed herself safe in her fool's paradise. One passage in this romantic correspondence stood out from all the others:

Why do you write so much of marriage to me, Beatrice? It seems that all the joy of loving will be taken from us when the world learns of our passion. If you become my wife you will cease to be my lover, and that would break my heart. Ah, my beloved. I desire you to be my lover always, as you were when Carlotta lived. Why bring matrimony into the midst of such a love and passion as ours?"

I read and reread these words, searing them into my mind. Of course I understood their drift. Dario had tried to feel his way with the dead woman. He had wanted to marry me, and yet retain Beatrice as his lover. Such an ingenious plan it was. No thief, no murderer ever laid a more cunning scheme than he, but the law looks after thieves and murderers. For a cheating man, the law is mute. There is no justice for those he betrays. Ah, but I have my own way of seeking a remedy.

Tying up the packet of letters again, with their sickening aroma and fraying edges, I drew out the last graciously worded missive I had received from Dario. Of course I heard from him every day. He was a most faithful correspondent. The same affectionate expressions characterized his letters to me as those that he had deluded his dead lover with. The only difference was that in Beatrice's letters he railed against the dreariness of marriage. In mine, he painted touching pictures of his desolation; how lonely he had felt since his dear wife's death, how happy he was to think that he would be a happy husband again — the husband of one so noble, so true, so devoted as I was. He had left the monastery and was now at home. He wanted to know when he would have the joy of welcoming me, his beloved, back to Vicenza?

He certainly deserved some credit for artistic lying. I could not understand how he managed it so well. I almost admire his skill, as one would admire a cool-headed burglar, who has more cunning and pluck than his comrades. I thought with triumph that though the wording of Cardano's will enabled him to secure all other letters he might have written to her, this one little packet of documentary evidence was more than sufficient for my purposes. And I was determined to keep it till the time came for me to use it against him.

And how about Gilda's friendly advice concerning the matrimonial knot? *A woman should not walk on the edge of a precipice with her eyes shut.* Very true. But if her eyes are open and she has her enemy within her clutches, the edge of a precipice is a convenient position for hurling that enemy down to death in a quiet way so that the world will not know about it. So, for the present I preferred the precipice to walking on level ground.

I rose from my seat. It was growing late in the afternoon. From the little church below me soft bells rang out. When the bells ceased ringing, I returned homeward through the shady streets.

On reaching the gate of the Signora Monti's humble yet picturesque dwelling, I heard the sound of laughter. In the shady orchard, I saw Paolo hard at work, his shirt-sleeves rolled up to the shoulder, splitting logs while Lilla and Santina stood beside him, encouraging his efforts. He seemed in his element, and wielded his ax with a regularity and vigor I did not expect from a man whom I was accustomed to see performing somewhat effeminate duties in attending me. I watched him and the young women for a few moments unnoticed.

If this budding romance were left alone it would ripen into a flower, and Paolo would be happier than I had ever been in my entire life. From the way he handled his wood-ax, I could see that he loved the hills and fields, the life of a simple farmer and fruit-grower, full of innocent enjoyments as sweet as the ripe apples in my orchards. I could foresee his future with Lilla beside him. Santina seemed to like Lilla too. Together, they would be content, living hale lives made all the more beautiful by the fresh air and the fragrance of flowers. Their evenings would slip softly by to the tinkle of the mandolin, and the sound of his family's singing.

What better future could a man desire? What more certain way to keep health in the body and peace in the mind? Could I not help him be happy, I wondered? I, who had grown severe because of brooding too long upon my vengeance, could I not bring joy to others? If I could, my mind would be lightened of its burden; a burden grown heavier since Beatrice's death. From her death, a new fury had been unleashed inside me, twice as wrathful. But if I could do one good act, it might help ease my soul's stormy darkness.

Just then Lilla laughed. What amused her now? I looked and saw that she had taken the ax from Paolo, and lifting it in her hands, was attempting to imitate his strong stroke. He stood aside with a look of admiration for her. The warm rays of late afternoon sun rained down on the tender scene. Poor Lilla. A knife would have made as much impression as her valorous blows on the knotty old stump she was trying to split. Flushed and breathless with her efforts, she looked more beautiful than ever, and at last, baffled, she handed the ax back to Paolo, laughing at her incapacity for wood-cutting. She shook her apron free from the chips and dust. A call from her mother caused her to run swiftly into the house, and Santina followed her inside. Paolo remained alone, working away at his task.

I walked to him.

When he saw me approaching, he paused with a look of slight embarrassment.

"You like this sort of work?" I said, gently.

"An old habit, Contessa, nothing more. It reminds me of my boyhood days when I worked for my mother. My old home was a pleasant place." His eyes grew pensive and sad. "It is all gone now, finished. That was before I became a soldier. But one thinks of it sometimes."

"I understand. And no doubt you would be glad to return to the life of your boyhood?"

He looked a little startled.

"Not to leave you, Contessa."

I smiled rather sadly. "Not to leave me? Not even if you wedded Lilla Monti?"

His cheeks flushed, but he shook his head. "I do not think such a thing possible."

"She is a grown woman, past marrying age. But there is plenty of time. She is beautiful, as you said, and something better than that, she is honest. Think of that, Paolo. Do you know how rare a thing honesty is? Respect it as you respect God; let her life be sacred to you."

He glanced upward reverently. "Contessa, would that I had a chance."

I smiled and said no more, but turned into the house. From that moment I was determined to give this love of Paolo's a chance at success.

So, I remained in Venice longer than I intended, not for my own sake, but for Paolo's. He had served me faithfully; he should have his reward. I took pleasure in seeing my efforts to promote his cause succeed. I spoke with Lilla often on insignificant matters and watched her constantly when she was unaware of my gaze. With me she was frank and fearless, but soon I found that she grew shy of mentioning Paolo's name, that she blushed when he approached her, that she was timid of asking him to do anything for her. By her reactions, I knew what was in her mind and heart.

One afternoon I called Signora Monti to my room.

She entered, surprised and a little anxious. "Is anything wrong with the service?"

I reassured her that everything had been impeccable and came to the point at once. "I would like to speak to you about your daughter, Lilla," I said, kindly. "Have you ever thought that she might wish to marry one day?"

Her dark bold eyes filled with tears and her lips quivered. "I have, but I have prayed, perhaps foolishly, that she would not leave me yet. I love her so much. I would be distraught if she married and moved away from me."

"I understand," I said. "Still, suppose your daughter wedded a man who would be like a son to you and who would not part her from you? For instance, let us say Paolo?"

Signora Monti smiled through her tears. "Paolo. He is a good man and I like him, but he does not think of Lilla. Rather, he seems very devoted to you, Contessa."

"I am aware of his devotion to me," I answered. "Still, I believe you will find out soon that he loves Lilla. At present he says nothing and is afraid to offend you, but his eyes speak, and so do hers. You are a good woman, a good mother. Watch them both and you will see for yourself that they love each other." I handed her a pouch I had filled with gold coins. "Inside you will find enough to cover Lilla's dowry."

She uttered a little cry of amazement.

"It is for whoever she marries, though I think she will marry Paolo. Giving you these coins is the only pleasure I have had for many weary months. Think well of Paolo, for he is an excellent man. And all I ask of you is, that you keep this dowry a secret till the day your daughter marries."

Before I could stop her, she seized my hand and kissed it. Then she lifted her head with the proud dignity of a Roman matron. Her broad bosom heaved and her strong voice quivered with suppressed emotion. "I thank you, Contessa, for Lilla's sake. Not that my daughter needs more than what my hands can give her; I thank the blessed saints who have watched over us. But this is a special blessing God sent to me through your hands, and I would be unworthy of it, were I not grateful. Contessa, pardon me, but I can see that you have suffered much sorrow. Good actions lighten grief. We will pray for your happiness, Lilla and I, till the last breath leaves our lips. Believe it. We will lift your name to the saints night and morning, and who knows but good may come of it."

I smiled faintly and sighed. "I am certain much good will come of your prayers, Signora, though I am unworthy of them. Rather pray for the dead that that they may be freed from their sins."

The good woman looked at me with kind pity mingled with awe. Murmuring her thanks and a blessing once more, she left the room.

A few minutes later, Paolo entered. "Absence is the best test of love, Paolo. Prepare everything for our departure. We will be leaving Venice the day after tomorrow."

And so we did. Lilla looked downcast, but Paolo seemed satisfied, and I knew from their expressions and from the mysterious smile of Signora Monti, that all was going well.

The Contessa's Vendetta

I left *La Serenissimma* with regret, knowing I should see it no more. I gave Lilla a smile when we parted and took what I knew was my last look of her. Yet the knowledge that I had done some good gave my tired heart a sense of satisfaction and repose—a feeling I had not experienced since I died and rose again from the dead.

On the last day of January, after an absence of more than a month, I returned to Vicenza. My many acquaintances and friends welcomed me back. Gilda D'Avencorta informed me the affair over Beatrice's death was a thing of the past—an almost forgotten circumstance. The carnival was in full riot, the streets were scenes of revelry. There was music and dancing, masquerading and feasting. But I ignored all the merriment and instead absorbed myself in preparing for my marriage.

Mirella Sichirollo Patzer

Basilica Palladiana

Chapter Twenty-Six

When I look back over those frantic weeks preceding my wedding day, they seemed like the dreams of a dying woman. Shifting colors, confused images, moments of clear light, hours of long darkness. All things coarse, cultured, material, and spiritual were blending into ever-changing new forms and bewildering patterns. My mind was clear, yet I often questioned whether I was not going mad; whether all the careful, methodical plans I formed were but the hazy wishes of a disordered mind? But no. Each detail of my scheme was too complete, too consistent, too organized.

I forgot nothing. I had the composed exactitude of a careful banker who balances his accounts with elaborate regularity. I can laugh to think of it all now; but then? Then I moved, spoke, and acted as if pushed by a force stronger than my own.

A few days after I returned from Venice, my coming marriage with Dario Gismondi was announced. Two days after it had been made public, while sauntering across the Piazza Castello, I encountered Gilda D'Avencorta. I had not seen her since Beatrice's death. She was cordial, though slightly embarrassed. "So your marriage will positively take place?" she asked nervously after several commonplace remarks.

I forced a laugh. "*Ma. certamente.* Do you doubt it?"

Her lovely face clouded and her manner grew still more constrained. "No, but I thought, I had hoped—"

"*Carissima,*" I said, airily, "I perfectly understand to what you allude; the love letters between Dario and Beatrice. I know better than to pay any heed to the foolish behavior of a man before his marriage, so long as he does not trick me afterward. The letters you sent me were mere trifles. In wedding the Signore Gismondi, I assure you I believe I secure the most honorable as well as the most handsome man in all of Veneto." And I laughed again heartily.

Gilda looked puzzled, but she was a conscientious woman, and knew to steer clear of this delicate subject. She smiled. "Then I wish you joy with all my heart. You are the best judge of your own happiness."

And with a wave she left me. No one else in my circle of friends appeared to share her foreboding scruples about my forthcoming marriage to Dario. It was talked of with much interest and expectation. Among other things, I earned the reputation of being a most impatient bride-to-be, for now I would consent to no delays. I hurried all the preparations on with feverish anticipation. I had no difficulty in persuading Dario that the sooner our wedding took place the better. He was as eager as I was, ready to rush toward his own destruction as Beatrice had been. His chief passion was greed, and the rumors of my fabulous wealth had aroused his hunger for it from the very moment he had first met me as Contessa Corona.

As soon as our betrothal became known, he became an object of envy to all the men who had tried to entrap me in vain, and this made him perfectly happy. I continued to give him costly gifts. And he, being the sole owner of the fortune I had left him, as well as that of Beatrice's, there were no limits to his extravagance. He ordered the most expensive, elaborate items, rare and antique jewelry to add to his increasing collection. He occupied himself morning after morning with tailors and shoemakers, and he was surrounded by numerous friends for whose benefit he flaunted his wealth till they became annoyed, though they kept their outrage to themselves.

And Dario loved nothing better than to torture the poorest of the men by the sight of his new horses, tack, rich clothes, and priceless jewelry. He also loved to dazzle the eyes of young girls and to send them away sick at heart, pining for his attention. Poor women. Had they known everything, they would not have envied him. Women are often too fond of measuring happiness by fine clothes and luxurious items.

My husband, because of his approaching second nuptials, had thrown off all signs of mourning and now appeared as spirited as any young man. All his old tricks of manner and speech were put forth to impress me. I knew them all so well. I understood the value of his caresses and fake lustful looks so thoroughly. He was anxious to enjoy all the dignity owing to him as the husband of an extremely rich noblewoman. Therefore he did not object when I set our wedding day for Fat Thursday, *Giovedi Grasso*. Then the fooling and mumming, the dancing, shrieking, and screaming would be at its height. It pleased him to know that our wedding ball was to be a masquerade; a display of Venetian masks and rich costume.

Because of my husband's recent bereavements, the wedding was to be as private as possible. It would take place in the Basilica Palladiana where we were married the first time. Since then, Dario's manner was somewhat curious. To me he was often apprehensive, and sometimes half conciliatory. Now and then I caught him looking at me anxiously, but his expression soon faded away. He was subject to fits of cheerfulness or moods of gloomy silence.

I could plainly see that he was in a state of unease and irritability, but I asked him no questions. If he tortured himself with memories, all the better. If he saw, or believed he saw, the resemblance between me and his dear dead Carlotta, it suited me that he should be disturbed and befuddled.

I came and went from the villa as I pleased. I wore my dark glasses as usual, and not even Giacomo followed me with his peering, inquisitive gaze. The poor man had been feeling poorly and had spoken little. He lay in an upper chamber, tended by Annunziata. Dario had already written to his relatives, asking them to take him home. "Why bother to keep him?" he had asked me.

True. Why bother with a poor old man, maimed, broken, and useless for evermore? After so many years of faithful service, turn him out, cast him forth. If he died of neglect, starvation, and ill-usage, who cared? He is a worn-out tool, his day is done. Let him perish. I would not plead for him. Why should I? I had made my own plans to see him well cared for; plans shortly to be carried out, of which Dario would know nothing about. In the meantime, Annunziata nursed him tenderly as he lay speechless, with no more strength than a baby, and only a bewildered pain in his upturned, lack-luster eyes.

One incident occurred during these last days of my vengeance that struck a sharp pain to my heart, together with a sense of the bitterest anger. I had gone to the villa early in the morning, and on crossing the lawn I saw a dark form stretched motionless on one of the paths that led to the house. I went to examine it, and recoiled in horror. It was my dog Tito shot dead. His silky black head and forepaws were dabbled in blood. His brown eyes were glazed with the film of his dying agonies. Sickened and infuriated at the sight, I called out to a gardener who was trimming the shrubbery.

"Who has done this?" I demanded.

The man looked pityingly at the poor bleeding remains, and said, in a low voice, "It was Signore Dario's order. The dog bit him yesterday. We shot him at daybreak."

I stooped to caress the faithful animal's body, and as I stroked the silky coat, my eyes were dim with tears. "How did it happen?" I asked in smothered accents. "Was the signore hurt?"

The gardener shrugged his shoulders and sighed. "No, but the dog tore his shirt sleeve with his teeth and grazed his hand. It was a small wound, but enough. He will bite no more, *povera bestia*, poor beast."

I gave the fellow five coins. "I liked the dog," I said briefly. "He was a faithful creature. Bury him decently under that tree." I pointed to the giant cypress on the lawn. "The coins are for you, for your trouble."

He looked surprised but grateful, and promised to do my bidding. Once more caressing the head of the truest friend I ever possessed, I strode into the house. I met Dario as he came out of his room. He was wearing a new white linen shirt, black velvet breeches, and fine black leather riding boots.

"So Tito has been shot?" I said, abruptly.

He gave a false shudder. "Oh, *si*. Is it not sad? But I was compelled to have it done. Yesterday I went past his kennel within reach of his chain, and he sprung furiously at me for no reason at all. See!" And holding up his hand he showed me three marks in his flesh. "I felt that you would be displeased to keep such a dangerous dog, so I had no choice but to get rid of him. It is always painful to have a favorite animal killed; but Tito belonged to my poor wife, and I think he has never been safe to handle since her death, and now that Giacomo is ill—"

"I see," I said, curtly, cutting his explanations short.

To myself, I thought of how much more valuable Tito's life was than his. Brave Tito, good Tito. He had done his best. He had tried to tear Dario's flesh; his instincts had led him to attempt to avenge the man he had felt was his mistress' foe. And he had met his fate, and died in the performance of duty. But I said no more on the subject. The dog's death was not alluded to again by either Dario or myself. My pet lay in his mossy grave under the cypress boughs, his memory untainted by any lie, and his fidelity enshrined in my heart as a good and gracious thing.

The days passed slowly on. To the revelers of the carnivale with their shouting and laughter, no doubt the hours were brief, but to me, who heard nothing except the ticking clock of my revenge, where every second brought me closer to my last and fatal act, the moments seemed long and weary.

In my carriage, I rode through the streets of the city aimlessly, feeling more like a deserted stranger than an envied noblewoman whose wealth made her the center of attention. The disorderly hilarity, the music, the color that whirled and reeled through the great streets of Vicenza this season befuddled and upset me. Though I was accustomed to the wildness of carnivale, this year it seemed out of place, a mere senseless distraction that seemed unfamiliar.

Sometimes I escaped the tumult and asked Paolo to drive me to the cemetery. While he waited, I would stare down at the freshly turned grass above Beatrice Cardano's grave. No stone marked the spot as yet, but it was not more than a couple of yards away from the iron grating that barred the entrance to that dim and fatal Mancini charnel-house.

I had a gruesome fascination for the place, and more than once I went to the opening of that secret passage made by the brigands to make certain it remained undisturbed. Everything was as I had left it, except the tangle of brush-wood had become thicker, and more weeds and brambles had sprung up, making it less visible than before and rendering it more impassable. By a fortunate accident I had secured the key of the vault. I knew that for family burial-places of this kind there are always two keys; one left in charge of the keeper of the cemetery, the other in possession of the owners of the mausoleum, and this is the one I managed to obtain.

On one occasion, alone in my own library at the villa, I remembered that in an upper drawer of an old oaken escritoire, was a ring of keys belonging to the cellar doors and other rooms in the house. I found them lying there as usual and they were all labeled. I turned them over impatiently, not finding what I sought. I was about to give up the search, when I noticed a large rusty iron key that had slipped to the back of the drawer. I pulled it out, and to my delight it was labeled *Mausoleum*. I immediately took it, glad to have obtained something so necessary to my plan. It would not be long before I would need it.

The cemetery was deserted at this festive season. No one visited it to lay wreaths of flowers or sacred mementoes on the final resting-places of their loved ones. Amidst all the joy of the carnivale, nobody gave a thought to the dead. In my frequent walks there I was always alone. I could have opened my vault and gone down into it without being observed, but I never did. I contented myself with occasionally trying the key in the lock, and reassuring myself that it worked without difficulty.

Returning from one of these excursions late on a mild afternoon toward the end of the week before my marriage, I strolled through the Piazza dei Signori, where I saw young men and women dancing a country dance with graceful, impassioned movements. The twang of a guitar and the metallic beat of a tambourine accompanied their steps. The dancers' handsome, animated faces, their flashing eyes and laughing lips, their many-colored costumes, the glitter of beads on the brown necks of the maidens, their red caps jauntily perched on the thick black curls of the men, painted a pleasant picture of vibrant life against the pale gray of the February sky.

I watched the dance with pleasure—so full of harmony and rhythm. The lad who thrummed the guitar broke out now and then into a song that matched the music perfectly. I could not distinguish all the words he sang, but the refrain was always the same, and he gave it in every possible inflection and variety of tone, from grave to gay, from pleading to pathetic: *How beautiful a thing to die, suddenly slain at the door of one's beloved.*

The stupid words made no sense, I thought half angrily, yet I could not help smiling at the young man who sang it. He seemed to enjoy repeating it, and he rolled his black eyes with lovelorn intensity, and breathed forth sighs that sounded through his music with earnestness. He had a charm about his handsome dirty face and unkempt hair, and I watched him with amusement, glad for the distraction from my intrigues and unhappy thoughts.

Soon, the dance ended and I recognized one of the breathless, laughing dancers. It was Ernesto Paccanini, who had taken me aboard his ship to Pescara. The sight of him offered some relief from a question that had been puzzling me for several days. As soon as the dancers dispersed, I walked up to him and touched him on the shoulder.

He tensed, looked round in surprise, and did not seem to recognize me at first. I recalled that when he had first met me, I had not yet purchased my dark spectacles.

"Signore Paccanini, it is I, Contessa Corona," I reminded him.

His face cleared and he smiled. "*Buon giorno,* Contessa," he cried. "A thousand pardons that I did not recognize you. I have heard your name spoken often and think of you all the time. Rich, great, generous. And on the verge of getting married too. Love makes everyone's troubles disappear, does it not?" He laughed heartily. Then lifting his cap from his clustering black hair, he added, "All joy be with you, Contessa."

I smiled and thanked him. I noticed he looked at me curiously. "Do you think my appearance has changed?" I asked.

He flushed with embarrassment. "We all change," he answered, lightly, evading my glance. "The days pass and each one takes a little bit of our youth away with it. One grows old without knowing it."

I laughed. "I see. You think I have aged somewhat since you saw me?"

"A little, Contessa," he confessed.

"I have suffered a severe illness," I said, quietly, "and my eyes are still weak, as you perceive," and I touched my glasses. "But I shall get stronger in time. Can you come with me for a few moments? I seek your help in a matter of importance."

He nodded and followed me.

Piazza dei Signori

Chapter Twenty-Seven

We left the Piazza dei Signori, and paused at a street corner.

"Do you remember Cesare Negri?" I asked.

He shrugged. "Oh, *povero diavolo*, the poor devil. I remember him well, a courageous fellow and fearless, with a big heart, too, if one knew where to find it. Now he drags his chains through hell. Well, no doubt he deserves it, but there are worse men in the world than Cesare."

I told him how I had seen Negri under arrest when I was in Pescara and that I had spoken with him. "I mentioned you, and he asked me to tell you that Teresa killed herself."

"Ah. Unfortunately I already know," he said sympathetically and sighed. "*Poverinetta*. Poor little one. So fragile and small. To think she had the courage and strength to plunge the knife in her own breast. Ah well, women will do strange things, especially over the love of a man, and there is no doubt she loved Cesare."

"If you had the opportunity, would you help Negri escape again?" I inquired with a half smile.

"Not I, Contessa. No, not now. The law is the law, and I, Ernesto Paccanini, do not wish to break it. No, Cesare must accept his punishment. It is a life sentence, and rather harsh, but no one can deny it is fair. When Teresa was alive, that was different. I might have considered it, but now, let the saints help Cesare, for I cannot."

I laughed as I met the audacious flash of his eyes. I knew, despite his denial, that if Cesare Negri ever got free of the galleys, he might just find the captain and his vessel waiting nearby. "Do you still own your brig, the *Laura Bella*?"

"*Sì*, Contessa, the Madonna be praised. And she has been newly rigged and painted. She is as trim a craft as any you will find in the wide blue waters of the Adriatic."

"I have a friend, someone related to me, who is experiencing some trouble. It is best for her that she leave Vicenza in secret. Will you help her? You will be paid well."

He looked puzzled and remained silent while he pondered my request.

I continued, noting his hesitation. "She is the victim of some cruel and malicious acts by a family member and is desperate to escape his vicious maltreatment."

His brow cleared. "Oh, if that is the case, Contessa, I am at your service. But where does your friend wish to go?"

I paused for a moment and considered. "To Civita Vecchia. From that port she can obtain a ship to take her to a further destination; anywhere she wants."

The captain's expression turned solemn and he looked doubtful. "Civita Vecchia is a long way from here, and it is winter with many cross currents and opposing winds. With all my heart, Contessa, it would be my pleasure to help you in any way I can, but I cannot risk sailing the *Laura Bella* so far in such adverse weather." He paused to consider something in silence. "But I know of another ship, and it might suit your friend's needs." He layed his hand confidentially on my arm. "It is a stout brig and leaves for Civita Vecchia next Friday morning."

The Contessa's Vendetta

"The day after Fat Thursday?" I queried, with a smile he did not understand.

He nodded. "Yes, exactly. She carries a cargo of Prosecco wine, and is very swift, very sturdy. I know her captain very well." He laughed lightly. "He is a good soul, but like the rest of us, he works hard to earn a good living. For someone as wealthy as you, money is of little consequence, but for people like us, well, we work hard and there is never enough to meet the needs of our families. Now, if you agree, I will approach him and make him an offer for passage in whatever amount of money you decide to pay, and I will tell him to expect one passenger. I can assure you, he will not refuse."

His suggestion fit with my plans perfectly and I offered to pay a generous sum for the passage.

The captain's eyes glistened. "That is a small fortune. I'd be lucky to earn that in twenty voyages. But I should not be impolite. Such good fortune cannot touch everyone."

I smiled. "Do not worry. I would never allow you to go unrewarded." I placed two gold florins in his palm. "As you said, money is of little consequence to me. Arrange this little matter without difficulty, and I shall not forget you. You can call at my rented villa tomorrow or the next day, when you have settled everything. Here is the address." I handed him my card. "But remember, in order to protect my friend, this voyage and her presence on his ship must be kept in the strictest confidence. I will rely on you to explain it as such to your friend who commands the brig going to Civita Vecchia. He must ask no questions of his passenger. The more silence, the more discretion. Then, when he has safely landed the passenger at her destination, he must forget all about her. Do you understand?"

Enrico nodded and winked. "*Si, si,* Contessa. He has a very bad memory, and it shall only become worse. Believe it."

I laughed and then we parted. As I walked away, an open carriage coming swiftly toward me attracted my attention. As it drew nearer I recognized the prancing steeds and the familiar livery. An elegant man clad in olive velvets and a cloak trimmed in Russian sables looked out, smiling and waving at the dancers.

Dario. My husband, my betrothed. Beside him sat the Doge's Grand Equerry, Giovanni Gabaldi, a most upstanding and irreproachable men, famous for his honorable conduct not only in Vicenza but throughout the Veneto region. He was so virtuous and unimpeachable, that it was difficult to imagine him even daring to be affectionate with his righteous, well-dressed wife. Yet I recalled a rumour about him; an old tale that came from Padua, of how a young and handsome nobleman had been found dead at his villa's doors, stabbed to the heart. Some say Gabaldi killed him, but nothing could be proved, so nothing was certain. On the matter, the Equerry remained silent, and so did his wife. Scandal seemed to elude this stately couple, whose behavior toward each other when out in society was a lesson in perfect etiquette. If dissension existed behind the scenes, no one knew, for they kept it well hidden from the world. I ducked behind a column as the carriage containing the two hypocrites dashed by.

I was in a reflective mood, and when I reached the market, the distracting noises of venders selling their wares of chestnuts and confetti, the nasal singing of the street-rhymers, the yells of *Punchinello* marionettes, and people's laughter frayed my nerves and tried my endurance.

To indulge a sudden impulse that took hold of me, I made my way into some crowded alleys, trying to find the street where I had purchased the clothes on the day I had escaped from the crypt. I took several wrong turns, but at last I found it.

The Contessa's Vendetta

The old rag-dealer's shop was still there, and in the same filthy condition of utter disorder. Like before, a woman sat at the door mending, but she was not the same brusque, warped old hag of before. This was a much younger and stouter individual, with a Jewish face and dark, ferocious eyes. I approached her. When she noticed my fancy dress and refined manner, she rose courteously and smiled with a respectful, yet suspicious air.

"Are you the owner?" I asked.

"*Si, signora.*"

"What became of the old woman who used to own the shop before you?"

She laughed, shrugged her shoulders, and drew her finger across her throat. "She killed herself with a sharp knife. She left behind a great deal of blood, too, for so withered a body. To kill herself in that fashion was stupid. She spoiled a rare Indian shawl that was on her bed, worth more than a thousand lire. One would not have thought she had so much blood in her."

I listened in sickened silence. "Was she mad?" I asked.

"Mad? Well, everyone certainly seems to think so, but I think she was sane, all except for the matter of that shawl. She should have taken that off her bed first before she killed herself. Yet, she was wise enough to know that she was of no use to anybody. She did the best she could. Did you know her, Signora?"

"I gave her money once," I replied, evasively; then taking out a few silver coins, I handed them to this evil-eyed, furtive-looking daughter of Israel, who received the gift with over-enthusiastic gratitude. "Thank you for your information," I said coldly. "Good-day."

"Good-day to you, Signora," she replied, resuming her mending and watching me curiously as I turned away.

I walked down the dirty street feeling faint and giddy. The death of the miserable rag-dealer had been relayed to me in a callous manner, yet I was moved by a sense of regret and pity. Poor, half crazy, and utterly friendless, the old woman had suffered betrayal and had wallowed in the same bitterness and sorrow as me. I shuddered and wondered if my death would be as violent as hers. When my vendetta was complete, would I grow old, shrunken, and mad? On a lurid day, would I also draw a sharp knife across my throat to end my life? I walked more rapidly to shake off the morbid thoughts that crept insidiously into my mind.

Earlier, the chaotic noise of the market had became unbearable. Now, I found it both a relief and a distraction. Two men in carnivale masks dressed in violet and gold costumes whizzed past me. A man leaned out of a colorfully decorated balcony and dropped a bunch of roses at my feet. I stooped to pick them up, and then raising my eyes, I waved to him in gratitude. A few paces on, I gave them away to a ragged child. Of all flowers in the world, they were, and still are, the ones I most detest. Dario had given Beatrice a rose on that night when I had seen her clasped in his arms. The red rose on her breast had been crushed in their embrace—a rose whose withered leaves I still possess.

In my rented villa there are no roses, and I am much relieved. The trees are very tall, the tangle of bramble and coarse brushwood far too dense. Nothing grows there but a few herbs and field flowers, unsuitable for picking, wearing or decorating. Yet to me, they are preferable than roses whose vibrant colors and lush aromas are forever spoiled to me. I may be harsh in judging such beautiful flowers, but their perfume now provokes a terrible memory I yearn to forget.

When I returned home, I discovered I was late for dinner. The worried expressions on Paolo's and Santina's faces faded moments after I walked through the door. Both had been watching over me anxiously. My brooding, long, solitary walks, and all the hours I spent locked in my room writing, worried them. Paolo helped me remove my gloves and mantle, biting his tongue as if to keep from asking me any questions.

I hurried through my dinner and then rushed to my room to change. I was to meet Dario and two of his friends at the theatre, and knew I would be late. I found him already seated in his box, looking refined and elegant in his golden embroidered waistcoat and white silk shirt with ruffles sleeves. His breeches were black brocade above white stockings and black shoes with gold buckles. On his wrists and fingers he wore the rings and bracelets I had asked Beatrice to give him from the stolen hoard. The jewels flared against the flaming sconces around us.

When he saw me enter, he and his friends rose simultaneously to greet me. Dario kissed me on the cheek with his usual enthusiasm, and handed me a gift of an expensive bouquet of gardenias set within a mother-of-pearl handle studded with garnets. I acknowledged his friends with a nod; both of whom I was acquainted with from long ago, and then took my seat next to Dario just as the comedy was about to begin.

The play was about a young wife, her old doting husband, and her noble lover. The husband was played the fool, of course. The climax of the comedy occurred when the husband found himself locked out of his own house in his nightclothes during a pelting rainstorm while his virtuous spouse enjoyed a luxurious supper with her admirer. My husband laughed heartily at all the poor jokes and stale adages. He especially seemed taken by the actress who played the wife; a cheeky, hotheaded liar who flagrantly flashed her dark eyes, tossed her head, and heaved her abundant bosom flamboyantly whenever she hissed out the words *vecchiaccio maladetto*, accursed villainous old monster, at her husband's humiliation. What shocked me the most, was how the audience sympathized with her, even though she was in the wrong.

I watched Dario with scorn as he smiled, nodded, and tapped his extravagantly shoed foot to the lively music. I leaned over. "Are you enjoying the play?"

His expression was jovial. "It's hilarious isn't it? The husband is so funny."

"The betrayed spouse is always made fun of," I remarked, smiling coldly. "Why bother to get married if one knows they will be held in contempt and made a fool of?"

He glanced at me. "Surely you cannot be angry. This sort of thing happens only in theatre, not in real life."

"Plays, *carissimo*, are intended to mimic real life, but I hope there are exceptions, and that all spouses are not fools."

He smiled and returned his attention back to the antics of the actors on the stage.

I toyed with the flowers he had given me and said no more as my mood turned sullen.

"You seem awfully bored or unhappy, or both," one of Dario's friends commented to me as we left the theatre. "Is something the matter?"

I forced a smile. "Me? If I seemed bored in your company, I apologize, for it would be most ungrateful of me."

He sighed. Although he was young and naive, he seemed to be more intellectual and more thoughtful than most men were. "That sounded almost like a compliment," he said, looking straight at me with his clear, candid eyes. "Yet I think your courtesy is contrived."

I looked at him in surprise. "Contrived? Forgive me. I do not understand."

He regarded me steadily. "What I mean to say is that

you do not seem to like men. Certainly, you compliment us and try to be sociable, but I sense you bear an inherent dislike for us and are skeptical of our motives. Why, I suspect you even think we are all hypocrites."

I laughed a little coldly. "You assume much about me. Your words place me in a very awkward position. Were I to tell you my real feelings—"

He interrupted me with a touch of his hand on my arm. "You would say we are all guilty of treachery. Ah, Contessa, we men have indeed many faults." He paused, and his brilliant eyes softened. "You have my sincerest wishes that your marriage will be a very long and happy one."

I did not know how to respond and did not even thank him for the wish. Rather, it angered me that he had successfully scoured my innermost thoughts with such accuracy. Was my acting that terrible? I glanced at him as we walked on, gathering my thoughts.

"Marriage itself is a farce," I said harshly. "The play has shown us how it will be. In a few days, Dario shall play the part of the chief buffoon; in other words, the husband." And at this, I burst out laughing.

My companion's mouth fell open and he looked aghast, almost frightened. An expression of aversion turned his face bitter. I did not care. Why should I?

Our conversation suddenly ended for we had reached the theatre's outer vestibule. My carriage was already drawn up at the entrance and Dario helped me step into it. Once I was seated, he stood next to his two friends at the door, and wished me a *felicissima notte*, a most happy night. I put my jeweled hand through the open carriage window. He stooped to kiss it lightly. Withdrawing it quickly, I selected a white gardenia from my bouquet and handed it to him with a bewitching smile.

Then my glittering carriage dashed away in a whirl and

clatter of prancing hoofs and rapid wheels. I looked back. Dario stood alone beneath the theatre's portico, a press of people still pouring out, holding the gardenia in his hand.

After a moment, I turned back around, recollected myself, and pitched the bouquet at my feet, savagely crushing it beneath the heal of my embroidered slipper. A nauseating, penetrating odor rose from the slain petals. Where had I inhaled such a cloying aroma before? And then I remembered. Beatrice Cardano had worn a gardenia in her corsage at the dinner party. It had been pinned to her gown when she lay dying. I hurled the thrashed bouquet out of the window.

As the carriage brought me closer to home, the streets were full of festivity and music, but I paid little attention to it. Rather, I looked out my window up at the quiet sky dotted with its countless luminous stars. I was vaguely aware of mandolins resounding from somewhere nearby, but my spirit was too numb to enjoy the delicate tones. My mind, always heightened, always alert, was now completely exhausted. My body ached, and when I arrived home, all I could do was change into my night clothes, and fling myself on my bed. I fell into the deep sleep of a woman weary unto death.

Chapter Twenty-Eight

All things come to those who wait. This, I knew well, and I had waited for a very long time. The time for vengeance finally arrived. The slow wheel of time had finally brought me to this day — the day before my strange wedding - the eve of my remarriage to my own husband.

All the preparations were made and nothing was left undone. The marriage ceremony was to be quiet and private, but it would be followed by a grand supper and a masked ball with one hundred and fifty friends, acquaintances, and members of the nobility. I spared no expense for this, my last performance in my brilliant career as the successful Contessa Giulia Corona. Everything that art, taste, and luxury could buy was included for this dazzling ball. After this, the dark curtain would fall on my completed drama, never to rise again.

And now, in the afternoon of this, my final act, I sat alone with my husband in the drawing-room of Villa Mancini, discussing several issues pertaining to the festivities the next day. The long windows were open. The warm spring sunlight lay like a veil of gold on the tender green grass. Birds sung for joy and flitted from branch to branch, hovering above their nests then soaring with perfect liberty into the high heaven of cloudless blue. Great creamy magnolia buds looked ready to burst into wide splendid flowers among the trees' dark shining leaves. The aroma of violets and primroses floated on every delicious breath of air, and around the wide veranda, climbing white roses had already unfurled their little blossoms to the balmy wind.

It was spring in Vicenza, a land where spring is lovely, sudden and brilliant in its beauty like angels from Heaven. And talk about angels. Had I not a veritable angel for my companion at that moment? No man could outshine Dario's charms; his dark eyes, rippling golden hair, a dazzling perfect face, and a physique to rival that of Hercules.

I glanced at him secretively from time to time when he was not aware of my gaze; an act made easy by the sheltering protection of the dark glasses I wore, for I knew that there was a terrible look in my eyes—the look of a half-famished tiger ready to spring on long-desired prey.

Dario was exceptionally cheery, and his happy expression and agile movements reminded me of some gorgeous tropical bird swaying to and fro on an equally gorgeous branch.

"You are like a princess in a fairy tale," he said. "Everything you do, you do superbly and with perfection. How satisfying it is to be so rich. There is nothing better in all the world."

"Except love," I returned, with a grim attempt to be sentimental.

His large eyes softened.

"*Si.*" He smiled with expressive tenderness. "Except love. But when one has both love and wealth, life is truly a paradise."

"So great a paradise that it is hardly worthwhile trying to get into Heaven at all. Will you make earth a paradise for me, Dario, or will you only love me as much, or as little, as you loved your late wife?"

He shrugged his shoulders. "Why are you always so fond of talking about my late wife?" he asked, irritably. "I am so tired of hearing her name spoken. I do not care to be reminded of dead people, and she died so horribly too. I have told you often enough that I never loved her. Certainly, I liked her a little, and I was quite shocked and upset when that dreadful monk, who looked like a ghost himself, came and told me she was dead. You can't imagine how horrible it was to hear such a piece of news suddenly, while I was actually at luncheon with Bea— Signorina Cardano. We were both stunned, of course, but my heart did not break over it. Now, you, I really do love—"

I drew nearer to him on the couch where he sat, and put one hand on his shoulder. "You really do love me?" I asked, in a half-incredulous tone. "You are quite sure?"

He laughed as I nestled my head on his shoulder. "I am quite sure. How many times have you asked me that absurd question? What can I say, what can I do, to make you believe me?"

"Nothing." In truth, nothing he could say or do would make me believe him for a moment. "But how do you love me? For myself or for my wealth?"

He raised his head with a proud, graceful gesture. "For yourself, of course. Do you think mere wealth could win my affection? No, I love you for your own sake. Your fine qualities, your virtues, have made me love you with all my heart."

I smiled bitterly. With me head still resting against him, he could not see the smile. I slowly caressed the back of his neck. "For that sweet answer, carissimo, you shall have your reward. You called me a princess just now. Perhaps I deserve that title more than you know. You remember the jewels I sent you before we met?"

"Remember them," he exclaimed. "They are my

favorites in all my collection. Such finery is fit for an emperor."

"And an emperor wears them," I said, lightly. "But they are mere trifles compared to other items of jewelry I possess, and which I intend to give you."

His eyes glistened with greed.

"If they are more elaborate than those I already have, they must be indeed magnificent. And they are all for me?"

"All for you," I replied, nestling closer to him, and playing with the hand on which the ring I had placed there sparkled so bravely. "All for my groom. A hoard of treasures; rubies as red as blood, sapphires as blue as the sky, emeralds as green as the lushest forest, diamonds brighter than the stars. What is the matter?" He had shifted restlessly. "All my treasures and wealth will be yours when we marry. All you need do is take them. I hope they bring you much joy."

A momentary pallor had stolen over his face while I was speaking in my customary harsh voice, which I strove to render even harsher than usual. But he soon recovered from whatever passing emotion he may have felt, and gave himself up to the joys of vanity and greed, the overriding passions of his dreadful character.

"I will be the richest and best-dressed man in all Vicenza," he laughed. "Everyone will envy me. But where are these jewels? Show them to me now."

"No, not quite yet," I replied, with a gentle disdain that escaped his observation. "Tomorrow night, our marriage night, I will take you to them. And I will also fulfill another promise I made to you." I touched my dark glasses. "Do you still wish to see me without my glasses?"

He raised his eyes. "*Sì*," he murmured. "I want to see you as you are."

"But I'm afraid you might be disappointed," I said ironically. "My eyes are not pleasant to look at."

The Contessa's Vendetta

"It doesn't matter. I will be satisfied if I see them just once. We don't have to have much light in the room in case the light gives you pain. I would not wish to cause you any suffering, no, not for all the world."

"You are very agreeable," I answered. "More than I deserve. I hope I may prove worthy of your affections. But to return to the subject of the jewels. I wish you to see them for yourself and choose the best among them. Come with me tomorrow night and I will show you where they are."

He laughed heartily. "Are you a miser? Have you some secret hiding place full of treasure like Aladdin?"

I smiled. "Perhaps I have. I fear I cannot trust my wealth to a bank. The jewelry I own is almost priceless, and it would be unwise to place such tempting toys within the reach of even an honest man. At any rate, if I have been miserly, it is for your sake. I have gone to great lengths to personally guard the treasure because it is to be your wedding gift. You cannot blame me for this?"

In answer, he kissed me. Strive against it as I would, I always shuddered at the touch of his lips. A mingled sensation of loathing and longing possessed me that sickened while it stung my soul.

"*Amore,*" he murmured. "As if I could blame you for anything. In my eyes, you have no faults. You are perfect; good and generous, the best of women. There is only one thing I wish sometimes—" He paused and knitted his brow into a frown as a puzzled, pained expression flitted into his eyes.

"And that one thing is?" I inquired.

"That you did not remind me so often of Carlotta," he said, abruptly and half angrily. "Not when you speak of her, I do not mean that. What I mean is, that you have ways and mannerisms exactly like hers. Of course I know there is no actual resemblance, and yet—" He paused, and looked troubled.

"Really, *caro*," I remarked lightly. "You truly do embarrass me. This belief of yours is most awkward. When I visited you at the monastery, you became quite ill at the sight of my hand, which you declared was exactly like that of your wife's. And now, you are doing it again. The same morbid notion has entered your head once more. Perhaps you think I am your late wife?" And I laughed aloud.

He frowned a little, but soon laughed also. "I know it sounds absurd Perhaps I am a little nervous. Tell me more about the jewels. When will I see them?"

"Tomorrow night during the ball, you and I will slip away together. It will not take long and we will return again before any of our friends miss us. You do want to go, don't you?"

"Of course, but I don't want to be gone for long because my valet will have to pack my clothes and personal items in preparation for leaving for Rome and Paris in the morning."

"That is the arrangement," I said, with a cold smile.

"The place where you have hidden your jewels is nearby?"

"Very near," I assured him, watching his reaction closely.

He laughed and rubbed his hands together. "But why not fetch them now and bring them here. Then we wouldn't have to leave the ball."

"Oh, goodness, I've accumulated far too many, and I do not know which pieces you would prefer. Some are more valuable than others and I have waited a long time to watch you make your choice."

He smiled craftily. "And what would you think if I made no choice at all. What would you say if I were to take them all?"

The Contessa's Vendetta

"You are perfectly welcome to them," I replied. "As many or as few as you wish."

He looked taken aback. "You truly possess a generous heart," he said.

"You deserve it. Good men are as rare as fine brilliants—difficult to find but wonderful to keep."

He caressed my hand. "No one has ever loved me as you have."

"Not even Beatrice Cardano?" I suggested, acidly.

He straighted and gave me look of disdain. "Beatrice Cardano. She was a mere servant and not worthy of my interest. It was only lately that she began to take advantage of the trust my wife had in her, and then she became too ardent towards me; a grave mistake on her part."

I rose from my seat beside him, struggling to maintain my composure while sitting so close to the murderer of my friend and his lover. Had he forgotten his own ardency towards Beatrice; the thousand tricks and spells by which he had captivated her heart, her spirit, and ruined her respectability?

"I grieve her death, and shall always continue to do so," I said, coldly and steadily. "Sadly, I am oversensitive and often, even small problems have an adverse affect on me. Speaking of Beatrice upsets me. It's best that I leave. Goodbye until tomorrow, when we will be finally married."

He came to stand before me and pulled me to him.

"Are you certain we should not meet again till we meet in the church?"

"*Si.* It's best that we each remain alone on our last day before marriage so that we have time to contemplate our future together. Besides, it will make us yearn for each other more."

He toyed with a loose curl beside my left cheek and I took hold of his hand. "I see you are still wearing your former wedding-ring. May I have it?"

"Certainly."

I smiled as I watched him draw off the plain gold band I had placed there nearly four years ago. "May I keep it?"

"Of course. I would rather not see it again."

"I promise you shall not." I slipped it into my purse. "I will replace it with a new one tomorrow—one that I hope brings you more blessings and good fortune than this one has."

And as his eyes turned to me with deceitful dreaminess, I fought back my hatred of him with every shred of strength I possessed, and let him kiss me. Had I acted on my true urge, I would have pulverized his foot with my heel, or slapped his face with brutal ferocity. I loathed him, bitterly, to the point that I felt ill at his caress, yet I managed to hide all signs of my hatred. All he saw was his elderly fiancé with her calm, courteous demeanor, chill smile, and parental tenderness; and he considered me an important woman of high-rank and unlimited wealth, who was about to make him one of the richest men in all of Europe.

He likely thought my resemblance to his dead wife was purely accidental. After all, similarities in face and body are common. Although my likeness to myself was astounding and troubled him, he was a long way from discovering the truth. How could he? Who would ever believe that someone who was dead and buried could escape from their grave?

Soon, I left him and made my way home. There, I found Ernesto Paccanini waiting for me. He was seated in the outer entrance hall and I bade him follow me as I entered my private salon. Unsettled by the splendor of the room, he paused at the doorway, and stood, red cap in hand, hesitating, though with an amiable smile on his sunburned face.

The Contessa's Vendetta

"Please come in and sit down. Do not let this gaudy display of silk and gilding prevent you from making yourself comfortable. After the sparkling waves and blue sky, and the sheeny white sails of your ship gleaming in the sun, this room must seem taudry to you. I would love to live a life such as yours. There is nothing better than the fresh air, the sun on your face, and the wind in your hair to truly feel close to Heaven."

At my words, he seemed to relax. Almost at once, he ignored the oppulent décor and costly luxuries around him and entered confidently, sitting himself on a velvet and gold chair with as much ease as if he had done so all his life.

"How true, Contessa." His teeth gleamed through his jet-black mustache while his warm southern eyes flashed fire. "There is nothing sweeter than a sailor's life. There have been many who encourage me to wed and start a family, but it is not so easy. The woman I wed must love the sea. She must be strong enough to wait through God's storms without fear. Her tender words must ring out loud and clear above the sound of the waves crashing against the ship when the wind is strong. And as for our children," he paused and laughed. "My children will have the ocean's salt in their blood, or they will be no children of mine."

I smiled at his zeal, poured out some Prosecco, and invited him to taste it. He smacked his lips in appreciation and raised his glass. "To your health, Contessa. May you live long and enjoy your life."

I thanked him, but in my heart I carried little hope that his good wish would come true. "And are you going to listen to your friends' advice? Will you marry one day?"

He set down his partly empty glass, shrugged, and smiled mysteriously. A sudden tenderness flowed in his keen eyes. "Who knows? There is a young woman. My mother loves her very much. She is as small and beautiful as Cesare Negri's Teresa." He placed his brown hand over his heart. "Her head reaches to here. She looks frail as a lily, but is hardy as a sea-gull, and no one loves the wild waves more than she. Perhaps, in a few months, when the white lilies bloom, perhaps I will ask her to marry me then." He raised his glass of wine to his lips and drained it off with a relish, while his honest face beamed with pleasure.

Always the same story, I thought, moodily. Love, the tempter. Love, the destroyer. Love, the curse. Was there no escape from this snare that trapped and slayed women's souls?

Chapter Twenty-Nine

Ernesto Paccanini snapped out of his enjoyable daydream and pushed his chair closer to mine. "And for your friend who is in trouble," he whispered in a low, confidential tone, then paused and looked at me as though waiting permission to proceed.

I nodded. "Go on. What have you arranged?"

"Everything," he announced, with an air of triumph. "All is smooth sailing. At six o'clock on Friday morning the *Rondinella*, that is the brig I told you of, will weigh anchor for Civita Vecchia. Her captain, old Antonio Bardi, will wait ten minutes or even a quarter of an hour if necessary for the—the—"

"Passenger," I interjected. "That is very kind and generous of him, but he will not need to delay his departure for even a moment. Is he satisfied with the passage money?"

"Satisfied." Enrico swore a good-natured oath and laughed aloud. "By San Pietro. If he were not, he would deserve to drown like a dog on the voyage. Though truly, he is not an easy man to please. He is old, cross, and crusty; a man who has seen so much of life that they are tired of it. Even the stormiest sea is a tame fish-pond to old Bardi. But he is satisfied this time, Contessa. I assure you, your friend will find him to be both dumb and blind when she comes on board."

"Perfect," I smiled. "*Mille grazie*, Enrico. I owe you a thousand thank-yous, but I have one more favor to ask of you."

In a light, yet graceful gesture, he bowed his head to invite me to speak. "Contessa, anything I can do, you have merely to command me."

"It is a small favor," I returned. "Would you take a small valise belonging to my friend, and place it on board the *Rondinella* under the care of the captain. Will you do this?"

"Most willingly. I will take it now if you wish."

"Yes please. If you don't mind waiting here a moment, I will bring it to you."

Leaving him, I went to my bedroom, and from a locked cupboard, I took out a leather bag, which I had secretly packed myself, unknown to Santina, with useful and necessary items. Most important among them was a bulky sack of gold florins. These amounted to nearly all that remained of the money I had placed in the bank at Pescara. I withdrew it in small amounts, leaving behind only a couple of thousand *scudi*, for which I had no special need. I locked and strapped the bag which bore no name on it and was of average weight to carry.

I handed it to Enrico, who swung it easily in his right hand. "Your friend is not wealthy, Contessa, if this is all she has for luggage."

"You are right," I answered, with a slight sigh. "She is truly very poor, beggared of everything that should be hers through the treachery of those who she once trusted."

Enrico was listening sympathetically.

"That is why I have paid her passage-money and have done my best to help her."

"You have a good heart, Contessa. Pity there weren't more like you. This friend of yours is young, without doubt?

"*Si*, quite young, not yet thirty."

"It is as if you were a mother to her. I hope she is truly grateful to you."

"I hope so too," I said, unable to resist a smile. "And now, my friend, take this." I pressed a small sealed packet into his hand. "This is for you, but you must promise me that you will not open it until you are home with your mother and the young woman you spoke. If its contents please you, as I believe they will, remember that I am overjoyed by your happiness."

His dark eyes sparkled with gratitude as I spoke, and setting the valise down on the ground, he stretched out his hand half timidly, half frankly. I placed my hand in his and he kissed it. Then I bade him farewell.

"I seem to be at a loss for words," he said, with a sort of shamefaced eagerness, "There is so much more I ought to say to you, Contessa, but for my life I cannot find the right words. I must thank you better when I see you next."

"*Si*," I answered wearily. "When you see me next, you may thank me if you wish, but believe me, I need no thanks."

I watched him leave knowing we would never meet again — he to his life of wind and sea, and I to—but I refuse to look ahead too far into the future. Rather, I preferred to go step by step through the labyrinths of my memory, over the old ground wet with blood and tears, not missing one detail on my dreary path towards the bitter end.

Later that evening I met with Paolo. He was melancholy and reserved, a mood which was the result of an announcement I had previously made to him, namely, that his services and those of Santina would not be required during my wedding-trip. He had hoped they would both accompany me, a hope which had partially soothed his vexation over my marrying at all.

His plans were now foiled, and if ever the good-natured fellow could be irritable, he was assuredly so on this occasion. He stood before me with his usual respectful air, but he avoided my glance, and kept his eyes fixed on the pattern of the carpet.

"Paolo. Joy comes at last, you see, even to me. Tomorrow I shall wed Dario Gismondi, the handsomest and perhaps the richest man in all of Vicenza."

"I know, Contessa," he said with the same obstinate expression and downward gaze.

"You are not pleased at the prospect of my happiness?" I asked.

He glanced up for an instant, then as quickly looked down again.

"If only one could be certain that you would indeed be happy," he answered, dubiously.

"And you are not sure?"

He paused, then replied firmly, ""No, Contessa. You do not look happy. Instead, you seem sorrowful and ill."

I shrugged my shoulders indifferently. "You are wrong, Paolo. I am well and very happy. Who could be happier? But my health or happiness matter nothing to me, and should matter even less to you. Listen, I have something I wish you to do for me."

He gave me a sidelong, half-expectant glance.

"Tomorrow evening I want you to go to Venice."

He was utterly astonished. "To Venice?"

"*Si*, to Venice," I repeated, somewhat impatiently. "You and Santina. There is nothing surprising in that. You will take a letter from me to Signora Monti. Paolo, you have been faithful and loyal so far, and I continue to expect implicit fidelity. You will not be needed here tomorrow after the masquerade ball has begun. You and Santina can go directly to Venice, and I want you to remain there till you receive further news from me. You will not have to wait long, and in the meantime," I smiled, "you can pay your respects to the lovely Lilla."

Paolo did not return the smile. "But—but," he stammered, perplexed, "if we go to Venice, we will not be able to wait upon the contessa. There is the portmanteau to pack, and who will see to the luggage when you leave on Friday morning for Rome?" He stopped, his vexation was too great to allow him to proceed.

I laughed gently.

"How many more trifles can you think of, my friend, to oppose my wishes? As for the portmanteau, you can pack it today. Then it will be ready. The rest of your duties can, for once, be performed by others. It is not only important, but imperative that you go to Venice on my errand. I want you to take this with you." I tapped a small square iron box, heavily made and strongly padlocked, which stood on the table near me.

He glanced at the box, but hesitated, and his gloomy expression deepened.

I grew a little annoyed. "What is the matter with you?" I said sternly. "If you have something you wish to say to me, then please, say it."

My irritation startled him. He looked up with bewildered pain in his eyes, and spoke with an eloquent appeal. "Contessa, you must forgive me if I seem too bold, but I am true to you and would go with you to death if need be. I am not blind, I can see how you suffer, though you try to hide it well. I have often watched you when you did not know it. I believe you have a wound in your heart, and it is bleeding, always bleeding. Such a wound often leads to death, just as if it were an arrow to the heart. Let me watch over you, Contessa; let me stay with you. I am very fond of you."

He stepped closer and placed his tentative hand on mine. "You do not know the look that is in your face sometimes. It is the look of one who has been stunned by a hard blow. You are even sadder than before, and the look I speak of appears more often. *Sì*, I have watched you, and lately I have seen you writing far into the night, when you should have been sleeping. Ah, Contessa. I can see you are angry with me now, and I know I should not have spoken so openly, but tell me, how can I go to Lilla and be happy when I know that you are alone and sad?"

I withdrew my hand from his clasp to stop his revelations. "I am not angry," I said, with quiet steadiness, and yet with a touch of coldness, though his expressions of affection had deeply stirred me. "No, I am not angry, but I am sorry to have been the object of so much anxiety on your part. Your pity is misplaced, Paolo, it is indeed. Do not pity me. I assure you that tomorrow I will have won all that I have ever sought. My greatest desire will be fulfilled. Believe it. No woman has ever been so thoroughly satisfied as I shall be."

Then seeing him still look sad and incredulous, I clapped my hand on his shoulder and smiled. "Come, wear a merry face for my bridal day. I thank you from my heart." I gave him a grave look. "For your well meant care and kindness, I assure you there is nothing wrong with me. I am perfectly well and happy. So, I can depend on you to go to Venice tomorrow evening?"

Paolo sighed, but was passive. "It will be as you please," he murmured, resigned to my request.

"Good. Now that you know my wishes, please ensure nothing interferes with your departure. And, please do me one more favor. Please cease to watch me. Plainly speaking, I do not like being under your scrutiny. No, I am not offended. Far from it. Loyalty and devotion are excellent virtues, but in my case I prefer obedience — strict and implicit obedience. Whatever I may do, whether I sleep or wake, walk or sit still, go about your duties and pay no

The Contessa's Vendetta

attention to me or anything that I may say or do. That is how you can best help me. Do you understand?"

"*Sì*, Contessa." He sighed again, and reddened with his own inward confusion. "You will forgive me, Contessa, for being so forthright? I feel I have done wrong—"

"I forgive you for something that never needs to be pardoned – an excess of love. Knowing you love me, I ask you to obey me in my present wishes, and thus we shall always be friends."

His face brightened at these last words, and his thoughts turned in a new direction. He glanced at the iron box I had pointed out to him. "That is to go to Venice, Contessa?" he asked, with more alacrity than he had yet shown.

"*Sì*," I answered. "You will place it in the hands of Signora Monti, for whom I have a great respect. She will take care of it till I return."

"I shall do as you wish, Contessa," he said, rapidly, as though eager to atone for his past hesitation. "After all," he smiled, "it will be pleasant to see Lilla. She will want to hear a full accounting of your wedding."

Somewhat consoled by the prospect of seeing Lilla, he then left me. Shortly afterward I heard him humming a popular love-song while he packed my portmanteau for the honeymoon trip, a portmanteau destined never to be used or opened by its owner.

That night, in contrast to my usual practice, I lingered for a long time over my dinner. Afterwards, I poured two full glasses of fine wine. Secretly, I mixed a dose of a tasteless opiate into them. I invited Paolo and Santina to join me and bade them drink it to privately celebrate my nuptials before they left for Venice. They both drained the contents to the last drop as we celebrated.

Outside, a tempest blustered with high winds and heavy, sweeping gusts of rain. Santina cleared the dinner-table, yawning as she did so. As usual, Paolo took my mantle and went to his bedroom, a small one adjoining Santina's, to brush off any dust and dirt from it.

I opened a book, and pretending to be absorbed in the story, waited patiently for about half an hour. Then I went softly to their bedroom doors and looked in. It was as I had expected; overcome by the sleeping opiate, Santina now lay on her bed in a profound slumber. Paolo too, lay in his bed in his room, the unbrushed mantle by his side. I smiled as I watched them; my faithful servants could not follow me tonight.

I left them to their slumber, and wrapping myself in a thick cloak that muffled me almost to the eyes, I hurried out into the dark storm toward the cemetary, the abode of the dead. Fortunately I met no one on the way. I had work to do there. Work that must be done. I knew that if I had not taken the precaution of drugging my devoted servants, Paolo might, despite his protestations, have been tempted to follow me. As it was, I felt I would be safe for at least four hours, when the opiate would wear off and Paolo and Santina would wake up.

I arrived at the crypt and went to work. Though I worked as quickly as possible, it took me longer than I thought. Hatred and reluctance slowed me down. This was a gruesome, ghastly work of preparation, and when I finished it to my satisfaction, I felt as though the bony fingers of death itself had been plunged into my very marrow. I shivered with cold, my limbs would scarce bear me upright, and my teeth chattered as though I were seized by strong fever. But the importance of my task kept me motivated and working until all was completed, until the stage was ready for the last scene of the tragedy. Or comedy? Betrayal by a spouse is a more bitter evil than death.

When I returned from my dismal walk through the

lashing storm I found Paolo still fast asleep. I was glad, for had he seen me in my plight, he would have had good reason to be alarmed concerning both my physical and mental condition.

I caught a glimpse of myself in the looking glass, and recoiled at the horrible image that reflected back at me. My eyes appeared haunted and hungry as they gleamed out from under a mass of disordered white hair. My pale, haggard face was set and stern. Glittering raindrops dripped from my dark cloak. Dirt and mud stained my hands and nails, and my shoes were heavy with sludge and clay. By my entire appearance and demeanor, it was obvious I had been engaged in some abhorrent deed too repulsive to be named.

I stared at my own reflection and shuddered. Then I laughed softly with a sort of fierce enjoyment.

Quickly I threw off all my soiled garments, and locked them out of sight. Arraying myself in dressing-gown and slippers, I glanced at the time. It was half-past one. The morning of my wedding.

I had been absent three hours and a half. I went into my salon and remained there writing. A few minutes after two o'clock, the door opened noiselessly, and a very sleepy Paolo appeared with an expression of inquiring anxiety. He smiled drowsily, and seemed relieved to see me sitting quietly in my accustomed place at the writing-table.

I surveyed him with an air of affected surprise. "Paolo. What has become of you all this time?"

"It was the wine," he stammered. "I am not used to drinking. I have been asleep."

I laughed, pretended to stifle a yawn, and rose from my easy-chair.

"Truly, so have I," I said, lightly, "And if I want to be a radiant bride, it's time I went to bed. *Buona notte,* Paolo."

"*Buona notte,* Contessa."

And we both retired to rest; he satisfied that I had been in my own room all evening, and I, overjoyed with what I had prepared out there in the darkness, without a single witness except for the whirling wind and rain.

Chapter Thirty

My wedding morning dawned bright and clear, though last night's wind still sent clouds scuttling rapidly across a fair blue sky. The air was strong, fresh, and exhilarating, and the high spirited crowd that swarmed into the Piazza dei Signori was anxious to begin celebrating *Giovedi Grasso*, Fat Tuesday. As the hours passed, people hurried to the cathedral, anxious to secure their places in order to catch a glimpse of the pageantry and brilliant garments of the few distinguished persons who had been invited to my wedding. The ceremony was to take place at eleven, and at a little before half past ten I entered my carriage, accompanied by Federica Marina, my sole bridesmaid, and drove to the church. Clad in my dazzling gown of blue and gold silk brocade with adornments of satin and silk taffeta ribbon, and with an intricate embroidered veil to cover my simply styled hair, I bore almost no resemblance to the haggard woman who had faced me in the mirror a few hours earlier.

A strange happiness took hold of me; a sort of half-frenzied merriment that threatened to break through the mask of dignified composure I must wear. There were moments when I could have laughed, shrieked, and sung with the energy of a drunken barmaid. As it was, I talked incessantly; my conversation flavored with bitter wit and pungent sarcasm. Once or twice Federica studied me with wonder, as though she thought my behavior contrived or unnatural. Paolo was compelled to drive rather slowly because of the pressing throngs that swarmed at every corner and through every thoroughfare. Masked celebrants yelled, street clowns romped about, and sharp bursts of colored bladders that people tossed into the air startled my spirited horses frequently, causing them to leap and prance dangerously, thus attracting more than the usual attention to my carriage. As it drew up at last at the door of the church, I was surprised to see such a large crowd. There were loungers, beggars, children, and middle-class persons of all sorts, who excitedly watched my arrival.

As per my instructions, a rich crimson carpet had been laid down from the edge of the pavement right into the church as far as the altar. A silken awning had also been erected, under which bloomed a miniature avenue of palms and tropical flowers. All eyes were turned upon me as I stepped from my carriage and entered the chapel with Federica. Murmurs of my vast wealth and generosity were whispered as I passed along.

One old crone, hideously ugly, but with dark piercing eyes, the fading lamps of a lost beauty, chuckled and mumbled as she craned her skinny neck to observe me more closely. "Oh, that poor woman. She has to be rich and generous to satisfy that money-hungry scoundrel she weds today – he who scoffs at the suffering poor."

Federica caught these words and glanced quickly at me, but I pretended not to have heard them.

The great bell of the cathedral boomed out eleven, and as the last stroke swung from the tower, the massive doors were flung more widely open. I heard the gentle rustle of my trailing robes as I began my walk down the aisle.

Ahead, standing before the altar, I beheld my husband. He wore a coat of dark blue velvet over a brocade waistcoat embroidered with silver thread. On his hands, wrists, and around his neck, he wore the jewels I had given him, and they flashed about him like scintillating points of light.

Inside the church, there were a great number of people, but my own invited guests, not numbering more than twenty or thirty, were seated in the space reserved for them near the altar, which was separated from the sight-seers by a silken rope that crossed the aisle. I smiled at most of them, and in return received their congratulations as I walked confidently towards the high altar. In my role as an older woman, I was without the escort of a paternal protector with only Federica to walk behind me.

The magnificent paintings and frescos on the wall round me seemed endowed with mysterious life. The eyes of the saints and martyrs were turned to me as though they reprimanded me - *Must you do this? Is there no hope for forgiveness?*

And in my mind came my stern answer. *No. If hereafter I am tortured in hell, now while I live, I must be avenged. No consolation or joy can be mine without my fulfilled revenge. And this I will seek as long as I breathe. For once, a man's treachery shall meet with punishment. For once, justice shall be done.*

As I walked, I wrapped myself in the somber, meditative silence. The sunlight fell gloriously through the stained windows; blue, gold, crimson, and violet shafts of dazzling radiance glittered in lustrous flickering patterns on the snowy whiteness of the marble altar, and slowly, softly, majestically, as though an angel stepped forward, the sound of music flowed on the incense-laden air.

I recalled my former wedding, when I had stood in this very spot, full of hope, intoxicated with love and joy, when Beatrice Cardano had been by my side, and had been tempted for the first time by my husband's handsome face and body; when I, poor fool, had never believed that either of these two people whom I adored could play me false.

I could see the admiration that broke out in suppressed murmurs from those assembled, as I paced slowly and gracefully up the aisle towards the devil's masterpiece who awaited me there. He smiled when I reached the altar and sank to my knees beside him in prayer. The music swelled forth with grandeur, the priests and acolytes appeared, and the marriage service commenced.

Soon came the blessing and exchange of rings. I drew the wedding-ring from my small purse that hung from my waist and looked at it. It was sparklingly bright and appeared new. But it was old - the very same ring I had drawn off my husband's finger the day before. It had been newly burnished by a skilled jeweler, and showed no signs of wear, as if it had been bought that morning.

As we placed our rings on the book the priest held, I glanced at Dario. His fair head was bent as if absorbed in holy meditations. The priest sprinkled them with holy water. Dario took the ring I had provided him to give me, and set it on my hand - first on the thumb, then on the index finger, then on the middle finger, and lastly on the ring finger, where he left it in its old place. As he did so, I wondered whether he recognized it as the one he had given me so long ago when we were first wed. But it was evident he did not. His calm remained unbroken. He had the self-possession of a perfectly satisfied, handsome, vain, and utterly heartless man.

The actual ceremony was soon over. The Mass flowed smoothly, and we, the newly-wedded pair, were required to receive Communion. I shuddered as the priest placed the Host on my tongue. What had I to do with the purity and peace this memento of Christ is supposed to leave in our souls? In fact, as I swallowed, I believed the crucified image of Christ with the pained eyes let me know that I would soon seal my own damnation. Yet, my husband, the true murderer, the arch liar, received the Sacrament with untroubled tranquility.

If I am damned, then he is double damned. Hell is wide enough for us to live apart when we get there.

Thus I consoled my conscience, and looked away from the painted faces on the wall; the faces that in their various expressions of sorrow, resignation, pain, and death seemed now to bear another look, that of astonishment— astonishment that a woman like me and a man like him had been permitted to kneel at God's altar without being struck dead for blasphemy.

Absorbed in my morose thoughts, I scarcely heard the close of the service. I was roused by a touch from my husband, and I returned to the moment to hear the organ music thunder through the air. All was over: my husband was mine; mine by the exceptionally close-tied knot of a double marriage; mine to do with as I pleased until death should us part. How long before death would come to us? And I began mentally counting the spaces of time that must elapse before the curtain closed on the final act of this, my long drawn plan.

I was still absorbed in this mental arithmetic, even while my husband offered me his arm before we entered the vestry to sign our names in the marriage register. So occupied was I in my calculations that I nearly caught myself murmuring certain numbers aloud. I checked myself and tried to appear interested and delighted, as I walked down the aisle with my groom through the rows of admiring spectators.

On reaching the outer doors of the church, several flower-girls emptied their fragrant baskets at our feet; and in return, I handed a bag of coins to Dario to distribute to them, knowing from prior experience that it would be needed. To tread across such a heap of flowers required some care. Many of the blossoms clung to my gown as we moved forward slowly.

Just as we had almost reached the carriage, a young girl, with large laughing eyes set like flashing jewels in her soft oval face, threw a cluster of red roses down in my path. A sudden fury possessed me, and I crushed my heel instantly and savagely upon the crimson blossoms, stamping upon them again and again so violently that my husband raised his brows in amazement, and the pressing people who stood round us, shrugged and gazed at each other with looks of utter bewilderment—while the girl who had thrown them shrunk back in terror, her face paling as she murmured, "*Santissima Madonna. Mi fa paura.* Holy Mother, she scares me."

I bit my lip with vexation, inwardly cursing the weakness of my own behavior. I laughed lightly in answer to Dario's unspoken, half-alarmed inquiry. "It is nothing—a mere fancy of mine. I hate red roses. They remind me of human blood."

He frowned. "What a horrible thought. How can you think such a thing?"

I gave him no response. He assisted me into the carriage with courtesy; then entering it himself, we drove together back to my rented villa, where the wedding breakfast awaited us.

This is always a feast of uneasiness and embarrassment. Everyone is glad when it is over; when the flowery speeches and exaggerated compliments are brought to a fitting and happy conclusion. Among my assembled guests, all of whom belonged to the best and most distinguished families in Vicenza, there was a pervading atmosphere of chilliness. The women were bored, jealous of my rich gown and jewels. The men were constrained, and could scarcely force themselves into even the semblance of warmth. They evidently thought that, with such wealth as Dario's, he would have done much better to remain a bachelor. In truth, the Veneto people are by no means enthusiastic concerning marriage. They are apt to shake their heads, and to look upon it as a misfortune rather than a blessing. *The altar is the tomb of love* is a very common saying.

It was a relief to us all when we all rose from the splendidly appointed table, and separated for a few hours. We were to meet again at the masquerade wedding ball, which was to commence at nine o'clock that evening. The highlight of the event was to be the final toasting of the bride after which there would be music, mirth, and dancing with all the splendor of royal revelry. At the end of the night, everyone would remove their masks and reveal themselves.

My husband escorted me to my private room, for I had many things to do such as to take off my bridal gown, don my ball costume for the night, and supervise Santina as she packed my trunks for the next day's journey.

The next day. I smiled grimly and wondered how Dario would enjoy his last trip. He kissed my hand respectfully and left me alone to prepare for the brilliant evening's feast.

Bridegrooms in Vicenza do not bother their brides with their presence or caresses as soon as they are married. Instead, they restrain their ardor to preserve the rose-colored mist of love as long as possible. They have a wise, instinctive dread of becoming overfamiliar; aware that nothing kills romance so swiftly as close and constant proximity.

And Dario and I, like other members of our rank and class, permitted each other a few moments of freedom. To my twice-wedded husband, I gave the last hours of liberty he would ever know. He left me to dress and adorn myself as most women do, believing I was eager to outshine others of my sex, and sow petty envies, mean hatreds and contemptible spites. But I was not such a woman. Tonight, I dressed only for Dario.

From my window I could see the Piazza dei Signori and I stepped out onto the balcony to watch the crowd's frolics. The foolery had begun, and no detail of it seemed to bore the easily amused folks who must have seen it all so often before. A vendor of quack medicines was making the crowd laugh. He was talking to a number of colorfully dressed girls and fishermen. I could not make out his exact words, but judging by his absurd romantic gestures, I could see he was selling an *elixir of love;* an elixir compounded, no doubt, of a little harmless honeyed water.

Flags flapped in the breeze, trumpets brayed, and drums beat. Musicians twanged their mandolins loudly to attract attention, and failing in their efforts, swore at each other jovially. The conflicting calls of flower-girls and lemonade-sellers rang through the air. Now and then a shower of confetti flew out from adjacent windows, dusting the coats of the passers-by. Clusters of flowers tied with favors of brightly colored ribbon were lavishly flung at the feet of bright-eyed peasant girls, who rejected or accepted them at pleasure, with light words and playful talk. Clowns danced and tumbled, dogs barked, and church bells clanged. Through all the waves of color and movement crept the miserable, shrinking forms of poor diseased beggars clad in rags that barely covered their halting, withered limbs as they pleaded for a coin or two.

It was a scene to bewilder the brain and dazzle the eyes, and I was just turning away from it out of sheer fatigue, when a sudden cessation of movement in the swaying, whirling crowd, and a slight hush, caused me to look out once more to determine what caused the momentary stillness.

The Contessa's Vendetta

A funeral cortege appeared, moving at a slow and solemn pace. As it passed across the square, heads were uncovered, and women crossed themselves devoutly. Like a black shadowy snake it coiled through the mass of shifting color and brilliance. After a few moments, it was gone. The depressing effect of its appearance soon wore away. The merry crowd resumed their folly and shrieking, their laughing and dancing, and everything returned to the gaiety of before.

And why not? The dead are soon forgotten. No one knew that better than me, I thought, as I leaned my arms lazily on the edge of the balcony. That glimpse of near death in my life had forever changed me. Strangely enough, my thoughts turned to methods of torture practiced upon vile criminals. For instance, the iron coffin where criminals were bound hand and foot, and then forced to watch the huge lid descending slowly, slowly, slowly, half an inch at a time, till at last its heavy weight crushed the writhing wretch who had watched death steadily approaching in agony, into a flat and mangled mass. Suppose that I had such a coffin now. I shuddered. No. He whom I sought to punish was too handsome and well-built despite his wicked soul. He should keep his magnificent good looks. I would not destroy that. I would be satisfied with my plan as I had crafted it.

I re-entered my room and called for Paolo, who was now resigned and eager to go to Venice. I gave him his final instructions and placed in his charge the iron cashbox, which, unknown to him, contained a small fortune in gold and silver and jewels. This was the last good act I could do. It was a sufficient sum to set him up as a well-to-do merchant in Venice with Lilla and her little dowry combined. And there was enough for a dowry for Santina too. He also carried a sealed letter to Signora Monti, which I told him she was not to open until a week had elapsed. This letter explained the contents of the box and my wishes concerning it. It also asked Signora Monti to send for Annunziata and poor old Giacomo at Villa Mancini, and tend to them both as well as she could till their deaths, which, judging by their ages, I knew could not be far off.

I had thought of everything, and I could foresee what a happy, peaceful home they would all find in Venice. Lilla and Paolo would wed, I knew, and form a happy family with Santina. Signora Monti and Annunziata would console each other with their past memories and in the tending of Lilla's children. For some time, perhaps, they might even talk of me and wonder where I had gone. Then gradually they would all forget me, for that is what I wanted – to be forgotten.

Si, I had done all I could for those who had never wronged me. I had rewarded Paolo and Santina for their affection and fidelity. Now, the path ahead of me was clear. There was nothing more to do except complete the deed that had clamored at me for so long to accomplish.

Revenge, like a beckoning ghost, had led me on, step by step, for many weary days and months in cycles of suffering. But now it paused, it faced me, and turning its blood-red eyes upon my soul, yelled at me to strike.

Chapter Thirty-One

The masquerade ball opened brilliantly. The rooms were magnificently decorated. The luster of a thousand lamps shone on a scene of splendor that befit the court of a queen. Some of the stateliest nobles in all of Venice were present, their breasts glittering with jeweled orders and ribbons of honor. Some of the loveliest women to be seen anywhere in the world flitted across the polished floors, delicate and graceful in a rainbow of brilliant colors and shades.

But handsomest among all, peerless when it came to his vanity, and absolutely faultless in his charms, was my husband, the groom, the hero of the night. Never had he looked so splendid, and even I, felt my pulse quicken, and the blood course more hotly through my veins as I beheld him, radiant, victorious, and smiling behind his Bauta mask. It covered his entire face with its square jawline, no mouth, and plenty of gilding. He had changed his garments too. Now he wore a wine-colored coat above a golden silk waistcoat and black brocade breeches. The brigand's ship pendant flashed gloriously around his neck below his cravat, while his golden hair reflected the light of a hundred or more candles. Around his wrist he wore a heavy, manly bracelet studded with brilliants that I well remembered, for they had once belonged to my father. Yet even more lustrous than the gems he wore was the deep, ardent glory of his eyes, dark as night and luminous as stars that glowed through his mask.

Some of the women present at the ball that night wore dresses the likes of which are seldom seen outside of Venice. Gowns sown with jewels and thick with wondrous embroidery that have been handed down from generation to generation through hundreds of years. As an example of this, Federica Marina's gold train, stitched with small rubies and seed-pearls, had formerly belonged to the family of Lorenzo de Medici. Garments like these, when they are part of the property of a great house, are worn only on particular occasions, perhaps once in a year; and then they are laid carefully away and protected from dust and moths and damp, receiving as much attention as the priceless pictures and books of a famous historical mansion. Nothing ever designed by any great modern tailor or milliner can compete with the magnificent workmanship and durable material of the festa dresses that are locked preciously away in the old oaken coffers of the greatest Venetian families; dresses that are beyond valuation, because of the nostalgic romances and tragedies attached to them.

Such glitter of gold and silver, such scintillations from glistening jewels, such magnificent embroidery, such subtle aromas of rare and exquisite perfume, such bejewelled masks; all these things that stimulate the senses surrounded me in full force this night; this one dazzling, supreme, and terrible night that was destined to burn into my brain like a seal of scorching fire. *Sì,* till I die, this night will remain with me as though it were a breathing, living thing; and after death, who knows whether it may rise again in some tangible, awful shape, and confront me with its flashing mockery and menacing eyes, to haunt me through all eternity. I remember now how I shivered and was startled out of the bitter reverie into which I had fallen when I heard the sound of my husband's low, laughing voice.

"You must dance, *cara*," he said, with a mischievous smile. "You are forgetting your duties. You and I are required to open the ball."

I rose mechanically.

"What dance is it?" I asked, forcing a smile. I noticed the dance area had filled up with men and women, the men's steps more athletic than that of the women who kept their upper bodies erect, their arms quiet, their movements minimal above the waist. "I suspect you will find me to be an awkward partner. It has been many years since I have danced."

He shook his head and his eyes narrowed. "You had better not disgrace me. You have to dance properly. You'll make us both look stupid if you make any mistake. The band was going to play a quadrille, but I told them to strike up a waltz instead. You'd better not waltz badly. Nothing looks so awkward and absurd."

I said nothing, but allowed him to place his arm round my waist and stood ready to begin. I avoided looking at him as much as possible, for it was growing more and more difficult with each passing moment to maintain my self-control. I was consumed with both hate and love. *Sì*, love of an evil kind, in which there was nothing admirable about it. I was filled with a foolish fury that battled with an urge to proclaim his vileness then and there before all my titled and admiring guests, and to leave him shamed in the dust of scorn, despised and abandoned. But I knew that if I were to speak out now and declare the truth of my past and his before that brilliant crowd, they would all think me mad. Besides, for a man like him, there existed no shame.

The slow waltz, that most enchanting of dances, now commenced. It was played *pianissimo*, and stole through the room like the fluttering breath of a soft sea wind. I had always been an excellent waltzer, and my step completed that of Dario's harmoniously. He glanced up with a look of gratified surprise as I bore his languorous, dreamlike movements through the glittering ranks of our guests, who watched us with admiration as we circled the room.

Then everyone present followed our lead. In a few minutes the ballroom looked like a moving flower-garden in full bloom, rich with swaying colors and rainbow-like radiance. The music, growing stronger, and swelling out in marked and even time, echoed forth like the sound of clear-toned bells broken through by the singing of birds. My heart beat furiously, my mind reeled, my senses swam as I felt my husband's warm breath on my cheek. I clasped his shoulder more closely and held his hand more firmly. He felt the double pressure, and his lips parted in a smile. "At last you love me," he said.

"At last, at last," I muttered, scarce knowing what I said. "If I had not loved you from the beginning, *caro*, we would not have been married today."

A low ripple of laughter was his response. "I knew it," he murmured again as he drew me with swifter and with more voluptuous motion into the vortex of the dancers. "You tried to be cold, but I knew I could make you love me, *si*, love me passionately, and I was right." Then with an outburst of triumph and vanity he added, "I believe you would die for me."

I pressed my body closer to his. My hot quick breath moved the feathery gold of his hair away from his ear. "I *have* died for you," I said. "I have killed my old self for your sake."

Still dancing, with his arms encircling me, and gliding along to the music of the dance, he sighed restlessly. "Tell me what you mean, *amore*," he asked, in the tenderest tone in the world.

Oh, that tender seductive cadence of his. How well I

knew it. How often had it lured away my strength. "I mean that you have changed me," I whispered. "I may seem old, but for you tonight, I will be young again. For you my chilled slow blood shall again be hot and quick as lava. For you my long-buried past shall rise in all its pristine vigor. For you I will be a lover, such as perhaps no man ever had or ever will have again."

My words pleased him and he pulled me closer to him in the dance. Next to his worship of wealth, his delight was to arouse the passions of women. He was very panther-like in his nature. His first tendency was to devour, his next to gambol like an animal, though his sleek, swift playfulness might mean death. He was by no means exceptional in this; many men are like him.

As the music of the waltz grew slower and slower, dropping down to a sweet conclusion, my husband led me to a table, and left me as he went to dance with a distinguished Venetian noblewoman who was his next partner.

Unobserved, I slipped out to make inquiries concerning Paolo and Santina. I learned they had departed. One of the waiters, a friend of his, had seen him leave. Paolo had glanced into the ball-room before leaving, and had watched me dance with my husband, and then with tears in his eyes had left without daring to wish me good-bye.

I accepted this information with kind indifference, but in my heart I felt a sudden emptiness, a dreary, strange loneliness. With my faithful servants near me I had been in the presence of friends, for friends they both were in their own humble, unobtrusive fashion; but now I was alone and lonely beyond all comparison; alone to do my work, without prevention or detection. I felt isolated from humanity, set apart with my victim on some dim point of time. The rest of the world had receded. Only Dario and I and God were all that existed for me; and between the three of us, justice must be fulfilled.

I returned to the ballroom. At the door a young boy faced me. He was the only son from a great Paduan house. Dressed in pure blue, as most boys are, with a white flower on his coat, and his dimpled face alight with laughter, he looked the very embodiment of a happy youth. He addressed me somewhat timidly, yet with all a child's frankness. "Is this not grand? I feel as if I were a king. Do you know this is my first ball?"

I smiled wearily. "Truly? And you are happy?"

"Oh, yes, I am ecstatic and wish it could last forever. And, is it not strange, but I did not know I was so handsome till tonight," he said this with perfect simplicity, and a pleased smile radiated his features.

I glanced at him with cold scrutiny. "And some one has told you so?"

He blushed and laughed. "*Si,* the daughter of the Venetian duke himself. And she is too noble to say what is not true, so I must be the most handsome young man here, just as she said, is it not true?"

I touched the flower he wore at his breast. "Look at your flower, child. See how it begins to droop in this heated air. The poor thing. How glad it would feel if it was once again growing in the cool wet moss of the woodlands, waving n the fresh wind. Do you think it could revive now if a young woman told it that it was handsome or beautiful? The same is true about your life and your heart. Pass them through the scorching fire of flattery, and their purity will wither like this fragile blossom. And as for being handsome, are you more handsome than him?" I pointed to my husband who was at that moment curtseying to a most beautiful woman in the stately formality of the first quadrille. My young companion looked, and his clear eyes darkened enviously. "Ah, no. But if I wore such manly brocades and silks, and had such rich jewels, I might be more like him."

I sighed bitterly. The poison had already entered this boy's soul. I spoke brusquely. "Pray that you may never be like him," I said, with somber sternness, ignoring his look of astonishment. "You are young, you cannot yet have thrown off religion. When you go home tonight, kneel beside your bed, and pray with all your strength that you may never resemble, even in the smallest degree, that man, so that you may be spared his fate." I paused, for the boy's eyes were dilated in extreme wonder and fear. I looked at him, and laughed abruptly. "I forgot," I said. "The man is my husband. I should have thought of that. I was speaking of another whom you do not know. Pardon me. When I am fatigued my memory wanders. Pay no attention to my foolish remarks. Enjoy yourself, but do not believe all the twitters and coquettery of young girls like the little Venetian duchess. *Arrivederci.*"

Forcing a smile, I left him to mingle with my guests, greeting one here, another there, jesting lightly, paying compliments to the men who expected them while striving to distract my thoughts with the senseless laughter and foolish chatter of the glittering cluster of people. And all the while, I desperately counted the tedious minutes, wondering whether my patience would endure until its destined time. As I made my way through the dazzling assemblage, Luciana Salustri greeted me with a grave smile.

"I have had little time to congratulate you, Contessa," she said, "but I assure you I do so with all my heart. Even in my most fantastic dreams I have never pictured a handsomer hero than the man who is now your husband."

I silently bowed my thanks.

"I am in a strange mood, I suppose," she resumed. "Tonight this scene of splendor makes me sad at heart, and I do not know why. It seems too radiant, too astounding. I would as soon go home and read a good book."

I laughed satirically. "Why not do it?" I said. "You are not the first person who, being present at a wedding feast has had depressing thoughts, just as if you were at a funeral."

A wistful look came into her poetic eyes. "I have thought once or twice of that poor, misguided young woman, Beatrice Cardano. A pity, was it not, that you quarrelled the same night she died?"

"A pity indeed," I replied, brusquely. Then linking my arm with hers, I turned her around so that she faced my husband, who was standing not far off. "But look at the Roman god I have married. Is he not a good reason to cause a dispute? Why even bother to think of Beatrice at a time like this? She is not the first woman who has quarelled with another for the sake of a man, nor will she be the last."

Luciana shrugged her shoulders, and kept silent for a minute or two. Then she added with her own bright smile, "Still, it would have been better if it had ended cordially between you over a coffee. By the way, do you recall our talking of Cain and Abel that night?"

"Perfectly."

"I have wondered ever since whether the real cause of their disagreement has ever been rightly told. I would not be at all surprised if one of these days someone does not discover a papyrus containing a missing page of Holy Writ, which will ascribe the reason of the first bloodshed to be over a love affair. Perhaps a woman drove the first pair of human brothers to desperation by her charms. What do you think?"

"It is more than probable," I answered, lightly. "Make a poem of it, Luciana, and people might say you have improved on the Bible."

I left her to join other groups, and to take my part in the various dances which were now following quickly one after the another. The supper was to take place at midnight. At my first opportunity, I looked at the time. Quarter to eleven. My heart raced, and blood rushed to my temples and surged noisily in my ears. The hour I had waited for so long and so eagerly had come. At last.

Chapter Thirty-Two

Slowly, with a hesitating step, I approached my husband. He faced a young woman who leaned against the wall. With his right palm on the wall beside her head, he was leaning forward prepared to kiss her. We had only been married for a few hours and already he was ready to betray me.

I swallowed down my fury and pasted a false smile onto my face. "Why there you are, Dario. I have been looking for you everywhere."

He turned swiftly around, his face red with embarrassment.

The young woman, her face scarlet, gave me a quick curtsey and with a rustle of her skirts, disappeared into a crowd of people.

I gave Dario my coldest, most stern look. "Permit me to remind you of your promise to come with me to see where I keep my treasures."

His angry frown at being interrupted disappeared as he recalled our previous discussion. He gave me a warm smile. "And I am impatient to fulfill it. Do we go now?"

"Now, if you wish. You know the private passage through which we entered here on our return from church?"

"Perfectly."

"Meet me there in twenty minutes. We must avoid being observed as we leave. But, make sure you wear something warm. In your room you will find a new cloak trimmed in sable. A small wedding gift."

"I am the most fortunate of men to have found such a considerate bride." He raised my hand to his lips and kissed it. "Are we going far?"

"No, not far."

"We will be back in time for the late meal, I hope?"

I bent my head. "Naturally."

He grinned. "I am delighted with your mystery tonight, *cara*. A moonlight stroll with my bride. There is even a bright moon to light our way."

"Yes there is." I gave him a seductive look as I ran my finger teasingly across his lips. "I promised to reveal everything to you this night — wealth, jewels, and your bride without glasses. You must trust me, for I promise you will not be disappointed. It will be a night to remember for the rest of your life."

He took my hand and kissed my palm with a lingering kiss emphasized by the heat in his eyes. "Then I look forward to our jaunt. I will meet you in twenty minutes at the passage you described. I promised the next dance to a young woman, and then I will leave to prepare to meet you."

And he turned his attention back to the dance floor where his eyes met with the same woman whom he had been about to kiss, who at that moment met his gaze and cast him a encouraging smile.

I watched him make his way to her, and sweep her into his arms as they glided onto the dance floor. *Dance, Dario, dance, now while you still can.* Biting back the curse that rose to my lips, I hurried away. Up to my own room I rushed with feverish haste, full of impatience to be rid of the disguise I had worn so long.

Within a few minutes I stood before my mirror, transformed into my old self as nearly as possible. I could not alter the snowy whiteness of my hair, but I restyled it to the way I used to wear it in the days before I was deemed to be dead with the plague. Because of the mask I had worn, my glasses had not been needed, and my eyes, densely brilliant, and fringed with the long lashes that had always been a distinguishing feature, shone with all the luster of a strong and vigorous young woman. I straightened myself up to my full height, and studied my lithe, shapely body. I laughed aloud in the triumph of my womanhood. I thought of the old rag-dealing woman who had said, *You could kill anything easily.* And so I could, even without the aid of a swift stiletto, which I now drew from its sheath and stared down at while I carefully felt the edge of the blade from hilt to point. Should I take it with me? I hesitated. *Si.* It might be needed. I slipped it safely and secretly into my purse.

And now the items of proof. I had them all ready and gathered them quickly together. First the items that had been buried with me: the gold chain upon which hung the medallion with Dario and Chiara's initials, the purse and card-case which Dario had given me, the crucifix the monk had laid on my breast in the coffin. The thought of that coffin moved me to a stern smile. That splintered, damp, and moldering piece of wood would speak for itself shortly. Lastly I look the letters sent me by the Gilda D'Avencorta, those beautiful, passionate love letters Dario had written to Beatrice Cardano when she was in Rome.

Now, was that all? I thoroughly searched both my rooms, ransacking every corner. I had destroyed everything that could give the smallest clue to my actions. I left nothing behind except furniture and small valuables, a respectable gift to the landlord.

I glanced again at myself in the mirror. *Si,* in spite of my white hair, I was once more Carlotta Mancini. No one that had ever known me intimately could doubt my identity. I had changed my fancy ball gown for a simple everyday one. I placed my mask back on too. Over this I threw my long fur-lined cloak, which draped me from head to foot. I pulled its hood well over my head and over my eyes. There was nothing unusual in such a costume; it was common enough to many Vicenzians who have learned to dread the chill night winds that blow down from the Alps in early spring. Thus attired, I knew my features would be almost invisible to him, especially since our meeting place was the long dim passage lighted only by a single oil-lamp that led into a private garden, and far from any other entrances or exits to and from the building.

Into this hall I now hurried with an eager step. It was deserted. He was not there yet. Impatiently, I waited. The minutes seemed hours. Sounds of music floated toward me from the distant ballroom; a dreamy waltz. I could almost hear the dancers' steps. I was safe from all observation where I stood. The servants were busy preparing the marriage supper, and all the inhabitants of the hotel were absorbed in watching the festivities.

Would he never come? Suppose, after all my planning and scheming, he should escape me? I trembled at the idea, then put it from me with a smile at my own folly. No, his punishment was just, and in his case, fate would be inflexible. So I thought and felt.

I paced up and down feverishly. I could count the thick, heavy throbs of my own heart. How long the moments seemed. Would he never come? At last. I heard a rustling and a heavy step. A wisp of his spicy cologne wafted on the air. I turned, and saw him approaching. He came to me eagerly, his heavy cloak trimmed with rich Russian sable falling back from his shoulders and displaying a glimpse of his elegant clothes beneath. He resembled a Roman god, framed in ebony and velvet.

He laughed, and his eyes flashed saucily. "Did I keep

you waiting, *cara*?" he whispered and kissed the hand with which I held my cloak muffled about me. "I am so sorry I am a little late, but that last waltz was so exquisite I could not resist it; only I wish you had danced it with me."

"You honor me with that wish," I said, as he put an arm around my waist and drew me close to him.

I led us toward the door that opened into the garden. "Tell me, how did you manage to leave the ballroom?" I asked, unclenching my teeth.

"Oh, easily, like I've done many times before. I slipped away from my partner at the end of the waltz, and told her I would return soon. Then I ran upstairs to my room, got my cloak, and here I am." He laughed, evidently in the highest spirits.

"I am glad you have agreed to come with me at all," I murmured as gently as I could. "It is kind of you to humor me in this little journey. Did you see your valet? Does he know where you are going?"

"He? Oh, no, he was not in my room at all. I dare say he is amusing himself with the kitchen maids. I hope he enjoys himself."

I breathed freely. So, no one would know of our whereabouts. We would be undiscovered. No one had as yet noticed our departure. No one had the least clue to my intentions. I gestured toward the door that led into the passage. Dario opened it and we passed through noiselessly. He paused to wrap my cloak more closely about me with feigned tenderness. I led him quickly across the garden. There was no one in sight. We were entirely unobserved. On reaching the exterior gate of the enclosure I asked Dario to summon a carriage.

"I thought we were walking because it was not far," he said with surprise.

"It isn't far, but I wanted to spare us any fatigue. It has been a long day, and it will be a long night," I reassured.

The Contessa's Vendetta

Satisfied with this explanation, he assisted me into the carriage and followed me.

"To Villa Guarda," I said as we rattled away over the rough uneven stones of the back streets of the city.

"Villa Guarda?" exclaimed Dario. "Where is that?"

"It is an old house," I replied, "situated near the place I spoke to you of, where my jewels are."

"Oh."

And apparently contented, he nestled back in the carriage, and put his arm around me, permitting my head to rest lightly on his shoulder. He drew me closer to him and my heart beat with a fierce, terrible joy.

"Mine at last," I whispered to him. "Mine forever."

He turned his face upward and smiled victoriously. His cool lips met mine in a close, passionate kiss. *Si*, I kissed him. Why should I not? He was as much mine as any purchased slave, but he deserved far less respect. He caressed me and I let him do so. I allowed him to think me utterly vanquished by his charms. Yet whenever I caught an occasional glimpse of his face as we drove along in the semi-darkness, I could not help wondering at his supreme vanity. His self-satisfaction was so complete, and, considering his approaching fate, so tragically absurd.

He was entirely delighted with himself, his fashionable clothing, and his conquest of me. Who could measure the height of the dazzling visions he indulged in? Who could fathom the depths of his utter selfishness?

Seeing someone like him, handsome, wealthy, and powerful, would not all less fortunate men feel somewhat envious? *Si*, they would and they do, but believe me, selfish males whose only cares are womanizing, gambling, and running carefree amongst society, should be despised and never desired. Their death has little impact, even in the circles of his so-called best friends.

I knew there was not a soul in Vicenza who was

attached to my husband. Not one would miss him, no, not even a servant, though he, in his superb self-conceit, imagined himself to be the adored lord of the entire city. Those who had indeed loved him, he had despised, neglected, and betrayed. Musingly, I looked up at him as he rested back in the carriage, his arm encircling me, while now and then a sigh of absolute delight in himself broke from his lips, but we spoke scarcely at all. Hate has almost as little to say as love.

The night was persistently stormy, though no rain fell. The gale had increased in strength, and the white moon only occasionally glared out from behind masses of white and gray cloud that rushed across the sky. Moon rays shone dimly, like a spectral torch glimmering through a forest of shadow. Now and again bursts of music, or the blare of trumpets, reached our ears from the more distant streets where the people were still celebrating Fat Tuesday, or the tinkle of passing mandolins chimed in with the rolling wheels of our carriage. But in a few moments we were out of reach of even these sounds.

We passed the outer suburbs of the city and were soon on the open road. The man we had hired drove fast. He knew nothing about us, and was probably anxious to get back to the crowded squares and illuminated quarters where the principal merriment of the evening was going on. No doubt he thought we showed poor taste in requiring to be driven out of Vicenza on such a night of feasting and folly. He stopped at last. The turrets of the villa were faintly visible among the trees. He jumped down from his box and came to us.

"Shall I drive up to the house?" he asked, looking as though he would rather be spared this trouble.

"The distance is short, we will walk," I responded indifferently.

And I stepped out into the road and handed Dario the

The Contessa's Vendetta

money with which to pay for our fare.

"You seem anxious to get back to the city," I said, half teasingly to the driver.

"*Si*, that is very true," he replied. "I hope to get many a good fare from the contessa's marriage ball tonight."

"The contessa is very rich," I said as Dario assisted me to alight. He kept his cloak well muffled round him so that the driver would not notice the elegance of his smartly tailored clothes. "I wish I were her."

The man grinned and nodded emphatically. He had no suspicion of my identity. He took us for a couple who had found each other at some public entertainment, and then hurried off carefully cloaked and hooded, to a mysterious nook known only to ourselves to complete our romantic escape. Bidding us a lively *buona notte*, he sprung onto his box again, jerked his horse's head violently round with a volley of oaths, and drove away at a rattling pace. Dario, standing on the road beside me, watched him drive away with a bewildered air.

"Could he not have waited to take us back?" he asked.

"No," I answered, brusquely. "We will be returning by a different route. Come." And taking him by the hand, I led him onward.

"Have we much further to go?" There was an irritable tone in his voice.

"A three minute walk will bring us to our destination," I replied.

He grumbled something indiscernible as he walked. The moon suddenly leaped forth through the clouds. Its rays spilled pallidly green and cold on the dreary stretch of land before us, casting a grim light upon the white tombstones of the *campo santo*, the cemetery.

My husband noticed them too and stopped suddenly. "A cemetary?"

In all his life he had never visited a cemetery. He had

always had too great a horror of death.

"It is where I keep all my treasures," I answered, and my voice sounded strange and harsh in my own ears, while I tightened my grasp on his arm. "Come with me," and in spite of my efforts, my tone was one of bitter mockery. "If I, an old woman, am not afraid, then you, a strong man, should not be."

And I led him on, unable to resist my determined pace, too startled to speak. On and on over the rank dewy grass and unmarked ancient graves. On till the low frowning gate of the house of my dead ancestors faced me. On, on, on, with the strength of ten devils in my hand as I gripped his arm. On, on, on, to his awaiting doom.

Chapter Thirty-Three

As quickly as it had appeared, the moon retreated behind a dense wall of cloud. Semi-darkness once more enveloped the landscape. Reaching the gate of the vault, I unlocked it. It opened instantly, and fell back with a sudden clang. He whose arm I held with my iron grip shrunk back, and strove to release himself from my grasp.

"Where are you going?" he demanded, in a faint tone. "This is madness. Aren't you afraid?"

"Of what?" I asked, endeavoring to control my voice and to speak without a shred of concern. "Because it is dark? Bah, we will have light very shortly, you will see." And to my own surprise I broke into a loud and coarse laugh. "You have no cause to be frightened. Come." And I stepped swiftly and easily over the stone step of the entrance, pulling him along behind me.

Inside at last, thank Heaven. I shut the gate behind us and locked it. Again that strange undesired laugh broke from my lips involuntarily, and the echoes of the charnel house responded to it with unearthly and ghastly distinctness. Dario stood perfectly still in the dense gloom.

"Why do you laugh like that?" he demanded loudly and impatiently. "It sounds horrible."

It took all my effort to keep myself in check. "Does it? I am very sorry. I laugh because our moonlight ramble is so mysterious and amusing, is it not?" And I stepped into his arms and kissed him deeply. "Now," I whispered, "Step carfully for the stairs are rough. We are going down into the grotto where all my jewels and money are. And it is all ours, yours and mine, my love, my husband."

And I led him down into the deep vault. Whether he tried to resist me or not I cannot now remember. I pulled him down the moldering stairway, setting my foot on each crooked step with the firmness of someone long familiar with the place.

But my brain reeled. Rings of red fire circled in the darkness before my eyes. Every artery in my body seemed strained to bursting. The pent-up agony and fury of my soul were such that I thought I should go mad or drop down dead before I could see my plan to its completion. As I descended I felt his hand turn cold and clammy in mine, as though he were chilled to the blood with terror. At last I reached the lowest step and my foot touched the floor of the vault. I released my grasp of his arm and I remained still for a moment, breathing heavily.

He caught my arm and and gripped it. "What place is this? Where is the light you spoke of?"

I gave him no answer as I moved from his side. With the tinderbox from my purse, I lighted up a brazier and one of six candles that I had earlier placed in various corners of the vault the previous night. The light was minimal and the vault was still cast in gloom. I did not yet want him to understand the nature of the place in which he stood. Still wrapped in my heavy cloak and hood that disguised my features, I watched him. What a sight he was in that abode of corruption. Striking, hale, and full of life, with the shine of gold gleaming from under the folds of rich fur that shrouded him. His gaze never left mine as I came to stand before him. With my hand, I gently brushed his cheek. With my fingers, I sensually traced his lips.

The Contessa's Vendetta

My husband sucked in a deep breath, letting himself get lost in the temptation of my touch. I spread his cloak apart and placed both palms on his chest, letting them roam downward, tracing a trail down to his middle.

He reciprocated and opened my mantle.

The gown I had chosen to wear permitted my breasts to spill over the edge of the fabric; a gown considered indecent by society's standards.

By his reaction, I knew he was enjoying my little act of seduction. He took me in his arms and kissed me hard on the lips, slipping his tongue into my waiting mouth.

I broke the kiss, and held his head in my hands as his kisses warmed my neck. "Are you ready for your surprise?" I whispered seductively in his ear. "I have some wicked things I want to do to you. If you are man enough, I can begin immediately."

Lust glowed in his eyes. Oblivious of the actual game I was about to unleash, he chuckled. "Let the games begin."

"Very well," I smiled. "Remove your mask and close your eyes."

As he stood with his eyes closed, I slipped from his arms and went to stand behind him. From a pocket inside my mantle, I removed a dark silk scarf and blindfolded him with it.

"This must be quite a surprise to need a blindfold," he said with just a hint of nervous lust in his voice.

"The blindfold is part of the surprise," I replied. "Do not worry. You trust me, don't you?"

He gave a slight grin. "You know I do," he said.

"Are you certain you cannot see anything?"

"Nothing at all," he said

I came back around to face him and placed my hand on his heart. It was pounding with potential possibilities. I waved my fingers in front of his face, but he gave me no reaction. Satisfied, I lead him further into the vault. "Put out your hands," I asked.

He did so almost eagerly and I bound them snugly together in front of him with a strip of silk fabric. I guided him closer to the wall and bade him sit on a small stool; another carefully chosen item I had placed there last night. I took his bound hands in mine and raised them above his head. From a hook high above I hung a longer silk scarf and tied it strongly to the scarves that bound his hands. Then to reassure him, I leaned forward and kissed him with depth and passion. When I pulled away, I could see his smile. I brought my hand to his chest and stroked it across him, down his torso. Sweat beaded on his forehead as I trailed my hand over his manhood, already hard against his breeches. And then I stopped.

"Do not stop. I want you," he whispered huskily.

"And you shall have me."

"Hurry," he said, his breathing ragged. He leaned back and sighed. I could tell he was trying to calm himself, trying to restrain his need. I could smell his scent, the taste of his mouth lingered on my lips.

"Very well." One by one, I lit all the remaining candles until the light within the enclosed space was dazzling. Then I reached behind his head, and removed his blindfold.

He looked at me first, his cheeks flushed with desire, and then he looked about the room. Suddenly, and with a violent shock, he realized the gloom of his surroundings. The yellow flare of the waxen torches revealed the stone niches, the tattered palls, the decaying trophies of armor, the dreary shapes of worm-eaten coffins. His eyes widened with horror and he sat as immovable as a statue clad in coat of mail.

"This is a vault. A tomb. A place for the dead. Get me out of here—" He broke off abruptly, his alarm increasing at my utter silence. He gazed up at me with wild eyes.

"Who in their right mind would come here on a wedding night? You told me you were taking me to where you stored your wealth. I demand to know what this is all about." His anxiety forced his voice to become louder; his chest heaved convulsively with a fear I could see he was trying hard to disguise.

"Hush. Have patience and keep your voice down. Consider where you are. You have guessed right. This is a vault, your own mausoleum, the burial crypt of the Mancini family and their spouses." I spoke in measured accents, tinged with some contempt.

At these words, he froze and he stared at me with a mixture of both shock and wonder.

"Here lie all the great ancestors of your wife's family, heroes and martyrs in their day," I went on with methodical deliberation. "Here your own flesh will molder. Here," and my voice grew deeper and more resolute, "six months ago, your wife herself, Carlotta Mancini, was buried."

He uttered no sound, but gazed at me like a handsome pagan god turned to stone. Having spoken thus far, I now held my silence, watching the effect of all that I had said, for I sought to torture the very nerves of his soul.

At last his dry lips parted. His voice was hoarse and indistinct. "You must be mad," he said, with smothered anger and horror in his tone. "Untie me and get me out of here." He glanced about him with a shudder. "Let's leave this horrible place. As for the jewels, if this is where you keep them, leave them here. We can send someone to fetch them tomorrow. Come on."

I raised my hand to stop his ranting and pointed to a dark object lying on the ground near us—my own broken coffin "Look," I said in a thrilling whisper. "What is this? Examine it well. It is a coffin of the flimsiest wood, a plague coffin. What does this painted inscription say? No, don't turn your head away. Look at it. It bears your wife's name. She was buried in it. Then how did it come open? And where is she who is supposed to be inside?"

He shifted uncomfortably where he sat. A new and overwhelming terror had taken instant possession of him. Mechanically and with shock, he repeated my words. "Where is she? Where is she?"

"Yes, where exactly is she?" My voice rang out through the hollow vault, its emotion no longer restrained. "Where is she? The poor, miserable, gullible victim, whose treacherous husband played the philanderer under her very roof, while she loved and blindly trusted him. Where is she?" I banged my fist against my breast. "Here, here. I promised you should see me as I am. I swore to grow young tonight for your sake. Now I keep my word. Look at me, Dario. Look at me, my twice-wedded husband. Look at me. Do you not recognize your own wife?"

Throwing my dark hood back and removing my mask, I stood before him undisguised. As though some defacing disease had swept over him at my words, so his handsomeness suddenly vanished. His face became drawn and pinched and almost old. His lips turned blue, his eyes grew glazed and strained to stare at me. There was a gasping rattle in his throat as he turned away from me with a convulsive gesture of aversion to avoid my gaze.

"No," he shouted. "Not Carlotta. It is impossible. Carlotta is dead, dead. And you. You are a madwoman. This is some cruel joke of yours; some sick trick."

He broke off breathlessly, and his large, terrified eyes wandered to mine again with a reluctant and awful wonder. He struggled to free himself, but I had tied him well. I approached, and stood silently before him. He regarded me with a searching, anguished look, first of doubt, then of dread, and lastly of convinced and hopeless certainty. He suddenly closed his eyes as though to shut out some repulsive object, and then broke out in a low wail like that of a man in bitter physical pain.

I laughed scornfully. "Well, do you know me at last?" I cried. "It is true that I am somewhat altered. My hair was once black, if you remember, but it is pure white now, blanched by the horrors of a living death such as you cannot imagine, but which," and I spoke more slowly and impressively, "you will experience yourself soon. Yet in spite of all these changes to my appearance, I think you know me. That is good. I am glad your memory serves you thus far."

A low sound that was half a groan and half a yelp broke from him. "Oh, no, no," he muttered, again. "This is some vile plot. This cannot be true."

I stepped closer to him. "Listen to me," I said, in clear, decisive tones. "I have kept silent, God knows, and patient, but now, it is my turn to speak. *Sì*, you thought me dead. You had every reason to think so. You had every proof to believe so. How happy my supposed death made you. What a relief it was to you. What an obstruction removed from your path. But I was not dead. I was buried alive."

He inhaled a sharp breath and looking wildly about, strove to wrench his hands free. "Think of it, husband of mine, you to whom luxury has been second nature, think of my poor body straightened, packed and pressed into yonder coffin and nailed up tight, shut out from the blessed light and air forever. Who could have dreamed that life still lingered in me, life still strong enough to split open the boards that enclosed me, and leave them shattered, as you see them now."

He shuddered and glanced with aversion toward the broken coffin, and yanked hard to loosen his hands. He looked at me with a burning anger in his face. "Let me go," he panted. "You are a madwoman. Liar. Let me go."

I stood erect, regarding him fixedly. "I am no

madwoman," I said, composedly. "I am Carlotta Mancini. You know as well as I do that I speak the truth. When I escaped from that coffin I found myself a prisoner in this very vault, this house of my perished ancestors who lived their lives with truth and honor. How they would recoil from your polluted presence."

He fixed his eyes on mine; they glittered defiantly.

"For one long awful night, I suffered here. I might have starved or perished of thirst. I thought no agony could surpass what I endured, but I was mistaken. There was an even greater torment in store for me. I discovered a way of escape, and with grateful tears I thanked God for my liberty, for my life. What a fool I was though, for I never imagined how those who professed to love me wanted me dead. How could I have known that I would have been better off dead than to have returned home."

His lips moved, but he uttered no word. He shivered as though with intense cold. I drew nearer to him. "Perhaps you doubt my story?"

He gave me no answer.

A rapid fury possessed me. "Speak," I cried, fiercely. "Or by God, I will make you speak." I drew the stiletto out of my purse. "Speak the truth for once. It will be difficult for someone like you, a man who loves lies, but this time, you *will* answer me. Tell me, do you know me? Do you, or do you not believe that I am indeed your wife, your living wife, Carlotta Mancini?"

He gasped for breath. The sight of my infuriated face, the glitter of naked steel before his eyes, the suddenness of my action, the horror of his vulnerability, all terrified him into speech. He found his voice at last. "Mercy, Carlotta. Oh, God. Surely you don't intend to kill me? Anything, anything but death. I am too young to die. *Si, Si,* I know you are Carlotta, my wife, whom I thought dead. You said you loved me today, when you married me. Why did you marry me? I was already your husband. Why?" And then his eyes widened as he comprehended. "I see, I understand it all now. But do not kill me, Carlotta. I am afraid to die."

I detested his groveling. As quickly calmed as I had been stirred into fury, I put back the stiletto. I softened my voice and spoke with mocking courtesy. "Rest easy," I said, coolly. "I have not the slightest intention of killing you. I am no vulgar murderer. You forget, I may be a passionate woman, but I am also a woman of flair, especially when it pertains to matters of vengeance. I brought you here to tell you of my existence, and to confront you with the proof. We have plenty of time to talk. With a little patience I shall make things clear to you."

He nodded, lifting his eyes to mine with a long, shuddering sigh.

I knelt by his side, pressed my face close to his, and laughed. "What. No loving words for me? Not one kiss, not one smile, not one word of welcome? You say you know me. Well, are you not glad to see your wife? You who were such an inconsolable widower?"

His face twitched, but he said nothing.

"There is more to tell," I said. "When I broke loose from the coffin, when I came home, I found my vacant post as mistress of my villa already occupied. I arrived in time to witness a very pretty pastoral play. The scene was in the avenue of Villa Mancini and the actors were you, my husband, and Beatrice, my best friend."

He raised his head and uttered a low exclamation of shock.

I paced a step or two and spoke more rapidly. "There was moonlight, and the song of nightingales. *Si,* the stage effects were perfect. I watched the progress of the comedy with great emotion, as you can imagine. I learned much that was news to me. I became aware that for a man of your large heart and sensitive feelings, one wife was not sufficient." I laid my hand on his shoulder and gazed into his face, while his eyes, dilated with shock, stared hopelessly up to mine. "And that within three short months of your marriage to me you took up a lover."

He shook his head.

"No, do not bother to deny it. Beatrice Cardano was a wife to you in all things but name. But I mastered the situation. I rose to the emergency. Trick for trick, comedy for comedy. You know the rest. As Contessa Corona you cannot deny that I acted my part well. For the second time, however, it was I who courted you, but only half as eagerly as you courted me. And I have married you for the second time. No one can deny that you are most thoroughly mine—mine, body and soul, till death do us part."

And I loosened my grasp of him. He writhed away from me as if he were a wounded serpent. His features were rigid and wax-like like those of a corpse. Only his dark eyes shone, and these gleamed with an evil luster. I moved away, and turning my own coffin on its side, sat down upon it as indifferently as though it were an easy-chair in a drawing-room. Glancing at him then, I saw a wavering light upon his face. Some idea had entered his mind. He watched me carefully, with a tinge of fear. I made no attempt to stir from the seat I occupied.

Slowly, slowly, his eyes looked past me to the stairway beyond.

"It is locked," I reminded him. "There is no escape."

He shouted out for help several times.

Only the sullen echoes of the vault and the wild whistle of the wind as it surged through the cemetary's trees answered him.

He bellowed out a yell, and then turned his eyes upon me, confronting me, the blood now burning wrathfully in his face, and transforming it back to something of its old

The Contessa's Vendetta

handsomeness.

"Untie me and unlock that door," he shouted with a furious attempt to loosen his ties. "*Troia*. Bitch. I hate you. I have always hated you. Untie me and unlock the damned the door. Now. You dare not do this. This is murder. You have no right to do this."

I looked at him coldly; the torrent of his words was suddenly checked when something in my expression daunted him. He shuddered and stopped his thrashing.

"No right," I said, mockingly. "I disagree. A woman once married has responsibility over her husband, but a woman twice married to the same man has surely gained a double duty. And as for 'dare not' there is nothing I 'dare not' do tonight." And with that I rose and approached him. A torrent of indignation boiled in my veins. I gripped him by the shoulders.

"You dare talk of murder," I muttered, fiercely. "You. You who have remorselessly murdered two women and our child. Their blood is on your hands. You are covered with it. Their blood be on your head. Even though I am alive, I am nothing more than the moving corpse of the woman I once was. Hope, faith, happiness, peace, all things good and great in me have been slain by you. And as for Beatrice—"

He interrupted me with a wild yell. "She loved me. Beatrice loved me."

"*Si*, she loved you, oh, that devil in the shape of a woman. She loved you." In a fury I could not restrain I pointed to one corner of the vault, where the torchlight scarcely illuminated the darkness, and there I pointed upward. "Above our very heads; to the left of where we are, the beautiful young body of your lover lies, festering slowly in the wet mold, thanks to you. The fair, lovely woman, now marred by slithering worms. The thick curls of her hair combed through by the crawling feet of vile insects. The poor frail body dead by—"

"You killed her. You, you are to blame," he bellowed, striving to turn his face away from me.

"I killed her? No, no, not I, but you. She died when she learned of your treachery, when she knew you were false to her for the sake of wedding a wealthy stranger. My poison put her out of torment. You. You were glad of her death, as glad as you were with mine. You talk of murder. You, the vilest of men. If I could murder you twenty times over, what then? Your sins outweigh all possible punishment." I spat the words at him with contempt and loathing.

This time my words struck hard. He cowered before me in horror. His cloak was loosened and scarcely protected him. The richness of his costume was fully displayed, and the gold ship necklace around his neck heaved restlessly up and down as he panted with rage and fear.

"I do not understand why you should blame me. I am no worse than other men."

"No worse. No worse," I shrieked. "Shame on you. You are an outrage to your sex. Learn for once what women think of unfaithful husbands, for it is obvious you are ignorant of it. You may believe that infidelity is no sin; merely a little social error easily condoned, or set right by the divorce court. *Si.* Books and the theatre may teach you so: in them the world is turned upside down so that vice looks like virtue. But, there is no meaner, no more loathsome object, so utterly repulsive to a faithful woman than a faithless husband. The cowardly murderer who lies in wait for his victim behind some dark door, and stabs him in the back as he passes unarmed deserves to be pardoned more than the man who blatantly disregards a wife's honor, position, and reputation, to be promiscuous. Infidelity is a crime; a low, brutal crime, as bad if not worse than murder, and deserves as stern a sentence."

A sudden spirit of defiant insolence possessed him. He pulled himself erect and joined his brows into a dark frown. "Sentence. How dare you judge me. What harm have I done? If I am handsome, is that my fault? If women are fools, can I help it? You loved me, Beatrice loved me; could I prevent it? I cared nothing for her, and even less for you."

"I know," I said, bitterly. "Love was never part of your nature. Our lives were but cups of wine for your false lips to drain; the flavor once pleased you, but now, don't you think the dregs taste somewhat bitter?"

He shrunk in my glare, his head drooped.

"And what of poor Chiara? No heart, no conscience, no memory," I cried. "That a despicable creature like you should live and call itself a man. The lowest beast of the field has more compassion for its kind. Before Beatrice died she knew me. Even my child, neglected by you, in her last agony knew me, her own mother. She being innocent, passed away in peace; but imagine if you can, the wrenching torture in which she died, knowing me, knowing everything. How her spirit must now curse you, her own father."

He raised his head. There was a starving, hunted, almost furious look in his eyes, but he fixed them steadily on me.

"See, here is the proof that I tell the truth. These things were buried with me." I threw the medallion and chain, the card-case and purse he himself had given me at his feet. "You will no doubt recognize them." I showed him the monk's crucifix. "This was laid on my breast in the coffin. It may be useful to you. You can pray to it very soon."

He interrupted me with a gesture of his head. He spoke as though in a dream. "You escaped from this vault?" he said, in a low tone, looking from right to left searching eagerly. "Tell me how—and—where?"

I laughed scornfully, guessing his thoughts. "You must think I am stupid, but it doesn't matter," I replied. "The passage I discovered is now cemented closed. I have seen to that myself. No living creature left here can escape as I did. Escape is impossible."

A stifled groan broke from him. He heedlessly kicked away the things I had tossed at his feet. "Carlotta. Please, take me out to the light, the air," he pleaded. "Let me live. Drag me through Vicenza. Let the world see see me dishonored, brand me with the worst of names, make me an outcast of society, only let me out of here. I will do anything, say anything, be anything, only let me live." He shuddered. "I am so young. Am I truly so vile? There are men who count their lovers by the score, and yet they are not blamed; why should I suffer more than they?"

"Why? Why?" I echoed, fiercely. "Because for once a woman takes the law into her own hands. For once, a wronged woman insists on justice. For once she dares to punish the treachery that blackened her good name and humiliated her to the world. Were there more like me, there would be fewer like you. A score of lovers. It's not your fault that you had only one. I have something else to say which concerns you. Not content with betraying two women, you tried again on a third. Yes, you wince at that. While you thought I was Contessa Corona, while you were betrothed to me in that character, you wrote to Beatrice Cardano in Rome. Very charming letters. Here they are," and I flung them down to him. "I have no further use for them. I have read them all."

The letters lay where they fell. His struggles to free himself had loosened his cloak so far that it hung back from his shoulders, showing a brooch formed in the Mancini crest that flashed on chest neck like a point of

The Contessa's Vendetta

living light.

I yanked it from him. "This is mine," I cried, "As much as this ring I wear, which was your love-gift to Beatrice Cardano, and which you afterward returned to me, its rightful owner."

I glanced down at his bracelet. "The rest of the jewels that adorn you were my father's. How dare you wear them? The ship pendant and the rest that I gave you are your only fitting ornaments—they are stolen goods, filched by the blood-stained hands of the blackest brigand in the country. I promised you more like them; behold them."

And I threw open the coffin containing what remained of Cesare Negri's spoils. It occupied a conspicuous position near where I stood, and I had myself arranged near it so that the gold and precious stones inside would be the first things to meet his eyes.

"This is where Contessa Corona's wealth came from. I found this treasure hidden here on the night of my burial. Little did I think then what dire need I would have for its use. It has served me well. It is not yet exhausted. All that remains is for you."

Chapter Thirty-Four

At these words he looked at the brigand's coffin, a faint light of hope as well as curiosity in his haggard face. I watched him in vague wonderment. He had grown old so suddenly. The youthful flush of his flesh had disappeared. His skin appeared drawn and dry as though parched from the sun and heat. His hair was mussed and disordered. Only his eyes showed his youth. A sudden wave of compassion swept over my soul.

"You are my husband and I loved you; my husband who I would have died for. Why did you betray me? I thought you were honest and a man of honor. If you had waited for the day after my death to take Beatrice as your lover, I might have forgiven you. Though risen from the grave, I would have left and told no one I was alive to allow you to be together. *Si*, if only you had waited, if only you had grieved for me even a little. But when you confessed your crime with your own lips, when I knew that within three months of the day we married, you had already cheated on me, when I learned that my love, my name, my position, were used to hide your affair with the woman I called my friend—God. Who could forgive such a betrayal? I am no different than anyone else, but I loved you, and in proportion to my love, so is the greatness of the wrongs you have done me."

He listened and a faint smile dawned on his pallid lips.

The Contessa's Vendetta

"Carlotta," he whispered. "Carlotta."

I looked at him. Unconsciously my voice dropped into a tender sadness.

"Yes, my name is Carlotta, and I am not a ghost. Does saying my name seem strange to you, Dario, my husband whom I loved as few women love a man? You who gave me no love at all? You who broke my heart and made me what I am?" A hard, heavy sob rose in my throat and choked my utterance. I was young, and the cruel waste and destruction of my life seemed more than I could bear.

He heard me, and a smile brightened his countenance. "Carlotta," he murmured. "Forgive me. I spoke in haste. I do not hate you. I will make amends for all the suffering I caused you. I love you and will be true to you. I will be yours and yours alone." His eyes searched my face for the reply to his words.

I gazed down at him with grief-stricken sternness. "Forgiveness? You ask too late. A wrong like mine can never be forgiven."

A strange silence followed. His eyes roved over me as if he was searching for some lost thing. The wind tore furiously among the branches of the cypresses outside, and screamed through the small holes and crannies of the stone-work, rattling the iron gate at the summit of the stairway with a clanking sound, as though the famous brigand, Negri, had escaped with all his chains upon him, and was clamoring for admittance to recover his buried property.

Suddenly Dario's face lightened with an expression of cunning intensity, and before I could understand what he was about to do, he tripped me with swift agility. The stiletto I carried fell loose.

Before I could react, he gripped it with his feet and raised them to his bound hands. With the stiletto now in his grip, he began cutting through the silk as if it were water. "Too late," he cried, with a wild laugh as he flung himself free of the ties and rose to his feet. "Now it's you who will die, bitch."

For one second the bright steel flashed in the wavering light as he poised it to strike. I dodged him. He turned toward me, the stiletto raised in his murderous hand. He held it with a desperate grip as he stepped closer.

A memory of that ravenous owl, that unclean bird I had fiercely fought off on the night of my living burial returned. My anger surged to new heights. It seemed I was possessed of intense strength, abundant courage. I raised my knee and kicked him hard in the groin. The knife fell from his grip. As he tumbled to the ground, his head struck a stone coffin. His glazed eyes looked up at me as I brandished the stiletto above him. Blood dripped from his head.

"Who talks of murder now" I screamed with bitter derision as he writhed on the ground in pain. "What a victory for you if you could have stabbed me and left me here for dead. Then a new world of lies would have been yours with the stain of my blood on your soul. You would have fooled the world, you with the stink of death upon you. And you dared to ask my forgiveness." I stopped short.

A strange, bewildered expression suddenly passed over his face. He looked about in a dazed, vague way. Then his gaze became suddenly fixed, and he pointed toward a dark corner and shuddered. "Hush," he said, in a low, terrified whisper. "She is here." He stretched out his arms. "Beatrice," he said.

With a sudden chilled awe, I looked at the corner of the vault that riveted his attention. All was shrouded in deep gloom.

With a moan he crawled backward as though the ghost he saw threatened him. He paused. His wild eyes gazed upward.

Did he see some horror there? Had the blow to his head struck him senseless?

He raised both hands as if to shield himself from an imminent strike, and then he uttered a moan and lost consciousness. Or dead?

I asked myself this question uncaringly, as I looked down on his inanimate body. The flavor of vengeance was hot in my mouth, and filled me with delirious satisfaction. True, I had been glad, when my poison had coursed through Beatrice's body and carried her to death, but my gladness had also been mingled with a touch of regret. Now, not one throb of pity stirred inside me; not the faintest emotion of tenderness. Beatrice's sin was great, but Dario had been the one to tempt her. His crime outweighed hers. And now, there he lay, white and silent in death and I did not care. Had his lover's ghost indeed appeared before the eyes of his guilty conscience? I did not doubt it. I would not have been surprised if I had seen her poor pale spirit myself, as I gazed down at the lifeless body of the traitor who had wrecked both our lives.

"Oh, Chiara," I muttered, half aloud. "We are avenged. You can rest in peace now, my beautiful child. Your father will go to hell for the wrongs he did to us, but is hell black enough to accept his malevolent soul?"

And I slowly moved toward the stairway. It was time to leave him. Possibly he was dead. If not, then he soon would be, for he had struck his head hard. I paused irresolute. The wild wind battered ceaselessly at the iron gateway, and wailed as though the voices of a hundred creatures lamented.

The candles were burning low, the darkness of the vault deepened. Its gloom concerned me little. I had grown familiar with its unsightly things, its crawling spiders, its strange uncouth beetles, the clusters of blue fungi on its damp walls. The scurrying noises made by bats and owls, who, scared by the lighted candles, were hiding in holes or corners of refuge, startled me not at all. In my current state of mind, an emperor's palace was less beautiful to me than this brave charnel house; this stone-mouthed witness of my struggle back to life with all of its misery.

The bell outside the cemetery struck one. We had been absent from the masquerade ball nearly two hours already. No doubt we were being searched for everywhere. It mattered not. They would never come here to look for us.

I walked to the stairs. As I placed my foot on the first step, I heard my husband stir. He seemed to come awake from his unconsciousness. I turned to observe him knowing he could not see me where I stood, ready to depart.

I watched as he murmured something to himself in a low voice, and groaned as he placed his hand on the back of his head, and pulled it away bloodied. He broke out into a laugh—a laugh so out of all keeping with his surroundings, that it startled me more than his attempt to murder me.

Slowly, with great difficulty, he managed to rise to his feet; and straightened his disordered clothes. He stumbled to the brigand's coffin, placed both hands on it to steady himself, and stared down into its contents of silver, gold, and a rainbow of gems. He took them carefully in his hands, seeming mentally to calculate their cost and value. Necklaces, bracelets and rings, he pulled out, one after the other, till his hands were overloaded with them. Against the candlelight, they blazed with lustrous color.

I marveled at his strange conduct, but did not understand it. I moved away from the staircase and drew nearer to him. Then I heard a strange, low rumbling like a distant earthquake, followed by a sharp cracking sound. A

The Contessa's Vendetta

gust of wind rushed round the mausoleum shrieking wildly like some devil in anger. The strong draught extinguished two of the flaring candles.

My husband, entirely absorbed in examining Cesare Negri's treasures, apparently saw and heard nothing. Suddenly he broke into a laugh. A chuckling, mirthless laugh such as might come from the lips of the aged and senile. The sound curdled the blood in my veins. It was the laugh of a madman.

"Dario," I called to him with an earnest, distinct voice.

He turned toward me still smiling. His eyes were bright, his face had regained its color, and as he stood in the dim light, with the clustering gems massed together in a glittering fire against his skin, he looked unnaturally, wildly handsome. He nodded to me, half graciously, half haughtily, but gave me no answer.

"Dario," I called out again, moved with pity.

He laughed again; the same terrible laugh.

"Beatrice? Do you love me?" Then he began to hum a mournful tune.

As the melody echoed through the dreary vault, my bitter wrath against him partially lessened. Compassion stirred my soul. He was no longer the same man who had wronged and betrayed me. He had the helplessness and fearful innocence of madness. In that condition I could not have hurt a hair of his head. I stepped forward, resolved to lead him out of the vault. After all, I would not leave him like this, but as I approached, he pulled away from me, and stumbled backward, while a dark frown furrowed his brows. "Who are you?" he yelled. "You are dead. How dare you come out of your grave."

And he stared at me defiantly and then he seemed to address some invisible being at his side. "She is dead, Beatrice. Are you not glad?" He paused, apparently expecting some reply, for he looked about him in wonder.

"You did not answer me. Why are you so pale?" He muttered, his words rambled forth in disjointedly. "When did you come back from Rome? What have you heard? That I have betrayed you? Oh, no. I love you. Oh, but I forgot. You also are dead, Beatrice. I remember now. You cannot hurt me anymore. I am free once more."

The strike on his head must have caused him to act like this, or had it suddenly released a madness he had long disguised?

Again I heard a hollow rumbling and crackling sound overhead. What could it be?

Dario hummed as he plunged his arm down into the coffin of treasure. He gave a shout of pleasure. He had found the old mirror set in its frame of pearls and it seemed to please him. He did not seem conscious of where he was anymore, for he sat down on the upturned coffin that had once held my living body. With complete apathy he gazed into the mirror at his reflection. What a strange and awful picture he made, vainly gazing at himself while surrounded by the moldering coffins that silently announced how little his vanity was worth, staring at himself in this alcove of skeletons.

I gazed at him as one might gaze at a dead body; not with loathing anymore, but mournfully. My vengeance was satiated. I could not wage war against this vacant, smiling, mad creature, out of whom the spirit of a devilish intelligence and cunning had been torn, and who therefore was no longer the same man. His loss of wit would compensate for my loss of love.

I tried to attract his attention again. I opened my lips to speak, but before the words could form themselves, that odd rumbling noise broke again, this time with a loud reverberation that rolled overhead like the thunder of artillery. Before I could understand where it was coming from, before I could advance one step toward my husband, who still sat on the upturned coffin looking at himself in the mirror, before I could utter a word or move an inch, a tremendous crash exploded through the vault, followed by a stinging shower of stones, dust, and pulverized mortar. I stepped backward amazed, bewildered, speechless, instinctively shutting my eyes.

When I opened them again, everything was in complete darkness. All was silence. The wind howled outside more frantically than ever. A sweeping gust whirled through the vault, blowing some dead leaves against my face, and I heard the boughs of trees creaking noisily in the fury of the storm.

I thought I heard a faint moan. Quivering in every limb, and sick with a nameless dread, I searched for my tinderbox. Then mastering my shaking hands, I struck a light. The flame was so dim that for an instant I could see nothing. "Dario," I called loudly. "Dario."

There came no answer.

Nearby, I saw one of the extinguished candles. Reaching for it, I lighted it and held it up with trembling hands. I could not stop my horror at what I saw and shrieked with shock. An enormous block of stone dislodged by the violent storm had fallen from the roof down over the exact place where Dario had been sitting a minute or two before. Crushed under the huge mass, crushed into the very splinters of my own empty coffin, he lay, and I could see nothing, except one white hand protruding—the hand on which his wedding ring glittered. Even as I looked, that hand quivered violently, beat the ground, and then lay still.

It was horrible.

To this day, in my dreams I still see that quivering white hand, the jewels on it sparkling with scornful luster. It appeals, it calls, it threatens, it prays, and when my time comes to die, I know it will beckon me to my grave.

A portion of Dario's mantle was visible. A slow stream of blood oozed thickly from beneath the stone; a boulder that could never be moved and that forever sealed him in his awful burial place. How fast the crimson stream of life trickled, staining his mantle with a dark and dreadful hue. Staggering feebly, half delirious with anguish, I approached and touched the white hand that lay stiffly on the ground. I bent my head and almost kissed it, but some strange revulsion rose up inside me and prevented me.

In a stupor of agony I found the monk's crucifix that had fallen to the floor. I closed Dario's still warm fingertips around it and left it there. An unnatural calmness froze my strained nerves. "This is all I can do for you," I muttered. "May God forgive you because I cannot."

Covering my eyes to shut out the sight before me I turned away. I hurried in a frenzy toward the stairway. On reaching the lowest step I extinguished the light I carried. Some impulse made me glance back. And what I saw, I shall see till the day I die.

Moonlight poured down a long ghostly ray from the opening in the roof caused by the fall of the great stone. The green glimmer, like a spectral lamp, deepened the surrounding darkness and fell distinctly on one object—that protruding wrist and hand, whiter than snow.

I gazed at it wildly. The gleam of the coffin's spilled jewels hurt my eyes. The shine of the silver crucifix clasped in those waxen fingers dazzled my brain. With a frantic cry of terror, I rushed up the steps with maniacal speed, opened the iron gate through which Dario would pass no more, and stood in the free air, face to face with a wind as tempestuous as my own passions.

With furious haste I shut the entrance to the vault locking and double-locking it. I did not yet fully believe that Dario was actually dead. *I am safe at last. He cannot escape.* I walked around the vault to make sure the secret passage was forever sealed shut. It was. *He cannot scream. He cannot struggle. He will never laugh any more, never kiss, never love, never tell lies to women anymore. He was buried as I was—buried alive."*

Muttering thus to myself with a sort of sobbing incoherence, I turned to meet the snarl of the savage blast of the night, with my brain reeling, my limbs weak and trembling, with the heavens and earth rocking before me like a wild sea, with the flying moon staring aghast through the driving clouds, with all the universe, as it were, in a broken and shapeless chaos about me.

I went forth to meet my fate, and left him behind.

Chapter Thirty-Five

Unrecognized, untracked, I departed from Vicenza. Wrapped in my cloak, and standing in a heavy stupor on the deck of the *Rondinella*, my appearance apparently caused no suspicion in the mind of the captain, with whom my friend Enrico had arranged the terms for my voyage. He was oblivious to the real identity of the passenger that had been recommended to him.

The morning was radiantly beautiful. The sparkling waves rose high against the still boisterous wind. The sunlight broke in a wide smile of springtide glory over the world. With the burden of my agony upon me, with the utter exhaustion of my overwrought nerves, I beheld all things as if I were in a feverish dream; the laughing light, the azure ripple of waters, the receding line of my native shores. Everything was blurred, indistinct, and unreal to me, though my soul would always peer down into those dark depths where Dario lay, silent forever. For now I knew he was dead. Fate had killed him, not I. Unrepentant as he was, triumphing in his treachery to the very last, even in his madness. Still, if I could have, I would have saved him, even though he tried to murder me.

Yet it was just as well the stone had fallen. Who knows what would have happened if he had lived. I strove not to think of him, and drawing the key of the vault from my pocket, I tossed it with a sudden splash into the waves.

The Contessa's Vendetta

It was over. No one pursued me. No one inquired where I went.

I arrived at Civita Vecchia unquestioned. From there, I travelled to Leghorn, where I boarded a merchant trading vessel bound for South America. Thus I lost myself to the world. Thus I became, as it were, buried alive for the second time. Only after several years passed, did I return to Vicenza to seek sanctuary at Monte Berico. There I am safely established and I seek no escape.

No one can trace in my care-worn face and white hair, any resemblance to the once popular and wealthy Contessa Corona, whose disappearance, so strange and sudden, was for a time the talk throughout all of the Veneto. On one occasion, I saw an article in a newspaper entitled MYSTERIOUS OCCURRENCE IN VICENZA and I read every word of it with a sensation of dull amusement.

From it I learned that Contessa Corona was being sought. Her sudden and unexpected departure, together with that of her new husband, formerly Dario Gismondi, on the very night of their wedding, had created the utmost excitement in the city. The landlord of the hotel where she stayed was making inquiries, as was the contessa's former servant, one Paolo Flamma. Police authorities were also seeking any information. If within twelve months no news were obtained, the immense properties of the Mancini family, in default of existing kindred, would be handed over to the Venetian government.

There was much more to the same effect, and I read it with numb indifference. Why do they not search the Mancini vault, I thought gloomily. Plenty of answers to be found there. But I know people well. They are timorous and superstitious. They would as soon hug a pestilence than explore a charnel house. One thing gladdened me, however; it was the disposal of my fortune. The coffers of Venice was surely as noble an heir as anyone could have.

As I told you at first, I am a dead woman. The world, with its busy life and aims, has naught to do with me. The tall trees, the birds, the whispering grasses are my friends and my companions. They, and they only, are sometimes the silent witnesses of the torturing fits of agony that every now and then overwhelm me with bitterness. For I suffer always. That is natural. Revenge is sweet, but who can remove the horrors of memory? My vengeance now recoils upon my own head. I do not complain of this; it is the law of compensation. It is just. I blame no one, except him, the man who caused my wrong-doing. Dead as he is I do not forgive him. I have tried to, but I cannot. Do women ever truly forgive the men who ruin their lives? I doubt it. As for me, I feel that the end is not yet. When my soul is finally released from its earthly prison, I shall still be doomed to pursue his treacherous spirit over the black chasms of a hell darker than Dante's in my relentless wrath, forever and ever.

But I ask no pity. I need none. I punished the guilty, and in doing so suffered more than they did. That is as it must always be. I have no regret and no remorse. Only one thing troubles me. One little thing; a mere foolish notion. It comes upon me in the night, when the moon peers down at me from heaven. For the moon sweeps in lustrous magnificence through the dense violet skies. I shut out her radiance as much as I can; I close the blind at the narrow window of my solitary cell, and yet no matter what I do, one wide ray always manages to creep in. One solitary ray that evades all my efforts to expel it. Under the door it comes, or through some unguessed cranny in the woodwork. I have tried and tried in vain to find the place of its entrance and stop it.

I cannot understand why that pale ray visits me so often. I see a white hand on which its ring shines. The hand moves. It lifts itself. The fingers point at me threateningly. They quiver, and then beckon me slowly, solemnly, commandingly onward to some infinite land of awful mysteries where light and love shall dawn for me no more.

Mirella Sichirollo Patzer

About the Author

Mirella Sichirollo Patzer lives in Cochrane, Alberta, Canada with her husband, two daughters, and rambunctious little grandson and granddaughter. She is also the author of The Blighted Troth and The Pendant.
For more information about Mirella, please visit:

http://mirellapatzer.com
http://historyandwomen.com

Made in the USA
Charleston, SC
19 July 2016